MOMENTS IN TIME

MOMENTS IN TIME

by

Paul T Kidd

Cheshire Henbury

First published in 2014 by Cheshire Henbury. Ebook edition published in 2014

Paperback version ISBN 978-1-901864-18-2

Ebook version ISBN 978-1-901864-19-9

British Library Cataloguing in Publication Data: A catalogue record for this book is available from the British Library.

Cheshire Henbury Email: books@cheshirehenbury.com

Web site: www.cheshirehenbury.com/moments-in-time

To my mother, who once said something to me and, unbeknown to her, set in motion a process that over the course of many years led to what is now before you. She never knew, nor did she live to see the result.

Also by Paul T Kidd:

Fiction
Enigma
A Tale of Two Deserts: Enigmatic Christmas Fables for the
    Modern Age
Encounter with a Wise Man: A Christmas Tale of Wisdom
Father Christmas Adventures: Unexpected Tales of Christmas
    Magic
A Father Christmas Story: Being a Tale of How Father
    Christmas Came to Be

Non-fiction
European Visions for the Knowledge Age: A Quest for New
    Horizons in the Information Society
Rapid Prototyping for Competitive Advantage: Technologies,
    Applications and Implementation for Market Success
Revolutionising New Product Development: A Blueprint for
    Success in the Global Automotive Industry
Agile Manufacturing: Forging New Frontiers
Organization, People and Technology in European
    Manufacturing

The future only exists in the imagination, the past only in memory. All we have is the present, moments in time that are doomed to slip away, forever flowing towards the far distant shores of life long past. Here in the present moment is where we create our regrets, or make our dreams come true. This is how life is; an inescapable law of nature, a universal truth, but ...

MOMENTS IN TIME

PROLOGUE

It is the age before our time and men's footprints have yet to leave their mark upon the planet. But the hand of a Titan is moving across the face of the earth; it is the hand of Prometheus and our era is beginning. Prometheus, however, favours his creation too much, and feeling sorry for them, advises them badly by showing them a trick that transforms humans into self-deluded tricksters.

What was this trick? It was but a simple deception. Humans, not wanting Zeus to take the best parts of a sacrificed bull, asked Prometheus for advice, and he told them to take the bones and to dress and hide them with a few bits of good meat so that they appeared to be the best and to hide most of what was best, with entrails and the like. And Zeus was deceived by this trick, picking what looked to be the best, only to discover that it was not, which angered him much and by way of punishment he denied men the fire that they could have used to cook the meat and to make for themselves a better life.

Yet again Prometheus foolishly acted in humankind's favour by stealing fire from the gods and thus, with the ability to make fire, the road to the development of human civilisation started. But this was too much for Zeus and as punishment, Prometheus was bound to a rock with unbreakable chains and an eagle was commanded to rip out his liver. Prometheus, though, being an immortal, could not die and at night his liver regenerated; thus the agony was repeated the next day and the next and so on for a countless age. And there he would have remained, caught in an eternal loop, if Zeus had not allowed Hercules to rescue Prometheus.

So it was that in the years ahead, humankind, having been taught badly by Prometheus, repeated their Promethean trick many times and increasingly so as the world began to shift and change into that which we know today. Thus it was that the age of science, engineering and technology emerged and with it the epoch of the industrial-age engineer, and the trick became so deep rooted in their culture that most were blind to this and they became like Prometheus, bound to the rock of the past with unbreakable chains, holding firmly to their beliefs.

Alas it seems that there is no Hercules to save our modern-day Prometheans and thus it is that engineers, along with scientists and technologists, in their delusions, lead human civilisation to the edge of doom. Who will set them free?

CHAPTER 1

Out of order comes disorder: this is one of the most fundamental laws of the universe, contrary to what some, being those who are inclined to say that *the risks can be managed*, mistakenly believe. Yet within the disorder there is order, but this, one might say, is hidden in plain view, so few see it.

As for the proof of the fundamentality of this law, this is there, waiting to be discovered in the everyday features of the surrounding world, left, so to speak, to enlighten and inform those who seek truth, rather than the reinforcement of faith – no matter in what form that manifests itself, be it science or religion, for in reality, both are, when stripped bare, but dogmas carried on by different means.

Care we to look, to examine, and, in the case of some – those who, similar to me, have been conditioned by education, training and practice, to think otherwise – to put aside beliefs, we would see a completely different universe from the one that presses for our attention through that which is obvious, that which can be seen, or that which can be explored through the limited tools that science has chosen as the means of investigating the mysteries of life.

And there we were, Helen, my fair and beautiful wife, and myself, another moment in time, similar to the many gone before, and the many to come, together, happy, looking

3

forward to the future. This is how it was, how it should have remained, but then there was a change in my life; an alteration in my circumstance that came about by means that defy full understanding. Whether in the telling of my story I will shed further light on what I encountered, this I cannot know as I begin to record my tale.

In reality, though, it does not matter what I may learn, for I am where I now am; my present conditions are entirely my creation, being the result of beliefs that, so ardently held for so long, brought me to that which, had I been more knowledgeable and wise, could have been avoided. This, if you have not already realised, is one of the great lessons of the human story, but few seem willing to learn.

Change is, as Buddhists will tell you, and if you care to ask, the only constant in this world and the universe. The great river of life flows forever onwards, unstoppable, washing away the old, bringing with it the new and with the passing of time everything returns to its constituent parts. Decay is everywhere. Ageing is all around. Beauty fades, sharpness dulls, memories are lost, and mobility declines. There is no escape from this endless process. The world is transformed, acted upon by forces over which there can be no control. Wind, rain and frost; they weather the rocks and turn them into dust. Leaves, once green and young, lose their brightness and fade, turning to brown, disintegrating. Seasons, they come and go, and of human life the same applies. People are born, they live, and they die. Elemental in their beginnings, embryonic cells divide and multiply to create the whole, but in the end to atoms they all return. Time will not halt nor wait for anyone. All are doomed to fade. Time is always the victor.

This is an irrefutable characteristic of creation, of life, yet there is a very old house in my village where not all these truths seem to apply – or is it the case that this building is actually a window, with glass all hazy and slightly distorted, through which a glimpse can be obtained of the true nature of the universe with all its unknown and, perhaps, unfathomable complexity? The Time House is what I have come to call this structure. Why such a name? I hear your unspoken question, to which I will provide an answer, but not just yet, for my tale is my response to this query. What I have to say at this stage is that this house has always been a place of great mystery; a puzzle.

Many have talked about this building, as people are inclined to do, gossiping and speculating, but only a small number, I later discovered, have taken the time to find out more, to enter in and to learn some of its rather surprising secrets. For these few, those curious enough to have explored its history and its peculiar capability, the Time House has revealed some of its secrets. I am one of these people – a rare breed, thankfully, for curiosity concerning this house has its dangers.

There will always be those who will speak about that which they know very little, not taking time to research their subject – this, alas, is human nature, with many being willing to condemn, to judge, to arrive at conclusions, knowing little or, worse, not wanting to know. This, I am afraid, is the

5

backcloth against which life proceeds and such ignorance and blindness hold back human development. History is, sad to say, the story of a constant battle, with the quest for truth set against that which people want to believe, with education and intelligence being no guarantee that truth will prevail; often the worst offenders are those who are too smart to think themselves so ignorant; this is arrogance, a trait that, in the modern world, can be found in abundance.

I am, I like to think, not a person who can be called ignorant or arrogant. Such was the extent of my delusions, shared in common with others; a person of good intentions, but afflicted by certain beliefs and participating in a collective delusion that made me more dangerous than I realised. And somewhere in my not too distant past I was a researcher, that apparently most highly educated type who, alas, all too often knows a lot about very little.

I will not delve into my past too much. All I will here report is that I am well acquainted with research techniques, not least of which is making oneself the subject of an experiment and experiencing directly the consequences; this being the truest test of the purity of the quest for knowledge. And this is what I did when, naïve and filled with a sense of being in control, believing that *the risks can be managed*, I became involved with this old house; a gateway to, perhaps, different laws of nature; ones that have, until now, not been contemplated, or maybe these are the laws of nature as they actually are, rather than as we perceive them using the narrow viewfinder we call science.

This building, this construction of man, is, it appears, a house built by two different builders – one working on the physical features, shaping it within the bounds of what is physically possible to meet the needs of those who would live there and make it their home, and the other, unseen, forming it into that which I will, in due course reveal. For the moment all I will say is that the result is that, within this abode, in this normal-looking building, time is not always the master. All around, this invisible and formless feature of our world, that which we call time, works its endless changes, but not in this dwelling. Here time seems to have been conquered; its ceaseless action has been subjugated to the will of ...? Precisely what? That is the question and what a question! But beware, for nothing about the Time House is as it seems! It holds surprises for those who venture in, and often proves assumptions to be incorrect.

Of the others who went before me, those whom I have already hinted at, those who have explored the puzzle of the Time House, of these there is not a single trace – swallowed up by time itself and lost forever, somewhere in the great continuum of eternity. Of course, I did not know this at the beginning; I only discovered the likely fate of these poor folk very much later in my adventure. Had I known in advance about these people and what most likely happened to them, I might have acted differently and I would not now have a tale to tell. Such is hindsight! Such is the delusion that *the risks can be managed*! It would have been better, though, to have exercised foresight, but I, similar to many in the contemporary world, do not take note of the warning signs and do not know when to stop.

The building in question is a few hundred years old. In the surrounding countryside there are other properties of similar age, all built by the well-to-do gentry of a bygone era that quietly slipped into history long ago, becoming first nothing more than memories to people who, with time, were destined themselves to be forgotten, they being of little interest to those who dwell in modern times, where people have more to do than can be possibly be done with the time that they have available and who are constantly being asked, and in some cases expected, to do even more, such is the lunacy of life in the early twenty-first century.

In all these houses, generations have come and gone. Babies have been born; they have become small children, have grown into adults, have had their own offspring, and then, as everybody must, they have passed away: all within the walls of these fine country homes. For these people, life was what it has always been, a confusing mix of joy and sorrow, with one event following on from the other, living always in the hope that when sadness descends, better times lie ahead. This is the eternal and unchanging nature of life; timeless. So it is that the cycle of life and death repeats itself with the passage of time and what was once new, and in pristine condition, deteriorates with time, being ceaselessly transformed. Nature's onslaught, which can be likened to waves perpetually pounding upon the shore, works its endless magic, turning the new into the old, but not so for the Time House.

I am now the owner of this old and enigmatic property. How this came about I will reveal as my tale unfolds, this being just one of the strange aspects of my story, but perhaps not the most extraordinary, as you will soon discover.

No one, so far as anyone can remember, has ever dwelt in the Time House, and given what I now know about the place, this does not surprise me. Perhaps for me there will be no choice but to live in this property, given the way events have worked out. But the house is not the sort of place one calls home, although there was once a time when I believed otherwise. This is because the building had, in times past, been a matter of discussion between Helen and myself, which is a matter that I will address in more detail later in my tale.

Here I will mention that Helen is inclined to indulge in fantasy, at least this is what I call her daydreams, I being a rational type of person, rooted in reality, ever ready to explain away the world or to justify myself purely in terms of facts. Helen does not think in this way, preferring instead to express herself through feelings and futures that could be; ones that could contribute to our happiness. She, perhaps wisely, sees the world that could and should be and not one that fulfils the demands of some heartless and cold logic that is solely based on evidence, without any regard to what people want and that which will bring meaningful happiness.

Returning back to the matter of the nature of the property, I now realise it is not a very welcoming house. I say this fully acknowledging that this statement is not just based on observable particulars; such is the shift that has taken place in my frame of reference. Cold and draughty the house is, for sure, for it was designed and built in a different age, when notions of comfort were far less developed. This is the reality of such an old building. But here I also mention that which I would never have even considered saying previously; put succinctly, the place is eerie, being haunted not by ghosts, but by that which is perhaps far worse. This of course, yet again, I did not know until too late, although even now I do not understand what it is that I have encountered.

I state here that I did not choose to own the property – it chose me, or at least that is how it seems! I have to admit that, when I first acquired the Time House, I did think myself very fortunate and the thought of selling did cross my mind, for it would certainly raise a lot of money. This, as you can see, is greed at work. How many woes of the world stem from the love of money? Far too many is the answer; we as a society, however, stubbornly refuse to acknowledge this.

Thoughts of selling are now irrelevant, however, since there can be, for the moment, no letting go of this property, for it has become my only refuge in the sea of uncertainty that I have created. But the house may have also become a trap in which I am ensnared. It is as if the old house holds on to me in a similar way that a barnacle clings to the hull of a ship. A link has been forged, one that may never be broken. We share, possibly, a common destiny; its fate is mine and I am bound to it, perhaps for eternity.

I find myself in a rather complicated and inexplicable position. How did I get myself into such unusual circumstances? This I wonder about. Why me?

I have started asking myself this question, but then I think, why not me? This is the nature of existence. Catastrophes are part of life. Cancer, accidents, the loss of a child, unemployment, the breakdown of a relationship, and so forth; all these are the elements from which life stories are constructed and they often come upon people unexpectedly, jumping at them, as if from nowhere, taking us by surprise, wrong-footing us, and often bringing despair. The question is not "Will any of these elements be part of a life journey?" but which ones and when. We may well ask, *why me?* but the truth is, *why not?*

Once I did think that most of what happens to us is largely indiscriminate; now I am not so sure. Events strike at people, regardless of who they are, coming at them at any time. These are the pieces of the jigsaw puzzle of life; a part of the tapestry that is woven for each and every soul as they journey through time towards their ultimate destiny, which is death, and what lies beyond, whatever people may believe that to be.

So it was with the Time House and me. But it seems that it was a purely random occurrence that led to the sequence of events that ended with my ownership of this property, yet the events themselves, the means by which I took possession, are extraordinary. Of course, some might say that my story is unbelievable, but I do not lie. What I here write did happen and it all began one holiday weekend during what had been a very hot and sunny summer.

My name is Benjamin Woodward and I am by profession a self-employed electrical engineer. I, similar to many, had thought myself master of my own destiny and my own time. That weekend I was about to learn otherwise.

I mention my profession here for it has a significant bearing on the strange events that transpired that holiday weekend, which now seems so distant, but which could in fact only be a matter of moments past, such is the confusion about time that I have created for myself. My line of work is also relevant because of the beliefs and values that I once held by virtue of being an engineer – *out of disorder, I create order*, this being a belief that I was eventually to learn is naught but self-delusion. I also once believed that *the risks can be managed*, which I now understand is nothing more than a euphemism for *we know we should not do this, but we are going to, regardless* – words most often spoken by people with vested interests, and most often these are people who call themselves scientists, engineers or technologists.

My experiences turned out to be a very poignant lesson, so I here recount to you my story in the hope that what transpired may serve as a warning to take heed of signs that point towards taking a different path, for I have become like Prometheus. And who will save me from this collection of self-inflicted circumstances?

CHAPTER 2

We were spending a few precious moments in time together before Helen's departure.

"Are you sure you don't want to come with me, Benjamin, love?" Helen asked, turning to me, while at the same time dabbing blusher onto her cheeks. There was hope in her voice and an expectation in the question that I might be enticed to change my mind. Looking at her, I smiled.

Her face, I have often thought, is a perfect match for her personality – soft and gentle. Helen is full of life; emotional, high spirited, yet sensitive and loving. The brownish powder she was placing on her still unblemished and youthful skin made her seem even more warm and cheerful. Age had not yet altered her complexion and she really did not need so much make-up, yet similar to many people she was self-conscious of her looks, fearing the effects of ageing more than was warranted.

"This is the last holiday till Christmas and its going to be really good weather. Shame to miss it!" she said, continuing to tempt me, while at the same time dabbing more powder on her face.

Helen was going off for the weekend to stay with her mother and father in Dorset. It was an annual pilgrimage. At the end of every August we spent a weekend with them, only this time I was not going and she was working hard to change this disagreeable fact. I should have listened to her.

Helen does not originate from Dorset. She is a local to the village where we live, this being located in the northern parts of England. Her ancestors had lived in and around our village for centuries and in the churchyard there are many gravestones bearing her family name, Dent. The reality of Helen's family roots lying in this village that we called home was a feature of my circumstances that was to shape subsequent events significantly; developments that were eventually to lead to the predicament in which I now find myself. But I am getting ahead of myself, so returning to the matter of Helen's parents, who, attracted by the milder climate in Dorset and the fact that a branch of the family live in that county, had retired to the small and attractive village of Abbotsbury, close by Chesil Beach.

What a sight that unusual beach is, with all those pebbles, literally billions upon billions of them, more than can be comprehended, innumerable, towering above the sea level. It would take an eternity of time and more to count them.

In places the tiny stones are piled up so high, it is as if one were atop a prominent hill in an otherwise flat landscape, but here one looks down not on green fields or forest canopy, but upon swelling water: the grey cold sea, hiding from view even more pebbles beneath its ever-shifting surface. And the short trek from the verdant landscape that sits behind this collection of stones, to the lapping waves that continually wash upon the shore, is a wearying and taxing journey that

14

saps away one's energy. The time taken for this journey just seems to go on and on, with that shoreline only coming closer at a remarkably slow pace. Each and every footstep taken towards the endlessly swelling and rolling waves is accompanied by sinking and sliding as the unstable surface pebbles give way as weight is applied, and the stones, relentlessly pressing uncomfortably into the soles of one's feet, serve to remind that the natural world has its own structure that was not designed to accommodate humankind. Those who bravely struggle to cover the short distance to the shoreline arrive knowing that this is a place most certainly better suited to some of earth's other creatures, being an environment based on both order and disorder, as though the two belong together, each needing the other.

This beach is nature's own barrier, protecting the village of Abbotsbury from the wild storms that frequently rage out in the English Channel. Like a giant lifeless sea snake washed up on the shoreline, with its tail-end lying at Portland in the eastern end of the county, this corpse of shingle hugs the Dorset coast for eighteen long miles in a westerly direction. It is by far the largest pebble beach in the world, created in a time before recorded history, at the end of the last ice age. The enormous forces of rising sea levels pushed and rolled these pebbles up onto the shore, until at last one of nature's great wonders was formed. Over thousands of years the endless action of the sea worked tirelessly to fashion this monster and it is a place of ceaseless amazement; incomprehensible in its enormity of course, but also timeless, a link to a distant age when there were few human eyes to take in this glorious view.

This seemingly endless mass of stones, stretching far in to the hazy distance, is, in many places along its vast length, similar to what it was when it was first created; remote and isolated, with seabirds being the only company. It is a place of solitude, a spot, in an otherwise forever-changing landscape, where time can be forgotten.

What a sharp contrast this is with the village of Abbotsbury, which is also old, but on a very different timescale, having stood nestling in the shelter of Chesil Beach for only a few hundred years. This charming place of attractive thatched cottages and houses, a creation of humankind rather than nature, is, during the summer months, full of tourists keen to experience the old-world charms that this delightful place has to offer. Similar to wasps drawn to a jam pot, they come in swarms, with holiday weekends being a particularly busy time. Local shops, ale houses and restaurants, if the weather is good, are guaranteed to do an excellent trade at such moments in time; and the coming weekend promised to be exceptional in terms of weather and therefore money.

But Abbotsbury is not a place to be over a holiday weekend if peace and quiet is what you are looking for. Yet, but a short distance away, there is the open space of Chesil Beach. Visitors to Abbotsbury often take a look at this amazing natural feature, wondering at its vastness, but these observers seldom take the time to venture far from the car parks. Even at busy periods, Chesil Beach remains as it has been for most of its ten thousand-year existence: quiet, deserted, untouched, and apparently boundless, with its beginning and ending points lost in the far distance, just like time itself.

Exploration, it seems, is determined by the path of convenience, acceptability, and the ease of the journey, with that which looks too unsmooth and difficult being left largely unexplored; who can tell what important knowledge remains undiscovered as a consequence of this?

It was early Friday morning and Helen and I were in our bedroom; half past six. Helen, seated on the side of the bed, was looking into the dressing-table mirror. Gazing back at her was what I can only describe as a picture of rare beauty and this is what I was contemplating as I lay in bed, watching her.

She was wearing a white bathrobe and sitting in a very feminine pose with both knees pressed together. Helen began to brush her blonde hair and then she paused and glanced round once more and spoke one simple word. "Well?" She was eager for a positive response to her previous persuasive words and took no measure to hide her keenness.

I wanted very much to say that which she desired to hear. Looking at her, now in her prime, I realised that I wanted to spend more time with her and here was an opportunity to do so, but work beckoned, calling me to pay attention to that which did not matter, at the cost of ignoring that which did. This, I now understand, is an all too common mistake. We always think that there will be more time, but the truth is this: every moment in time has the potential to be our last, but this is not how we live our lives.

I smiled back, wanting to show the depth of my desire to please her. "You know I want very much to come with you," I began to say with feeling, "but I have far too much work. I am sorry, but this weekend will be a chance to catch up on all the office work that I've been neglecting for the past few months. I have to stay here, Helen, and deal with the admin work."

Oh, how much I wanted to go with Helen. Helen! The woman I love, the woman I live with, the woman I want to have children with. But on this occasion I knew, with regret, that it was not possible for me to join her.

This was plain foolishness. What was I thinking? I worked for myself and I should have been master of what I did, but I now understand that work was my unforgiving master, that my occupation had become an end in itself and that this, similar to many aspects of the modern world, lacked a meaningful purpose.

I was lying back, resting my head on the pillow. Rising up and moving over to Helen and then kneeling on the bed, I placed my arms around her young body, feeling the warmth, and I gave her a hug. She turned her head and looked into my eyes and our lips met, joined in a sweet kiss of love. I was aware of Helen's soft lips gently pressed against my own, stimulating, sensual. I savoured the moment of being with her in this way, so precious, so ephemeral; brief moments in time when, together, we were as one, unified and inseparable. Then I said tenderly, "I love you."

"I love you too," she replied, continuing to gaze into my eyes, smiling sweetly as she did so. It was a moment of magic; to be savoured, remembered, and repeated, I was certain, many times in the years that lay ahead.

"I'll miss you," I responded, speaking with the depth of feeling that only comes when barriers between two people have dissolved away. "I wish I could come with you," I continued, lightly stroking her hair as I spoke, "but I need to sort out the administrative work; you know, accounting books, business correspondence, and so forth. Boring, I know, but there is no escape from it. It needs doing and I don't see other opportunities ahead. It's now or never. Seize the moment, as they say."

"I understand. But it's a shame to miss out on this. We don't often get such good weather at holiday weekends. And I'll miss you too."

I kissed her again and then held her tightly and, feeling Helen's warm body against mine, pleasant and reassuring, I was reminded of how much I would miss her. It seemed at that particular moment in time that time itself had stopped and just stood there waiting for us to end our embrace, allowing us a few seconds, stolen from time itself, before it, that never-ending flow of moments, continued on its relentless advance into the infinity of the future.

Helen and I both have busy working lives. She too sometimes has to work weekends so there was no look of disapproval in her angelic face and no tone of chastisement in her voice. That soft, fair, round face, with blue eyes and shoulder-length blonde hair, and that voice so light and warm; I was indeed a lucky man to have such a person in my life.

Sweet person that she is, she accepted that this was how it was going to be, just as I would have done if our positions had been reversed. But it did not stop her continuing to entice me to change my mind, to pester me in the hope that I might give way. "Are you sure?" she asked. "You could bring some work with you."

"There's too much to do," I responded. "I wouldn't be able to bring all that I needed and I'd be bound to forget to bring a vital document. Better to stay here and get it sorted once and for all." Then by way of compensation I suggested, "Perhaps we could go away one weekend in September to make up for this."

Quickly flashing through my mind were images of Helen and myself enjoying a romantic weekend in some idyllic rural place; perhaps on our own in an old cosy cottage, exclusive and charming, or maybe in a suite, in some luxury country-house hotel, full of branded items and standardised features that would render us feeling that we could in fact be anywhere in the world, such is the overly corporate nature of most contemporary hotels.

"Sounds perfect," was her enthusiastic answer. "Just you and me, on our own, but that doesn't mean that I don't want you to change your mind about this weekend. We could have two weekends away."

Making no response to this with words, I fell back onto the pillow, pulling Helen gently towards me. She gladly followed and we lay there for a few moments in time, bound together by our love. I touched her hair and then I gently ran the back of my hand down the side of her face. No words passed our lips. It was one of those still, quiet moments when two people are just happy to be united, peacefully bound together, certain in the knowledge of their love, and that this is how it would be for many years to come.

But time was pressing. Helen had a long journey before her, one that would consist of busy motorways and Friday traffic, and it would take a long time to get to Dorset. Ahead of her lay a drive that would be far from pleasant, given the number of vehicles she expected to encounter. There would be people heading home for the weekend, as well as commuters and business travellers going about their daily routines, and others getting away early to miss the holiday rush. All these, combined, would serve to slow the journey. And, as for me, I still had another day's work ahead of me before a weekend spent preparing invoices, filing letters away, reading magazines, working my way through junk mail, and getting my accounting books up-to-date. This was the consequence of running a small electrical engineering business and employing two electricians, along with two apprentices. And we had been very busy over the preceding three months with the inevitable result that there was a backlog with the administration and paperwork.

"Better get moving," I said with a hint of reluctance in my voice, but wanting also to make a start, to begin to engage with the new day and to make of it what we, who are in control, want to make of it; every day is ours to shape according to our will.

So it was that our attention, with mixed feelings, returned to the business of preparing for the coming day, for our journeys over the coming days, which would begin at exactly the same moment in time: Helen's, planned and known, with its own potential for uncertainty; mine, as it turned out, unexpected and unknown, full of complex uncertainty – the universe demonstrating yet again, teaching unwilling pupils, its clear lesson that *out of order comes disorder*.

Helen rose and then resumed brushing her hair, which was now messier that it had been before she had started to brush it. She still looked beautiful though, even with her hair in a tangle. She gazed into the mirror, applied a few strokes of her paddle brush and, with this simple act, soon restored order; a clear demonstration of my belief that *out of disorder comes order*.

I too rose and began the early-morning rituals that signalled the beginning of yet another day; most likely, I thought, destined to be much the same as those that had gone before, for in truth I was controlled by the needs of my business, but being somewhat self-deluded, I was not keen to admit this.

I dressed and then went downstairs. While I made coffee and toast, savouring the aroma of both, allowing the scents to stimulate my brain, Helen finished packing her bag and before long she was down in the hall, ready to depart, looking as she always did, the smart, independent and modern lady that she is, full of vitality and determination.

We sat in the kitchen, eating and drinking, enjoying the few moments in time that we had left together before the modern world, with all its demands, pulled us into its ceaseless activities, most with little meaning or purpose. As we did so, we chatted about what she would do while at her parents' home. "What are your plans since you're free to do as you please this trip?" I enquired, curious to know, as we had not yet found the time to discuss this; which is rather typical!

"I'm going to see some old friends who are on holiday nearby."

"No doubt there will be plenty of reminiscing about old times," I suggested teasingly, "talk of dreams for the future and the inevitable discussions about babies. When and how many, I believe, is the usual subject matter, is it not?"

"Yes, of course, dear. Girl talk! It's timeless! What else is there to chat about?"

She was joking, responding as she always did when I teased her, showing the sharpness of her wit.

"And when is your sister coming down to Abbotsbury from London?" I asked.

Now there was a notable change in her demeanour, as was always the case when we talked about Caroline. A slight hint of tired acceptance of fate came into her tone as she began to speak on this matter.

"On Sunday, but just for the day. She won't allow more than a day for such visits. And she's bringing a new boyfriend with her as well. I'm curious to know more about this latest conquest, but I doubt that a lasting relationship will emerge; there have been too many before him. She always abandons her boyfriends quickly in favour of someone else she fancies."

Helen's sister can be likened to a butterfly, always flitting from one flower to another, never settling on one for long. But she is a pretty butterfly, nevertheless. Helen and her sister are both very attractive. Caroline is more materialistic and ambitious than Helen; a very driven person, but yet someone who seems to be endlessly searching for that which is undefined and elusive, with never enough time to do what matters in life.

Looking back, reflecting on that moment in time from the vantage point of my present position, with the benefit of that which I have so recently experienced, I can see now that Caroline is yet another person living the collective delusion that, through her actions, she creates order in her life.

Helen sat in silence for a few brief moments, slowly sipping at her black coffee, lost in her own private thoughts.

Breakfast was soon over and it was time for partings; that moment in time when the one who does not want to leave on her own has to say goodbye to the one that does not want to stay on his own. But it would only be for four days. On

Monday evening Helen would be home and we would be reunited. We embraced and kissed, a lingering embrace, a long kiss, as though time did not matter. But it did. Neither of us wanted to let go. Reluctantly I did so. Then I picked up Helen's bag, heavier than I imagined it would be for such a short trip, and carried it out to the car. Helen collected her handbag and followed.

"Have a safe journey," I began, after I had stowed the bag in the car boot, "and give my love to your parents."

Helen smiled. Those last moments in time and that loving and accepting smile, the warmth of expression, will forever remain with me, burned into my memory as though a brand, stamped on my consciousness; painful!

"I will. And don't worry, I'll be okay. I'll ring you as soon as I get there."

"I love you," was my reply. "Have a nice time. Say hello to your sister for me."

"I will. Love you too," responded Helen warmly as she reached out once more to embrace me. Then she let go and in a jiffy she was in the car, engine running and ready to depart.

The car, a dark blue Ford, was only a few months old so it still had that aroma of newness; the smell of plastics, solvents and sealants that lingers in new vehicles, reminding owners of the moment in time when they first took possession of the car, but which now was already part of the familiar, slowly descending into just another vehicle destined ultimately, with time, for the scrap heap.

It was time to go and I was soon standing on my own at the end of the drive, watching her car disappear into the distance, and then she was gone. All alone for four full days; I was missing her already and feeling a sense of emptiness that I did not want in my life, but perhaps teaching me that I should be making an effort, while I could, to enjoy what I had, for one day, without doubt, one of us would experience a loss that would be permanent; it was just a question of when.

It is an unsettling feeling being on one's own when one is used to having a partner there with you all the time. And I was experiencing exactly that sensation; I felt as if an essential element in my life had been removed, leaving me with a strange feeling that I had, until that moment in time, not previously experienced, such was the good fortune in my life not ever to have encountered grief. For a brief moment in time I understood, on a smaller scale, a little bit of the emptiness of the bereaved; those who have lost forever someone central to their existence. Still, there was work to do, so I went back inside. I did not know it at that moment in time, but I too was about to undertake a long journey, and not the one I would have been able to predict if anyone at that instant had asked. At that moment in time I had no inkling of the strange events that were to happen over the weekend, for all seemed as it should; the routine of another day was about to begin. Order reigned supreme.

My expectation was that it would probably be late on Monday night when I would see Helen again; all the holiday traffic on the roads would hinder her return, turning her journey into a slow progress homeward. There, at that moment in time on the Friday morning, Monday evening seemed an age away, but in reality the time would fly away; all I had to do was to keep myself busy and not notice the moments slipping by and then she would be back and all would be as it should be.

This, then, is exactly what I set about ensuring – filling my hours with activities that would hide from me the passage of time.

CHAPTER 3

The village where we live is just a small place, with forty or so dwellings of different ages. Some of these date from the eighteenth century, a few are Victorian, but many were built in the 1930s. Most of these homes are comfortable ones built for people who could afford such comfort, in eras when few were in such a fortunate position. How times have changed; now it is the majority who are able to pay for comfort, even if this comes in varying degrees.

At the centre of the village there is a large grassed area, which is just called the village green; a relic of a time when local peasants used it as common pasture. This was one of the few rights of ordinary folk in harsh times, when people were prisoners of a feudal system that bound serfs to lords, for life, for all time, across the generations, forever, or so it seemed to those who lived in that long-past age. Change, for all it is a constant, can at times seem as though it is absent.

The village green is neatly divided into four parts, four quadrants, by the roads that run into the village, roads that cross at the middle point, dissecting and dividing the neatly mown grassed area. Here is proof that from disorder humankind creates order, for the grass is kept free from the invasion of weeds by the regular use of herbicides and the greenness is ensured by continual application of synthetic fertilisers. Both these chemical products are icons of the modern age, the result of endeavours of scientists, technologists and engineers over the years, applied to ensure that order is maintained, transforming precious and non-renewable natural resources into tools that bring this order, all in the name of the free-market economy. But nature, secretly, quietly, and slowly responds in ways unexpected and unforeseen, trying to teach those caught up in their collective delusions that disorder will prevail; only those for whom the lesson is intended – they never learn.

At the crossroads stands an old way-sign giving directions and distances to nearby villages and to the town where I work. This road sign dates back to the late 1940s, an age when the movement of vehicles was slow enough to allow signs that people could only read when in close proximity. How different from the modern world, where road signs are large and brash, communicating their messages to busy people travelling at speed with no time (lest they lose money) to stop and read.

Next to this junction, surrounded by grass, is a small circular duck pond, occupied by several pairs of wild mallards and, on occasion, by itinerant Canada geese; these are the only natural aspect to this idyllic English country village scene. And everyone knows when these birds are present by the racket that they make, ceaselessly calling to other Canada geese that may happen to be passing by in the sky overhead, or any person within earshot who may care to listen to this noisy but natural cry.

Most of the older properties in the village are clustered around the village green. Some are terraced and some are detached, but most have no gardens to the front, since there is a perimeter road of gravel running around the grassed area; a dividing barrier between house and the associated ownership of property, and the grass, and its association with common land.

The newer Victorian and twentieth-century houses are mostly located along the lanes that run out of the village; roads that radiate away from the centre like tentacles reaching out to nearby villages. And just as the gravel track that circles the village green once served to indicate status, so now do the roads leading out of the village, for location is status. Many who live in the homes dotted around the village green tend to think of themselves as being superior to those who live in the newer properties built along the lanes. The nature of social standing changes with time, but it is always there, somewhere, adapting, taking on new forms as time goes by.

Our home is one of the 1930s detached houses; originally three bedrooms, also with a bathroom (but without a toilet), and downstairs a kitchen, a dining room-cum-sitting room, a lounge (once normally only used on very special occasions) and an outside toilet. Now, though, it has been radically transformed, by both improvement and extension, so it is similar to other modern homes, equipped with all fashionable facilities and over-burdened with labour-saving devices and entertainment equipment that is full of functions and capabilities destined never to be used – the delights of modern living and its associated technology; where would we be without it?

Our house is situated on the road that I travel along, just about every day, to the small town, ten miles away, where my business premises are located; both I think are conveniently situated; one for enjoying the pleasantness of the English countryside, the other providing access to a town where many people live, creating the marketplace for the services I provide, with the hope that in exploiting the market I do not spoil the rural features that I value – yet another collective delusion, which, similar to the majority, I subscribe to because I do not want to face the consequences of this not being so.

At half past seven I set off for my office. The sun was shining brightly, the sky was blue and there was no trace of clouds. It was already warm; the beginning of an idyllic summer's day. Helen was right, it was going to be a beautiful weekend, but alas for me, all I had to look forward to was being shut away behind a desk while the majority made the most of the glorious weather. Life can be very unfair at times.

On my way to the office I passed an old house that stands on its own a short way outside the village. There was a For Sale sign by the front garden gate, again! Most people in the village always referred to this property as the Old House, for it has no name, or, at least, no one knew if it had a proper name. Originally someone might have christened it but, if so, whatever that name was it had long ago been forgotten with the passage of time. This is the very same building that I now call the Time House.

It is an ordinary-looking eighteenth-century detached property, standing in about two acres of land. To the back a high brick wall encloses a large garden. The dwelling appears to be in fine condition, which I have always thought remarkable given that it is over 250 years old and has never been occupied within living memory.

At the front there is another (tiny) garden, enclosed by a small, white picket fence. The house itself has three storeys and a pitched roof covered with stone slabs quarried from the nearby hills. The front elevation of the building has been rendered with lime mortar and painted cream. The decoration of the window frames and the front door is dark green and the two colours give the house a feel of a property that has been transplanted to the site from a bygone age. Positioned high up, in the centre of the building, just below the eves, is a date stone that announces, to all who care to look, that the house was built in 1750, five years after the Jacobite rebellion of 1745.

There is no telling what scenes of history may have been played out before the house, what it had witnessed and, if it could speak, what secrets it would reveal; and many secrets it did have, as I was on the verge of discovering.

It is, without doubt, an attractive-looking property of character, even if the colour scheme is somewhat dated. It is also well-maintained, with well-kept gardens, but it is also an enigmatic house and there are many local stories about it.

Perhaps the word story is not quite the right one to use here; maybe legends would be a more appropriate description of that which people speak of relating to this property. The tale, for example, of the mysterious people who dwell in the house, but whom nobody has ever seen, or the people who come and go, not wanting their identity to be known, which again nobody has ever laid eyes on; plainly ridiculous nonsense, easily explained by the well-known phenomenon that in the absence of information people will invent facts, and I mean all people, including scientists, engineers and technologists.

I have already mentioned that no one lived there, or had ever done so, as far as anyone knew. And here one can say, for sure, that no occupants had ever been seen by anybody and this was an aspect of the building that locals had talked about for as long as anyone could remember, which contradicts the tales, abovementioned, that many tell. Contradiction! Yet another quirk of human behaviour!

You might think that a house apparently unoccupied would be subject to vandalism. But there was none. Not a soul ever went near the place and that included bored teenagers with nothing better to do than to destroy the world around them. The place was charmed in this respect. Some said that it was haunted and that is why there was no vandalism; no one dared to go near the house!

Obviously though, to be rational about it, the house did belong to someone. Repeated attempts had been made to sell it, but without luck as it happens, since a For Sale sign was a regular sight outside the property; a fact that many chose to ignore when speculating about the property, which I can tell you was a regular occurrence. So, it can be said that with respect to its saleability the house was jinxed – no one wanted to buy it.

I continued driving along the narrow lane. It is a quiet country road and in the summer season, with the hawthorn hedges in full leaf and wild plants growing along the roadside, it was an enjoyable journey and a passage along the lane was usually accompanied by sightings of wild animals. At night, foxes or rabbits could often be seen darting across the road, momentarily illuminated by headlight beams, their eyes shining as if they were bright gems glowing in the darkness. In the daytime it was common to see wild pheasants running along the hedgerows and the occasional stoat could sometimes be spotted, shyly peeping out from the grass verges, only to quickly disappear again at the approach of a vehicle. There was life in the narrow strips of grass, vegetation, bushes and trees that lined either side of the lane; life that few now took time to notice; life that had been in the English landscape since time immemorial.

Soon I arrived at the edge of the town. Green fields now gave way to houses and neat, well-maintained gardens. Then some commercial properties appeared and this where my journey ended.

Ten minutes to eight and all my employees were waiting for me; forty minutes early! All of them were keen to get on with the business of the day and to finish early so that they could start their holiday weekend as soon as possible:

they all had plans. It is amazing how, when it comes to the use of the time of others, people can show little urgency, but when the matter of one's own time is at stake, then the opposite often applies.

The fact that all my employees had made holiday plans, and would not therefore be available over the holiday weekend, was another significant factor in the events that were about to unfold. Had it been another weekend, I might never have visited the Time House, sending in my stead one of my electricians; thus it was that one of life's chance happenings put me in the wrong place at the wrong time. Or maybe it was a random event that placed me at the right place at the right time. In the end it is all a matter of perspective. Perhaps it was my destiny that I should make the journey that has led me to where I now find myself.

This particular Friday was much the same as others, just routine. All four of my employees were working on the rewiring of a large old house in town and with luck it would be finished by early afternoon. I would then visit the property and make my contribution by inspecting their work and issuing the owner with the necessary certification; an increasingly common feature of the modern world, over-regulated and formalised to an extent that previous generations would, no doubt, find over-burdensome and perhaps also unreasonable.

After the four of them had departed to continue with their appointed tasks, and having quickly glanced at the morning's mail, adding it to the pile that had accumulated on my desk, which was now far too great to realistically give proper attention to its constituent parts, I set off for my first appointment of the day – another old house that needed rewiring, and for which I had been asked to provide a quotation.

On leaving my office I picked up a portable heater that we had just serviced for one of my commercial customers. It may seem odd to be servicing heaters in the summer, but actually this is the best time to do the job. It is a quirk of life that the time to service equipment and the time to use it often do not coincide, and success in the latter is often dependent on the proper selection of the former. This is how it is with machines that are only used seasonally and which are left unused for long periods of time. There seems to be a law at work determining that such apparatus is inclined to go wrong just when it is needed the most. And when this happens there is inevitably a panic to get the item fixed quickly. So I had managed to convince some of the businesses I serve that timely maintenance of electrical equipment was preferable to responding when they fail – timing is of the essence in many aspects of life, especially when it comes to ensuring order.

Planning, and knowing in advance what is required, can also be a significant means of saving time in many circumstances, as well as the key to avoiding arguments later on; time spent in planning and preparation is very rarely wasted. Thus, when I left the premises of this old property, I was armed with agreement on all important matters that would affect the price of the job to be undertaken and all was clear concerning exactly what the work would entail. I had laid the foundations of the order that I so much valued and saw as being the natural state of the universe. I then visited an electrical wholesaler to replenish stocks of items that had been depleted as a result of the contract we were just about to complete. Again, holding stocks is another time saver, avoiding unnecessary trips to suppliers; yet another feature of my ordered world. You can tell by all this that I am an engineer, one of the creators of the many artefacts of the modern world; from disorder I create order.

The day was turning into a real scorcher. Beads of perspiration formed on my brow as I placed the materials into the boot of the car; this was not the sort of weather for occupations that involved exertion. As I worked, I reflected on how fortunate I was not to have to undertake very much in the way of manual labour, for at that time of the year excessive physical activity could be very unpleasant in such heat. It is perhaps a measure of the progress made in western society that what was at one time the predominant nature of labour – (often) hard physical effort – has now been replaced by office-type work, but not all involving significant use of mental faculties; even those with university degrees and claiming a professional status are repeatedly engaged in nothing more than following prescribed behaviour, coming to supposedly innovative solutions to problems, which in reality are often naught but realisations of that which is acceptable, within (often limited) prescribed bounds; such is the nature of collective delusions, which endure simply because these delusions are perceived as being better than facing the discomforting and sometimes disturbing nature of reality.

Those that toil in field, factory or office will one day be liberated from this, when, having made their contribution to society, they are allowed to retire. So what may at times seem like an endless trudge, as people move through life, working away until they are, frequently, unable to work no more, does at last reach a terminal point; all, with time, comes to an end. But when this happens is not always within the power of individuals to determine, as they are ultimately controlled by forces, economic and social, over which they have little or no control. I on the other hand see myself differently, being able, I reasoned, to do that which I wished; I was in control, creating in my own life, through planning and preparation, circumstances whereby nothing could disturb my ordered world.

My reflections came to an end when, just as I had finished loading the items, my mobile telephone began to ring. I immediately started to wonder if this would be another call from some sales person, working in a call centre, located who knows where, operating in a business environment that has become increasingly intrusive, where companies deem it their right to waste the time of busy people, trying to sell them products and services that are of no interest. Looking at the display screen I ascertained that it was Helen calling. Shutting the boot lid and leisurely sitting back on it to take the call, I began to speak with Helen, taking advantage at the same time of the opportunity to enjoy, for a short while, the warmth of the day.

CHAPTER 4

"Hi, love," I began. "How's the journey going?" I was curious to know how bad the traffic was, but my question also reflected the reality of moments in time spent in conversation, much of which is concerned with what seem to be trivial matters, but which nevertheless are the building blocks of two lives shared and lived as one.

"Okay. Everything is fine so far. The roads are busy, but not too bad. I'm at a motorway services at the moment, just south of Birmingham."

"I'm missing you already," I said sadly, knowing that while the contact with Helen was a welcome one, it also served to remind me of the moments in time we were spending apart.

"Missing you too," she responded. Then she changed the topic of our conversation, not wanting to dwell on our separation. "Come on. Let's talk about a different subject. What have you being doing?" she enquired, trying to be cheerful.

I told her about my movements and tasks so far that morning and of my plans for the rest of the day. Not exactly exciting material, but she asked so I obliged by giving this account. So, as if to emphasise its everydayness, I said, "Not very exciting, just a normal day." Then I remembered the Old

House and I added to the statement the news: "The Old House is up for sale once more."

I knew that she would know what I was talking about. We had often talked about the property and sometimes discussed buying it. But it had always been beyond our price range, not to mention that I had grave concerns about purchasing such an old building; so such talk had, in the past, been wild fantasy. It was a dream that Helen liked to indulge in from time to time and I was happy to go along with this as it made her happy to do so.

"Again!" she responded excitedly. "Perhaps we should think about buying it! We might get it for a good price, given that whoever owns it is evidently keen to sell it and no one wants to buy it. We could renovate it and then sell it for a profit."

I had heard this many times before. Every time we discussed the matter, Helen always believed that the owners would be willing to accept a low offer just to be rid of the property. I had my doubts, but it was, however, my engineering training that shaped my response to her statement. "Perhaps there is a good reason no one ever buys it," I said, sounding very serious. "As I have mentioned previously, maybe there is a structural problem. And even if we did buy it and renovate it, we too might not be able to sell it." Then I jokingly added, "Perhaps it's haunted!"

"Be serious, love," she replied. "I know your concerns – you mention them over and over again – but you should try to use your imagination and not be so driven by facts. What we want, our dreams, our happiness, they are just as important as facts, perhaps more so."

"Sorry, but we've talked about this before. You know that I'm concerned about purchasing any property that is so old. Just look at my office building. It dates from the same era and is dogged by structural problems that the landlord can't afford to fix. No, I think that the Old House is best left well alone."

These last words were prophetic as it turned out.

"Look, even if we couldn't sell it," she continued, "it would make a lovely family home. Plenty of rooms, a big garden, and countryside all around; it's perfect."

At that moment in time, without my present knowledge, putting aside my concerns about the structure, I admitted that she was entirely correct in this. It was actually an idea that had occurred to me previously, one that I had pondered on several occasions, but I had kept such thoughts to myself. It would indeed make a good family home. It was an ideal place to raise children. For a moment I worked with this idea. I pictured in my mind imaginary children, our children, a boy and a girl, playing happily in the garden, with the summer sun, warm and bright, adding to the idealistic image that had formed in my head. Then my thoughts shifted to a clear, cold and crisp winter's day, snow on the ground and the children building a snowman. Oh yes, it certainly seemed perfect in my mind's eye.

"Darling, are you still there?" enquired Helen, interrupting my daydream. I had been quiet for too long and she was wondering if we had been cut off – the curse of modern mobile telephony, and certainly not a regular characteristic of traditional landline telephones.

"Yes," I replied, "I'm still here. I was just thinking about what you were saying. I still have reservations, but if you're really serious, perhaps we could have a structural survey undertaken and then we could think about it in the light of the facts. Do you want me to get the property details from the estate agent? I know the proprietor. I sometimes undertake work for him."

"Facts again! Always facts! But, no, let's wait till I come home then we'll discuss it further. We need time to work out how much we can afford. No point wasting time chasing after that which is out of our price range, even if I am very attracted to living in the house. You see, even I can take on board facts!"

"Fine," I responded, happy to go along with her line of reasoning. "We can talk about it next week."

"Oh, I forgot to tell you that there is some pizza and chilli con carne for you in the freezer," she informed me.

I appreciated her thoughtfulness in leaving food ready prepared for me. It would certainly save time, freeing more of that precious resource for my work. "Thanks. I'm looking forward to eating them," I replied. "But I would rather be sharing them with you than eating alone," I added, sincerely.

"Okay, love. I think I need to get moving again; must push on. I want to get to my parents before the traffic starts to build up later. I still have a fair amount of driving to do. I'll phone at my next stop. I love you."

We are the sort of people who are always taking time to say how we feel, that we love each other, which we do, very much. We also take time to cuddle and we do that a lot as well, but this we would not be able to do until Monday night and I looked forward to it, knowing that what I now missed would soon become possible once again, such is the surety of being young, knowing that there is much time still left – but it is a delusion.

"I love you too," I replied, adding, "Drive safely. Speak to you soon. Bye."

"Bye," she responded and then she disconnected. I placed my mobile telephone in my shirt pocket. It was time to get on with the rest of the day's business.

I drove back to my office and set about the tasks that needed to be completed. And so time passed. Outside the temperatures soared as the day wore on. My employees returned and then disappeared to start their holidays, leaving me once more on my own. There was one more call from Helen, who by two o'clock was just one hour away from her parents' home. At half past three she called again to say that she had arrived safely.

After her final call I collected together some material to read that night, leaving the rest on the desk. My intention was to spend time in the office on Saturday, working through the piles of documents that had accumulated over the months, but to try to do as much work as possible sitting in our garden, making the most of the good weather.

On my way home I undertook the inspection and testing of the rewiring work that my electricians had just completed, found that all was well, and arrived at my house at about five o'clock.

It had turned out to be a very hot day, exceedingly hot in fact. The back of our house faces south and the sun, relentlessly beating down on the windowpanes, had raised the temperature in the rear rooms to unbearable levels. Having forgotten to close the curtains, the place was as though it were a hothouse.

Unlocking and throwing open the French windows and stepping into the garden, I was greeted by the joys of a summer's day. The sounds of buzzing insects filled the air. There was colour everywhere: many shades of green, yellow, red, and the blue sky, endless and vast, arching overhead. The heat of the sun was still strong though and too much to bear for long.

I sat on a garden chair in a shaded spot for some time, consuming cold drinks, but did not eat the food left for me, preferring instead to have a light snack.

The hours passed by and still I felt no inclination to go indoors, choosing to stay where I was and to continue reading the journals that I had brought home. Seven o'clock; I went back inside to pour myself a whisky – single malt, aged and matured, its elegance defined by time. I picked up my mobile telephone and rang Helen. We chatted for a while and then said our goodnights.

I continued to sit outside and watched the sun setting; as though slowly falling from the sky, it dipped below the horizon and then was gone, leaving an orange glow in the atmosphere, which with time slowly faded, giving way to that not-quite dark of a summer's night.

This was a scene that had been played out every day since the planet had first formed, a reoccurring act predating human life. Such aspects of the natural world are measured on different timescales to human existence, the latter being no more than the time taken for the blinking of an eye compared with the age of the earth, the solar system, and the universe. And years, months, days, hours, minutes and seconds, the defining parameters of time, are only human notions, inventions of a scientifically oriented world, where time has become the defining characteristic of life. Such measures allow for counting and reckoning, but do not explain the mystery of time – they say little of the secrets of time that have yet to be revealed and of all the events and lives stretching back into the origins of humanity somewhere in the darkness of an unrecorded past.

I did not know it at that moment in time, but I was watching the last sunset of my old life. The next day my life changed forever. When the sun went down that Friday evening, it was not just the sun that disappeared, but also my old existence; one can say that it passed away. When I awoke the next morning, when the sun rose again, it was not just a new day that greeted me, but a new beginning; a new dawn and a new reality, where time was, I initially thought, mine to do with as I pleased.

CHAPTER 5

Saturday morning dawned, the rising sun heralding the prospect of more weather similar to that of the previous day: fine, sunny, and hot. This new day, similar to every one that had gone before, had the potential to be just as other days had been, but it also held the possibility of the unexpected, such is the uncertainty of life. But there was one certainty at that moment in time, the sureness that it was going to be another blistering summer's day – definitely not one for working but, alas, my commitment was to labour rather than to pleasure.

Six o'clock and the brightness of the early-morning sun illuminated the bedroom, rays of light streaming through the gap that I had deliberately left between the curtains. I lay abed thinking of what might have been, of Helen, of togetherness. At that moment Helen would be in her bed, slumbering, peaceful and lost in dreams, while all about her the natural world was alive with activity; endless, timeless, and enduring. And I could have been there with her.

I thought of Helen for a few moments; of the pleasure of lying next to her while she slept and of her warm skin, smooth and soft to the touch. But the business of the day kept sneaking into my mind and in doing so it drew my attention away from this vision of beauty, spoiling the comforting images, intruding into my private world in the same way as an unsolicited door-to-door salesperson or a talkative stranger on a train does; unwanted, unwelcome, but an inescapable aspect of the modern world.

If only there were more time for quiet moments such as these, for reflection, free from the intrusions that masquerade as living. Life, it seems, no more has the desert to offer as a place of solitude where one can retreat to, but has itself become a kind of desert in the most negative sense of the word; a spiritual desert, filled with emptiness, superficial activities and devoid of real meaning or purpose.

I wanted to stay in bed, to lie there, thinking of Helen. But I had resolved to make an early start in the hope that I would at least be able to get away from the office by mid-afternoon and spend some time at home, in the garden, making the most of the warm summer sunshine. Days such as these can be unforgettable when coupled with pleasurable activities; moments in time that linger in the memory, warm thoughts long after the warmth of the day has given way to colder times. But not today, for this would be one where labour would have my primary attention and because of this it would be just another day among many spent in the pursuit of earning money.

I knew it did not have to be this way. The previous evening I had read journals while sitting in the garden and this had not been an unpleasant experience, even with work to do, although it would have been even more enjoyable without the demands of business.

I had concluded that, by occupying myself on Saturday, dealing with matters that required my presence at the office, I would then be able to spend the rest of the weekend at home, gradually working my way through the backlog of activities left undone from previous months. At least that way there would the consolation of knowing that the holiday period had not been completely spent in my workplace, and this would certainly be much better than shutting myself up in the office for three days while summer proceeded on its happy way outside, without me. Of course, at that moment in time I was completely unaware of the strange occurrences that were about to unfold in the coming hours; events that would change my life forever.

It was late August, so even though the previous day had been very hot, the temperature had dropped during the night to the point where dew had formed on the grass. Tiny droplets of clear water clung to the green blades, but these would not last very long. Soon they would evaporate, burned away by the brutal sun, and be gone, but only temporarily. Ephemeral they were indeed, but rare they were not. Return they would, but only when the conditions were right.

I stood by the window, looking out over the garden, our garden, the one we had made together, but it was too early in the day to appreciate the splendour of the view. My brain was still numb and calling out for caffeine, so I took hold of my dressing gown, and while walking to the kitchen to make some coffee I slipped my arms into the sleeves and secured the garment in place, tightening the belt so that I was now no longer dressed as nature had made me.

It is a strange fact that it is often the small and seemingly insignificant aspects of life that give most pleasure; a cup of freshly brewed coffee at the break of day, or taking in the silence of the night, or watching the world come to life in the early dawn, or lapping up the warmth of an open fire in the depths of winter. Or just being with Helen; my thoughts had drifted back to Helen again. Even just thinking about her was a source of pleasure, but being with Helen would have been even better.

I could not afford to spend too much time lost in my thoughts, being set upon a plan to use my time to clear the accumulation of administrative tasks and other activities that I had put off till another day. Should I have done this? Would it not have been better to have found the time to deal with these matters? The phrase *no time like the present* drifted into my consciousness. Too late now though for such regrets. So, consoling myself, I considered that there would be plenty of time later for indulging myself in small pleasures. At that moment in time I did not realise how prophetic this thought was.

My drive to work was, more or less, similar to every other journey that I had made to my office. Once more I passed the Old House, the Time House as I now call it. Again I drove down narrow country lanes; byways that had been there for centuries and along which people across the generations had moved, as time marched continually onwards. And yet again I found myself unlocking the front door of the office, letting myself into a building that was also old, with a history of its own. This was only a small and insignificant history in the great scheme of life, death and existence, but nevertheless a history important to the people for whom the building had been part of their lives. And at the moment in time it was part of my life and I was contributing to its story, just as those who had gone before me had done.

In this respect it was similar to all buildings; it had a storyline, a sequence of events, lost in the past, in the minds of those who had lived their lives in and around it, complete with moments of joy, moments of sorrow and a whole bundle of moments for which no classification is necessary, being the everyday events that form together the moments in time of which a person's life is composed.

It had been half past seven when I arrived at my workplace. At five minutes past eleven, the telephone rang – the defining moment of my life as it turned out.

We are normally closed over the weekends so I wondered why anyone was bothering to call. My immediate assumption was that it was someone who did not know our business hours. For a moment I hesitated. "Should I answer it, or not?" I asked myself. I pondered this question for a few seconds. It continued to ring. Perhaps it would not have mattered. Some actions and outcomes are meant to be, an inescapable part of one's destiny; if not today, then perhaps the next.

The moment of indecision was over; my curiosity had got the better of me. I picked up the handset. "Hello," I said.

"Benjamin? Is that you Benjamin?"

It was a familiar voice: Harry Mellor. "Yes, Harry, it's me. What's wrong?"

I had instantly assumed that Harry had a difficulty and was in need of my help. He knew too well my business hours and would not be trying to contact me over a holiday weekend if he did not have an urgent problem requiring my attention.

Harry Mellor is an estate agent and I sometimes carry out work for him. This usually involves checking domestic electrical installations as part of the structural surveys that Harry undertakes for house buyers, or, on occasions, repairing electrical faults in empty properties that are on the market. It turned out that it was for the latter reason Harry had phoned.

"I'm really glad that I managed to catch you. I expected that you would be closed given that it is a weekend, and a holiday weekend, but I thought that I would see if you were around."

"You're lucky this weekend, Harry," I replied. "Helen has gone to her parents and I'm catching up on a backlog of paperwork."

"The pleasures of running a business," Harry responded with a note of sarcasm in his voice. "I have to work every public holiday, except Christmas and New Year, so you don't realise how lucky you are."

"That's one way of looking at it, Harry," I stated, wondering as I did so why he was complaining about an element of his life that was there by choice. He could easily work regular hours by becoming an employee. But I suspected that would not suit Harry, just as it would not fit well with me, for independence, not being reliant on others, and a sense of being in control of one's life are often what motivates those who pursue careers as proprietors of small businesses.

"What can I do for you?" I enquired.

"I was wondering if you would do me a favour," he began to explain. "There seems to be a problem with the electrics in one of our empty properties and I want to get it fixed quickly as I am worried that it might be dangerous."

"What exactly is wrong?" I asked, attempting to form a better picture of the circumstances.

"Yesterday evening I was showing a woman around that Old House just outside the village where you live ..."

"The Old House! What a coincidence!" I said, interrupting Harry's explanation. "Helen and I were talking about that place yesterday. She has this idea that we should consider buying it."

Harry, being a salesman to the core of his being, was quick to respond. "I'd be happy to show you around," he replied in response to the information I had just furnished him with.

"Okay, but Helen and I agreed to talk in more detail about the matter first. I'll get back to you about that. But sorry, I interrupted what you were saying."

Harry continued, "Yes, that's fine. Don't forget I am here if you need further information. Now, back to what happened yesterday. During the visit, the lights started flashing on and off. And then the lady said that she received an electric shock when she touched a light switch. So, you see, I am concerned. I don't want anyone to be killed, or to have a fire in the property. Can you take a look this morning and see what's wrong, and, if there is a fault, fix it?"

Coincidence is a very interesting concept. Science, of course, has no place for the consideration of non-causal connections, yet humans do find meaningful relationships among events, which has been formalised into the concept of synchronicity; occurrences that are meaningfully related. Who has the right to say that synchronicity does not exist? That, it seems, is the core problem with those who adhere to the ideologies of science, engineering and technology – similar to their theological counterparts, they do claim rights and in doing so lay the foundations for their blindness, for most then become attuned only to that which reinforces their beliefs, dismissing all that does not fit with these, as a lack of *right mindedness*. And of that which underlies coincidence? Is it just an accidental alignment of events or thoughts that create that resonance in the mind which we call coincidence, standing out from the normality of what are otherwise apparently unrelated moments of time, or is there a hidden force at play? Again, science has no room for such considerations, for there is no purpose; the universe is just a machine, as we are too; what a frighteningly sterile view!

They are those who call such alignments serendipity, when events are fortuitous, or just plain bad luck when they are not, implying that these are just matters of chance, but others may say it is one's destiny at work and in doing so imply, perhaps, that there is a hidden hand guiding us towards

55

places and moments in time that have already been written in the manuscript of our lives.

I am an engineer, *out of disorder I create order*, so in my case I would have veered towards the former, but now, having been drawn into a complex sequence of events of a most peculiar nature, I am not so sure. And the measure to which my worldview has been transformed by the events that I have yet to recount to you can be measured by the fact that what I have just written, about synchronicity and so forth, I would never have previously entertained as being valid.

All moments in time are interconnected and there are consequences that follow on from one's decisions and actions. Of these truths I am now certain, but as an engineer I do not act in a manner appropriate to this fact. What I do is to respond to instructions and I was in no doubt at that moment in time that Harry was now issuing me with instructions, and I, being an engineer, dutifully obeyed, for there was a job here for me that was important and could not wait. The safety of life and property was at stake and it would have been unprofessional of me to leave the task until Tuesday. I also realised that the matter was important for Harry as well, not just for the reasons that I have just mentioned, but also because holiday weekends are a busy time for estate agents. Serious house hunters, and also the not so serious, those at a loose end and looking to fill up their time over the holiday, would be out in force over the three days, visiting estate agents and arranging viewings.

"No problem, Harry," I said. "I'll take a look this morning."

"Do you mind going on your own?" he asked. "I'm really busy this weekend."

"Okay. I'll be over in about thirty minutes."

"That's fantastic," he responded with a tone of genuine appreciation in his voice. "See you in about thirty minutes then," he continued, "and I'll make a sketch for you, showing where the incident occurred and where the fuse box is located. Bye."

"Bye," I said in return. But Harry had already put the telephone down and I was left talking only to myself. I could tell from the tone of his voice that he was feeling a little stressed and it was only the beginning of the day. There were three full working days ahead of Harry and if he were not careful he would end up having a heart attack. He was at the age when many people first start to experience heart problems and in addition he was overweight; he therefore seemed a prime candidate for coronary disease; the great terminator, in numerous parts of the industrialised world, of many people's time on earth. Such is the progress that has been made in western civilisation!

My intuitive sense that Harry was feeling stressed was confirmed when, half an hour later, I arrived at the estate agent's office. Harry was rushing about, trying to find some property leaflets for a young couple. It struck me that better organisation would help considerably to reduce Harry's stress by saving time, which he could then use more profitably; *out of disorder I create order.*

There were also other potential house buyers in the office, apart from the young couple, and Harry's sales assistants were fully occupied. If this level of activity continued over the rest of the weekend, I became more convinced that Harry would be spending time in intensive care at the hospital, and very soon.

Harry glanced at me and hurriedly shouted over, "I'll be with you in a few moments."

I waited patiently. After a few minutes Harry found what he was looking for and handed the leaflets to the couple and then excused himself and came over to me.

"Benjamin, thanks for coming," he began, rather flustered. "Come through to the back office and I'll give you the keys and show you my sketch."

"Harry, you look stressed," I noted, showing genuine concern.

Harry was a bundle of energy and always seemed highly strung, even at the best of times, but now he appeared on the edge; nervous, strained, about to explode.

"It's the usual holiday weekend rush," he jokingly replied, adding, "I'll be okay."

We went through to the back office, a poky little place not at all similar to the modern, stylish setting of the front office. Harry sat down in a swivel chair behind an old teak-veneered desk dating from the 1970s. He motioned for me to take the chair on the other side of the desk, so I was seated facing Harry. He placed his hands, palms down on the desk, looking eager to get back to the business taking place out front.

He did not look his age, which I knew was fifty-nine. Instead I thought I was sitting in the presence of a person twenty years older. This premature ageing was, I assumed, the result of pressure of work. But there was no time for such reflective observations. Not seeing the need for initial small-talk, Harry went straight to the point of our meeting.

"So, let me tell you what happened. Truth is I did not observe all that transpired. The lights flashing on and off I did see, but as for the woman getting an electric shock, that I did not witness. She said that she touched the light switch on the first-floor landing. Perhaps she just imagined it. I really don't know. Here," he said pointing at a sketch he had made, "you can't miss it. The switch is close by a large horizontal timber beam that is buried in the wall – a lintel. A long time ago the house was bigger than it is now. Parts of the property were demolished in the late eighteenth century. What was originally where this beam is, I do not know, perhaps an opening or maybe the landing was larger than it is now."

"And the main fuse box – where is that located?" I enquired.

"In the cellar," replied Harry. "There is a door under the stairs and steps down to the cellar."

"Right, I'll take a look for you. It could be that your client experienced static electricity, but I'll check the switch to make sure it's not faulty."

"Here are the keys for the front and rear doors," said Harry, passing them over to me. I noticed that his hand was shaking, not a good sign that Harry's health was in a favourable state. "The front door is very heavy," Harry mentioned. "Just give it a good push. When you've finished you can keep the keys and drop them back in here on Tuesday morning. I have another set if I need them. Truth is though, that's unlikely judging by past experience. Very few people seem to be interested in the house."

"Why is that?" I asked with a genuine air of interest. "Does it have structural problems?"

"You said Helen was interested in the house. I'll tell you no lies, Benjamin. It's perfectly sound. That surprised me when I first put the house on the market, many years ago. Most eighteenth century buildings usually have problems, often fairly serious ones. Normally it's damp, or dry rot, or woodworm, and so on, and occasionally the foundations need underpinning, but the structure is, as they say, sound as a bell."

"So why does it never sell?" I enquired, curious to learn as much as I could.

"I don't really have a good answer to that question. No one has ever been able to properly explain to me why they don't want to buy the house, but I myself do feel that it does not have a very welcoming atmosphere."

"You mean it's haunted?" I said jokingly.

"Don't joke about matters such as that, Benjamin. I've been in this business for forty years and I've come across all sorts of houses and some of them … well, what can I say? They have left me with very bad feelings. Glad to get out of them. Didn't want to be in them on my own; always in and out as fast as possible."

"Thanks, Harry, that's very reassuring. Now I'm really looking forward to visiting the Old House."

"Don't worry! This one's not like others that I've experienced. It just does not feel very welcoming. That's a bit of inside information for you in case you are serious about the property."

"Okay, thanks. I'll bear that in mind during my visit. And out of interest, who actually owns the house?"

"I have no idea, Benjamin. That's another strange aspect to the place. I've never been able to establish that. My instructions always come via a solicitor, Dome and Smith, just along the road. They won't speak about the owner. Apparently they have instructions not to reveal the vendor's name."

"You have certainly managed to paint a mysterious picture of the place, which is in keeping with what villagers say. In a way I'm looking forward to my visit."

Harry glanced at his watch. "Better get back in there," he muttered wearily, looking towards the door. "Time and tide wait for no man."

"You should take it easy, Harry," I returned with a tone of concern in my voice. "Take time for yourself and your family. Work can always wait, but the time we have with our loved ones is all too short and very precious. You never know what is going to happen. Take a holiday weekend off, Harry, and enjoy time with your wife and children."

"I know, you're right, but you appreciate what it's like when you are self-employed or run a small business. Work takes up a lot of time. There's always some task that needs doing and if I don't do it, there is no one else who will. I can only expect my employees to do so much."

"I understand what you mean, but still ..." I didn't elaborate the point further. I knew Harry understood; he just was not prepared to re-order his priorities. This was not a problem that I could solve for him, so I let the matter drop. "Okay, I'm on my way. I'll let you know what I discover. If major work needs doing I'll discuss it with you first. Otherwise I'll fix the problem if it is only minor."

"That's fine. I'll leave that to your judgement."

I left Harry to his harassed way of life and set off for the house. As always it was an uneventful journey, as all the previous ones had been, a pattern repeated many times as I travelled from work to our home in the village, and back again, but this was the first time that I had stopped at the Old House. So in this sense it was different, though just how out of the ordinary this was to be, at that moment in time, I had no inkling of.

CHAPTER 6

It was just after noon when I arrived. At the side of the property was a farm gate that led to the attached land that surrounded the house. I pulled into the opening leading to the gateway, turned off the engine, climbed out and then removed my toolbox from the boot of the car.

There were no car-parking facilities at the property: no drive, no garage. Obviously, no one who had owned the house had possessed a car and I suppose that this lack of modern amenities was a result of no one ever living there, at least not within living memory. This outdatedness was, as I was about to learn, a feature of the house; it lacked most of the facilities associated with a modern lifestyle.

Walking the short distance from the car to the front gate, carrying my toolbox, I was full of anticipation and a sense of discovery and exploration. Stopping, I paused for a moment to examine the building. The imagination is a very peculiar aspect of the mind; once informed that a house has an atmosphere, that it might be haunted, the imagination starts to play tricks. While I stood there, taking in the view and inspecting the external details more closely, which I had never done previously, I thought I saw out of the corner of my eye, in one of the first-floor windows on the east side of the house furthest away from me, the shape of a man, a dark figure, just caught for a moment at the edge of my field of vision. I quickly turned my view fully towards the window in question, but there was no one visible.

I had a feeling that I was being watched, which is a very weird sensation. How can one sense being watched? But I was conscious that eyes were upon me, even if I could not see anyone. Then, as suddenly as the feeling had come over me, it was gone.

Harry had said that the place was not very welcoming, but I dismissed the idea that there might be some other-worldly reason for this. Logic prevailed. I told myself that the house was empty. What I had experienced was my subconscious mind reacting to Harry's observations – and the result was just an imaginary figure manufactured by my brain.

The small white gate creaked slightly, but only slightly, when I opened it, suggesting that it had been cared for – no rust here. Walking slowly up the garden path to the front door I continued to observe my surrounds by glancing about and then I stopped and decided to phone Helen to tell her that I was about to enter the house we had spoken about only yesterday.

There was no delay, no waiting, wondering if there would be an answer, for the connection was there, almost in an instant and then came the voice that I was always glad to hear. "Hello darling," she said in a soft, sweet welcoming tone.

"Hi, love," I replied. "I've got a surprise for you. I'm standing on the doorstep of the Old House, key in hand, about to unlock the front door."

My revelation was indeed a surprise for Helen, but not an unpleasant one.

"What on earth are you doing?" she responded, sounding astonished. "We agreed we would talk some more before taking further steps."

"Relax, dear. This has nothing to do with our conversation. I am here on business. Harry Mellor, the estate agent, rang me this morning and asked me to look at the electrics. There may be problem with them."

"How exciting! I don't mean about the electrics, of course, but to go inside. Now I wish I had stayed at home." For the moment our feelings had reversed. Now it was Helen who was sad that she had not stayed, rather than me being regretful that I had not gone with her.

"I thought you might appreciate a running commentary as I explore the place," I told her. But to be honest, I was feeling isolated and in need of company, so I was glad of her presence, even though it was only through voice contact. Modern technology is such a wonder, for through it I was able, to some extent, to be with Helen and to share with her the experience of my first encounter with the house. In my hand was a device, a mobile telephone, which linked us together, even when we were far apart. And this was, in its most basic form, when reduced to its elementary components, just oil and rock, transformed by engineers and technologists into a meaningful item of value. It was yet further proof to me that out of the disorder of the natural world, engineers create order.

Helen's response was tinged with an air of anticipation. "Oh, yes please! Tell me what you see and what your initial reaction is. This is thrilling."

"Right, but first I must unlock and open the door, so hang on while I do that."

Having told Helen this, I placed the key in the lock, unlocked the door and turned the handle to open it. Harry was right: the front door was heavy. I pushed hard against it and with a bit of effort the door swung open. This was my first encounter with the workmanship and materials of an age long past; how different from the lightweight, almost insubstantial quality of modern doors, and perhaps the modern world itself.

"The door's really heavy," I observed, "but I managed to get it open by applying some effort. That's one item that will need replacing if we buy this house. Now it's time to go in."

Picking up my small toolbox that contained all the equipment that I would need, including a powerful torch, I gingerly stepped over the threshold into the entrance hall.

"Well, what's it like? Tell me!" she impatiently demanded.

"It's pretty dismal in here, love. An effect I'd say of the dark-stained wood panelling in the hall and on the stairs and the fact that the house has a north-facing front elevation. But it seems much brighter upstairs on the first-floor landing."

The brightness I noticed on looking up the stairs and this, I later discovered, was the result of a south-facing landing window through which warm sunlight was streaming.

"Not a promising beginning then," Helen noted, sounding a little disappointed. "So what else can you see? Tell me, tell me," she insisted, sounding now even more impatient.

I began to explain to Helen the particulars of the house, giving her a fairly detailed account of what I could see, along with my impressions and thoughts.

When I entered through the front door I found myself standing in a large square hall with a red carpet, not a wall-to-wall fitted carpet found in most modern homes, but one in the old style, with a border of polished wooden flooring showing around the sides. The carpet looked new, even though it was obviously not. What struck me immediately was how clean the property was. I had expected to see dust and cobwebs, but there were none to be observed. I had also expected a smell of dampness, or mustiness, but the air was dry and fresh. This was unusual.

Several panelled doors were positioned around the hall leading off to the downstairs rooms. Each of the doors was very wide, much more so than those found in modern houses. To my right there was a wide staircase ascending to the first floor. All the wooden wall panelling, along with the doors and other woodwork, were coated with a dark-brown wood stain, creating a very dismal appearance. The panelling occupied the lower parts of the walls and above this there was wallpaper – a very elegant wall covering in fact, but again obviously very dated, being made of cloth rather than paper. And the ceiling was painted a light green.

I could not conceive of a more effective way of reducing the appeal of a house than what greeted me on first entering this old property. A coat of paint, if nothing more than plain white, would transform this unwelcoming sight into a far friendlier one. This, I began to think, might be the problem; the reason the owners had never been able to sell the place. On entering, a prospective buyer would be greeted by not just a gloomy hall, but also an immediate awareness that the place was in need of modernisation.

Helen's response was predictable and reflected my own thoughts. "The décor alone is enough to put anyone off buying the property. A period feature it may be, but it's not one that I could live with and I can't imagine many other people putting up with it. And I suppose decorating the hall and stairs, and the landings that lie upstairs, would be a mammoth undertaking. It doesn't sound as though it is a ready-to-live-in property."

"I think you're right about that, love," I responded.

To my left I noticed a bank of light switches – three switches all together, arranged horizontally. This is what I had come to investigate, so it was necessary that I should start my investigations, and here was a good a place as any to begin.

"So what are you going to do now?" Helen enquired.

"I was just looking at some light switches. They are old; the black and round type that date back to the 1930s. I suspect that I'll be facing wiring that is just as old and therefore in very bad condition."

I was used to dealing with older wiring, but only from the perspective of removing it completely and replacing it with modern plastic insulated cables. Technologies change: time is a great innovator. In the 1930s, before the age of plastics, cables were covered with rubber. With the passage of time this material deteriorates, as does other matter in the world. Ageing results in a loss of the properties that make it suitable as a covering for cables, as an insulator, as the means of keeping the deadly electricity safely away from human touch. With time, as with some people's personalities, rubber becomes hard and brittle, and when it is disturbed, the rubber tends to crack and break away, again not unlike those who with the passage of time have become grumpy and unsociable; solitary figures that have broken their links with society and their fellow creatures.

If the circumstances that I fully expected were realised, then the electrical installation in the house would be in a very unsound condition. But I was to be surprised in this respect.

"I'm just going to try these switches first before moving on," I informed Helen, so that she would be aware of what I was doing; this, after all, was not a visit to view the property with a mind to deciding about a possible purchase.

Systematically, I started to explore the functioning of these switches, looking out for oddities that might provide glues to the problems that Harry had explained earlier. Starting on the left, I reached out and touched this first switch, and with my forefinger I flicked it downwards and the downstairs hall light came on, functioning just as it had done, back somewhere in a simpler age, when electricity had still been a novelty. I then moved to the next, again flicking it downwards, and a wall light came on halfway up the first flight of stairs. Finally I reached the third and last switch and moved it to the on position. This time there was no outcome, no light obvious to me, burning bright, illumining the murky place where I stood, but this was not unexpected, since it probably controlled a light on the upstairs landing. Because it was so bright up there I was unable to ascertain if an electric light had come on. But, on walking over to the stairs and gazing upward, I saw with some relief that the landing light was lit. I say with relief because I have learned that, in older properties, several problems can often be found when one starts to look for them, so to discover that a particular light, power socket and so forth actually work just means one less item for the fault list.

"These lights work," I told Helen, "so now I'm going to take a look at the downstairs rooms."

This was just straightforward curiosity about the house for Helen's benefit as well as my own. By taking a closer look, taking note of the layout of the chambers, room sizes, decorative details and so forth, and reporting to Helen as I went, we might be able to come to some initial decision about its suitability for our needs.

"Okay," replied Helen, again showing her impatience to learn more.

I resumed my running description of the house, providing Helen with the (disappointing) details of the features and décor, as I went on my journey of exploration.

First I entered a front room, the one immediately to the right of the front door, which lay on the west side of the dwelling. The internal door, as with the external one, was made of solid oak, which I could ascertain from the amount of effort I needed to expend to open it and my knowledge of wood grains; such is the detail of the knowledge that I have always sought to acquire in my quest to be an engineer of quality; whether I acquired wisdom concerning the use of this knowledge is, I must now admit, very doubtful.

This door and the others as well were more items on my already-developing mental list of features that would need replacing. As to that which was revealed on entering this room, this just added further to my impression of an aged and largely untouched building in need of a significant amount of modernisation. The room itself was bare; no carpet or rug adorned the floor and no pictures were hung on the walls, and not a single item of furniture could be seen. As for the décor, it was not much of an improvement over the entrance hall. The wooden floor was stained to match the dark wood panelling on all the walls, but in this case the panelling ran all the way up to the ceiling, which was whitewashed, and in the centre of the wall opposite the window there was a large stone fireplace with a tiled hearth. The room was cold and uninviting.

Leaving this chamber I crossed over to the other side of the hall and entered the other front room. This, I can tell you, was very different from the one I had just left. It was, once more, devoid of furnishings, but the wooden panels only extended a few feet up from the floor and were coloured a light green. The walls above were white, as was the ceiling, and as for the other woodwork – the doorframes and skirting board – these were painted light blue. It was a much lighter room than its counterpart on the other side of the hall and much more pleasing to the spirit.

Having conveyed these details to Helen, she responded by saying, "I suppose that the whole house must be similar. It looks as though it needs complete redecoration. But what of the room sizes – are they big or small?"

"Very big compared with modern standards; plenty of space for furniture without feeling overcrowded," I reported, while also informing her that I was about to explore the rooms at the rear of the property.

Passing through a second door on the south wall of this front room, I then entered a further downstairs chamber, which turned out to be more agreeable, for it was much lighter, being again decorated in light colours and benefiting from a south-facing aspect. The sunlight illuminated this room, creating a warm and welcoming atmosphere in what was otherwise a rather cool abode.

"What about the kitchen? What's that like?" Helen enquired, still curious to know more about the décor and the facilities.

The kitchen was located on the opposite, west side, of the house. To gain access to it I had to pass through a further door, which lead me to a small and plain rear entrance hall, at the far end of which was located (what I assumed was) the rear door to the property. On passing into this space I was faced with one more door, immediately opposite me, which I discovered led to the kitchen. This was, as I expected, very dated. There was the usual cast-iron cooking range, a feature of many kitchens in old English country houses.

"It's not good," I informed Helen, "very antiquated. There's not a single modern feature in here. It's as if it were an exhibit in a museum. It needs stripping out completely and refurbishing."

"Oh dear. Sounds as though it's going to be very expensive!"

"Yes, my mental list of needed improvements is already fairly long and growing with every room I visit. The whole house is probably in need of the addition of most modern amenities. So the cost will be purchase price plus tens of thousands of pounds for renovation." I then added the obvious question, "Still interested?"

"I'm not sure," Helen replied, with doubt evident in the tone of her voice.

"While you're pondering the matter I need to get on with the job that I came to do. I want to examine the fuses in the cellar. I'll ring you again later when I go upstairs."

"I'll be waiting for your call. Love you."

"Love you too. Bye for now."

CHAPTER 7

Having temporarily finished taking Helen through a guided verbal tour of the premises, I ventured into the cellar to find the fuse box.

Here I will now tell you about what I discovered concerning the wiring in this building, for this was, as I have already hinted, a surprise to me. I learned on closer inspection that the wiring, while being of rubber as I had initially suspected, was in very good condition; there was no sign of the ageing that I had anticipated. I quickly identified the lighting circuit, and, removing the fuse box cover, I checked for loose connections, the presence of which might account for the lights flashing on and off. All was sound. So the mystery remained.

After checking the other wiring in the cellar and replacing the fuse box cover, I returned to the hall where I quickly disassembled one of the light switches to ascertain the state of the wiring. That too was insulated with rubber, but was also in excellent condition. I replaced the cover and turned towards the stairs. It was time to venture up to the first floor and then up further to the next. I briefly recalled the figure of the man I thought I had seen at the first-floor window. My spine tingled at the thought. Suddenly goose bumps appeared on my skin. It felt as if someone, or a creature, had brushed against my hair, and my scalp reacted by becoming itchy and I had to scratch it.

I tried to calm my thoughts. "It's just my imagination," I muttered to myself. And with a determination not to allow the circumstance of being alone in an old and rather mysterious house to get the better of me, I quickly headed for the staircase and then bounded upstairs, my footsteps thudding on each stair, but with the impact softened by the carpet.

And there I was, on the landing, facing the very spot that Harry had marked on his sketch, the place where the lady had supposedly received an electric shock from a light switch. And there was the large horizontal timber beam that Harry had mentioned. But I was astonished and a little perplexed by what I saw.

The first-floor landing was not what I had expected to see from the information that Harry had provided. The floorboards were covered with the same red carpet as that on the stairs and in the hall, and at the north end, where I had moved to and now stood, there was a window. The layout of this part of the landing was similar to the hall on the ground floor, with a doorway located on the west side, at the bottom of another flight of stairs that led up to the second floor. This door opened into the first-floor west-side bedroom. But there was no doorway on the opposite side of the landing, just a wall.

I was standing facing east, and to my right, at the south end of the landing there was another large window. I walked over to this window. Here was my first sight of the rear garden, a section of which was enclosed by a high brick wall. The garden was in surprisingly good condition considering that the house had stood empty for such a long time. Evidently, someone was being paid to look after it, or so it seemed!

From this south-facing window I could also see, to my left, the outline in the ground of what seemed to be foundations, as if a building had once stood there. This, I assumed, must be the part of the house that was demolished. Pondering the scene for a little while, I considered what lay before me, and I then decided, based on the evidence, for I was after all an engineer, that what I was looking at was indeed the remnants of a wing, or an extension, on the rear of the east side of the house.

The sun was shining strong and warm with its light beaming in through this south-facing landing window, warming my skin; pleasant as this sensation was, I moved away and turned my attention to the horizontal timber lintel. Glancing at Harry's sketch, I again looked at the wall, confused by what I was seeing.

"Must be the wrong floor," I muttered to myself.

I stood before an opening in the wall, over which the wooden beam was placed to support the wall above. Harry had not mentioned any opening. Beyond this, a wide corridor ran directly towards the east gable-end wall of the house. On the left side of this space there was a door that, I assumed, led into the front north-facing chamber – the room where I imagined I had seen a dark figure watching me. On the right side there was just a wall.

There was no sign of the light switch where Harry had indicated it should be. Looking at this opening and observing no light switch led me to the obvious conclusion that I was definitely on the wrong floor. And then I walked to the north end of the landing and headed up to the next floor. Here once more I was to be surprised and perplexed by what I observed, for no horizontal timber beam could I see. There was also no light switch where Harry had indicated it should be. I opened all the doors and looked into each room in turn. These upper-floor chambers were obviously all bedrooms; each one had a window, but no furniture or carpets, and there was no sign of a timber beam in any of them, or on the second-floor landing. I tried the lights in each room as I entered; they all worked.

This was indeed a mystery and I was now confused. Perhaps Harry had not been very accurate in conveying information to me, so I headed back down to the first-floor landing and entered the front room located on the west side of the house. This was a very large chamber extending from the front of the property right to the back, and, as a consequence, the builder had provided three windows, one in the north-facing wall, another one in the west gable-end wall, and a further one in the south-facing wall. I liked this room very much as it was bright and warm, and its large floor space plainly marked it out as a candidate for a master bedroom. But that was not my concern at that moment in time for I was intent upon finding this large timber lintel with its nearby light switch that Harry had described. There was still no sign of it in this chamber.

I returned to the landing and to the opening in the landing wall. This was the only horizontal timber beam that I could find, but as for a light switch I still could not find one. This must be the place that Harry was referring to. I looked more closely for a light switch, then I walked under the beam towards the east side of the house and as I did so I felt a strange tingling sensation in my body. I stopped for a moment, wondering what had just happened.

But the sensation was gone as quickly as it had appeared, so I continued to look for a light switch. There were none to be seen, and in fact I noticed that in the east side of the property there was no electric ceiling light in the corridor where I now stood. So I walked back through the opening to the west side and, as I did so, I experienced once more that peculiar feeling, that slight irritation, that sensation, undefined, and slightly unpleasant. I stood for a moment in time looking at the wooden support buried in the wall; this large piece of timber that, through its strength, held in place above it, most likely, a considerable amount of stone or brickwork, depending on what had been used to construct the inner walls of the house.

Then I noticed that shapes and words had been roughly carved into the wood. The writing was obviously a sentence, but it was a very cryptic one. I looked more closely. The carving read: *Alpha and omega, beginning and end, and in between an eternity of time for those who wander into here.*

"Now what does that mean?" I asked myself, speaking aloud, for I was truly puzzled. I read it several times over. I recognised of course the biblical connection in the sentence: alpha and omega, beginning and end. But it was a puzzle and evidently one that I was not going to solve by staring at a piece of wood. Probably it would forever remain a mystery to me. Now, with the benefit of experience, I do understand its meaning, and its clear nature as a warning message.

While gazing at the carving I also examined the shapes cut into the wood. These were symbols that I recognised, markings that I had seen before. They were several of these; many were curved lines in the shape of loops, similar to a piece of string folded back on itself and crossed over, some were daisy wheels, and others just concentric circles. And where had I seen these previously? I recalled that it was in books where I had first set eyes on these peculiar patterns and here I was, face-to-face with them in reality. No pictures these, but actual carvings, shaped ages ago by a long forgotten and nameless craftsman. And I also knew immediately that there was one aspect to these that was out of place. These symbols did not belong in a house built in 1750. In buildings dating from a century earlier, from the 1650s, one might well find such carvings on doors, rafters and so forth, but not in a house from 1750.

These were apotropaic symbols, supposedly having the power to avert evil influences or bad luck. They belonged in a much more superstitious age than 1750. In the seventeenth century they were common, placed on buildings to protect against witches and witchcraft, which were part of the beliefs of the peoples of that time. But by 1750, these marking were no longer routinely placed in and on buildings. So why were they carved into this horizontal timber beam? My curiosity was becoming increasingly aroused by this strange building; I wanted to know more.

I searched my mind for a rational explanation and eventually concluded that the wood must have been removed from an older building and reused in the construction of this property. Perhaps this older construction had stood on the site of the present house. Yes, surely this was the explanation.

It was just after I had reached this conclusion that I was struck by another thought – there was an anomaly! It did not at first register with me, but it leapt to my attention as I was gazing at the carved words and symbols. What occurred to me was that Harry had not mentioned an opening in the wall below the timber beam. In fact his description had been very precise, unmistakably indicating that the timber beam was most likely a remnant of the original design, which had included a part of the building that had been, for reasons unknown, demolished.

I stepped for a second time into the east side of the house and in doing so I experienced once more the tingling sensation; this I found to be rather odd, for it was evidently linked with passing under the timber beam, but this made no sense to me at all. Once I was on the other side I examined the south-side corridor wall on my right, making sure that I took careful note of all the features that I could see; it seemed as though it were an ordinary wall, with nothing to alert me to what was about to occur.

Passing back under the beam I went to the south-facing landing window. Looking through the small panes of glass I examined once more the marks in the ground, the place where part of the house once stood; demolished long ago, back in the late eighteenth century, so I had been told. Opening the sash window, I looked out to my left, where I could just discern that there was a window, obviously indicating what I already knew, that there was a room on my left, on the other side of the wall that ran from the opening to the place where I now stood; but where was the doorway? There was no entrance on the landing or in the corridor than ran from that mysterious opening along to the east-side gable-end wall. So I pulled my head back in, closed the window and quickly headed back along the landing. On reaching the opening in the wall I once more stepped through it. I carefully examined the corridor wall yet again; it seemed solid enough, so I concluded that the room must have been sealed up.

It now occurred to me that it was very strange indeed that a whole room should be completely placed beyond use in such a way, which added more to the mystery of the place. I leaned against the wall in question, pondering this mysterious and unseen room, when suddenly I found myself falling backwards. I put my hands out to try to break my fall. It was an instinctive reaction and fortunately I landed well, on a carpeted floor, and I did not hurt myself. But for a moment I thought that I was dazed and that I was dreaming. I lay there glancing around me. Where once there had been a wall, the one that a few seconds before I had been leaning against, there was now just open space. The wall had completely disappeared. There was no trace of it; no marks on the floor, or the ceiling, no seam in the red carpet to indicate that there was a join, not a single trace. I was lying on the floor in the room that had moments before been sealed, only it was not closed up anymore. I looked over my shoulder, expecting to see the south-facing window that I had a few moments before seen when I stuck my head out of the landing window, but there was no frame or glass to be seen.

Now I was sure that my mind was playing tricks with me, yet another work of my own imagination, or perhaps the result of my fall; had I banged my head? Standing up, which I did not find difficult, I found that I was not in any way disoriented or unsteady on my feet; all was as it should have been in this respect. Contemplating what had, until a few moments before, been hidden behind the wall, I discovered before me a floor space. This in itself was no surprise for what else might I have expected? What had not entered my thoughts was the sight that I now beheld, for here was a floor that ran beyond where I knew the south wall of the house was located.

Here I note, once more, that I had, only minutes before, carefully looked out of the south-facing landing window, taking note of the details of what I could see, and what I unmistakably observed was the outside south-facing wall and the window frame in what had been a closed-off room. With the mysterious disappearance of the internal wall, I found myself standing in a space that should have had an external south-facing wall and window; but there was no wall or window to be seen; these were not there, and they should have been. What I could perceive was part of the house that no longer existed; a phantom wing, demolished long ago, consisting of stones, bricks and mortar, and timber that belonged in the eighteenth century, but not in the twenty-first. I was staring into part of the house that was no more, seeing a view of the property that no one had looked upon for over two centuries!

"This cannot be," I stated aloud to myself. "How is it possible? Walls do not just disappear, and floors do not run beyond solid external walls into spaces that no longer exist."

I began to think that I had started to experience hallucinations. That was the only realistic explanation. Harry was right about this house – it did have an atmosphere and it evidently was affecting me more than I had realised. What presented itself to me was an illusion, an apparition that would disappear and become what it should be, what I knew it was, if only I could bring myself back to reality. So I waited for my mind to stop playing these games and for the wall and window to reappear. I blinked my eyes repeatedly, even holding them shut for several seconds, expecting all to be right again when I opened them.

Alas, this did not happen. The scene in front of me did not change, but stubbornly remained as it was. I stood there for what seemed a long time, but it may actually only have been a few minutes. I did not notice the passing of time, so I am unable to state exactly how long I did wait there, in disbelief, looking at this apparition of the past. But eventually I moved, because I was beginning to feel uneasy just standing, gazing, as though incapable of action. I sensed for a brief, uncomfortable moment that I was not alone, that I was being watched, yet when I glanced about me there was not a single person to be seen.

When no one appeared and with all obstinately remaining as it should not be, I decided that I had had enough, and I walked back under the beam once more to the first-floor landing. My heart was beating fast and I felt my stomach muscles begin to tighten and then I realised that I was becoming unnecessarily anxious. I went and stood by the north-facing landing window, just to peer through it, to be reassured that all was well. There was my car as I had left it. It was a heartening sight, being one that spoke of normality. I took a few moments to calm myself by breathing slowly and deeply. My composure started to return and, bracing myself, I slowly walked back over to the opening and then passed once more into the east side of the house; but all was just as I had experienced it a few moments before. I found myself yet again looking into the demolished wing of the house and then the realisation dawned on me that perhaps what I was seeing was real and not a mere figment of my imagination, an invention of my mind. It was time to decide my next steps.

CHAPTER 8

For a brief moment I was unsure what to do. Perhaps I should have left the house at that moment in time, this being an option I did consider; it would have been the wisest course to follow. I am, however, an engineer, one of a modern breed of people who, along with scientists and others calling themselves technologists, have long since forgotten what wisdom is. Perhaps they never knew. Maybe what happened to me would have just been part of a future that was never to be, just one of the many that occur over a lifetime, if only I had departed at that moment. *If only!* How often do we say that? If only I had stayed. If only I had gone. If only I had not done this. If only I had done that. If only we had taken a different design decision. If only we had taken note of the warning signs. If only we had not built that nuclear reactor. If only we had not spread deadly chemicals on crops for the sake of improving the productivity of what is, without doubt, a most inefficient way of growing food. If only we had not squandered the world's oil resources. If only we had not told people that *the risks can be managed.* Oh, how life now, and in the future, would be different, perhaps better.

Yes, of course, but we have no way of knowing. We can only look back from some future vantage point, a place of safety, a point of reflection, calm and cool, and say, *if only.*

And if you believe this, then you are as self-deluded as those, such as me, who should know better.

At that moment a desire coming from deep within my subconsciousness kept me there; an irresistible force called curiosity. I was curious. A little frightened for a few seconds, yes, but I wanted to know more about this mystery. Call me stupid if you want, call me foolish, but there was an aspect to the circumstances in which I found myself that drew me onwards into the events that followed. The moment of indecision was over. I decided to stay.

While I was standing, looking into a part of the house that no longer existed, into an image of the past, I recalled the man whom I thought I had seen at the first-floor window – the dark figure. Was he real or just an illusion? If real, was he sinister or benign?

The entrance to the room where I believed I had seen this man now lay behind me. I had not yet entered that front east-side chamber; perhaps I had avoided doing so, lest I encounter some unpleasantness that would spoil my day.

There was the door; all I had to do was to open it to reveal the truth. I summoned up the courage to enter, to establish if indeed there was anyone there. Perhaps this too was foolish; but, alas, this human characteristic called curiosity, it drove me forwards. But maybe, if there was someone present in that room, he could provide answers. Or he might just add to the mystery. There was only one way to find out!

Slowly I approached the doorway and placed my hand on the handle, turned it and cautiously opened the door. I peeped in, inspecting what lay within the chamber. I looked over to the window, behind the door, and up at the ceiling. There was no one inside, but to my surprise the room was fully furnished, with a bed covered with sheets. There was also a dressing table and a number of chairs. I had expected a chamber as bare as the others that I had entered earlier, devoid of all those items that make a place a home, but instead I found a comfortable bedroom, ready to be used. But the style was not of my own time; it was old fashioned and, I assumed, dated back to the eighteenth century.

Looking through the window, I sensed that there was an aspect to the world that was not quite right, with some features missing, but what, exactly, did not register with me straightaway. Then I realised that familiar objects outside, those that we take for granted and which form the backcloth of life, were absent. The trees! No trees!

In the fields opposite the house, situated along the sides of the road, there are a number of very old and mature trees – oaks, ash, elms, and so forth. Large trees such as these are very common around the village where I live, and there are many of them lining the country lanes that weave among the fields of lush green – byways that create an intriguing pattern in the landscape.

The trees are highly visible from all around the village. They stand large and looming, adding to the ambience of the locality, even though they can be a nuisance at times, especially when one of these is uprooted in a strong gale, and, always in the autumn, depositing their leaves in gardens and along the country lanes. But they add colour to an autumnal season that is often damp and drab – a time when memories of summer's pleasant warmth are still fresh, and there is still a longing for more of the joy of the summer just past. And in winter, nature's naked time, deciduous wood provides a timely reminder of how devoid of foliage the English countryside can be during the time of long dark nights when nature is mostly asleep, slumbering until called once again to wakefulness by warming days and lengthening hours of sunlight. And when the snow falls it collects on the branches, a Christmas-card scene, prompting older folk to yearn for a time when the pace of life was slower and existence was more peaceful. The good old days, they call these times, when life was, they claim, better, but in truth not in the ways that matter most, for premature death, unnecessary illness, and poverty were commonplace. Yet the snow-clad branches are ephemeral: here today, gone tomorrow, victims of that eternal constant called change. Time rolls forever onward.

I looked out on the world and I realised that the trees were indeed there, but I was gazing at a scene that no modern person had ever seen. No living eyes had beheld the sight that was now before me. All who had observed what I now saw were dead, laid long ago in their graves in that eternal slumber called death, for the trees that now appeared before me were much smaller, just tiny saplings at the beginning of their long lives, not many years past the moment when they first sprouted forth from the ground to begin their slow journey upwards, beginning at some moment in time back in the eighteenth century. And there was no metalled road passing by the house, just a dirt track. My car was nowhere to be seen; it was gone, being parked in another age. And from my vantage point on the first floor, looking out across a landscape devoid of the mature trees that were so recognisable to me, I could see the village, but not as I knew it. Many of the houses that I was familiar with were no longer to be seen. They had vanished – the modern ones that is, for all the old ones were there, although looking very different from what I was used to.

Fear gripped me. I was confused, alarmed and frightened. I turned and ran from the room and headed back at great speed, passing under the horizontal wooden beam into the west side of the house. As I did so I experienced that strange tingling sensation yet again. Every time I passed under this strange wooden lintel, always there was this peculiar sensation.

I went straight to the north-facing landing window. There was the lane, but it had changed from a few seconds past into that which was very familiar. What I saw before me was the road, as I knew it, with a tarmac surface and fully grown trees lining the route. And there was my car. How could this be? What was happening?

Amidst all the confusion that I was experiencing at that moment in time, my mind was active as I searched for explanations. Then I made a link. I had found an association and it was as if a light had come on – an epiphany. It was what Harry had said to me that eventually clicked in my mind, making all the connections; it was the incident that had set in motion a train of events that had brought me to the house, to that very specific moment in time. The sensation, I realised, that I had experienced when passing under the horizontal wooden beam was very similar to an electric shock. These are an occupational hazard for an electrical engineer and, over time, I had received several of them. But the sensation that I was feeling was similar to an electric shock from a very low-voltage source – not dangerous. It was akin to that administered when one accidentally touches those electric fences that farmers use to keep sheep and cattle confined in a particular part of a field; unpleasant, but safe to people and animals. The lady who had been viewing the house claimed to have received an electric shock from a light switch near the beam. What was different here was that, at least for me, there was no light switch, just an opening where there should have been a wall. This might at least explain why the lady reported receiving a shock; there must be, in the area around the beam, electricity, but created by what? And how was it transmitted, there being no cables or other conducting material?

So the fog in my mind had cleared a little. I realised that there could only be two explanations: I was either imagining that I was seeing into the past when I was in the east side of the house, or I was travelling through time, to a distant moment long ago, a lost and forgotten point in the past that, as with all such moments, had come and gone, and become part of the great continuum of history. Logic reasserted itself. It must be the former; it is impossible to travel back through time, I reasoned; the universe is a place of order, with one moment in time following on from the previous one. But deep down, far beyond the realms of reason, I was beginning to doubt this rational view of what I had encountered.

I walked downstairs, opened the front door and stepped out into a searing summer's day. The hot air, touching my skin, reasserted my sense that reality was the explicable, the familiar, and that all that I had just encountered was inexplicable, discomfortingly unfamiliar, alien and disturbing, and just a fantasy. I made my way to the lane, crossed over to the opposite side and paused there, looking at the property and in particular at that first-floor window on the east side of the house. I remained at the roadside for several minutes, mulling over what I had experienced.

Where I was standing, facing south, I was exposed to the full sun; the shade of the trees that lined the lane lay in the field behind me. It was too hot to remain where I stood for long, so I quickly got out my mobile telephone and called Harry. His telephone rang for a few seconds and then there was a response. "Hello, Mellor Estate Agents," said the voice in a friendly way. It was Harry. He was trying to sound welcoming, but again I sensed that he was stressed.

"Hi Harry," I began, "Benjamin here. I just wanted to check with you about the location of the light switch where the lady claimed she received an electric shock. It is on the first floor, adjacent to the wooden beam in the wall? Is that correct?"

"Yes, that's right. Did you identify the problem?"

"No, not yet. I just wanted to check with you that I am looking at the right switch," I replied, pretending that I had found the switch in question. "And were there problems with the other light switches in the first-floor rooms on the east side of the house?"

"No, they were fine," responded Harry, sounding a little worried.

"So the light switches in the first-floor front room and the back room on the east side of the house were both okay?" This I stated, reiterating the point, while wanting to be absolutely sure about what Harry had seen.

"The light switches in both of those rooms were fine when I tried them," Harry declared. "Is there a serious problem with the wiring? Is that what you're getting at?" Harry asked, starting to sound alarmed.

"No, Harry, I'm not saying that. I just wanted to establish with you that those switches were okay when you were here. Now I'm clear," I said, adding, "The wooden beam looks interesting, very old I'd say. And the carvings – they are odd, are they not?"

"What carvings? And what do you mean, interesting? It's just an old wooden beam," replied Harry. "How interesting can an old piece of plain wood be?"

"You mean you didn't notice the words and symbols cut into the timber?" I enquired, trying not to sound surprised.

"Are we talking about the same piece of wood, Benjamin? I saw the beam. It's just a piece of old timber with no decoration. I know! I've been all over that house many times! There's nothing carved in the wood. Believe me, I would know if there were. I told you it was a strange place. It's making you see that which does not exist."

I did not want to discuss this further with Harry, so I said, "Yes, maybe you're right. I just find the place a curiosity. Stimulates the imagination wondering what the house was like when it was first built. The décor, the wing that was later demolished; ever thought about these matters, Harry? What the place looked like?"

"To be honest with you, I haven't. Does this mean that your interest in the property is growing?" he asked, sounding hopeful.

"Possibly," I responded, trying to sound uncommitted, for I did not want to give him false hope. "I'll get back to you about that after I have spoken with Helen."

"Tell you what," replied Harry, perhaps sensing a sale in the air, "hang on to those keys for a while, and show Helen around when she gets back from her parents'."

"Right, I'll do that. Thanks. You've told me what I wanted to know. I'll give you a ring when I have news about the electrics. Okay?"

"Okay. That's fine. I am busy. I'll have to go. Bye."

And Harry put the telephone receiver down, and I returned my mobile to my shirt pocket.

"So, Harry," I said to myself as though I were still talking to him, "you have told me what I wanted to know. There are two rooms on the east side of the house, except I can only see one room. What should be the other room is just an extension of the landing area leading into the part of the building that is not supposed to be there. And the carvings in the beam, well, Harry, you can't see them, but I can. And there's no light switch – except there is, at least for you, Harry, but I can't see it! That's just fantastic."

I started to wonder what exactly I was going to tell Harry, given that I could not see the problem light switch. It was, without a doubt, time for me to head back inside. I crossed the lane, but first I made my way around the side of the house to the back.

I was soon in the rear garden, close to the house. Further away from me, enclosing the garden, was the tall brick wall. I looked at the brickwork on the rear wall of house, which had not been rendered, and compared it with that of the garden wall; there was a distinctive difference in the amount of weathering that had taken place. The garden walls were, to some degree, weather-beaten, with the mortar between the bricks eroded away, but not as much as I would have expected after 250 years. But the house walls were a different story, because here the mortar was not at all weathered. Nor did it look as though these walls had been re-pointed with new mortar at some time in the past. Very strange!

In the garden area where I stood, I looked down at the remains of the wing that had been demolished. I followed the line of the foundations, walking along them. I estimated that it must have been a fairly significant part of the house that was knocked down, which only raised in my mind the question of the reason for this. Why would anyone remove such a large part of a building? Was there an ambience in this wing that spooked the owner so much that he felt it necessary to demolish part of his house, to obliterate it completely?

Glancing up at the window of the rear first-floor room on the east side of the house I was in no doubt that, at least from the outside, the wall and window contained within it represented the end point of the house. There was no extension wing.

I returned to the front of the property, intent on re-entering and making another closer examination of the upstairs, and I soon found myself up on the first-floor landing, staring up at the beam and the mysterious words carved there, wondering what they meant. Was it a cryptic message from a previous owner? Was it a warning? These questions appeared in my mind, but I ignored them for I was too clever by half to engage in pondering such ridiculous notions; better to stick with facts. But, whatever these words and symbols meant, it was clear that Harry had not seen them, and that was a fact, though not a very comfortable one.

How the house on the first floor appeared to Harry, I could only guess at. From what he told me, on the east side of the house there must have been a door to the front first-floor room, the entry being located on the landing between the front wall of the house and the mysterious beam. What I beheld was just a wall without a doorway. The door to that front chamber was located in the east side of the house, in the landing area that lay beyond the opening. And what I saw in that landing area, which led off to the non-existent part of the house, must to Harry have been another room, so I assumed that there was another door located on the landing between the beam and the rear south-facing wall of the property.

This was just speculation, for I could see none of this. My view was the same as the one I had encountered when that wall had just disappeared into thin air; a sight that I had tried to dismiss as just a trick of an over-active imagination. But now I was past that stage. Harry had confirmed for me that our perceptions of reality were very different, leading me to conclude that what I was experiencing was, I reluctantly concluded, unique and very special.

So it was that my rational thinking and the power of logic began to give ground to that other side of life, the supernatural and the mystical, which is today so much ridiculed that to speak of it invites branding as an oddball; only crazy people talk about such things, which might be why those not crazy at all do not speak about them when they are encountered.

Of the mystery that was before me, there was only one explanation that I could formulate, and this was that, through some inexplicable means, I was seeing and experiencing the east-side part of the house as it was when it was first constructed back in the eighteenth century. But it was not just the internal features that appeared to me as they were at that time, but also the outside world, because the view from the window in the front east-side room had revealed a landscape different from the one I knew.

Although initially I did not want to accept this explanation, there was no doubt in my mind now about what I had encountered, about what I was seeing. The images forming in my brain were not the result of my imagination; all that I saw was real. I was not dreaming, but travelling back in time!

Up to this moment I had not yet ventured very far into the east side of the house and I had no knowledge of what lay in the phantom wing. And at that moment in time I made up my mind – I wanted to explore further, to see what lay beyond what was visible from just stepping into the east side of the house. It was time to find out what surprises lay waiting for me in the mysterious south-east wing. I told myself that *the risks could be managed.*

CHAPTER 9

I crossed under the beam again, experiencing once more the tingling sensation, a feeling that was already becoming very familiar to me. I was a little apprehensive and perspiration had formed on my brow, so I walked slowly towards where there should have been a window. As I approached the opening in the south wall, I began to take in and form an impression of the south-east wing. My initial feelings, developed from inspecting the foundations of the demolished part of the building, were confirmed; it was indeed a large section of the house, and I again wondered why it had been pulled down, but it was reassuring to know that the risk associated with what I was about to do could be managed.

I stopped and stood just before the opening that led into the phantom wing. One more step and I would be walking into the unknown, perhaps placing myself in great danger. So far I was in a part of the building that did actually still exist in my own time, but that was not the case for the demolished section of the house.

It was then that I heard the voice for the first time. This was another part of the mystery that I was experiencing, and it was one that I would encounter several times.

"Are you going to be able to get back?" it asked. "Will you become trapped?"

It was a soft gentle voice, but nevertheless I was disturbed to hear it.

"Who's there," I said in reply. There was no response. "Who's there? Show yourself." But all was quiet.

I did not move forward for the experience had halted my progress and what the voice had asked was a valid question, so much so that I was more concerned with the content of the questions and their implications than with the fact that I was hearing a voice that had no obvious physical source.

I stood on the threshold of the south-east wing of the house for several minutes, wondering what to do. Before me I could see that the landing area extended further into the demolished wing. A few feet in there was a wall that ran two thirds of the way from the east side towards the west-side walls of the wing. Turning a corner towards the south, the wall then led to what was the south wall of this part of the building, and in doing so this interior wall formed a room, leaving a corridor that ran down the west side of the wing. And it looked as though at the end of this passage there was another staircase that led down to the ground floor. But to be absolutely sure about this I would need to enter the south-east wing and move along this corridor.

It was a natural reaction to hesitate, to waver at this moment, at this point of decision, not only because of the voice I had just heard, but also because what I was about to do seemed unnatural. But I could not stand there forever, gazing into an apparently empty corridor. Some action on my part was needed, so, putting aside my reservations, my fears, my concerns, and telling myself that the risks could be managed, I gingerly stepped forward and then paused. I was now standing in the south-east wing and with this came the confirmation that it was no ghostly apparition, but real, physical, and very solid. Moving backward one step into the main body of the house confirmed that I could actually get back. I was correct – the risks could indeed be managed. So I slowly moved forward a few more steps. Taking a very cautious approach, I stopped once again, and then retraced my steps backward into the house proper. It seemed that I was able to move back and forth as I wished, so the question of becoming trapped was well answered by practical experience, and the worry that had formed in my mind on hearing that mysterious voice dissipated. I was now ready to move down the corridor, to set off once more into the unknown that now lay before me. I could see that on the left side of the corridor, towards the end, there was a door, presumably leading into the room, and at the very end there was indeed a flight of stairs leading down to the lower floor.

A few moments in time was all it would take for me to walk the length of the corridor, descend the stairs and to discover what lay waiting for me down there. I have to admit now that thoughts of going back, of giving up this adventure, were not to be entertained. My curiosity had got the better of the doubts that the voice had raised in my mind about what I was doing, and I was now fully committed to exploring the mystery of this part of the house.

I was excited by the prospect of discovery and exploration, but I was not reckless, or at least this is what I thought. I proceeded with care, for I knew not what lay ahead of me, or for that matter who, for it was entirely possible that I might encounter someone, the owner of the property perhaps, and I was not sure about the reception I would receive. After all, how would anyone react if they found a stranger wandering around their home?

My slow walk down that corridor began. With every step I drew closer to the stairs and my journey into the unknown deepened. I began to speculate about what other oddities I might find. I might just find a doorway back into my own time, or a gateway to a world of endless wandering through time and space. And what creatures might lurk there? All seemed possible given the circumstances that I now found myself in. Such thoughts awakened in me a feeling of fear, so I tried not to dwell on the possible unpleasant discoveries and to remain alert to my surroundings.

I drew level with the doorway on my left. Stopping, I turned towards the door and slowly moved my hand towards the handle, listening as I did so for sounds, noises that might indicate the presence of another person. Anxiety returned and my heart was pounding in my chest once more, and I paused, frozen in time and space. All was quiet. No movement was evident, either inside the room or elsewhere. The whole house was still and there was no more of that voice, asking awkward and inconvenient questions, which were nevertheless founded in wisdom.

Resuming motion, I gently began to open the door. Peeping through the opening gap as the door moved, I tried to ascertain if indeed I was alone. As the door moved further ajar and more of the room came into view, I scanned the emerging scene; still no sight or sound that might indicate the presence of a fellow human being, or other creatures. But I did notice that this room, as with the bedroom, was furnished. And the style was that of the mid-eighteenth century and not of the modern age – my time.

Eventually the door stood wide open and stepping into the room I checked behind the door to ensure that there was nobody hiding there. I was alone. Glancing around at the décor and the room furnishings I saw that all looked brand new. There were two leather-upholstered armchairs that stood either side of the fireplace, a mahogany desk positioned near the window with a chair close by, and a rug on the floor. On the desk there was a glass inkwell, complete with ink and a quill pen and also a leather folder. I wondered what might be inside; perhaps some interesting documents?

On both sides of the fireplace bookcases were fitted into the alcoves. I moved over to one of these and selected a book at random, removed it from its shelf and opened it. It was dated 1748, but it did not have that musty smell that one associates with old books. The paper was still in pristine condition and the book, judging by its state, appeared not to have been read or even thumbed. This room, I surmised, must be a study, a place of quiet and solitude, with only books and perhaps a good glass of fine cognac for company.

I placed the book back in its position on the shelf, went over to the window and looked out over the ground at the rear of the house. There was the garden wall, but the soil was bare as no one had yet endeavoured to add plants – no grass or roses, just bare earth, with clumps of weeds growing here and there. There was no sign of anyone outside.

A feeling of excitement was starting to grow inside of me. I liked this exploration of a different age and I began to fancy myself as a time traveller.

Keen to move on, I decided to examine, on my return, the contents of the leather folder lying on the desk. I made my way to the doorway and back into the corridor, and then walked a little further, ever so quietly, to the top of the stairs, where once more I halted and listened. Standing by the banister I very carefully leaned slightly over it to try to see more of what lay at the bottom of the stairwell.

The stairs were in two sections, with four steps down, leading to a half-landing, at which point the stairs continued downward to the right, at a ninety-degree angle to the first set of stairs. The part of the ground floor that I could see, which was very little, was covered with red clay tiles. Unable as I was to discover very much from my vantage point, the only way to ascertain what lay below was to make the descent.

At this point I was now much more confident and I was ready to embark upon the next stage of my exploration. But then I heard the voice again. It asked questions similar to those posed previously, and this caused me once more to stop. "What if you cannot get back into your own time? What if there is no way back?"

I looked around, seeking the source of the voice, but there was no one to be seen anywhere. I had demonstrated to myself that I could go back, but on hearing this voice I began to panic and I was gripped by a fear of being trapped, locked in a time and a world where I did not belong, where I would be out of place. I started to feel uneasy with what I was doing and my recent confidence ebbed away. For all the excitement and curiosity that I felt, a less adventurous disposition began to seem the better course. I did not want to become a prisoner of an alien world. I thought it prudent, therefore, to return, so I turned and retraced my steps along the corridor, back into the main part of the house. I passed once more under the beam, into the west side of the house, and immediately headed for the north-facing landing window.

When I looked out of that window the sight that greeted me came as a welcome relief, for there, exactly where I had left it, was my car. The view was just as it should have been, as I knew it, a landscape with all elements present – a picture of life in the early twenty-first century. This came as a great relief to me. Then I felt a little stupid. I had panicked for no reason. All was well. I had passed to and fro into the east side of the house several times and on each occasion I had been able to return to my own time. I had also stepped back and forth a number of times across the boundary between the house and the phantom wing and experienced no difficulties. Thinking about these facts for a while was reassuring; I am an engineer and I always rely on facts. My confidence started to return and my disposition towards exploration and adventure came back. "The risks can be managed," I confidently declared.

"So it seems that I can come and go across this time barrier," I said to myself, continuing to speak aloud. "I can step into the now non-existent wing of the house, and this causes no problems."

But what of the voice! It was, I confess, a mystery, for it sounded as if it were in my head, but at the same time it was real enough to create the impression that there was someone close by speaking to me, but there was obviously no one near to me. "It's just a trick of this place, part of its weirdness," I said to myself.

So, having yet again dismissed the warnings, and secure in the knowledge that there was a way back to my own time, I resolved to continue. Looking back I can now see that this behaviour was all too familiar. We do this all the time in the modern world and I, as an engineer, may be one of the worst offenders. How often do we hear of concerns about science and technology brushed aside by those claiming to know better, who proclaim that the benefits are such that risks are worth taking? *The risks can be managed*, cry the vested interests. And yet when disaster does strike – and let us be in no doubt here that it does strike – people shrug their shoulders and say, this is the price we pay for progress. Nothing ventured, nothing gained. This is a manifestation of the delusion that humans can control the forces of nature and, out of disorder, science and technology can bring order. It is an assumption that renders scientists, engineers and technologists potentially very dangerous people, especially when they entice politicians and policymakers with their beguiling collective delusions – perhaps a case of the blind leading the blind?

I quickly went back the way I had just come, now fully determined to uncover the mystery confronting me. I reached the top of the stairs in the wing and without further hesitation began my descent. Carefully placing my feet on the stairs, allowing my weight to be transferred to each foot very slowly, so that I did not make a noise, I moved downwards. I was attentive to sounds that might alert me to the presence of anyone, always watching for signs that might signify that I was not alone.

Occasionally glancing back over my shoulders to reassure myself, I continued my descent.

I need not have worried. I was alone. Very soon I reached the bottom of the stairs and stood on those red clay floor tiles, so recently laid, that covered the ground floor. And there was no one there. The walls were lined with shelves, but each shelf was as bare and empty as on the day they had been fixed in place. On the north side of the room was a doorway, which I assumed led into the main part of the house, to a part I had already visited, though in my own age, but when I tried to open this door I discovered that it was locked. There was also another door, not leading into the house but outside to the garden. This I was able to ascertain, since next to it was a small window through which I could see the outside. The way back into the main house was the route I had come, or, via a journey outside and around the side of the house, through the front door, if it were unlocked, that is.

I walked around the ground floor at the bottom of the stairs for a few moments. The place was devoid of furnishings, so I decided to step outside, to pass through the doorway, into the world of the eighteenth century. Beyond the door there was a world unknown to me. The major events of history I knew about from history books, but of the customs and habits of the time, of the small details of which life in reality is composed, I knew very little beyond that which I had seen in television costume dramas. I did not know how people in this area would talk, what the local news was, who lived nearby ... The list of what I did not know seemed endless; I was truly ignorant of what lay before me. Then it occurred to me that if anyone saw me they might think me a bit odd, for my clothes would be very unfamiliar. More than unfamiliar – to them, I would be dressed in the strangest way, for outside, men of that era wore frock coats, breaches, stockings, and tricorne hats. Still I had no other option. If I were to continue with my adventure I would have to proceed as I was, dressed in clothes from the twenty-first century, and deal with issues as they arose. I was committed now and was not prepared to go back.

So it was with great determination and resolve that I headed for the external door. With growing confidence I boldly stepped out into the world of the eighteenth century, an age that had long ago passed into history, but which for me was about to become a reality – a living place, full of people working through the moments in time that constituted their lives, as well as the place of artefacts and customs unknown to me. Somehow or other I would have to cope with this uncertainty, relying upon my ingenuity and what knowledge I had from my own time to deal with whatever came my way. And it was not long before I was faced with circumstances that necessitated some quick thinking on my part.

CHAPTER 10

What I encountered was an immediate challenge in the form of people from the eighteenth century, at the front of the house, in the lane, demanding my attention. I will explain.

On passing through that rear door I found myself in a warm day, at some moment, I know not exactly when, over 250 years before my own time. I learned later that the year was 1750. The weather was very similar to that which I had left behind me, only it was not so hot. White puffs of cloud drifted across an azure sky and a cooling breeze blew from the east. I found it hard to pinpoint precisely the specific month, but it was evidently summer time.

As soon as I stepped outside I heard raised voices coming from a place not too distant from where I was positioned. The noise originated at the front of the property and indicated that two people were arguing. But one voice was much fainter and lighter than the other and sounded to be that of a child. The other plainly belonged to an adult, a very annoyed man by the tone and content of what I was hearing.

I quickly moved along the side of the property, but I was careful for I did not want to reveal myself. I had no intention of speaking to them, or becoming involved. I just wanted to know more about what was happening and to reconfirm that I was indeed in a different time to my own era.

Near to the front of the house I paused and stood with my back against the side wall of the building. I could hear the man shouting, angrily. "Little rat," he yelled in a loud voice full of fury. "I will beat you to a pulp."

On hearing these words I became alarmed. It sounded as if the argument, if indeed that was what I was overhearing, was about to deteriorate into violence. I poked my head around the corner, just enough to observe what was taking place.

I saw a young man, probably in his early twenties, holding a young boy by the lapels of his jacket, a boy who could not have been more than ten. The older of the two obviously had an unfair advantage and should not have been treating the young boy so, but I was in a different age when values and rules were unlike those which I was accustomed to.

The assailant, who was cursing, using the foulest of language, was shaking the little child, and then suddenly and with great force the man threw the boy to the ground. I heard a hollow thud as his little body hit the grass by the side of the dirt track, such was the force used against the poor child, who cried out in pain, as the fall had hurt him. The boy began to sob and beg for mercy.

"Now to teach you a lesson, you little bastard," said the man, full of venom.

No sooner were these words uttered than I saw a hand, within which was grasped a cane, rise into the air; the man was about to strike the boy with his stick. The hand hovered in the air for a moment while the aggressor focused on delivering as hard a blow as he could muster. What happened next was an instinctive reaction on my part. I ran forwards from the spot where I was observing all this, not at all thinking about the consequences, either for my own safety or the impact that my strange appearance would have upon the man or the boy. I bounded along the front garden path and jumped over the low gate located in the fence that marked the boundary between the property and the lane. As I did so the man landed his first blow on the child's body. The boy rolled slightly on to his right side, raising his left hand and arm to protect his head and face. The cane struck him hard on the raised arm. The little fellow cried out once more in great pain. "Ow!" the boy yelled. "Leave me alone," he added, while continuing to cry.

I reached the boy's assailant just as he was raising his cane for a second time, preparing to land another heavy blow on his victim. I grabbed the walking stick just as the man's hand was elevated as far as it would go. Jerking the cane from his grasp I pushed the young fellow down on to the ground, shouting at him as I did so, his tricorne hat flying off as he went down. He landed on his side a few feet from me on the grass verge.

"That is enough of that," I said in a firm and determined voice. "Leave the young lad alone. Whatever he has done, he does not deserve to be treated in this way."

The young man was taken by surprise by all this and for a few moments he lay on the ground, dazed. I reached out and pulled the little boy up. He too was shocked by my intervention, but he was evidently hurt and grateful for my timely involvement. There were tears in his eyes and rolling down his face and he held onto his left arm, cradling it, protecting it, ensuring that it came to no further harm. "Stand behind me," I told him. He was more than glad to do so.

The young man lying on the floor had now recovered from the initial shock of having his cane taken from him and his undignified fall to the ground. He looked very angry and in a moment he sprang to his feet. He seemed ready to have a go at me as well and was, I am sure, on the verge of doing so, when a troubled expression came over his face. He looked me up and down and then seemed unsure of himself. "What the hell do you think you are doing?" he yelled furiously. "How dare you push me down? I will give you a beating too." With that he made a lunge for the cane, which I was still holding in my right hand. I quickly stepped out of his way and he went flying, ending up lying face down in the dust on the road. He was stunned by this for a few moments, and then he rolled over on to his side, looking up at me.

I decided at that point that I should dispose of the cane. Taking hold of it with both hands, near the ends, I placed it into a horizontal position, lifted it up then brought it down with great force, bringing my right knee up at the same time. The cane snapped in half and I felt a sharp pain across the area just above the knee where contact was made. With both pieces in my right hand I threw them far into the field adjacent to the place where we stood.

The look of anger and astonishment on the man's face was all too visible. He clambered to his feet. This was my first opportunity to examine his style of dress. I must admit that he looked rather elegant, very much the 1750s man, dressed in a knee-length fawn-coloured frock coat, but lacking decoration – a practical day coat, I assumed, which I was later to learn is called an undress coat. He also wore a brown waistcoat with embroidery, a white shirt and dark-brown breaches and black knee-high riding boots. His hair was long and black and tied back at the rear of the neck with a large black ribbon. And as for me, I was acutely aware that my clothes were extremely odd by comparison, being dressed as a twenty-first century man, and that my hair was cut short; it was really obvious that I had not given any thought to blending into this world; but I am an engineer, and not used to thinking through the full consequences of my actions.

What I also observed was that his frock coat, breaches and riding boots were covered with dirt from the dusty road surface. Stuck to his coat sleeves were bits of dried grass from his first fall and his hair was disorderly. I sensed that this would just add to his displeasure.

He stood, feet apart, a short distance away, arm out, with finger pointing at me. His face was flushed. He was breathing very heavily, so intense was his anger. "Do you know who I am?" he asked, rhetorically. "Do you know who I am? No one does this to me. No one!"

He was unmistakably enraged and I also sensed a cold murderous air about his tone, but I was not going to be spoken to in such a way. "I have not the least idea, nor any interest for that matter, in whom or what you are," I stated.

I had responded in a manner that he was not expecting. He examined me again. I could see that look of uncertainty had returned. He was obviously not accustomed to being addressed in such a way. But he also recognised that an educated man was confronting him. Evidently he also knew that I was not a local, for my voice was very different from that of the young boy's. He turned to look at the house and then examined me once more. A big grin crept across his face for a moment, and then a serious and dangerous expression appeared. "I know who you are," he said, trying to sound superior. "You are the stranger who had this new house built. There has been a lot of talk about you. I had heard that the newcomer was supposed to be from the American Colonies." Then he added, in a derisory tone of voice, "Is that the way they dress in the Colonies? That is not the attire of a gentleman in this country."

He had not said much, but what he did say and the way that he spoke convinced me straightaway that he was a disagreeable type. I was determined not to let him get the better of me. He was obviously a bully and used to getting his own way. "My business is my own and how I dress is not your concern," I said with a threatening tone, "and in future," I continued, "you will keep away from my house. And, if you lay another finger on this boy, you will answer to me. Understand me well – hurt him again and I will come looking for you."

I had said *my house* without thinking, but of course it was not mine, at least that is what I believed. Subsequent events would eventually challenge this belief, but I am jumping ahead slightly. For the time being, all I will say is that I did not realise it at that moment, but by speaking to him and threatening him in such a way, in front of the little boy who was well below my adversary's social level, I was humiliating him. There would be repercussions from this incident at a later point in my adventure.

The man stormed over to where his hat lay, picked it up and placed it back on his head. He brushed himself down with his hands and when finished he again pointed his finger at me, saying, "You have not heard the last of this. What is your—"

I interrupted him. "Did not anyone ever teach you that it is rude to point?"

Once again he looked at me, finding it hard to believe that anyone would dare to speak to him in such a way. "Damn you. What is your name man? Come on. Tell me."

"You can go to hell," I replied. "You probably will do if you go around behaving in that manner."

I could see that he was completely frustrated. He was getting as good as he gave and losing. He decided to cut his losses and he turned and departed, walking along the road, venting his anger and frustration on the world about him by occasionally kicking at stones that lay on the dirt track. He was heading towards the village, a place I knew well, but in reality had no knowledge of in that time, which, for me, lay a long way back in history.

"It seems that I have made myself an enemy," I said, turning to the boy. Then I enquired after the boy's injuries. "Are you badly hurt?"

"Only a little," he replied. "I will be fine. It hurts, but it would have been worse if you had not helped me."

"What is your name?" I enquired.

"Samuel," he replied. "Samuel Jones."

"How old are you?" I continued, trying to discover more about the boy.

"I do not know, sir," he replied, rather embarrassed.

I was very unfamiliar with the era, so I naïvely asked, "Why do you not know?"

"I do not know why, sir. It does not seem important. Is it important?"

I paused for a moment, but then I decided against pursuing the topic further. "No, I suppose that it does not matter," I replied, recognising that the passing of time here did not seem to have the same importance as it did back where I had come from. I then eyed the young fellow and I could see that as regards dress he was not exactly a reproduction in miniature of the style of his assailant; Samuel's clothes were of much poorer quality, although similar in appearance, except that Samuel did not wear riding boots, but instead wore a pair of simple buckled shoes, and a pair of stockings up to his knees, which is where his breeches ended.

Rather than interrogating the boy further about his own circumstances, I introduced myself. "I am Benjamin Woodward," I told him. Then I asked about my adversary. "Who is that man?"

"Him! He is the son of one of the local gentry. His name is Walter Smythe."

"Why was he so angry with you? Why did he hit you?" I enquired, conveying also my genuine concern for Samuel.

"For not much reason," Samuel replied. "I did not greet him or acknowledge him as we passed. He expected me to tug my hat and avert my gaze from his. But I did not. I do not see why I should. He is no better than me really."

"And because of that he set about beating you," I said, somewhat astounded.

Samuel was not interested in talking about Walter Smythe or what this arrogant man had just inflicted on him, but instead wanted to know about me. "Have you really been to the American Colonies?" he asked excitedly, with a sparkle of youthful curiosity in his eyes.

I knew with great certainty that Samuel had never been more than a few miles from his home in the village, for this, in those days, was the norm, and there was, before me, no evidence to suggest otherwise. And within the confines of the boundaries defined by walking distance, he was, most probably, destined to spend his whole life, never venturing into the wide world to explore its treasures and to discover some of its secrets. In the time in which I now found myself, much of the planet was still unexplored and only a tiny minority ever got to travel and to experience its delights.

I am fortunate to have been born in an age when global travel is much more common for ordinary people, and I had done a fair amount of travelling, including several visits to the United States. Plus, I had been exposed to the benefits of television, bringing the world, with its enormous variety, colour, vibrancy, pleasures, as well as its tragedies and sadness, into my home. Compared with Samuel and others of his time, my experience of the world was on a par with explorers and adventurers of the mid-eighteenth century, people such as Captain James Cook, who had sailed the seas, visiting exotic places and discovering strange new lands. So, when I replied to Samuel's question I was not lying to him. "Yes, Samuel, I have been to America ... I mean to the American Colonies; many places in fact, as well as other countries such as those in Europe and further afield."

Samuel's eyes and mouth opened in amazement. He looked at me, full of awe. Never in his wildest dreams had he imagined that he would one day encounter someone who had travelled the world. "Tell me about those Colonies," he begged. "Please!"

"I am not sure I have the time, Samuel," I began.

"Oh, please! Just a little bit," he pleaded.

He was so insistent and I was so taken by his openness, his simple character and his innocence that I found it impossible to refuse him. He had not been conditioned and affected by the modern world of the twenty-first century and just accepted that I was who I said I was. There was no concern that I was a stranger, someone who potentially might harm him and therefore someone to be avoided. There was just a basic human instinct of trust and curiosity. So I began to mention a few facts and matters to satisfy his hunger for knowledge. But I was careful not to talk about places that did not yet exist, although I think I may have referred to geographic and climatic characteristics of the North American continent that were still unknown in Samuel's day. Of this I cannot be fully sure, for I do not have a detailed knowledge of what was known in 1750. But I had decided that it was harmless to mention what I knew, for I assumed that the world, and human history, could not possibly change by telling a small child, living in such an insignificant place, of such matters. But was I correct in this assumption? Later on I would have my doubts.

"Well, Samuel," I stated, "I have travelled widely. I have been to many places in the American Colonies, along the east coast and deep inland as well. It is a vast place, much bigger than where you live, Samuel." To illustrate this point I picked up a small piece of dead twig and drew a small square in the dust. "See this square – this represents England, where we are now." Then I drew another square, many times bigger, next to the small one. "This square represents the American continent," I said. "See how big it is compared with England and so varied as well. There are vast areas that look just the same as what you see around you here with green grass and trees, but there are also enormous forests as well. And tall mountains with snow-capped peaks and large open spaces, covered with tall grass, that just go on and on for hundreds of miles, without a soul in sight."

I glanced at Samuel; he was enthralled by what he was hearing. I realised at that moment in time that this was probably one of the few times in his still short life that he was receiving education or intellectual stimulation. I continued with my description. "The weather varies enormously as well. In the summer it is really hot in the centre of the continent, but in the winter it changes and becomes freezing cold. When it snows it stays on the ground for ages and the world around is all frozen and lifeless. But in the south, it is much warmer," I said, pointing to the lower part of the square that I had drawn. "Here there are a lot of desert areas, as well as lush warm climates. And the cities in the American Colonies, they are amazing! Some of the older ones, such as Boston, are big and are still growing. And there are all sorts of people in them – rich and poor, skilled and unskilled, traders and soldiers, white skinned and the native North Americans. It is a fabulous place and, for the most part, more equal than here. No one over there would expect you to pull at your hat every time a gent passed by. All is new, more fresh, more alive, more exciting."

I do not know if Samuel understood all that I told him, for I was not used to conversing with children, especially a child from the mid-eighteenth century, and I knew nothing of his educational achievements, if any. Nevertheless, soon we were sitting on the grass verge and so it was that I continued to entertain and to educate Samuel in the delights of the American continent. Samuel just sat and listened, wide eyed, spellbound by what I was saying and I did not notice the time passing by, moments in time slipping away, minutes spent in a different age. So engrossed in my conversation was I that I did not notice the two ladies approach.

Samuel had seen them in the distance, walking along the lane, heading for the village, but had not mentioned them. They were not within my field of vision for I had my back turned towards the direction from which they came. Eventually they drew closer and then paused but a few feet away, listening to the accounts of my travels. I was in the middle of describing my visits to the cities of New York and Boston. Samuel placed his hand on my arm, shook it and nodded towards the ladies, indicating that we were not alone.

I stopped talking and turned towards them and was completely taken aback by what I saw before me. Samuel and I both rose to our feet. "Helen!" I said, sounding surprised. "What are you doing here?" I was addressing myself to the younger of the two, who was smiling. It was Helen! No doubt about it! But how could it be?

On my calling her Helen, the smile disappeared and was replaced by an expression of curiosity. She turned to the other lady, an older person, as if to ask, "Who is this madman who calls me Helen?"

The second lady had a similar appearance to the younger one and from this I assumed that they must be mother and daughter. This vision of my dear Helen looked back at me and, the smile returning to her face, she spoke to me in the gentlest and friendliest of voices. "I think you must have me confused with someone else of your acquaintance. My name is not Helen. And please forgive us. You must think us rude, but we could not help overhearing what you were saying about our American Colonies. From the little that I did hear, I found it most interesting."

Thus began our polite conversation, a trait of that age, and one that is increasingly not found in modern western civilisation, caught up as it is in the dogma of economic growth; we are, after all, according to science, nothing more than complex biological machines, and what machine needs polite conversation? This is progress!

My facsimile of Helen then turned to Samuel, saying in the most gracious way that I have ever heard anyone speak, "Hello, Samuel. I see you have found a new friend. How are you and how are your parents?"

"I am fine, thank you very much, Miss Lucy," responded Samuel, "and Ma and Pa are both well. Thank you for asking."

Samuel had by now picked up his hat, which had lain discarded on the grass after his encounter with the dangerous Walter Smythe. The manner in which he stood and spoke indicated to me a respect for the younger lady, a respect that he obviously did not share for Walter Smythe. Looking at her, observing her beauty and the kind way in which she behaved towards Samuel, I immediately understood why.

It was a beauty that I was familiar with. How strange, to step into this distant age, this world so alien to me, and to meet someone who was so similar to Helen in her appearance. No, I am wrong to say so similar. Every aspect of her face was just as if Helen was standing before me. I felt so moved by a familiarity and love for Helen that I could have, at that moment, stepped forward and hugged this apparently identical twin, this spitting image, as if it were Helen herself. I had to remind myself that this was obviously not she.

I became conscious that I would appear very strange to them dressed the way I was. But I recalled that Smythe, being ignorant of colonial dress, had assumed that I was clothed as might be a traveller from what I called America, which they knew as the American Colonies, and I hoped that this would also explain my unusual appearance to the two ladies.

Having obviously finished addressing Samuel, the younger lady, whose name I had learned from Samuel was Lucy, turned to me. There was an awkward moment of silence. I was embarrassed by my mistake in recognising her as Helen, but it was a mistake easily made. I was also unsure how to address myself to her, not being familiar with the customs of the age and not being sure that what I had seen on television, in costume dramas, and read in classical books was at all correct. But the young lady was obviously not one to stand on ceremony, being more direct than I assumed was acceptable for the age and for a woman.

"Please forgive my forwardness, but are you the owner of this lovely new house behind us? I ask this for you are

123

obviously a stranger to these parts and we, that is my mother and I, had heard that a stranger, someone from the American Colonies, was responsible for its construction. And given that you were talking of that place and your unusual mode of dress … I assumed …"

"Lucy dear," interrupted her mother gently, "the gentleman does not have to answer your questions."

Turning to me, and addressing me directly, I discerned an experienced and self-confident person whom, I will admit, I found attractive, for she was also beautiful, but in a more mature way than her daughter. She spoke, saying to me, "I am sorry if my daughter has offended you. Please forgive her; she has a curiosity and a forwardness that lead her to speak in a way that can be inappropriate at times. It is her nature. She is very high spirited, but she has a kind heart and means well. With time she will learn to behave as the lady she is, to be more demure." Then turning to her daughter she said, with a note of desperation in her voice, "Although I may be an old lady before that happens."

There was a tone of affection in her voice and a slight smile on her face as she spoke these gentle words of reproach. I could see that she expressed herself more in the way of jest and fun, as if sharing some secret joke, and I sensed that perhaps the older lady recognised in her daughter her own wilder side that had, many years ago, been tamed to the standards and expectations of her times.

The daughter laughed, demonstrating that Lucy was not at all embarrassed by what her mother had said and she held her head high, showing herself to be also a mature person, and her manner spoke of experience of life beyond that which her present circumstances might suggest.

"There is no reason to apologise," I began. "Directness, curiosity and forwardness: these are all admirable qualities where I come from, even in a lady." Then directing my comments at the younger of the two, to Lucy, I said. "As you can see from my dress and hear from my voice, I am a stranger in these parts. I was in the house when I heard a disturbance in the lane outside and I came out to investigate. I found young Samuel here being attacked with a stick by a very unpleasant fellow by the name of Walter Smythe."

At this news the two ladies were both shocked. Miss Lucy quickly moved to where Samuel was standing and placed her arm round him, showing motherly concern, and in a way that only a woman can. "Poor Samuel," she began. "Are you hurt?"

"A little, Miss Lucy, but I am all right now. He only hit me once before Mr Woodward stopped him. Smythe was very angry, but Mr Woodward stood up to him."

"Well done, sir," said the mother. "Well done! It is about time someone dealt with him. He is a big bully. I do not know what his parents were thinking, the way they brought him up; takes after his father, though, who was also spoilt rotten when he was a child, and that turned him into the most arrogant of men. And he has gone and done the same with Walter. Now look at him – empty, rotten and full of pride; a complete waste."

"Mr Woodward, sir, I cannot thank you enough for rescuing poor Samuel here from that awful man," Lucy said, genuinely appreciative of what I had done.

"Oh, dear," began her mother, "here we are talking to one another and we have not even introduced ourselves. Please, forgive us. What must you think of us? We stand here learning of your good deeds, of what you did to save little Samuel, and we have not even bothered to tell you who we are. I am Marjory Dent and this is my daughter, Lucy."

I heard the name Dent and in an instant my mind made the connection. Dent was Helen's family name. The people before me must be distant ancestors of Helen, which might explain the close resemblance between Lucy and Helen – a random matter based on genes, though how that had resulted in such a close resemblance, I did not know. On realising the kindred connection I wanted to know more about Lucy, about her own relatives, about her family history, but how to find out without seeming over inquisitive and possibly offending Lucy?

In response to Mrs Dent, I said, "Seems to be a day for informality. But do not worry – where I come from informality is the norm. I am Benjamin Woodward." And then I shook hands with both ladies, which surprised them. Sensing this, I just said, "That is the way we greet people where I come from."

In my conversation with these ladies I was careful to avoid stating that I had come from the American Colonies, preferring instead to say, *where I come from*, for I did not want to lie to these nice people, and this seemed the best way of avoiding matters that would be difficult, nay impossible to explain.

"Oh, well, not to worry," said Mrs Dent. "Now Mr Woodward, you should come for tea tomorrow afternoon. I am sure Lucy will be delighted to learn more about your travels," adding, "Is that not so, my dear?"

"Oh, yes! Please do come," added Lucy. "Sundays can be so dull around here, even more so than the normal dullness of other days. Please say you will come. I would love to learn more about the American Colonies."

My question concerning how I could discover more regarding Lucy had been answered. Here was an opportunity to learn Lucy's story, her history and about her world, so strange and unknown to me. But I was a little cautious, for I had not planned on this. I was making friends in a time that I knew very little of and in a place where I was, as everyone had noticed, a stranger. But what could I do? It would have been impolite to refuse and I was eager to find out more about the Dent family. Under the circumstances, I accepted.

"Thank you for such a kind invitation. I would love to come. I accept. I look forward to it. What time?"

"Oh, do not worry too much about the time. Let us say three o'clock tomorrow afternoon, but if you come earlier, or later, then not to worry, for you would be just as welcome. Would that be suitable for you?"

I noted again the imprecision concerning time and I found it hard to imagine people in my world being so inexact about such matters.

"Yes, that is perfect," I said. "And where—"

Mrs Dent interrupted me, anticipating what I was about to ask. "Yes, of course, you do not know where we live do you? Are you familiar with the village yet?" she asked.

"Reasonably so," I replied.

"Overlooking the village green, there is a large house, Elm House, not as big as some houses in these parts, but big enough."

I was very familiar with Elm House, for it is still called this in my own time. It is a bay-windowed Georgian property, one of the better ones in the village, located overlooking the duck pond. "I think I know the one you mean."

"Do not worry! We will be keeping an eye open for you. We look forward to your visit and getting to know you better," said Mrs Dent.

"Yes," added Lucy. "You can tell me about all the interesting places you have visited."

"I will do my best, but that is a fair number," I replied.

"The more the better," Lucy said, smiling, and with a hint, I thought, of interest that went beyond curiosity.

"Come, Lucy. Let us be on our way. Goodbye for now. We will see you tomorrow. Come, Samuel. You can accompany us and we will see you safely home."

Samuel looked at me as if to say that he did not want to go.

"Time to go now, Samuel," I said. "I will tell you more another day."

He smiled and said. "Oh, yes, please."

Why I said this I am not sure for I should, at that moment in time, have already realised that I was becoming involved, and already losing sight of the reality of my circumstances, of interfering in something that I did not understand; but I am an engineer and my sense of reality is determined only by what I am prepared to accept as relevant.

So it was that the three of them set off for the village. Lucy occasionally glanced back, and when they reached a bend in the lane, she waved and then they disappeared from view. What was in that wave I did not know, but in time, as with all such matters, this would become clear.

"Oh, dear," I said aloud to myself, "I am being drawn into a different world. I hope that I do not get too involved. And Lucy, she is so similar to Helen in her ways as well as her looks."

I could have here followed a different path, chosen not to become involved. Can you see now how a lack of wisdom leads us to actions that, with hindsight, we would avoid given those circumstances again – if, that is, we are fortunate to be gifted with such retrospective reflections and have not become trapped in mind-sets and ways of behaving that preclude the humility to admit we were wrong. I can tell you that many modern scientists, engineers and technologists are not gifted with such humility, though I would not have admitted such to myself at the moment in time when I embarked upon my adventure. Such are the unbreakable chains.

I crossed the road and went back into the house, intrigued by what was happening, by what I was experiencing, and excited that seemingly I was able to fit in to this distant time. Common sense should have told me to get away from that era, to run, to stop meddling in that which I did not understand, to retreat from that moment in time long past, back to my own world where I belonged. But I felt a lure that was hard to resist and so it was that I began to be drawn into events that would eventually lead to my present predicament. You see, in the end, the risks are shown not to be manageable, as you will soon discover. Does this sound familiar? It should, for evidence of this is to be found all across the modern world; it is just that we choose not to see this. *Out of order comes disorder.*

CHAPTER 11

Retracing my steps, I headed back to the rear door of the house. As I did so I heard that voice again, warning me, telling me not to be so foolish. "You are being drawn into another world. Do you really know what you are getting involved in?" it asked.

And I replied to it, no longer wondering who or what the voice was. I was beyond the state of being surprised and just accepted it as part of the strangeness of my new circumstances. "I will be all right," I responded, but in a way that was also meant to reassure myself.

The voice, however, did have an effect upon me, for I began to think more deeply about what I was doing. All sorts of worries rushed through my mind, but chief among them was the matter that the voice had first raised, a concern that I thought I had laid to rest. Evidently I had not. Prising its way into my consciousness was an unpleasant and frightening prospect that I might become trapped in this alien era. This idea was an unwelcome visitor that sent a shiver down my spine. Then the voice spoke again, raising new possibilities.

"So you think you can go back," it stated. "You have convinced yourself of that because you have demonstrated that it is possible to go back, and you have tested this several times. But what if the opening through time has closed during that period you spent in the lane, while you were busy talking to Samuel, to Lucy, to her mother? Perhaps it was only open for a short duration! Or perhaps you might become trapped for other reasons."

The voice had made a valid point, but it was not yet finished with me. "Have you any idea how long you have been away from your own age?" it asked. "Is it hours? Or have several days or even months passed by?"

To this I had no answer for I had no way of knowing; this was a measure of my ignorance, my folly, my arrogance. What did I know of the mysteries of time and a universe that could, completely unexpectedly, and defying all that is known, link one moment in time with another, separated by over 250 years, with an amount of history in between that no one could fully record? Then it flashed into my mind that what had brought me to this far distant point in history – call it a time warp, or a time portal, a distortion in time and space; it does not matter what name is used – whatever it was, might have been a fluke occurrence that had allowed me to become a time traveller. Perhaps the voice was correct – perhaps the opening had closed and I had missed my opportunity to go home.

But far worse was a new anxiety that the voice raised in my mind when it asked its next question. "What if you step back not into you own age, but into another era, one different from this one and your own? Perhaps you might end up wandering through time for an eternity, forever passing from one age to another, never growing old, never to return to your rightful place in the history of the universe!"

I was now afraid, yet the answer to these questions and the reassurances that I sought were but a few moments in time away. All I had to do was get back inside the house, head upstairs and pass once more under that strange wooden beam. And this is exactly what I did. I was inside the house in a moment, shutting the rear door behind me and then heading at great speed back up the stairs, along the corridor. I hoped as I went that all would be well and that I would end up back in the same moment in time that I had left behind.

Then, before me, I saw a welcome sight: the opening in the wall. I was, in a few moments, standing by the north-facing landing window and could see, with great relief, my car, just where I had left it. I resolved at that moment in time to leave and go home, before I got myself into trouble. But just as I was about to do so, I remembered the leather folder. I had forgone an examination of the wallet in favour of exploring the house further. And in my rush to end my first reconnaissance I had forgotten all about the wallet. Now I was feeling regret that I had not taken a look when I had the opportunity.

That the wallet might contain documents providing some information about the owner was the thought that entered my mind. I did want so much to find out what the wallet contained. Surely it would not hurt to go back for it. It would only take a few seconds. What can happen in such a short time?

I had managed to convince myself that it would be all right to return and that I would be safe. But to make sure that I was not placing myself in danger, for I was now inclined not to tempt fate, I would go and get the folder and bring it into my own age. I had been lucky on my first visit into the world of the eighteenth century, but I might not be so fortunate a second time. Best therefore to keep this, my next visit, very short. Once I had collected the wallet I could look at its contents in a more relaxed way and then return it, when I had finished reading what the wallet contained. I resolved on this course as the best solution, so I quickly re-entered the past, headed for the room in question, took the leather folder and was soon back in the present.

Satisfied that my little plan had worked, I sat down on the stairs and began to explore the contents. I was extremely surprised by what I saw. There was a letter addressed to me. This is what it said:

Dear Mr Woodward,

We have carried out your instructions and arranged for you the purchase of the land and the construction of the detached property using the funds that you provided. All accounts have now been settled with the builder and other tradesmen and we have inspected the house and grounds and found them to be satisfactorily completed. All that remains for us to do is to complete the legal formalities of ownership. With this letter you will find the title deed for the land and buildings; you should sign where indicated. Also enclosed is our bill, which has been paid from the monies that you supplied. A detailed account of how your funds have been spent is also provided for your scrutiny. A balance of one thousand guineas remains from your fund and we are holding this money in a client account in your name until such time that you instruct us further with regard to these monies.

We remain at your service,

Yours most sincerely,

Dome and Smith Solicitors

I looked at the other documents. Sure enough, these were the title deeds, made out in my name, Benjamin Woodward. I was shocked and stunned by this revelation. "How has this come about?" I asked myself; I was now even more baffled by what was happening, and still only half believing what I had seen and read.

It was indeed a mystery. Perhaps it was just a coincidence, for it was entirely possible that the person who had instructed the solicitor to arrange the construction of the house might have also been called by the same name as me. But I wondered for a moment about this, thinking about whether there were other explanations. Then a thought occurred to me; an idea triggered by what I had learned from those stories where people travel back in time and end up changing the past with subsequent knock-on effects in their own era as events ripple across the ages. Perhaps I had done the same. As a result of making contact with people in the eighteenth century, of my interfering with and saving poor Samuel Jones from his attacker, of conversing with him about

America, and accepting Mrs Dent's invitation to tea on Sunday afternoon, perhaps all these actions, so small and insignificant in themselves, or so they seemed, had altered the course of history. But then I realised that the folder had been on the desk before all these events had occurred. So now I was even more concerned and I began to wonder if that first simple act of just stepping under that wooden beam had set in motion a long chain of actions that had led to my ownership of the property.

This seemed highly unlikely, but then thoughts of chaos theory came into my mind. Small changes can cause significant events to happen, the so-called butterfly effect: a butterfly flaps its wings in Beijing and hours later it rains in New York as a result. Could this be what happened as a consequence of my first passing under the beam; my very initial small steps; my first, and at that moment in time, unknowing visit to the eighteenth century?

Then the voice spoke again, raising these very concerns. "You are dealing with matters that you do not understand and as a result of your curiosity the whole course of history may have changed. You do not know what may have happened just by stepping into the eighteenth century and what resulted from conversing with Samuel about America. Perhaps it left him with an urge to go there. Perhaps he went to places he would never have gone and undertook actions that he would otherwise not have, which created a legacy, the effects of which rippled across the centuries."

I recognised that this might well be true and that I had no way of knowing, but I am an engineer; out of disorder I create order. The fact that I am also not well versed in the learning of other disciplines, that I post-rationalise to explain what happens in terms that I find acceptable, that I ignore warning signs, that I do not understand the complexity of natural systems, that I believe that the risks can be managed … I am too clever by half to let such matters interfere with my worldview.

Being this way inclined, I stubbornly continued along the path that all right-minded people must follow, asking myself how such ripples could affect the ownership of the Time House. I might well have already interfered in events and changed the future, but this was not likely to have influenced the matter of who owned the Time House. No, there was obviously some other dimension to this, some deeper mystery and this made me more determined to continue; I wanted to know more about the Time House, it origins and its strangeness.

The voice had raised the prospect that I might have changed the course of world events, but I was not repentant. While at school I had been extremely interested in history. I had wanted to read the subject at university, but my father influenced me against that, encouraging me to follow a vocation, arguing that an engineer could always do other jobs, but that only those qualified in engineering could practise this subject. Needless to say he was himself an engineer. But I had no regrets about choosing electrical engineering. It had led me to undertake research that had provided me with a PhD, and while this was a qualification that I no longer used in my present work, it left open the possibility that I might, one day, return to the world of research. For the moment, however, I was fulfilling another dream – to be my own boss, to run my own business – and I was happy for the time being in pursuing this ambition. But my love of history had never left me. My inquisitiveness about the subject had developed over time. On my bookshelf at home I have many history books, covering many different topics and historical periods. And I now saw an opportunity, a chance to follow another dream.

The Time House had taken me on a journey through time, to a different age, and, so far, on each occasion that I had stepped across the barrier into the past, I had returned safely to my own era. If I could be sure that I would not become trapped in the past, if I could put aside the concerns that the voice had raised about this, then what possibilities lay before me? What if I were to go on other journeys into the past? I could, with the Time House, do that which historians desire most: to be part of the period that they study, to experience the times for themselves and to witness events first-hand.

This was the possibility that now tempted me. A whole new way of life might open up for me. I had before me the chance to explore history from within, to experience it as events actually happened and unfolded. Now, as a result of being an engineer, I had the chance to be a historian, to learn about history in a way that no one had ever done before. As a bonus I had one thousand guineas at my disposal to fund my adventures. All I had to do was to sign my name on the title deeds; I would then have in my possession not only a house but also a doorway into the past.

It was an exciting prospect. I thought for a moment about what the voice had said and as I did so I began to convince myself that all would be well. No misfortune would befall me. I would take all the precautions necessary to minimise the risks, which, I argued to myself, would be enough to warrant my incursions into places that I now realise I did not belong. I would be able to come and go as I pleased and to return to my own time without difficulty. Oh, how wrong I was!

At that moment in time all my worries evaporated. Concerns about interfering with time, of modifying events and changing the course of history, did not arise anymore. I was going to become a time traveller. About this my mind was made up. I replaced the documents in the folder and walked back into the past.

Now sitting at the desk, taking out the title deeds and turning to the page where my signature was required, I picked up the quill pen and dipped the nib end into the inkwell. It was strange writing with such an instrument. It lacked the strength of modern pens and I found it impossible to sign my signature in the normal way, so I ended up, in effect, writing it slowly. Then it was done. The house was mine. All I had to do was to take the documents to the solicitor and collect my money.

I placed the pen on the desk and covered the wet ink that was my signature with some sand, which acted in those days as a means of absorbing excess liquid, for blotting paper had yet to be invented. When I was sure it was dry I shook the paper to remove the sand and then replaced the documents in the folder, which I then picked up. Holding it in my hand I took one more glance out of the window. The sun was much lower in the sky, telling me it was early evening. I was hungry and I wanted to eat. It was time to slip back into my own era and to mull over what I was going to do next. I looked at my watch – eight o'clock in the evening. But was it?

Once again I passed back into my own time without difficulty. My confidence about the stability of this gateway into the past was growing. So far it had not let me down and deep down my unarticulated thoughts were shifting to the view that this is how it would remain; doubts introduced by the voice were disappearing, swept away by the excitement of the prospect of exploring the past.

Returning to my own age I collected my tools and went downstairs, passing out through the front door, locking it and then heading to my car. But there were aspects of my surroundings that had changed: the world was different. This was not quite the place that I had left behind many hours earlier.

The first discrepancy I noticed was that although my watch was telling me that it was evening, eight o'clock, the height of the sun in the sky and the temperature suggested otherwise; these signs pointed to early afternoon. I checked with the clock in my car – just after one o'clock. Yet I knew that more than one hour must have passed since I had first entered the house, given all that had happened. I reset my watch to twenty-first century time.

It was clear that even thought I had spent several hours in the eighteenth century, this had amounted to no more than a short period in my own time, if any length at all. I was eventually to discover that this was entirely correct, but I did not realise until much later the implications – the advantage of being able to exist in two worlds, but to lose very little time, if any, in my own; it seemed that I was able to acquire moments in time without cost. But there is always a price to pay!

Before getting into the car and driving home I looked around. What was it that had changed? My surroundings were definitely different, but in what way exactly I could not immediately tell. The differences, you see, lay not in the bigger picture, but in the smaller details and it took a while for me to realise this. At first sight most of the world seemed to be as I had left it and there were no extensive modifications to suggest that anything was amiss, but closer inspection did reveal some changes. I stood and looked for a moment, trying to recall the landscape. Then I realised what had happened. There was a flicker of light in my mind, which turned into a dawning of an understanding that there was one building missing. It was one of the older ones in the village, and one that could always be seen when approaching along the lanes that led to the village green; a house made visible because of its tall chimney stacks. This, now, was absent.

I also then noticed that a number of trees looked different as well, and there were some located where there should only have been grass. What is more, I discovered that where once there had been oaks, there were now ash trees. Also, there were more elm trees than I recalled, as if the great loss of elms that had occurred in the 1970s as a result of the spread of Dutch elm disease had never happened. The road also looked different, as it was in need of resurfacing, yet I knew that it was fine previously, since I drove down it just about every day, and I recalled that it had been repaired and resurfaced only five years earlier.

This was perplexing and it should have served as a warning that I was meddling in matters that I did not understand. I now realise that I was over-confident and that I had created for myself an illusion of control, which, alas, is an all too common mistake when it comes to matters of science, engineering and technology. It was this arrogance and lack of humility in the face of forces beyond my comprehension that led me to ignore the warning signs, to disregard my observations of what are now the obvious effects of my visit to the eighteenth century, and to just head home without any care for the impact of my actions on the world; all I was engaging in was the result of my belief that I was in control and that a state of order would prevail. What foolish optimism, which is, alas, typical of the society from which I had acquired my values and beliefs!

So it was that I began my homeward journey with the title deeds for the Time House safely by my side. Soon I was in my own twenty-first-century property, the place Helen and I called home. There was mail lying on the floor. On picking up the bundle, I found that there were several envelopes addressed to myself and some with Helen's name on them, mostly junk mail and a few bills.

One letter stood out from the rest – it was franked and bore the name of the sender: Dome and Smith Solicitors. Now, the name Dome and Smith had become very familiar to me during the course of the day and here for the third time within the space of a few hours was another reference to this firm of lawyers. Hence, I was more than curious to know why they were writing to me, for I'd had no previous dealings with them. I shut the front door and headed for the kitchen to read the letter. This is what it said:

Dear Mr Woodward,

Further to your request that we instruct estate agents to place your property on the market, we have now done as you required and I am pleased to inform you that the sale of your property will be handled by Mellor Estate Agents. The proprietor informs me that all steps have been taken to advertise the house and I will keep you informed about the progress.

We remain at your service,

Yours sincerely,

Dome and Smith Solicitors

What can I say about how I felt on reading this letter? Several times I read it through, thinking perhaps that it had been sent to me by mistake. But this did not seem credible. The fact of the matter was that, before me, I had a letter that indicated that I was the owner of the Time House. Not more than thirty minutes had passed since I had signed the title deeds, but the reality of the circumstance was that this had actually happened 250 years ago, and here now the very same solicitors who had corresponded with me in 1750 were sending me another letter about the house. Once more I was blind to the warning signs. I should have realised that I had ventured into very dangerous territory, though instead of being concerned I found myself very excited to learn that I was indeed the owner of Time House. But then I heard the voice again, which surprised me for I had thought that it was only connected to the Time House. "Are you not concerned as to why you would want to sell the house, having just acquired it?" the voice asked.

I have to confess that this question made me a little uneasy, but only for a short while. What was going on here? I did not know it at that particular moment in time, but what I was experiencing were the complexities of time. Events somewhere in the past, occurrences that I had yet to experience, had led me to decide to sell the house, but at that moment I had no idea what they were!

That actions taken within one lifetime have consequences within that generation, this I understood from my experience of living. But what was now becoming

144

apparent was that my deeds back in the year 1750 were also having consequences in my lifetime – not just for the world about me, such as those that I had observed as changes in the surrounding landscape, but also for me directly.

This is a truth that cannot be escaped, a law of the universe that we all experience but very rarely take time to contemplate. The world is the way it is for a reason: somewhere back in other eras, someone acted and changed an aspect of their world, and regardless of the action and its worth, the effects rolled onwards across the ages, as if they were like ripples radiating out across a pond when a pebble is thrown into it. Small and perhaps insignificant deeds from many centuries back, such as the planting a certain tree at a specific spot, affect the world today in ways that the initiator could never have imagined. All those seeds, the results of countless seasons of growth and renewal, spread across the land by birds, wind and animals can form offspring, new trees that would never have been, but for the action of one person, anonymous, unknown, and now forgotten, at some place and some moment in time in the distant past. And what events occur under these trees and what do they cause by way of accidents?

No one can foretell all that follows from their deeds. This is the nature of time and also its essential mystery: a continuum of events, large and small, all affecting the way the world develops. And, knowingly and deliberately, I was interfering in this process, learning as I went that not all is linear, as one would expect; the world is in fact highly nonlinear. But at that point I was far from understanding the nature of time and its interdependencies, with one action intertwined with another, and also its potentially chaotic nature – part of the prevailing disorder of the universe that is at the same time part of its order. At that moment in time I was still labouring under the illusion that *out of disorder I created order*, but in actual fact I was doing the opposite, or was it that the universe was restoring disorder in response to the order that I was trying to create?

I glanced at the clock in the kitchen: nearly two o'clock, but for me it felt as though it were much later for I had experienced several hours in another age and was feeling very hungry.

I knew that I should phone Harry, but what to tell him? I pondered this for a while and then an idea came to mind. I was aware that now I did not need an excuse to go back to the house for the property was mine. But did I have a set of keys of my own? Unsure of the answer, I knew I needed to keep, for a while, the keys that the estate agent had supplied, and fortunately Harry had given me permission to hold onto them. So I thought that the best course of action was to tell him that I had found no problems, not untrue, but that I would go back again on Sunday afternoon to check one more time, just to make sure. That way I would be able to justify my presence there, if he were turn up, for I was now set on exploring the past and my first step would be to return to the Time House to keep my Sunday afternoon appointment with the Dents. That night I would search my home to see if keys for the property had appeared there.

So I telephoned Harry. Someone else answered the phone. "Hello. Mellor Estate Agents. Can I help you?" the voice asked.

"I want to speak to Harry," I replied.

"Harry? There's no one by that name here."

I thought that someone was playing a joke on me. "Come on," I demanded. "Harry Mellor. Let me speak to him."

"Oh," said that voice on the other end of the telephone. "Harry Mellor."

"Yes, Harry Mellor."

I was not prepared for what came next. "I am sorry, sir, but Harry Mellor died five years ago."

To say that I was shocked by this revelation would be an understatement. "*Died?*" I said, sounding astonished. "But …" I was going to say more; however, it dawned on me that I was on dangerous ground. I did not know to whom I was speaking and I did not want to say too much.

Then the person on the other end of the telephone line said, "Can I help you?"

I paused briefly and then I said, "No. It was Harry I wanted to speak with. Sorry. I didn't know," adding by way of explanation, "I've been away for some time. Tell me, what did he die of?"

"It was a heart attack. Don't know much more than that. Sorry I can't help you."

"It doesn't matter. Thanks anyway. Bye."

I put the telephone down, feeling stunned. If this was true, that Harry was indeed dead, then the world had changed more than I had realised. Then I heard the voice again. "See?" it began. "Because of what you have done – the simple act of signing a piece of paper – someone is now dead. And how many more lives have you wiped away?"

I felt responsible. The euphoria that I had experienced on discovering my own private gateway into the past now gave way to remorse. "What have I done?" I muttered to myself. "What have I done?"

I stood for a moment, quiet with my own thoughts, not just feeling sorry for Harry, but also for myself. Truth be told, I was feeling sorrier for myself than for Harry. Then the voice continued. One word was all it said at first: "Helen!" There was a pause and I was not completely sure what point it was trying to make. "Is Helen still part of your life?" asked the voice. "Has she ever been?"

This was a nightmare prospect, but I knew how to find the answer to these questions, for throughout our home there are many photographs of Helen and myself. First I went to the lounge. There on a sideboard was a photograph, exactly where it should have been, of Helen and myself, taken a few years back while on holiday in France. So at least I knew that Helen was part of my life, or at least had been. But was she still? I bounded up the stairs and into our bedroom. There was the photograph of us together, taken one summer while on another holiday, this time in Dorset, and there in the wardrobe were Helen's clothes, as well as other personal effects lying around our bedroom. But this did not fully reassure me. The only way to be sure that she was fine and well was to speak to her.

I sat down on the bed and took out my mobile telephone. Selecting Helen's number I pressed the dial button and waited, anxious to hear her voice, to be quite sure that all was as it should be. Her mobile rang many times, just adding to the suspense and increasing my concern. But eventually it was answered. It was Helen. I was relieved to hear her voice.

"Hi, love," she said. "I have been waiting for you to ring me to finish the guided tour of the house."

"Sorry," I replied, "I forgot. I was engrossed in trying to find out what was wrong and the time just slipped by."

"Are you still at the Old House?"

"No, I came home as it was lunch time."

"And did you find problems?"

"No, I didn't. I'm going back there tomorrow to have a longer session."

"See what comes of working over holiday weekends? If you'd come with me none of this would have happened. How are you going to deal with that backlog of paperwork if you spend all your time taking on new work?"

"Very true, dear. Very true!"

I must have sounded a little depressed when I said this, for quickly Helen sensed my mood and asked, "What's the matter?"

"Oh, I'm just feeling lonely and I wanted to hear your voice again. The sound of your voice, well, it's just … reassuring."

"Are you okay, love?" she asked, now even more concerned by my tone of voice.

"I'm fine, Helen," I replied, trying to sound convincing. "It's such a long weekend without you here. I wish now that I had come with you. I'm really missing you and I wanted to hear your voice and to just talk with you."

"Ah, that's sweet," she said, sounding much touched by my words. "I miss you too. I wish you'd come. It's lovely here. So have you managed to do any of the work that you planned to do?"

"I've done some, but not as much as I wanted to," I replied, which of course was true. But I also knew that if I had not become involved with the Time House I would have certainly completed much more, and given that I planned to return there on Sunday, most likely a lot more.

I was starting to feel much better now that I was talking with Helen. "It's good talking – you're making me feel better already," I informer her. "You going away for the weekend brings home to me how much I love you. I can't wait till Monday evening."

"I know what you mean, love. I have the same feeling," replied Helen. "I love you," Helen said, in a soft gentle voice. Continuing, she then said what I really very much wanted to hear. "Look, we're both missing each other, so I'll come home a bit earlier on Monday. If I leave here really early, I could get back to you just after lunchtime. How does that sound?"

"Perfect. I'm looking forward to that," I responded, sounding very pleased. "We should never do this again. Next time I have work that needs doing on a holiday weekend, the work can wait. Being with you is far more important."

I was genuine about this. My adventure in the Time House was making me realise how important time is, especially moments spent with someone you love. Work can always wait; it will still be there tomorrow, but loved ones might not be. Deep inside we all know this is true, but do we act accordingly?

"You're right," replied Helen. "I really do love you and I can't wait to be with you again."

"I love you, Helen," I told her with affection and then I blew her a kiss over the telephone. Helen reciprocated, sending me one back.

"I'll ring you again tonight, before I go to bed," I said.

"I'll be waiting for you. Speak to you later then. Bye, love."

"Bye, sweetheart."

There the conversation ended. I was feeling much better. All was well with Helen. She was still there and we were together, a couple and in love. It was a relief to know this, but I still did not know what she knew about the Time House. I resolved to explore this issue with her when I telephoned that night. As for why the voice had sought to raise the matter of Helen with me, this I could not understand. I realise now, of course, why it did so, but now it is too late.

CHAPTER 12

Thoughts of work had slipped right out of my mind. The rest of the day I spent idle, at home, reflecting upon what had happened to me, of my experiences and the opportunities for more adventures that lay ahead. Yes, I was sorry about what had happened to Harry, but I reasoned in the end that it was not my fault. I had told him about taking life in a more relaxed way, of the need to spend time with his family. I convinced myself that Harry's demise was the sole responsibility of Harry and that when he'd been alive he'd had within his grasp the means of changing his fate: his priorities were such that he had just chosen not to exercise that power. Harry walked the path of his own choosing and paid the price. He could have taken another road through life, but he did not, and that was the end of my reflections on the matter.

After changing into more casual clothes, and with a salad sandwich, a bottle of cold beer and my thoughts for company, I stayed in the garden all afternoon. I lay on a sun bed, by the French windows, safe in the shade provided by the awning, but nevertheless warm. The effect of the food and alcohol made me feel drowsy so I closed my eyes and drifted off into the world of sleep.

It was a restful sleep, perhaps surprisingly given what had transpired that day. I was not at all bedevilled by disturbing dreams and I felt completely refreshed when I awoke. Looking at my watch I was taken aback. Seven o'clock! The hunger that I had felt earlier had abated, but I decided to eat. In the freezer in the garage I found the chilli con carne that Helen had made for me. While it was defrosting in the microwave oven I found some bread from Thursday's trip to the supermarket. With the passage of time it had become a little stale, so when the chilli con carne was completely warmed through I placed the bread in the microwave and warmed it slightly to refresh it.

Back in the garden once more, eating the food, I began to wonder about what I would do the following day. I also considered the possibility that the next time I passed though the opening in the Time House, I might find myself in a completely different age. It occurred to me that if time were running at different rates either side of the mysterious barrier that divided my own world and time from that of the village back in 1750, then I might never be able to visit the Dents on Sunday afternoon. What if that moment in time, relative to my side of the time portal, had already passed by, because of this different rate at which time progresses? If it had, becoming, so to speak, a moment in time long past, which of course it was in another sense, this would mean that I would miss my appointment. Perhaps Mrs Dent and her daughter Lucy had sat there waiting for me to turn up and, when I did not, had dismissed me from their immediate thoughts, and eventually had forgotten all about me. I might knock on their door only to find that several years had gone by, or, worse still, Lucy had grown old, with her mother long dead. What then would she think on seeing me just as I was twenty or thirty years earlier?

I pondered this for a while. It made me realise even more that I knew little about time, and that humankind was ignorant of its nature and that what science had to say about it did not at all encompass what I was experiencing. Physics tends to see time as an illusion. This is because for deterministic systems, for example those produced by Newton and Einstein, the equations are valid regardless of the direction of time; if time runs forwards or backwards, this does not matter, for deterministic equations still give the same predictions. But there is another perspective that comes from chaos theory, which states that what can be called the arrow of time runs only in one direction, and that is forwards. This is in essence because of the irreversibility of many highly complex natural processes; biologically I grow old, but I cannot become younger, for what leads to ageing is irreversible.

Neither of these views, however, provided an explanation, for what I had encountered was not time running forwards or backwards, or the reversibility or irreversibility of complex natural processes. My encounter with time seemed to be based on interactions, and very complex ones! Hence, I began to formulate a different perspective on time and one where I found the reassurance that I was looking for. This, you should understand, is what scientists, engineers and technologists have a tendency to do, and its validity only stems from our status; we are rational people, therefore what we say is valid, unlike others who, being irrational and lacking status, should not be believed; you can trust me because I am a scientist, or because I am an engineer, or because I am a technologist!

I visualised a helix running through space, representing the passage of time. Any point on that helix corresponds to the here and now for someone, for anyone who had ever existed, those in the past, in the present, and the people of the future. I postulated that individuals were inserted into this helix at various points, this being their date of birth, and then they left it, this helix, at the time of their death. Plainly this implied that human consciousness existed outside of time and space. I did not feel it necessary to link this with any particular religious perspective. To me it seemed that most beliefs were based on the existence of spirit or soul separate from the human body. It did not seem important to me to think about this aspect. If you do not yet realise, this is what scientists, engineers and technologists do all the time, that is, ignore that which does not fit with their theories, worldviews, etc. It is called reductionism, and it is simultaneously both powerful and very dangerous, for it not only provides the means of solving complex problems, but also encourages the delusion that what is ignored is in fact not important or, worse, does not exist.

So I went on to consider how someone on one part of the helix might find a way back, or even forward, into another part. "How might that happen?" I asked myself. I came up with an intriguing answer to this question. What if the helix was in motion? What if it was wriggling about as a worm does when it seeks to move forward? Perhaps it was just as if it were a large spring being acted upon by forces that pushed it sideways, causing dents, distortions and loops to appear. Perhaps it sometimes doubled back on itself and two points on the helix, representing different moments in time, came into contact with each other. At such occurrences perhaps a bridge, a gateway, between two ages might form.

It was an interesting theory, but it soon dawned on me that it was one that suggested danger. If the helix was indeed in motion, being pushed about, then it was possible that the gateway might easily shift backwards or forwards to another point on the helix; or worse still for me, if I were on the wrong side of the gateway, the bridge might be broken, and then I would be trapped for the rest of my life in an alien time. This was not the reassurance I had been seeking.

The concerns that the voice had earlier that day raised with me now seemed all too real. I had in effect created for myself a good reason not to have anything more to do with the Time House. I had produced a theoretical explanation, a hypothesis, which justified the issues thrust into my mind by the voice, concerns that I had managed to convince myself were unjustified. To go back through this opening, this bridge to another age, back into another time, would surely be an act of folly!

Unhappy that I had not arrived at a theory which supported that which I wanted, I considered my hypothesis again and wondered if it could explain how I had been able to spend several hours in the past, while time moved forward only a little back in my own world, if it had advanced at all, for this I was not sure of. I visualised the helix again. I saw it in my mind's eye, bent back on itself and touching a point way back in the past.

Speaking aloud to myself, I began to state what I thought I had learned. "So this bending would provide me with a portal to travel back in time. Now, as time advances, I should be moving forward along the spiral, but when I pass back through the gateway again to return to my own age, I arrive close to the moment in time when I departed."

This was not entirely a clear statement, but I moved on to state what I believed was the reason for this. "For that to happen," I said continuing, "the point on the helix representing my time, bent back, making contact with some distant point, must be sliding along the helix, twisting around and around the helix as it does so, ensuring the link with my own era remains exactly at the moment in time when I left, but allowing times past to advance forward."

This it seemed was a plausible but complex explanation, but it did not explain what I was experiencing. I was still unclear how I could return on Sunday afternoon in my own time, and find that it was Sunday afternoon in 1750. Surely I would return to a time … Actually I was unsure what time I would return to. Then I imagined a metal spring being subjected to the same process and recognised that it would soon end up all twisted, distorted and unwound. I was not, however, dealing with the physical, with metal, but with time and space and I knew from my physics that space could be distorted by gravity. And gravity might well be the force that was acting upon the helix.

I realised that by starting to formulate this theory I was dealing with a high degree of complexity, and in truth this was not a theory at all, just metaphysical speculation. But I am an engineer, so what I say has credibility, even though it may well be nonsense. That I was creating as many questions that I was trying to answer was also not a problem, for I am an engineer, and who dares challenge me?

At this point I gave up on this theorising, which was in reality no more than conjecture given respectability because of who I am. There was only one way to find out how the gateway to 1750 behaved and that was to go back through it. If I never investigated it, by actually using this opening, this portal, I would never know. There were risks, yes, to be sure, but there would also be rewards. I resorted to that familiar, meaningless and over-used cliché: *the risks can be managed.* This is the nature of science and technology, and I was undertaking a scientific experiment, using what I had discovered, to learn more about time, but also to study history at first hand. To understand some details about the mysteries of time and space, surely this was a goal that justified the risks. How often has this been used as a justification for scientific and technological endeavours? How often have people convinced themselves that the answer is yes, the risks are worth taking, when all reason says that the answer should be no, they are not?

I decided to sleep on the matter and to make a final decision on Sunday morning whether to return to the Time House.

The night was closing in. Eventually darkness enveloped the part of the world where I lived and the sky became dotted with twinkling stars – moments in time from millions of years past reaching my eyes after travelling incomprehensible distances across the vastness of space. I was looking at the past, a time before humans walked the earth, moments in time when nature had not been touched by the corrupting hand of man.

I had been lost in my thoughts for several hours. I decided it was time to retreat indoors. Outside it was becoming chilly, but inside it was still very warm – heat stored in the fabric of the house would keep it that way all night.

I went to bed, telephoned Helen, switched off the bedside lamp and waited for her to answer. She too was in bed, waiting for my call, so there was no long ringing and waiting. I had intended to ask her questions to see if she knew about my ownership of the Time House. But we quickly slipped into pillow talk; we spoke of matters small and insignificant, but which collectively were part of the interwoven fabric of our lives. Not wanting to disturb the mood with serious, materialistic issues, such as ownership of property, I decided to leave the subject of the Time House to rest for a while. We chatted for thirty minutes or so and then said our goodnights. I was surprisingly tired even though I had slept during the afternoon and I quickly slipped into another peaceful sleep; evidently I was still blind to the warnings that had passed before me that day, for if I had taken note of them, I am sure my dreams that night would have been nightmares.

CHAPTER 13

Seven o'clock. I was awake, refreshed and fully resolved on the course of action that I would follow. Previously I had wondered whether, on returning to the eighteenth century that coming Sunday afternoon, I would end up at the right time to visit the kindly Mrs Dent and her daughter Lucy, who was so much the image of my dear Helen; perhaps too similar in looks and manners for my own good.

Might I, by some additional strangeness within the peculiarities of my already extraordinary circumstances, not arrive at that appointment, which I now admit was, deep within me, so much longed for? This was a matter that needed to be determined, and there was only one way I was going to find out – I would have to make that journey! But I was intent on discovering more about how time progressed while I was away from my own age, so I decided to undertake an experiment. This involved taking two clocks with me. One of these I would hide in the west side of the Time House in my own era, while the other I would take with me through the portal and secrete in the east side of the house in the eighteenth century. This would allow me, on returning from 1750, to see how much time had elapsed while I was visiting the past and compare this with the passage of time in the twenty-first century.

Amidst the excitement of my adventure, all thoughts of work had now left me completely. I was involved in a voyage of discovery and exploration far more interesting and unique than work, yet I did not recognise at that moment in time that I was also embarking on a different journey, one of self-discovery that would lead to an enhanced awareness of the limitations of my worldview and a realisation that I was, as much as any religious devotee, caught up in an ideology, bounded by dogma, and trapped by beliefs that bore no correspondence with the great ocean of truth that lies before us all. As with most involved in science, engineering and technology, I shared the collective belief, the collective delusion, that all matters pertaining to these domains are neutral, not at all reflecting the values of those who practise these disciplines; and if those who follow these professions produce undesirable or damaging outcomes, then this is because of an abuse and not because of some inherent flaw that renders scientists, engineers and technologists potentially very dangerous people; I, we, most of us, choose to see only that part of the great ocean of truth that fits with our beliefs, and because nearly all of us are *too clever by half*, we do not even recognise that we are ignoring the rest!

I had before me a once-in-a-lifetime, perhaps even a once-in-an-eternity, opportunity, and I was going to make the most of it.

At seven o'clock on a holiday Sunday morning – with the working week over, with exertion in the past, for the moment at least, with thoughts of work banished, and with the start of the coming labour of the new week delayed by a holiday Monday – the majority of the population, especially those in employment, want to lie in bed: to sleep, to recover from the preceding week's efforts and the associated early-morning waking; but not me.

I am a morning person, a lark as they say, accustomed to rising with the sun in summer, and well before it in winter. At the other end of the day, just as the autumn of the day is passing into winter, dying, I begin to drift off into sleep, when some, the people who are like owls that is, are just coming, it seems, full awake. I was never one to engage in late night studies, preferring instead to tackle my work before the rest of the world was stirring. This is the habit that I developed while at university. It has remained with me since.

Here you have a hint of nature's endless variety at work, for not all have, following a good night's sleep, a mind fresh and ready for learning, for absorbing knowledge, and engaging in those timeless activities, spent by students across the ages, preparing for examinations – those moments of time bounded by rules, when some of this knowledge would be released in moments of recall, never destined though to evolve with the passage of time, through life's trail of experiences, into wisdom.

Being, as I have just indicated, a person of the quiet dawn hours, I normally wake at about five, and rise immediately, not being inclined to linger, reasoning that there is an eternity ahead for such, when, being dead, I will lie still without end. Seven o'clock was therefore very late for me – a lie-in unplanned and much needed, given that I had gained some time in my life, lived in effect through a day longer than twenty-four hours. But it was more than just this extra-long day, this additional time that I had acquired, which had delayed my waking and kept me from my normal routine of getting out of bed at a moment when others are still intent on sleeping; my tiredness was also induced by the excitement that I had experienced, and also, to some extent, by my worries and the concentration of the senses that comes with the presence of possible danger; all this, taken in sum, had inflicted its toll on me.

Once I was awake and thoughts of time travel and the coming adventure began to surge through my mind, I soon found my brain becoming active and the thought of lying abed, contemplating my actions, did not appeal to me. The room was also filled with brilliant sunlight, stimulating my senses, further adding to my inclination to rise and begin a new day.

Here started the same routine followed every day, as regular as the ticking of a clock, and as predictable as sunrise itself. Now out of bed, now slipping on my bathrobe, now heading downstairs, now preparing my morning coffee, now sitting in the lounge, sipping at this delightful and stimulating brew, I began to plan my next steps. Soon the caffeine, passing into my bloodstream, began to work – I was alert and sharp and what I had to do now became very clear.

The plan unfolded in my mind, as if it were a map being laid out before me, with all the important features clear and defined. Sunday morning would be spent at home. I would call Helen sometime before eating a light lunch. Then would come the moment in time I was most looking forward to, and with great anticipation also – the walk to the Time House, a slow one for it would be, once more, a day that all sun lovers adore. And then, on arriving at this place where two ages had come together, forming a bridge between two very different times, I would embark upon the final steps of my journey back into 1750 and then arrive as planned, and expected, at the house located in 1750, which would lead, by another walk, to my final destination, the home of Lucy and her mother.

And my planning did not stop with my arrival at the Dents' home, for I also foresaw my departure, sometime later, and the retracing of my steps, and my safe arrival back in my own age, which would be, I expected, just as I had left it; these were planned actions with the only thoughts of consequences being the ones that I was willing to accept as valid, and any that were not, in my eyes, legitimate were just the inventions of those ignorant of science, engineering and technology, the mark of those who did not understand, or did not want advancement, for I am an engineer and what I do is progress; all that oppose must therefore be lacking in some way. That there are consequences which I do not acknowledge, which I inflict upon the world through my ignorance and limited understandings, this is a price that the world pays for people such as me being so bound up in ideology. And my ideology is engineering.

Of what lay between my arrival and departure, those moments in time spent with Lucy and her mother, these I anticipated would be interesting, entertaining and pleasurable – not at all the prelude to the greater disaster that awaited me, one which must ultimately befall all foolish and arrogant enough to believe that what they do cannot go wrong, or that all measures have been taken to minimise the risks. *Out of order comes disorder*: it is a fundamental law of the universe.

And when this journey into the unknown was over, and I was safely back home, this would be a crucial moment in time, for then I would decide what I would do on the following day – the holiday Monday. If my experience from the previous day, from the Saturday, was repeated and I returned back to my own era, close to, or exactly at, the moment in time that I departed, then on the holiday Monday I would exploit this unforeseen feature of the time gateway to my advantage.

My mind was distracted, being focused on a new, mysterious and exciting aspect to my life. What I should have been doing at this moment in time was directing my attention towards that which had kept me from spending the weekend away with my wife – my work. Instead, I found myself engaging in gardening as a way of passing away the hours that lay between the present and the rapidly approaching moment in time when I would once more become a time traveller. These activities helped to take my mind off the Time House and, as with all activities that engross the mind, time advanced without being noticed, minutes and hours slipping away, never again to be seen, except perhaps by me, positioned as I was on the threshold of becoming the master of time – what folly, but how typical of our modern age with all its impressive science, engineering and technology.

It is not hard to understand why impressive achievements deceive some individuals, leading them to accept the madness of shaping technologies that reflect values which speak of people who have lost touch with their humanity, who see resistance and concern only as barriers to be overcome or to be ignored, and not as the warning signs that they are. The mindset is clear; things are the way they are because there is a process at work that ensures that the best always emerges. And this is the thinking of social Darwinists, for that is what many scientists, engineers and technologists are, which leads them to the notion of the one best way, that which is best, because this is what emerges with time, with competing technologies, processes, methods, tools, etc. eliminated because they are inferior. There is no alternative to what predominates, even though the evidence shows that there is. But those caught up in these ideologies have no room in their minds for evidence.

Lunchtime arrived and I had forgotten to telephone Helen. I tried to ring her, but there was only an automated response; either she was busy or it had not been possible to make a connection. If it was the latter then I assumed that she was somewhere with a weak signal or she had her mobile telephone switched off.

So it was that lunch was consumed, satisfying the hunger that had been intensified by the physical activities of the morning, but this is just trivia, small detail, in comparison to the significant problem that suddenly presented itself to me. How could I have forgotten this and not foreseen such a problem? What to wear? This question was one that now threatened to upset my well-laid-out plans, showing that I had not actually fully considered all aspects of what I was going to do.

The reality was that I had no clothes that suited the styles of eighteenth-century dress. But, not letting such matters stand in the way of implementing that which I knew was right and had to be done, I came to the convenient conclusion that the clothes that I had been wearing the previous day, along with a corduroy jacket, would be best, until, that is, I could find garments that would enable me to blend in with the dress of the age. Problem resolved!

Two o'clock arrived, as it always does one minute after thirteen fifty-nine hours, and I was ready to depart. I set off on my journey, full of anticipation, ensuring that I maintained a gentle pace, not wanting to exert myself in the midday heat, which would result in perspiration and a smelliness that I abhorred, although I knew that I was heading for an age where body odour was the norm – a feature of the past that has now largely disappeared thanks to modern deodorants and antiperspirants, these being the fruits of science, engineering and technology put to the service of humanity. What false image of engineers you have! Do you not know that we invent, that we are the creators of the modern world? Intensive care technology, pharmaceuticals, mobile phones, cars, domestic appliances, computers, trains, central heating, deodorants, fast food, throwaway cups, tasteless vegetables, overcrowded roads, mountains of discarded plastics, chemical weapons, unnecessary energy consumption, mindless and repetitive manual work, dwindling oil reserves, environmental pollution, global warming, loss of biodiversity, nuclear reactors that melt down ... Yes, indeed, we create the best of all possible worlds, far better than the one that nature provided. Can you not see that we deserve a higher social status than that which we actually have? Or is it the case that we have the social status we deserve?

My route was typical of many thousands of English country lanes scattered across the land, and the scenery on either side of the byway was very English indeed. Nowhere else in the world does one come across such a beautiful landscape – the creation of man, not of nature, and increasingly depleted of that which nature provides and needs. Encompassing modern and old, the natural and the manmade, it seems eternal, but is not, for across the ages different agricultural practices have provided their own unique features, none so attractive and productive than nature's own way, mostly ignored, not understood, and not at all suited to maintaining the vested interests of large agrichemical companies and industrial-scale farmers.

Routes that meander across this world of fields and hedges are numerous – lanes of ancient origins, following tracks that were laid down by wanderers and travellers from times long past. But very often the hedgerows are not so old, dating back to a more recent period, between the mid-eighteenth and mid-nineteenth centuries, the time of the Enclosure Acts that resulted in open swathes of land being enclosed by fences and hedges – an innovation not technological, being in character mostly social, organisational and methodological, but which enabled technological innovation in later periods.

It was not a long walk; only twenty minutes had passed since I left my home, when I found myself standing in front of the Time House. Once more I glanced up at the upper floors, recalling the previous day's sighting at the upstairs window. This was an aspect of events that had slipped from my mind with all the excitement of my adventure. The memory of that brief glimpse of a dark figure looking out of the window came flooding back, casting an unwelcome shadow over an otherwise rosy day.

Then I heard the voice again, which had been silent since Saturday. It spoke to me, in a measured tone, saying, "Beware the creature at the window."

"What creature?" I replied. "It was only a figment of my imagination, or an optical illusion, the effect of light on glass."

"Perhaps," the voice said, "or maybe there was someone at that window."

I recalled the dark figure that had, I admit, seemed sinister. Or was that just a characteristic that I had assigned to it? Perhaps there had been someone there. Perhaps it was a projection of someone from another time. After all, a house that could take me back to another age might be capable of other tricks.

Then the voice spoke again, but never showing signs of emotion – always calm and unhurried, patiently seeking to divert me away from my chosen course. "You do not know what you are getting involved with. Turn back," it said. "Turn back before it's too late. You do not have to do this. You can go home and forget all about the house, about Lucy. You are in deep water and in danger of drowning. Get out now while you can."

"I don't want to turn back," I responded. "There are discoveries to be made, new knowledge to be gained and mysteries to solve. I need to find answers to the questions raised by yesterday's experiences. The only way I can find these answers is to return to the house."

"It is not a question of need; it's an issue of wanting," the voice said, continuing with its efforts to dissuade me from continuing. "You don't need to go back; you want to go back. There's a difference! You have a choice. You could decide not to return, to give up this notion of time travel. There is always a different path to follow."

Previously the voice had only raised with me concerns that might affect my safety, such as not being able to find my way back to my own era, or it had tried to frighten me. Now it seemed to have changed tack and was shifting to a different level. I concluded that the voice had reasons for arguing against my returning to the Time House and that this was an inexplicable part of its mystery. Strangely, I did not question what the voice was, or whose it was. Now of course I do know, but at that moment in time it was a curious feature of a unique experience, and one that did not seem out of character with what was occurring. Mystery is a feature of life that the modern world seems to dislike, preferring instead clear answers to all questions. But, paradoxically, science is beginning to demonstrate that life and the universe are far more mysterious than many had ever realised. Perhaps some aspects of both should remain that way. Can we truly ever achieve knowledge of everything? Do we want to? Should we?

Such thoughts shaped my answer, for, as with most modern people from the age of science and technology, my values have been moulded by the foolishness of a culture that arrogantly believes that we can eventually know it all.

"It's the nature of humanity to investigate, not just because of need, but also because of wanting to know," I replied. "That's what makes us different. We explore and advance, not just because we are fulfilling needs, but because we want to discover the world, we want to uncover new knowledge, and we want to move forward."

"That's also what gets you into trouble as well," returned the voice. "Perhaps you need to be more circumspect in what you choose to explore and discover, rather than stumbling blindly into circumstances that could be avoided. That too is a capability that differentiates humanity from other creatures. It is called foresight, but to exercise this one needs wisdom, which is notably absent from science, engineering, and technology."

The voice had made a good point; however, I felt disinclined towards such reflections. I had an appointment to keep, a moment in time that called me to attend to matters planned, and this involved re-entering the Time House. I looked at my watch; nearly half past two.

So it was that once more I walked up the path to the front door, inserted the key and entered the Time House. It was also my house. No longer was I there as a visitor, a provider of services to the estate agent, but present as the owner, fully entitled to be in the building, to enjoy my property as I saw fit and to stay for as long as I wanted. And this was a good feeling. At that moment I knew that if a representative from the agent arrived, I would not need to explain myself in detail to whomever it was. Then I recalled what I had discovered about Harry – his untimely departure from this world, brought about from another act of ignoring warning signs, of thinking that all would be well. But in Harry's case, all was, plainly, not all right – he had died as a result of choices he had made. So, if a sales agent did appear, then I knew it would not be Harry. That he was dead and that this might have been a consequence of what I had done in the house on the previous day, or more correctly just outside the house back in the year 1750 – this I refused to consider. I told myself once more that I was not to blame for Harry's death. What was different as a result of my actions was that the consequences of Harry's lifestyle had caught up with him sooner than I expected, for catch up with him they surely would; it was just a question of when.

I did not lose any time: having hidden one of my clocks in the kitchen, noting that it was precisely half past two, I was, in a moment, upstairs on the first floor landing, and there it was, the portal, just as it had been before – an opening in the wall leading into the south-east wing of the house, and, I hoped, into the year 1750, precisely at the moment in time that would take me to Lucy's front door exactly at the time we had arranged.

I stepped through the gateway, feeling as I did so the electrifying sensation that told me that the house was working its magic, transporting me back (I expected) hundreds of years, but to what age exactly? This I was intensely keen to discover as quickly as possible. I walked into the bedroom on the first floor; it was just as I remembered it from the day before. Looking out of the window at what beheld me there, that too, as far as I could recall, was just as it had been on the previous day. Here in this room I hid my second clock.

"So far so good," I said aloud to myself, perhaps feeling the need for the comfort of the reassuring words that I spoke.

Then I was in the mysterious south-east wing and then in the study; all seemed exactly as I had left it the evening before. I glanced out of the window; there was no one in sight. I listened carefully for any sounds coming from downstairs or outside; there were none. "Excellent," I told myself, once more speaking to myself words of reassurance, convincing myself that all would be well. And all was well as far as I could tell.

It was now or never, for this was the moment in time that I had waited for. I would not make my three o'clock appointment if I dawdled. I am a punctual person and putting aside Mrs Dent's willingness to accept my arrival at whatever time I chose to make my appearance, I put caution to one side and boldly marched out of the study, down the stairs and across the chamber below; then, on opening the door, I stepped out into what I hoped was the summer of 1750.

Having made my way along the side of the house to the front of the property I was very soon in the lane, a place already of memories, and also of learning, for this is where I had my first experiences of a world that to me was alien, given that I came to this far distant age with values and beliefs that none of the people who inhabited 1750 would have understood or accepted. And yet, strangely, I soon found that I was able to fit into this unfamiliar world.

My adventure of the preceding day had been confined to the very small area on the track directly outside the Time House. Now, I was about to penetrate deeper into this place, into a time long past, embarking upon a journey further into the unknown, and with consequences that perhaps I could have foreseen, had I taken note of the warnings, had I opened my eyes and seen the world in its true complexity rather than the mechanistic and reductionist version that passed for my version of reality.

I was, I have to confess, just a little nervous, but this did not hold me back. That I should be nervous is of course natural, as this is the way of humans in such circumstances.

I set off along the lane towards the village, but it was a very different byway to the one I had just walked along when I travelled to the Time House in the twenty-first century. Here my surroundings were more as they had been for the many centuries that followed the felling of the great forests that once spread across the country. It was more natural in the sense that nature was not subjected to the mindless onslaught that lay in the future, yet the land still bore the mark of humankind. Gone were the hedgerows, not just those along the side of the lane, but also those that lined the farmers' fields. Before me was an open landscape. I was used to seeing the English countryside as a system of fields, visibly demarcated by lines of hedges, at least in places where these had not been uprooted in the name of progress, which, in this case, presented itself under the guise of large-scale, intensive, industrialised agriculture – good only in terms of producing large quantities of produce, but of questionable quality, and bad from all other aspects, the ones that really matter, the ones our future existence depend upon. This is one of the industrialised world's greatest achievements – the unnecessary destruction of the natural world, driven by the greed of a few, and blindly supported by engineers! *Ours is*

*not to reason why, but to unquestionably do our employers'
bidding.*

The lane that passed by the Time House was no more
than a dirt track, heavily rutted by centuries of coming and
going by wagons, the wheels of which had churned up the soft
earth, creating permanent channels along which all vehicles in
subsequent ages would follow, except of course in my own
time. Ways such as this did exist in my world, but only as
access roads to farms located well away from the metalled
roads that were an essential part of a modern transport system
– the benefits of modern engineering and technology. And yet,
for all the convenience of the modern, I have to say that I
found the journey back to the village more pleasant than the
outward one. I did not have to worry about speeding cars that
might pose a danger. I was now in an age where the fastest
vehicle was a horse-drawn cart or coach, and given the state
of the roadway, the speed of such a means of transport would
be no more than a few miles per hour. Yet, although this
aspect of the journey did seem very quaint, I was well aware
that I was now in an era where hardly anyone travelled very
much at all – perhaps a feature of the past that will have to
become, once again, part of our over-consuming world.

Many of the inhabitants of the period that I was
visiting, as I have already mentioned, lived out their lives
within a few miles of where they were born. And part of the
reason for this was the lack of good roads. This stands in
sharp contrast with the modern age of the twenty-first century,
where transport is varied in means, more or less ubiquitous in

coverage, and accessible to just about all; the age of mass transportation, with all its benefits along with its many problems that defy resolution; all that is offered are palliatives that address symptoms. It seemed to me at that moment in time, with the benefits of being able to experience transport in two widely different ages, that problems are not actually addressed, and do not disappear with time; they just change in nature, but they are always present, providing opportunities to develop technological fixes, which are not solutions, just ways of avoiding the social and economic innovations that the world so badly needs.

And I was also conscious of the fact that I was in an era of great inequalities and ignorance. Relative to my own time I was now in a backward place: one where people died from ailments that modern medicine has, largely, long since banished, at least from the developed world. Of course, it is true in my own age that diseases, many avoidable and curable, still afflicted the undeveloped regions of the planet, but that only served to remind me that the work of spreading the fruits of human progress and development more widely had still not concluded. Some might say it had only just begun, and to a large extent they would be right. But, what I, like most scientists, engineers and technologists, had failed to recognise was that our modern battle against disease was also partly founded on ignorance of nature, for increasingly bacteria in the modern world are evolving and developing resistance to the antibiotics upon which we have become so reliant; such is our own ignorance and a perfect example of how technological fixes, in the end, fly in the face of that great truth, that nature will find a way to restore disorder.

I did not realise it at that moment in time, but here at work was a universal law; in eliminating the disorder of nature and bringing order through our scientific approach to medicine, nature was fighting back to restore its natural state of disorder. It is a battle we cannot win, and back in 1750 no one knew about this, and as for the age I had come from, few still realised the power of nature to overcome our best endeavours to control the world. Most people in the early twenty-first century were still living the delusion that order would prevail, including myself and the majority of all other scientists, engineers and technologists; collective denial of reality! When will these people grow up and begin to develop a more mature approach, instead of seeking to bludgeon nature into submission?

One thought that passed through my mind as I journeyed to my appointment with the Dents was that what I was about to experience might be compared not to a journey through time, to a place in the distant past, but to a visit in my own age to some far less fortunate undeveloped country. For this, it seemed to me, summed up some of the problems of the world; most of it is caught in a time warp, one of a more primitive existence, reflected not in physical living conditions but in the prevailing attitudes towards the environment, towards other living creatures and towards fellow human beings. Economy has dominance and other issues play second fiddle to this – not a recipe for a happy, meaningful or more certain future. My own world hid from the vision of many its true nature, its undeveloped characteristics, through the veneer of a sophistication derived from an illusion of progress generated by material possessions, fancy technology, amazing engineering achievements, and blind arrogance.

These were the rather serious thoughts that accompanied me as I walked along the lane. Why I should have been so reflective did not at the time bother me. Later I realised that this too was a consequence of the folly I was engaging in. In this respect I see myself as being fortunate, for my experiences did, in the end, open my eyes to the stupidity of the contemporary world.

My deep reflections on the nature of modern life came to an end when the sense of expectation associated with my visit to Lucy and my curiosity with respect to my surroundings began, as I drew closer to the village green, to dominate my mind. What greeted me were both the familiar and the unfamiliar. All post-1750 construction was of course absent and this meant that only the original core of the village was present. This consisted mainly of what I referred to as the older properties that were built around the village green and a few cottages scattered here and there along the country lanes that led into the centre of the settlement. Only here, in 1750, they were not at all old.

I emerged from one of these byways, onto the village green, and stopped to look around, to take in the view and to savour a sight that no living person had seen for over 250 years – the village as it was in the mid-eighteenth century.

Save one solitary figure sitting on the grass by the duck pond, there was no one to be seen, but there were many animals, mostly sheep, but also some cattle, grazing on the grass. Here was the proof of what I had learned from the study of history, that the large grassed area in the centre of the village was originally common land. And, as it was common land, poorer farmers used it for grazing. This was yet another glimpse of life in this period. Scenes such as the one now before me could be found in hamlets and villages all over the country. Yet no one, except me, knew that within a few decades all this would be swept away by increasing industrialisation and land reforms that would lead to the creation of a new and more efficient system of agriculture. And this knowledge, of what was to come, would have to stay locked away in my mind, for I was firmly resolved not to reveal what I knew about the future. To the people with whom I was about to come into contact, these events were to be their future and hence they should remain unknown, but to me they were just history. I had already seen the relatively small effects in my own time of my previous visit and I was not about to magnify them by interfering in the past and forewarning anyone about what lay just around the corner. I was here only as an observer; I was not going to become involved and that is how I intended matters would stay. That was my good intention at least, but I did not know how hard it would be to keep to this.

CHAPTER 14

The solitary figure sitting by the duck pond was Samuel Jones, dressed exactly as he had been on the previous day, this being, I assumed, because he did not have much in the way of clothing. He knew about my visit to the Dents and was undoubtedly sited where he was so that he could, once more, speak to me. As soon as I emerged from the lane he jumped up, waved and ran over to where I had paused.

I greeted him, saying, "Hello Samuel," not being really sure what I should say, and not wanting to influence him further with my alien knowledge and opinions. The truth is, I would have preferred not to have seen the boy, but he was obviously excited about his encounter with me on the previous day and wanted more of that experience. This of course did not surprise me. It did not take much imagination to realise that life for Samuel Jones must have been fairly unexciting. And the arrival of someone such as me, a visitor from a far-off strange place, would have stimulated the curiosity of any child, but especially this one, for I could see that he was intelligent. It was a sad thought to know that millions similar to him, across history, had been denied the opportunity to use that intelligence, denied the chance to become educated and knowledgeable. How much human talent has been wasted over the ages simply because of lack of opportunity? This at least is one aspect of the world that has changed to a certain extent with time, but not fully. Perhaps what has not changed is that many in my own time, as in all eras, choose not to know, preferring instead to limit their knowledge, understanding and awareness to matters with which they feel comfortable and that do not disturb long-held beliefs and values!

"Hello, Mr Woodward," he replied enthusiastically, greeting me with a pleasant smile that spoke of an equally pleasing personality, which I had already concluded, based on our previous encounter, the boy possessed. This warm smile was worn on a face of innocence, conveying an air of trust. Once more I briefly reflected on the difference between the two ages; there were no stark warnings in this time and place from parents to their children about avoiding talking with strangers. This was a timely reminder that there are many aspects to modern living that are far from being ideal and that serve to illustrate the point that quality of life cannot just be measured by economic indicators, scientific progress, technological wonders, and engineering achievements. In the end, none of these are a substitute for a safe, unpolluted environment where people can be content and happy. And this implies that people should not be, as they have become in the early twenty-first century, servants and slaves to the mindless and soulless world of economics, science, engineering and technology. There is a choice about this, which groups with vested interests, such as engineers, do not want to address, as they pursue their own agendas that will, if persisted in, lead us all to becoming bound in a metaphorical darkness from which there will be no escape.

These reflections were an unwelcome intrusion, and I was surprised how quickly they formed in my head, for I had never had such thoughts previously.

I do not know if there was a delay in my response to Samuel's greeting, but I did evenly venture to ask if Samuel had been waiting for me, even though I knew he had, which he quickly confirmed in his response. "I thought that I would wait for you and be your guide, since you are new to the village."

This seemed a genuine kindness born of a spirit that is often now not to be found in modern western civilisation, leading one to wonder if, indeed, what exists in the Europeanised world is in fact a civilisation at all, or just a large group of people being preyed upon by greedy entrepreneurs and business people, who see no value in citizens other than how much money can be extracted from them. So it was that I replied, "That is very kind of you," appreciating the value of this simple act.

"So where do you live?" I asked, curious to know more about Samuel. This I must add was a genuine interest, not just idle social chatter, for I recognised that I liked Samuel, and deep within me there was a desire to help him, to guide him on his way through life. This was a natural human response, instinctive in character, but not at all compatible with the cold logic that had determined that I, in this age, would be no more than an observer, not becoming involved in the lives of the people whom I would meet.

Samuel turned to his right, lifted his small arm and pointed. "In the shop over there," he said. "Ma and Pa run the village shop."

It was indeed a small arm, for Samuel was a child of the eighteenth century, and was not as well-nourished as children in the developed nations of the modern world – yet another reminder of the significant differences between the two ages.

I was acquainted with the property that Samuel had just identified as being his home. In my own time it is the village post office and small convenience store. It is much bigger than the tiny shop to which Samuel was pointing, but I could see familiar features in the frontage that still remain in place in my own age. And glancing at Samuel's facial features I recognised many similarities with the postmistress who now ran the shop. Only her surname was Hamlin, but that might have been her married name.

I enquired if Samuel worked in this very small shop, selling, I supposed, a limited range of products, this not being an age of excessive and unsustainable consumption – a delight of the industrial era, which as of 1750, had still to be inflicted on the world. "Oh yes, every day, except Sundays," Samuel replied.

My questioning then shifted to the matter of Samuel's education, starting with a very straightforward enquiry: "And what about school? Do you attend school?" The reply was that

Samuel did not go to school as his parents did not have enough money to pay for one. And saying this he hung his head slightly as if conscious of the differences in financial standing that lay between us. For a moment the brightness of his soul dimmed a little, as he must have realised, as did I, that school for him was a luxury that would forever remain unattainable, most likely ensuring that he would spend the rest of his life illiterate and uneducated.

"And there is no church school in the village that you can attend? No place where you can gain even the most basic elements of an education?"

"No, sir. But every evening Ma teaches me reading, writing and sums. She is clever, my Ma. She went to school. But there is no school here." By way of recognition of his circumstances he added, "And there will never be, at least not for the likes of me."

I was curious about his mother, so changing the subject I asked, "So your mother does not come from the village then?"

"No, sir. She is from London."

"London! That is a long way away. How did she end up here?"

It transpired that the answer to this question was more enlightening than I expected. "She found a job in one of the big houses outside the village. Actually it is the one where that Walter Smythe lives. My Ma worked for his father. That is how she met my Pa. He worked in the gardens. Then my grandfather passed away and Pa inherited the shop. By that time Ma and Pa were courting, so they got married and gave up their jobs, which did not please old Mr Smythe."

"I see," I said knowingly, immediately recognising that in this fact of Samuel's parents' life there was perhaps the core of the reason for Smythe's hostility towards Samuel – a case of a son inflicting punishment on another son, a punishment for the sins Samuel's parents had inflicted on his own. "So would that be a possible reason why Walter Smythe reacted so badly to you yesterday?" I enquired, seeking confirmation of my hypothesis.

"Yes, sir. It is not the first time he has done that. He is a bully and most people around here are frightened of him, except you of course. And for that I am glad." Samuel was evidently please with what had happened, but he added, "Although I fear that he will not stop his bullying just because of what you did yesterday. Smythe is arrogant and thinks he can do whatever he likes to those below him."

I found what Samuel had just told me very disturbing. Someone needed to deal with Walter Smythe before he seriously harmed Samuel. But should this person be me? I, after all, had vowed not to become involved, to be nothing more than an observer in this age – make no bonds, do not interfere, let affairs take their course, no matter what!

"Right, I will have a think about what to do with him," I said reassuringly. But what exactly I was going to do, I had no idea. Already I was being drawn in to their world, feeling deep within me an instinctive desire to address an injustice, even though I was just an observer; so much for my naïve beliefs, of which I now know I had many.

"So come on, then. Show me where Lucy and her mother live," I said, wanting to change the subject, but also resolving to ask Lucy more about Walter Smythe and his vendetta against poor Samuel. But Samuel had not finished, and he asked me about that which I really did not want to speak further, having already probably said too much the previous day.

"Can I ask you a question? About the American Colonies?" Samuel enquired, diffidently.

I had no choice. What could I do? Say no, and disappoint the poor child. "Yes, all right. What is it you want to ask?"

"Do you think that I could ever go to the American Colonies? Not now! I mean when I grow up. I would really love to become an explorer, just as you are. I want to travel, to visit strange places, and to experience the world. Living here for the rest of my days is not what I want to do."

I looked at the boy and wondered what I should say. Should I, as an observer, be influencing Samuel? But how could I not do so? So I sighed and crouched down at his level so that our gazes met. In his eyes I saw the joy of youthful curiosity, which I could not ignore. "Samuel," I began, "if going to the American Colonies is what you really want to do, then do it. Do not let anyone or anything stand in your way. Learn as much as you can from your mother. Learn to read, to write and to do sums. Use that knowledge as a starting point.

Learn about the world. Read as much as you can. If you do not have any books, try borrowing them from someone, Miss Lucy for instance. Never let anyone tell you that you cannot do it. Follow your dreams. It is the only way to true happiness, although it is not the easiest of journeys."

I was being surprisingly philosophical and to an extent that I had never been before. This was a measure to which my circumstances were already beginning to change me, to act upon me in ways that I still cannot fully comprehend.

Samuel smiled at me. His inner being now seemed even more illuminated, as though my words of encouragement were charging a battery somewhere inside his mind, driving the light of life to shine more brilliantly. And I wondered what that might lead to, how that might change the world in ways that I could never imagine.

I had an appointment to keep. I looked at my watch. It was already past three o'clock. "Time for my appointment," I said. "Where do I have to go?" The reality of course was that I knew exactly which house was my destination.

I rose. Samuel pointed at a familiar property. Elm House. Standing at an upstairs window I could see Lucy looking out, watching. She smiled and waved at me. I returned the smile and waved, reciprocating her gesture of warmth and, although I did not know it at the time, friendship. I turned to Samuel. "Remember what I have just said. Be sure to follow your dreams." Then I gently touched the back of his head in a gesture of truth warmth, turned, and walked away from Samuel, leaving him standing, watching me, his mind full of new thoughts, new ambitions, and new dreams. But after a few paces I paused, turned and looked back. "I will see you when I leave later this evening. If you are not around I will come to the shop."

Samuel smiled. "I will be waiting," he responded enthusiastically.

I smiled back and then turned and resumed my walk towards the house.

Upon knocking on the door it was opened by a maid. "Please come in, sir," the young woman said plainly and politely. "You are expected. Mrs Dent is in here, sir," and she led me to one of the many doors in the large entrance hall. She knocked and entered. "Mr Woodward, madam," she said, curtsying as she spoke.

The maid allowed me to enter and then she departed, shutting the door behind her, leaving me alone with Mrs Marjory Dent.

So there I was, thinking of myself as an observer in a different time, someone just passing through, but I was on the cusp of doing that which I was resolved not to do: of becoming involved in a world where I did not belong, and this act of stupidity would have consequences. I am an engineer – out of disorder I believe I create order, but in reality this is not so.

The scene was now set. All that was necessary was for me to follow the sequence of events that would demonstrate to me the folly of my naïve and ill-informed beliefs; the universe was about to show me that nature will not be subjected to the will of humankind, no matter how hard we try, no matter how sophisticated our technology, no matter what we may seek to engineer to make that happen.

CHAPTER 15

At last I was in the home of Lucy and her mother – present as a guest, but one who was evidently invited for reasons beyond just neighbourliness and good manners. There I was, standing in the drawing room of their elegant Georgian house, which overlooked the open space that was, and still is, the village green, and I was a visitor, a unique one, experiencing what many explorers of new worlds must have felt: a sensation of anticipation tinged with concern that comes from what is unknown and uncertain.

At that moment in time I was poised on the cusp of a new life, for what had not yet dawned in my mind was the realisation that I had already become involved. I can see now that I was naïve to think that I could be just an impartial bystander in this age, that I could just come and go as I pleased and not be affected by what was going on around me. I did not realise it at that particular moment in my travels, but I was presently to learn that such a position is impossible to maintain and that I would very soon be consciously discarding this role and actively becoming engaged with the lives of the people around me. Events were about to unfold that would challenge me, tempting me to change the course of history using knowledge from my own period. What should have been a sightseeing journey through time was soon to become an emotional roller-coaster ride. What is more, danger would stalk me and my very life would be at risk. But for now all was peaceful. The quiet before the storm, that gentle time when all seems right with the world and peacefulness fills the mind and heart, and all is sweet content.

"Mr Woodward," Mrs Dent said in greeting me and welcoming me into her home, warmly and confidently, demonstrating through her manner that at some stage in her life she had acquired much experience of acting as hostess. "Do come in. Make yourself comfortable. Lucy will be with us in a moment."

"Thank you," I replied, as this was the only way I knew of responding, and I was making an extra effort to act in as respectful a way as possible, being unsure of what was expected of me. This is the problem that comes with venturing into the unknown, for customs are part of culture, which changes with time as society evolves and standards change.

She offered me her hand, and being a person of the twenty-first century I accepted it as I would any other and shook hands with her, as I had done on the previous day. She may have expected me to kiss her hand, as people once did long ago, but it was not obvious to me that this was her intention, so I believe that she found my action unorthodox, but she was not easily flummoxed. She was a lady of good breading, well used to dealing with social gatherings, and much experienced at hiding her reactions.

Mrs Dent must have sensed my slight awkwardness for she continued by saying, "No need to stand on ceremony here. We have never previously had a visitor from the American

Colonies. I know you behave differently over there, so let us just be informal shall we?" doing her best to make me feel comfortable, which I very much appreciated. I thought it considerate of her, which elevated my opinion of her. There was, here, not the snobbishness of someone who thinks herself superior, but a kind-hearted person, willing to accept me as I was and as an equal. This surprised me, but perhaps it should not have done, for what I knew of her era mostly came from watching period costume dramas on television and who is to say that these are historically accurate? Perhaps, as in my own time, people behaved in the mid-eighteenth century according to their personalities, and why not? Some aspects of life are timeless, and what more so than human actions in such circumstances?

I then heard a repetitive dull thudding coming from outside the room, one thud coming after the other, and moving downwards, coming closer to the door; it was the sound of someone moving quickly down the stairs. Mrs Dent heard this also. "That will be Lucy," she said, adding, "Full of energy she is. Quite a handful!" And into the room she came – Lucy in all her splendour; alive, engaging, and beautiful, as though she were Helen.

I now looked at her in a different light. Gone was the surprise of yesterday's meeting, overshadowed by my encounter with Walter Smythe. There was time now for closer observation, for reflection, and my thoughts immediately and naturally turned to her resemblance to Helen. About this I had not been mistaken. It had not been an error on my part, for looking at her once more, seeing her with time to examine and consider, I realised that she did indeed closely resemble my Helen. But her behaviour and character were also in many ways similar to Helen's. From her looks I also judged that in her age she also had yet another likeness. And at that moment in time, looking at her, deep within me I felt emotion stirring.

I sensed also that I stood in her presence this time in a different light from the previous day. No longer was I seen as a stranger, an oddity from a far distant place, but as someone they regarded as worthy of their friendship, for I judged that she was genuinely happy to see me, and I for my part was also glad to see her, for I did like her very much, which should not come as a surprise given that she was virtually the same as Helen in all ways.

Before me was someone enchantingly beautiful. She had rosy cheeks and a mischievous smile. Her blonde hair was curled and pinned up at the back, exposing the rear of her neck, similar to how Helen also sometimes wore her hair, but without the curls. And her complexion was soft and smooth, unmarked by the passage of time, as is Helen's. As for her clothes, these did her no justice at all by the standards of my time, but that is the way with fashions from periods long past, from far-off days; and fashion is one aspect of our lives that does change, and whether for the better is a matter of opinion.

The dress she wore was in my eyes ridiculous, as underneath she was wearing a pannier, extending the garment each side of her, but leaving the front and back flat, this being the mode of dress of women in the mid-eighteenth century.

The material was sky-blue satin, with intricate embroidered patterns on the front, and her bosom was to some extent exaggerated, being pushed upwards by the effect of wearing what I assumed was a corset. Even so, the features of her body were clear enough: she had a figure that made her appealing, being one that had not suffered from the effect of pregnancy or excessive eating. In all she was a sight to behold, and I pictured her in more modern attire and judged her to be a real beauty.

For a few moments I gazed at her. Feelings were beginning to stir inside me. I was fascinated by her and I was being drawn into her life. How could I help myself though? For here before me was Helen. And I could see she was reciprocating these feelings and she did not try to hide them. This is the reality of life; here I was, committed to the one I loved, yet before me was what seemed to me to be the same person. What could I do? I was lost already and I knew it, and I did not resist; it seemed pointless to try. Married man meets other woman, feels the stirrings of physical attraction, starts to fall in love, and then ... This is yet another aspect of life that never changes.

"How nice to see you again, Mr Woodward. You are most welcome in our home," Lucy said with a warm and welcoming smile.

I replied by thanking her, adding that I considered it to be a pleasure to be there. But I said no more than this, being still a little unsure of myself, and not having enough worldly experience to feel confident in that most unusual of circumstances.

Fortunately Mrs Dent was confident, for what she had before her was a scene, I supposed, that must have been played out many times in her life; a guest feeling awkward and self-conscious, in need of reassurance; someone to be put as ease. "Come now, Lucy," began her mother in an authoritative but friendly voice, as she began the process of alleviating my discomfort. "Sit here on the settee. And you, Mr Woodward, sit next to her."

We did as we were told, but immediately I began to wonder if Lucy's mother were about the business of matchmaking. For I had already assumed – by the lack of both reference to a male figure in our conversations and a ring on Lucy's left hand – that Lucy was single. And I, seeming to be a person of some wealth, must surely have been a possible candidate for the position of Lucy's husband, at least in the eyes of her mother, if not also in Lucy's mind as well.

Having organised us both, Mrs Dent pulled a chord by the fireplace, and I heard a bell tingle somewhere in a far distant part of the house. She then proceeded to sit down in the armchair opposite and continued speaking. "Tea will be with us in a few moments. I do hope you like fruitcake, Mr Woodward," she said rhetorically. "Fruitcake suits me well, I must say," she continued, ensuring that there were no discomforting periods of silence by regaling me with the story of her love of fruitcake – how it had developed, how her dear late husband had taken, one Christmas, to the enjoyment of this spiced and exotic cake, and how, ever since, it had been a part of the Dent household.

There were no delays in bringing the tea and cake to the drawing room, this being so I believe because all was arranged and ready, so in what seemed no time at all, there was a light knock at the door, which was opened by the maid who had first greeted me on my arrival. Following her was another maid carrying a tray, upon which was placed what was to be our tea, which consisted of buttered bread and a large fruitcake. Arranged on the tray were also the means that would help us consume these delights – Mrs Dent's best English china, Royal Dalton, or some such similar brand, and her silverware, spoons and forks, and also a knife to cut the cake. I surmised that this paraphernalia was only brought out for special occasions or distinguished visitors. Such a time-honoured tradition could be found in many a household across the land and it is also one that I recall my own mother indulging in. This is another aspect of life that had not changed. As I said previously, there are facets of our world, our existence, that never change and are as eternal as the passage of night into day and then back into darkness once again.

The tray was placed on the table that stood next to the chair in which Mrs Dent was now sitting. "I will take care of that," Mrs Dent said to the maid, who responded by curtsying and saying, "Yes, madam," showing her mistress due respect. It was a time of order in society, and everyone knew their place in that order, and woe to anyone who questioned it.

The maids left the room and Mrs Dent said to me in the most genteel way, "Would you like some buttered bread?"

"Yes, please," I replied, adding, "Buttered bread, how very English. I must confess that I have not eaten bread in this way for a long time." This was a true statement, for eating bread just spread with butter was not my preference and normally I would not do this, there being more interesting spreads and fillings available in the twenty-first century.

"And you, Lucy dear, will you have some?"

"Yes please, Mama." Lucy's response sounded both innocent and captivating at the same time, luring me, drawing me closer to her, creating the bond that should not have been made.

Lucy turned, smiled at me and asked, "What would you eat in the Colonies for afternoon tea?"

Now I was faced with inevitable questions linked to America. They wanted to know more about this curious place and its new and different customs. "It is common to eat smoked turkey or Virginian ham, and then to have some buttermilk biscuits," I responded, trying to sound as familiar as I could, but also recalling my knowledge of colonial fare from the time I had spent in New England.

Fortunately, I had, during my time in that part of the United States, visited many traditional restaurants in small towns and villages, communities that had retained their colonial heritage and were exploiting it for commercial gain. Tourists, both American and foreign, were all too eager to absorb what was on offer, as though it were genuine. The only

200

point of distinction between the two was that overseas visitors took more time to take in the experiences. For many Americans it was enough to say they had seen whatever it was that needed to be seen. Superficial perhaps, but that is how matters often are in that part of the world. But this is not the case for all: there are always exceptions, and it is a mistake often made, sometimes with dire consequences, as can be seen throughout history, to judge a society as homogeneous, uniform, with the sins of some unfairly attributed to all. The same applies to scientists, engineers and technologists, for not all are as blind as the majority, and there are those more reflective and concerned about the implications and consequences of their actions, and would, I am sure, be open to developing new and different approaches more appropriate to the early twenty-first century with all its complex problems, which could easily overwhelm humankind, pushing governments towards actions that would be completely abhorrent and unacceptable under more normal circumstances. This is the danger, the risk, that we face, and the descent has already begun, but there is little or no awareness of this, and no appetite to reflect on this fate; this also can be seen in history, and the outcome is never a happy one.

"Turkey? What is turkey?" Lucy asked, obviously just as eager as young Samuel Jones to know more about this strange land called the American Colonies. I was evidently among people eager to learn, a characteristic of people across all eras.

"Turkey is a North American bird, similar to goose, I suppose," I replied, trying to provide a comparison to which they could relate, "but much bigger, and without all that fat," I added.

This bird, so familiar in the twenty-first century, with its associations with Christmas, was still, in 1750, largely unheard of, and here I was, introducing to these people knowledge that most likely they should not have. This is how easy it is to act in a way that can, in turn, lead to unforeseen consequences of a most significant kind; there is no way of knowing, yet the modern world behaves as though this can never happen. And the reasons? There are many: over confidence; a lack of humility; ignorance; not knowing what one does not know; over-reliance upon and a belief in the power of technology that is not borne out by close examination of historical facts; the dehumanising mindset that refers to people as being part of a nameless mass, as *others*, as if they have no right to decide and must accept, without question, what science and engineering want to impose upon the world because these are good, and not at all a result of values and beliefs.

The inherent neutrality of science, engineering and technology is a nonsense dogma that has been inflicted upon the world for far too long, and the damaging consequences are now all too clear to those who care to look.

You can already see, in what I am writing, how much I have changed!

During the course of my response to Lucy's question, Mrs Dent, using a pair of tongs, was in the process of placing a piece of buttered bread onto a plate, undertaking this simple task with great precision, ensuring that the item was placed neatly in the centre of that particular item of crockery. Then, after attracting Lucy's attention with the words "Lucy dear," which prompted Lucy to rise from her seat to take on the role of waitress, the plate was taken from her mother and then handed to me. Mrs Dent placed one more slice onto another plate, which she also passed to Lucy. Lucy's mother then slowly rose, as if some affliction hampered faster movement, but I was never to be told if there was an ailment, and on reflection, I think it may have been the stiffness encountered when sitting in one position for a lengthy period of time; a trouble that comes with age, but one easily alleviated by regular stretching exercises. But there was, in that time and place, no understanding of this.

Moving away from her chair, my hostess went over to a small cupboard sited in an alcove to the right of the fireplace. Taking a small key, which was attached to a thin silver chain hung around her neck, Mrs Dent unlocked the cupboard, removed a tea caddy and returned to her chair.

Tea – a commodity item in my time, but in the mid-eighteenth century a luxury so valuable that people in Mrs Dent's position would not leave it with the servants. And so began a tea ceremony – the careful preparation of the drink that is quintessentially English. First the precious leaves, all black from their fermentation, were spooned into the tea pot; I counted three, one for each of us, I suppose. Then hot water was poured into this receptacle, from which whiffs of steam drifted, until the lid was placed over the aperture. I noted that the water would have no longer been at boiling point, which is essential to achieve a good-quality brew. Then we waited patiently – a few minutes of silence as we all gazed at the tea pot, as though wondering what was going on inside. Occasionally I glanced at Lucy, as one does when one is taken by a beautiful face and the forces of attraction have started their work. Mrs Dent noticed, as she did for most of the small and seemingly insignificant happenings taking place around her. And what she observed I could see she liked and approved of.

We were now in the final stage of the tea ceremony. "So, Mr Woodward, do you take milk and sugar with your tea?" Mrs Dent asked, polite as ever, and always attentive to the needs of her guest.

"No," I replied, "Black, just as it comes from the pot please." And so it was that the tea was poured, with the pot raised up high, and the tea cascading down into the cup, swirling around, the turbulence helping to entrap some extra oxygen, that which reacts with the tea to enhance its flavour.

This was my first encounter with eighteenth-century food. I discovered that the bread was different. It was wholemeal, but much courser than what I was used to and also much saltier. It did not appeal to my tastes, but I was a guest in their home, so I did what I thought to be polite and ate what I had been given, that which had been so lovingly and carefully positioned on my plate; they were ignorant of the world from which I came, of its foods, and of its concerns for healthy eating, and I was not going to begin teaching them about such matters. What they gave me, I assumed, was the norm for their day. They knew no better, and I accepted this, just one of several occasions when I had to do so. Yet another of the unforeseen consequences of travelling to a different age – we tend to forget such small details of history, lost as they are against backcloth of the major events that are recorded in written historical accounts. But step back in time and then all these small details present themselves, combining to form the whole picture of an age that has largely been forgotten; this perhaps is the destiny for most small details and their associated moments in time.

While I was eating, Lucy placed a cup of tea on the small table next to where I was seated, along with another plate upon which there was a slice of rich dark fruitcake, similar to the type that I had eaten as a child at Christmas time. "Thank you," I said, after I had swallowed what I was eating. And after finishing the bread, I started on the fruitcake. All was silent in the room while I ate, the quiet that comes before the storm. As soon as I had finished, their questions came.

It was Lucy who started. "I have," she began in the endearing manner in which she engaged in conversation, "often wondered what the American Colonies are like. Many times I have pictured the place in my mind, imagining the appearance of the landscape, and what the native peoples are like. I would very much like to go there one day, Mr Woodward. Please tell me what you can about this mysterious place. Tell me all."

"Yes, Mr Woodward, tell us about the American Colonies," added Lucy's mother. "So far away! It is hard to believe that we are so fortunate to have someone living in our midst that has travelled so much and so far. You will be the subject of talk in every house for months to come. It will guarantee you many invitations."

"Yes, well," I began speaking slowly, trying to give myself time to think, to make sure that I did not reveal that which had to remain unknown to these people. I paused for a moment then resumed. "It is a place a great variety. There is so—" I did not get chance to finish my sentence.

"Where did you live?" asked Lucy, interrupting, seemingly wanting to go straight to details pertaining to myself, rather than wanting to listen to the generic information that I had decided would be my best way of dealing with their questions. These were indeed formidable women, not ones to be put off from asking direct and pertinent questions. I liked this, even though such forthright questioning placed me in a difficult position.

"I lived for a while in Boston," I began to explain, once more speaking slowly, thinking carefully about what I was saying. "Then I travelled for a long time," I continued, "not settling anywhere, just doing work here and there. I visited many cities during that period, New York, Washington, Philadelphia, and many other places, mostly small towns that you would never have heard of. I also went further west, visiting frontier settlements, but I eventually returned to Boston."

No aspect of what I said was untrue as I had spent time in America when I was a university student, and I also felt that it would not be appropriate to tell lies to such nice people. This was an aspect of my time travelling that I had not anticipated, and in the back of my mind I did for a moment wonder whether I had taken the right decision to use the gateway in the Time House. This would not be the last occasion I would be visited by these misgivings. Later events would amplify my concerns and lead me in the end to question my whole relationship with the Time House. But the moment of doubt was gone in a jiffy, and the conversation continued.

"And will you be returning to the American Colonies?" asked Lucy. "Or does the fact that you have had a house constructed here signify that your travelling days are over? Will we be seeing more of you?" It was obvious that this was not an innocent question, but an indirect way of telling me that she, Lucy, wanted to see me again. I was flattered, and I too wanted to spend more time with her.

When Lucy had asked these questions, I immediately saw an opportunity to provide my hosts with a possible explanation, if I were suddenly to disappear as a result of deciding never again to use the Time House to return to 1750. "Very pertinent questions," I responded. "And my reply is that

I am not sure. I have been thinking about returning once my business here is finished."

"So you are not taking up residence here?" asked Mrs Dent, sounding a little disappointed.

Here I ventured another glance at Lucy, and she too, I ascertained from her facial expression, would have preferred that I had said that I would be settling in the village. So I quickly added, "I have not finally decided about that matter at the moment. I have acquired the house that you have just mentioned, but I am not sure yet if I will take up residence. Once my business is finished, I might decide to have a long break and live in the house for a year, taking time to explore more of England."

"Oh, I see. And you mentioned you had business here, Mr Woodward. What line of business are you in?" Mrs Dent enquired, continuing her probing questioning.

I noticed that Lucy was sitting quietly, listening carefully to what I was saying.

"I am an engineer. I have an engineering business."

Now, being ladies of the eighteenth century, they had very little knowledge, if any at all, about the subject of engineering, or what it involved, and, as I expected, Mrs Dent did not pursue the matter further, not wanting to emphasise her ignorance of such matters. In this respect her lack of understanding of engineering and the work of engineers is also a feature, surprisingly, of my own world in the twenty-first century. And people should know more about this subject, for it has an impact upon our world, both positive and negative, with the latter not being just a matter of misuse; the damaging consequences of engineering is a subject far more complex than such a simple issue and not at all understood by engineers; they live in the brilliant light of their glowing achievements, so much so that they are blind to the damage they inflict on people and the natural world. Yet it does not have to be like this, but this involves following a different path, transforming a profession into one quite different, and for that to happen, first there has to be acceptance of the mistakes made, the inappropriateness of current practices, and an improvement in the quality of people taking up engineering as a career, which will not happen until engineers start to change their beliefs, values and behaviour.

"And what other places in England do you want to visit?" asked Lucy, who now seemed very keen to become involved in the conversation.

I replied by telling her that I needed to take a trip to the nearby town to see my solicitor, and that I wanted to see London, but that I had yet to give the matter my full attention. No doubt there would be other places that would, in due course, attract my interest, and none of this was untrue. I had formed in my mind a plan to collect the money that was, I had already assumed, mine, and it seemed to me that the following day would be a good one to do so. I had also begun to consider a more adventurous journey, to London.

"London. Oh, Mama, it would be so nice to visit London. To see all those well-known places and buildings!"

"Nice? I do not think so. I lived there for a short time when I was young lady. Full of rouges! Now if you want to go somewhere nice, Bath would be the place, or Lyme Regis in Dorset. London is no place for a respectable young lady such as yourself. I could write to your uncle in Abbotsbury and you could visit him. I am sure that he would be delighted to have you stay and would be happy to take you to Bath."

The mention of Abbotsbury confirmed to me that I was in the company of Helen's ancestors. It was to Abbotsbury that Helen's parents had moved, precisely because a branch of the Dent family lived there. And it was also at this point that I recalled that Helen had once mentioned to me that far back, in the mid-eighteenth century, there had been a tragedy in her family among those who lived in our village, but the details of this had been long forgotten.

Here was an opportunity to find out more about this misfortune, but then it occurred to me that the event or events might not yet have happened. It also immediately dawned on me that what was to occur might well involve the people with whom I was now sitting, given that they might be the only Dent family in the area. And this was a disconcerting thought, to have an inkling that a calamity might be about to befall these people, but not to know what and, perhaps even worse, not to be able to warn them. This was yet another matter that I had not foreseen, for even if did know what lay ahead, I surely could not tell them. Thus I decided to leave the matter alone for the time being; it could wait for another moment in time.

For the present I decided to probe further about the Abbotsbury connection.

"So you come from Abbotsbury?" I asked, not seeking to hide my curiosity. "The village next to the enormous shingle beach," I added.

Mrs Dent replied, "You are correct. There is indeed such a beach. It is called Chesil Beach. And yes I do know Abbotsbury very well. My late husband and I were born and brought up in Abbotsbury. Do you know the place, Mr Woodward?"

"I have once been there, a long time ago, before my present existence," I responded, adding, "but it seems as if it was in a different age, such is the time gap. It is one of the few places in England I have visited. I went to see Chesil Beach."

"It is a grand sight, is it not, Mr Woodward? A very grand sight indeed! Shingle! Shingle! Shingle! Everywhere shingle."

"So it is," I returned, "very impressive! Nature does create beautiful structures, far more wondrous than that which humankind has ever produced."

"Seems a small world sometimes, does it not," was all Mrs Dent said. She then glanced over her shoulder towards the open Venetian window and then looked at the clock on the mantelpiece. "Four o'clock. How time flies! And it is such a nice day outside. A little too hot for me though. I prefer to stay out of the sun. Lucy dear, why not take Mr Woodward into the garden and have a little walk? The garden is so beautiful on days such as this. I am sure Mr Woodward would love to see it."

Lucy had been quiet for a while, lost in her own thoughts, perhaps reflecting on what could be. I do not know, for she never told me, and now never will. But I will always remember how her face lit up when her mother spoke those words.

"That would be nice," Lucy said, smiling. She looked at me, eye-to-eye contact, and once more I felt that stirring that forewarned of the bond that was about to be forged. I could plainly see that she was happy at the idea of being alone with me, and I again wondered about her mother's motivations. "Would you like to have a stroll in the garden?" Lucy then asked.

"Yes, that would be very pleasant. It is a nice day and a garden is where one should be on such days."

"I share your sentiments," Lucy responded, "for I do love the colour and scents of an English garden on a warm summer's day."

So we left Lucy's mother sitting in her chair and made our way out into the garden. The warm air greeted us and our eyes were exposed to the sight of flowers in full bloom, it being, so I had discovered, the height of summer. The air was filled with the scent of blooms, that which Lucy had expressed her love for only a moment before. But, unlike other seasons, when impressions are dominated by the visual, here there was also audible stimulation, adding to the impression of nature, busy, and at its peak of activity, for the garden was alive with the sound of buzzing insects as they hopped from flower to flower, or journeyed on their way to destinations that would forever remain to us a mystery. Bees were hovering over flowers, doing what they had done for close on sixty million years, attracted to the sweet nectar by the flowers' vibrant colours and patterns signalling the plants' desire to perpetuate themselves with the help of these curious creatures, architects of amazingly regular structures in their hives – here once more an example of nature's own engineering, differentiated from man's fumbling efforts, by the achievement of a harmony with the rest of nature, a sophistication that even in the twenty-first century engineers are still not even close to being able to conceive, being as they are trapped in the time warp of industrial thinking, with its emphasis on brute force and ignorance. Engineers are far from achieving such a mental leap forward, and at a stage in the human story when such an intellectual and spiritual advancement is desperately needed, they dwell in the past, holding onto that which has long ceased to be relevant, arguing for more projects that involve concrete, steel and chemicals, the very products of engineering endeavour that have created the problems that now seemingly defy solution. More of what actually is the cause of our problems is all they have to offer. They are truly like Prometheus, bound to the rock of the past by unbreakable chains that they cannot even see.

The scene in the garden reminded me of trips Helen and I had made to country houses, now no longer in private hands, but preserved as part of our cultural heritage and open to the public to earn revenues for the upkeep of these ageing properties and gardens. But here in 1750, all that lay in the future. Country houses were still under the ownership of the landed gentry, and how outraged and appalled they would be if they knew what I knew, of the fate that awaited their beloved homes.

CHAPTER 16

The garden was large and well-planted with flowers, shrubs, large bushes and some small tress. At the furthest point from the house, at the bottom of this large garden, there was a small orchard, mostly stocked with several different varieties of apple trees, but there were also other types of fruit trees as well – plums, cherries, pears, redcurrants. And we strolled along the path that led away from the property towards these fruit trees, walking close together, and occasionally coming into physical contact, which neither of us sought to correct. This familiarity, this lack of concern to ensure a proper distance was maintained, was not what I expected from a lady in an age that was so much bound up in formal behaviour.

As soon as we were out of sight of the house she started to talk to me as though we had known each other for a long time. "Benjamin," she said, emphasising further this familiarity. "You do not mind if I call you that when we are on our own, do you? Mr Woodward is so formal. Mama insists that we call you Mr Woodward, but I prefer to call you Benjamin."

"Benjamin is fine with me. To tell you the truth, I am not used to being called Mr Woodward. Where I come from everyone calls me Benjamin."

"Good. Then from now on I shall call you Benjamin. Except, that is, when Mama is with us. She is not as bad as some parents when it comes to tradition, but she can be very formal at times."

I listened. I sensed that this conversation was leading somewhere. It had a purpose.

"What is it like, the journey to the American Colonies? I know it is long, but what is it really like? In my mind I imagine that it is fairly harsh and difficult, and perhaps also dangerous."

We had reached a garden bench, out of sight from the house, and here we stopped and sat together, feeling the warm sunshine on our skin, made bearable by a slight breeze that blew from the north-west, bringing cooler air from the Arctic, which was unusual for that time of year.

I thought for a moment about the long-haul flights that I had taken to get to America. I recalled the cramped conditions, the boredom, the horrible airline food, and the unlikable or over-talkative people whom I had sometimes had the misfortune to be seated next to. I judged that, apart from the speed of the journey and the nature of the surroundings, it was still a disagreeable experience, and while the nature of the unpleasantness had changed since the day when sailing vessels took six weeks to make the journey, it was still not an enjoyable passage.

I looked at Lucy. "It is unpleasant," I began. The journey is long and boring, the food is awful, and the company can be disagreeable." I paused for a moment, looked into her eyes, and once more felt that stirring of emotions. Then I enquired as to why she was asking about the journey.

216

She smiled at me. That sweet smile, a smile that could capture a man's heart, and make him vulnerable to love's enchantment. I knew that I was in danger of developing a relationship with Lucy; her similarity to Helen made this almost inevitable. I could have escaped if I had wanted to, but I knew that deep down I did not want to. I could have risen at that moment in time and walked away from her. But it would have been very rude to leave and I know it would have hurt Lucy if I had done so; nevertheless I could have done it. The truth is that I wanted to stay, to be alone with her. So I remained seated next to her.

"I was curious. I have never travelled and have no knowledge of such matters," she replied. Then she was quiet for a moment and I sensed she wanted to say more, but perhaps she had thought better of the idea, and hence she remained silent. I decided now was an appropriate time to probe a little into her background.

"Tell me about yourself."

"There is not very much to say, really," she said, suddenly seeming rather reserved. "I have lived most of my life here in this house, except for the short time when I was married, and I lived about four miles from here. But when my husband died, I came back to live with my mother. Two widows together!"

"I did not realise you are a widow," I responded. "I am sorry. When did your husband die?"

"Oh, it is over nine years ago now; time enough to move on, for the wounds to heal, but never long enough to be truly over it."

I had no experience of bereavement, so I did not know of what she spoke, and could only express an understanding and sympathy based on human kindness, rather than personal experience, so I said that if I had upset her then I was sorry for that.

"No, you have not upset me," she returned. "Time is a great healer, but there are some emotions and experiences that remain with you to the end of your days, and losing a loved one, especially one so young, when we had so much to look forward to, is so hard. You see, he was only twenty-one. Poor Henry; he still had the rest of his life ahead of him, and then he caught typhoid fever."

I am no medical expert, but I knew that the survival rate in the eighteenth century for those with typhoid fever was fairly low. It was largely a matter of luck, for there were no antibiotics to treat the disease, and in the end it all came down to being strong enough to resist and ride out the infection. "I am sorry," I stated once more, not being able to think of words or phrases more original.

"No need to be. This is life. It happened and it cannot be changed. But come, we are becoming sad and miserable discussing such matters. Let us talk about that which is more cheerful."

Responding to the cue, I asked the obvious: "So your surname is not Dent?"

218

"No, it is Bamford." And, as she finished speaking she once again looked me in the eye, smiled, and placed her hand on mine, my left hand, which was resting on my knee. Continuing to gaze at me, she spoke her meaning in a way that mere words could never do. I responded by placing my hand over hers. She smiled once more. I turned my hand so that I was holding hers in mine.

"How can this be?" she asked. "Only twenty-four hours have passed since we met, and I hardly know you, but I feel as if I have known you for much longer, that somewhere we have met before."

Here is a mystery, for there are times when we meet people, and instantly there is an attraction, a bond, a unity. It is rare, yes, and perhaps fortunately so, but it does occur, and it had happened to me; no slow development of friendship here, just immediate oneness.

"I know what you mean. It is as if we have been together for eternity, that there are no barriers between us."

Eye contact yet again, intense, gazing at one another, both momentarily lost, both of us smiling. Her hand was warm and soft, and with it resting in mine it was as if I were with Helen. Then Lucy spoke. "Please come again. Do not go back to the American Colonies! Not yet, at least. Please!"

I wanted very much to return to see her again, so I responded positively. "Of course I will come again. As for the American Colonies, they are a long way off, both in time and distance. We will see about that one day, but for now I will remain here."

She was obviously pleased to hear me say this. "We have so much to talk about. I know people will say that this is infatuation, but I know it is not. There is a connection between us – a bond, a link that defies all logic. I just feel that I want to spend my time with you. It is an emotion that I thought I would never feel again. But then, when I saw you yesterday, it was as if my whole world was illuminated by a bright light. We were destined to meet."

I recognised this sort of talk. It was exactly how Helen speaks to me at times when she is in a reflective mood and inclined to refer to matters such as destiny, that which the modern world has no time or place for anymore; superstitious nonsense!

"I understand," I replied, smiling.

She thanked me and then she gave me a little kiss, a small peck on the cheek. This surprised me as I had always thought ladies in the 1750s would not be so bold or so forward to behave in such a way. But we were holding hands, which she had initiated, so perhaps I should not have been so taken aback.

Our conversation was interrupted at that point by the sound of Mrs Dent calling into garden from the Venetian window in the drawing room. "Lucy dear, where are you? Do not spend too much time in the sun. It will spoil your complexion and make you look old before your time. Bring Mr Woodward back in."

Lucy shouted back, "We will be with you in a moment." She then looked at me one more time, still holding my hand. I stared yet again into her eyes and felt that tug once more. Lucy gazed right back into my eyes. She was bold, to be sure. A more timid person would have avoided my stare, but not Lucy. She just looked straight into my eyes, and it was true what she had said, that there were no obstacles between us. There was a moment, only a brief one, when we were one. Then she spoke again. "There is an aspect, a manner about you," she said. "I do not know what it is, but you are not at all similar in any way to anyone else that I have met before. You are full of knowledge, experience and life. You have an air of mystery about you. Your clothes, your mannerisms, your attitude to the world – these are all different from what I know, to what I have found in others."

Time changes people!

I did not respond immediately. Yet more eye contact, just staring back at her, looking directly into her deep blue eyes, speaking unspoken thoughts, in silence. I allowed myself to gaze at her. "We had better go back otherwise your mother will come looking for us," I eventually said.

"Yes," agreed Lucy, "she will." Then she let go of my hand, stood up, straightened her hair and composed herself. "Time to go in," she said. And then she started to walk back to the house. I followed and caught her up and we walked side by side, she careful to maintain a respectful distance between us.

Back in the drawing room Lucy sat on the settee again with me sitting by her side, with her mother standing opposite us.

"Now, my dear," Lucy's mother said addressing herself to Lucy, "Mr Woodward does not need me to keep him company. So I will leave you to entertain our guest. It is time for my afternoon rest, so I am going to have a lie down."

Turning to me she then said, "It was nice to meet you, Mr Woodward. Please call again. This is the first time that we have had a visitor who has travelled from the other side of the world. I am sure that Lucy would love to hear more about life there."

"Yes, Mama, I would."

I rose and said, "It was gracious of you and Lucy to invite me. And I will certainly call again. Thank you." Then Lucy's mother left the room and I sat down again. Lucy and I were alone once more.

While walking in the garden an idea had occurred to me, and I wanted to ask Lucy about this. "Lucy," I began. She looked at me with anticipation. "Would you do me a favour?"

"Yes, Benjamin. What?" Lucy's response showed a keenness to please that she took no trouble to hide.

"Before I arrived today I was speaking to Samuel Jones, who was waiting for me on the village green."

"Yes, I know. I saw you both."

"He is a bright boy. His mother is teaching him to read and write, but I think he would benefit from a person teaching him who is more educated. So I was wondering if you would help him, by teaching him English."

"Yes, Benjamin, I would be happy to help."

"Good. Thank you. I will tell him on my way home this evening. Could you start tomorrow, say in the afternoon?"

"Yes, tomorrow afternoon will be fine."

"If you want you can use my house. There is plenty of room and the back door is always left unlocked. Just go in and use the room at the top of the rear stairs."

"That will be nice. I will do that. It will make a change to get out of this house."

"I am going to ask Samuel to come with me tomorrow morning to town. I have a few jobs to do. So, shall we say three o'clock?"

"That will be fine. Any time would be fine. I have all the time in the world. I will be there."

We sat there speaking about Samuel, about life in the village, of her mother and late father, painting a picture of her life, providing for me greater insight into her world, her existence, her history. And as the conversation developed, she too learned more about me, my history, my life, and not just from what I said. And when I next looked at the clock on the mantelpiece I was surprised to see how time had slipped by, and it was now half past six, and, as much as I wanted to stay, I also wanted to get back to the Time House.

"It has been an interesting afternoon," I informed her. "I have enjoyed being with you, and talking with you." Then I rose. "But I have to go. I will see you tomorrow afternoon."

Lucy got up from the settee, not hiding the look of disappointment on her face, and led the way out of the drawing room to the hall.

"Say goodbye to your mother for me. Tell her thank you for the tea and cake."

All she said was, "I will."

I looked at her once more and then she opened the door and I stepped out into the world. I began walking, but could not help looking back. Lucy was standing in the doorway and she waved, and I returned the gesture, just as I had done on my arrival. Then she shut the door and I headed across the village green.

Samuel must have been looking out for me, for he emerged from the village shop and ran towards me. We met near to duck pond.

"Hello, Samuel," I began. "I have some good news for you. I asked Miss Lucy to give you reading and writing lessons at my house and she agreed. You start tomorrow afternoon; three o'clock. Is that all right with you?"

"Oh, yes! Thank you, Mr Woodward. I like Miss Lucy. She is very pretty."

"Yes, I know, Samuel, but that is not important, is it? What is vital is that you learn to read and write well, so that you can fulfil those dreams of yours. Now finally, before I go, I want to ask if you would like to earn yourself a shilling."

"Oh, yes, please," Samuel said eagerly.

"Tomorrow morning I am going into town and I want you to be my guide. Do your mother and father have a horse and trap?"

Samuel responded with a positive reply to this question, so I asked him if he thought his parents would allow me to borrow it to travel into town. Again he gave a positive response, adding that given what I done the previous day, his parents would be happy to help me in any way that I asked. So I told him to meet me outside my house at nine o'clock sharp on the Monday morning. And, after our visit to town, when we returned, I told him that he would have his first lesson with Miss Lucy at three o'clock. I then ended our conversation by telling him to run along home.

"I will see you in the morning," were my parting words, to which Samuel responded by saying, "I am looking forward to tomorrow. I will be on time. Good evening."

Young Samuel ran off back to his home, happy as a lark, and I set off for my own house, for my own time, my own world, but with a head full of thoughts. It had certainly been an eventful day.

CHAPTER 17

Back in the Time House I immediately went upstairs to the opening that would return me to my own era. I looked at my watch – seven o'clock. Then I realised that I had not bothered to hide this device, which had been invented in the 1860s and had therefore no place in the mid-eighteenth century. This was a blunder on my part and just one further way in which I could end up contaminating the past and changing history; I would need to be more careful on future visits. I quickly recovered the clock that I had placed in the bedroom – seven o'clock. Passing under the timber beam back into what I hoped would be my own era I collected the clock that I had hidden in the kitchen – half past two in the afternoon!

Here was clear proof; I had been away for over four hours yet time had not moved on since my departure. All had stood still, frozen at the point in time when I had left for 1750. Now I was as sure as I could possibly be that I was able, safely, to visit the past and not lose any moments in time at all in my own age. Thus, I would be able to return to 1750, call in on the solicitor and collect the money, live for years in the eighteenth century, spend time with Lucy, travel and explore places, and be gone from the twenty-first century for no time at all. This was perfect. I considered myself to be blessed in many ways. I had acquired both a house and money, I was able to explore history without losing moments in time in my own era, and I had met someone special, a replica of Helen. What more could anyone ask for? What I had discovered in the Time House was beneficial, and I could no longer see any drawbacks to making full use of the gateway to the past. The risks, most definitely, could be managed. I felt that I was in control, which is what I was used to, being an engineer – *out of disorder I create order*.

I immediately left the Time House and returned home to collect some items that I would need for a longer stay in 1750, items that would make my time there more conformable and safe.

Once I was among the familiarity of the twenty-first century artefacts that define our age, the many items that clutter our lives, which no one in the eighteenth century could have ever imagined, I put together a small bag of clothes, underwear, a toothbrush, toothpaste and other such similar modern comforts. Even though I was fascinated by the past, I was not prepared to subject myself to unnecessary hardship nor to neglect my personal hygiene while I was away, and I knew that most of what I had in my bag would make a big difference to the quality of my life. This is one way in which our perceptions of comfort have changed with time, and a measure of how far we have come, at least in material terms. I also prepared some food to bring with me: sandwiches, boiled eggs, some bacon, fresh fruit, biscuits, and such forth. All that came enclosed in a factory-produced packet, I unwrapped. I placed that which I would not immediately need in biodegradable plastic bags and the rest in plain brown paper bags, not wanting to contaminate the eighteenth century with items that had no place there.

My major concern was illness. What if I should fall ill while visiting the past? I knew that I should take some precautions. The lack of safe drinking water was one worry. Fortunately the Time House did have a modern water supply, so good-quality water was available; all that I had to do was to step back into my own time and make use of those facilities. I therefore packed into my bag some empty glass mineral water bottles, from which I removed the labels. I also packed a glass wine bottle, complete with cork, with labels removed. These I intended to take with me on any journeys that I might take, so that I could carry some water and wine with me. Rummaging through my camping kit I also found some water sterilisation tables, since carrying sufficient water for a long trip was plainly infeasible.

The other concern that I had was minor ailments such as headaches, diarrhoea, and such like. I therefore took from the medicine cabinet a number of medicines to treat such conditions. About the major illnesses of the 1750s I knew already from history books, but I hoped that my immunity, based on the vaccines and inoculations that I had been given during my life, would be adequate, but I had no way of knowing this. I was not, however, going to let such a small detail as this stop me. Although I base all my decisions on facts and evidence, I only do so when I find this convenient – I am an engineer.

I checked to make sure that I had the documents that I would need to present to the solicitor, and then I departed, along with my travel bag containing the food and medicines that I had prepared. Not long afterwards I was back in the Time House. I hid some of my supplies, and then slipped back into 1750.

I had no plan about how long I would spend in the past, for it did not seem to matter anymore, for when I returned after spending time in 1750, it would still be the Sunday afternoon of my departure, and I would be able to return home and speak to Helen, and be there for her on Monday afternoon when she came back from Dorset. I was in control!

Having organised myself in the front east-side bedroom, I took my food to the rear study in the south-east wing and sat there throughout the evening, until it was time for bed.

I slept that night, for the first time, in the Time House, and my sleep was peaceful. No thoughts about that stranger, that unexplained figure, whom I had seen at the window on the Saturday, disturbed my mind. I was now convinced that what I had seen was no more than an optical illusion or a figment of my imagination. Nor did I hear that mysterious voice again, which was a relief, for its arguments against what I was doing I did not want to hear; it was far too wise for my liking.

The night was an uneventful one, as I concluded it should be, for as far as I was concerned there was no one to make it otherwise, and I awoke next morning fully refreshed and looking forward to the adventures of the coming day.

Just before nine o'clock I was at the front of the property waiting for Samuel to appear. Right on time I saw a horse and trap, driven by Samuel, appear from around the bend in the lane, and soon he was drawing up outside the house.

"Good morning, Samuel," I said, greeting him. "Well done! I see that you have acquired our means of transport."

"Thank you and good morning," he replied with a big smile.

"Now, you are sure that your mother and father will not need the horse and trap today?"

I asked this because I wanted reassurance that Samuel was acting in a proper way and was not going to get himself into trouble with his parents.

Samuel assured me that all was being done with his parents' full knowledge and agreement. "Quite sure," he replied.

"Good, then let us be off. First port of call is Dome and Smith Solicitors. Do you know where they are?"

I was relying on Samuel to be my guide as the town I was about to visit would be very different from the one I knew, with all the changes that have taken place since 1750, especially since the early 1990s, when development mania seemed to have gripped the place, along with just about every other city and town in the country – a mark of the unsustainable consumption that accelerated significantly about that time, and which has continued to increase ever since.

Samuel replied to my query by saying, "Yes, Mr Woodward, sir."

"Lead on then." And so we set off, and I then took the opportunity to mention to Samuel what I had wanted to say on the previous day.

"Samuel, when we are together on our own, or with Miss Lucy, you can call me Benjamin. When there are other adults around, call me Mr Woodward, as I think that is how they will expect you to address me."

Samuel glanced at me, looking pleased. "Benjamin! I can call you Benjamin! Most adults I know do not allow children to call them by their Christian name. They say it is disrespectful."

"I know, Samuel, but it is not really and I am not used to being called Mr Woodward all the time. So Benjamin is fine."

"Thank you," responded Samuel.

"You are welcome. Now, tell me, how long will it take to get to where we are going?"

"About forty-five minutes," was Samuel's reply.

"Good, that means we should leave for our return journey no later than two o'clock to be back in time for your first lesson with Miss Lucy at three o'clock."

So we travelled on. I took careful note of my surroundings, not wanting to miss anything. Samuel left me to my thoughts and quietly observed my intense interest in what lay all about, an interest that was made obvious by my constant turning, shifting about on my seat, looking over my shoulder, and rising from where I was sitting to get a better view.

Eventually some buildings came into view and, as we drew closer, I recognised one of them; it was the place from where I ran my business. Only there was one major difference between the building as I knew it and what now appeared before me – the stone slab roof that I was so familiar with was not there, the building being instead roofed with a straw thatch.

"That building over there, Samuel, what is it?" I was eager to know the answer, to discover what he knew of the place.

"That is just a house. Some old woman lives there. I do not know her, though. I have seen her when I have passed by."

We journeyed onwards and soon we stopped outside a small building that bore the name of Dome and Smith Solicitors.

"Wait here for me, please, Samuel. I will not be too long," I said, while climbing down from the trap, feeling inside a slight apprehension, some doubt, for I did not know if this firm of solicitors had actually met Mr Woodward. What if I was exposed as a fake, a fraudster? I could end up in prison, and then what would become of me?

I hesitated, a moment in time of indecision, which was evident to Samuel, for he looked at me, wondering why I did not step forward. I quickly responded. "I am just reflecting on what is, for me, a big step – finally completing the formality of legal ownership of the house." I reached out and picked up the document wallet that had lain on the seat between Samuel and me. "Here goes," I said, trying to sound confident. Then I disappeared into the solicitors' office and emerged not long after with all that I needed, and, most importantly, confirmation that I was now the owner of the Time House, and a bag of money, just enough to cover the expenses for the day. I had arranged to call into the office again on my way back to the house to collect the remainder of my one thousand guineas, which the solicitor needed to obtain from the bank just across the street.

There had been no moments of doubt concerning my identity and I noted how different that was compared with the modern age where I continually have to prove that I am who I say I am – Benjamin Woodward. It is as though one can no longer engage in any kind of transaction – to work, to buy, to sell – if one does not bear a sign that proves entitlement to make a transaction; it is the monster of distrust and control, which seems increasingly to preoccupy the minds of administrators, bureaucrats, managers, government officials and the like. We are blindly heading for a world where all will have to carry a mark of identification, whether that be a card, or an electronic device on our wrist, or some device embedded under the skin, and this will, I am sure, eventually become a legal requirement, enforced by both legal measure and the necessity of having such an identification before one can even buy the most basic of items – water, bread, warmth ... And as for those who will speak out against this, you can be sure that the engineering profession will not be lining up to resist. To them, it will be yet another interesting technical challenge, another opportunity to demonstrate that they do their employers' bidding, helping them to reap the business rewards that will come from the vast outlay of money, the billions that will be spent on implementing and operating such a system. Lawyers, doctors, architects, the true professions, will lead the opposition, for it is well within their professional code of conduct and tradition to speak out on such matters.

As for engineers and technologists, what will they have to say? It is not difficult to answer this question. They will warn not of the human rights implications, of the big brother world that this will lead to, but of the high-risk nature of the endeavour in terms of the technical challenges; of the problems associated with specific technologies being combined in ways that are unproven and on a large scale not previously attempted; of the need to establish requirements through formal and rigorous analysis; of the need to define the specific issues that are being addressed before converging on solutions; of the need for realistic deadlines; of the need to avoid improper use, as if the whole scheme were not in itself an improper use of the talents of engineers and technologists.

Reflections of this kind were becoming a norm in my life but, strangely, I did not reflect on why that was so.

Back up on the trap, I made another stop. It was to a tailor, where I arranged for some new clothes. The tailor told me that he only made to measure, but the sight of my money convinced him that he could adapt an existing current order to my measurements. As it happened he had an order nearly ready for someone of similar measurements to my own. It turned out that this person was none other than the rouge Walter Smythe, who would no doubt be very put out to learn that his order would now be delayed.

Having agreed with the tailor that I would call back after lunch to collect the clothes, I wanted, in the intervening time, to explore the town to see how it had changed from the place that I was familiar with, so I asked Samuel to give me a guided tour.

What a curious experience it was, riding through the familiar streets of a location I knew well, but seeing it as it had been 250 years before my own age. Most of the town consisted of timber-framed buildings with thatched roofs. Some of these were destined to stand the test of time and would survive to my own era, for I recognised several, albeit with slightly different facades to the ones that I was familiar with. One of the main differences was the loss of the thatch, which on all the buildings that had survived had been replaced with roofs of stone slabs, or manufactured red clay tiles, all regular and standardised.

Most of the buildings were entirely new to me. Somewhere between 1750 and the twenty-first century these unfamiliar buildings had been demolished to make way for more modern constructions in later eras. I saw for the first time what had originally stood on the sites where, in my own time, buildings from the late Georgian, Victorian, Edwardian and twentieth-century periods now stood. Looking at the town as it was in 1750 I was stuck by its homogeneity, the sameness of most of the timber-framed buildings. I realised, perhaps in a way that no one else had ever done, how much variety in architecture had resulted from the distinctive styles of each period and how these differences had contributed to what people appreciate. I saw and understood how each generation had imprinted on the town its own unique contribution. Here I could see the consequence of stagnation, of listening to those voices that advocated preserving towns and buildings as they are. To do so would be to create a relic of the past, to stifle innovation, and to elevate the past above the present as being superior in its contribution to architecture. I saw plainly how people in one age create an inheritance, a legacy for those who follow, and I also, at that moment in time, realised that the same applied to science, to engineering, to technology. The importance of choosing to create a legacy that future generations will appreciate requires a different approach to that which now dominates; this implies thinking about how our actions will be judged, and this alas is not of concern, for if it were, then some of that which is done in the name of science, engineering and technology would not be. More reflections!

And so the morning passed by. I was starting to feel hungry and I guessed that Samuel was too, although he did not say so. "Do you want to eat?" I asked.

Samuel's face lit up at the thought of food, and a smile appeared. "Yes, please," he said eagerly.

"Where can I buy some food? Perhaps a pie."

"The butcher sells meat pies. Very nice pies! Pork, beef, chicken, game; all very nice pies indeed!"

I was surprised that Samuel was familiar with game pie, for in my own time it is an expensive luxury, but then I recalled that in times past, before industrialisation, game such as rabbits, pheasants, and other edible animals were considered as wild creatures that belonged to no one, and were therefore part of the diet of all. Then began, in the minds of men, for it was mostly men and not women, the growth of the idea of ownership of nature, of its resources, leading eventually to the confirmation, through law, of the landowners' rights to that which dwelt on their land, and to some extent, in times past, that which could be found beneath it. This marked the beginning of the modern world, which has set its soul on plundering the planet of its resources regardless of the implications for the present and for future generations.

"Then take me to the butcher," was my response to Samuel's admirable sales efforts on behalf of this purveyor of meats.

Off we went and within a few minutes we were outside a butcher's shop. Still in the trap I looked in through the shop window. I could see that there were large carcasses hung on hooks. The butcher was slicing meat for a customer. He was working on a wooden work surface that had large parts worn away as a result of an unrecorded age of cutting away at lumps of meat with sharp knives, which had in turn taken its toll on the workbench. The floor was tiled with marble, quite elegant I thought, which also spoke of material success in this line of business; and to add quaintness to this scene, the tiles were covered with sawdust.

I purchased two small game pies – one to share with Samuel and one to take back to the house to keep me supplied for a few days. I would need to start learning the habits of this age, the daily visit to the shop, for here there were no refrigerators to preserve food, to slow down the ageing process – one of the great achievements of the modern world. Science, you see, on the one hand helps us, while at the same time destroys us; we have not yet acquired the knowledge, the sophistication, the wisdom to achieve the former without the latter. The time we have left to do so grows short!

I asked Samuel about liquid refreshments, to which he responded that I should purchase a jug of beer from the Cock Inn. I considered this to be a good idea for I did not want to drink the local water lest it be contaminated with diseases to which I had no resistance. Beer, I assumed, should at least be free from bacteria, if it was fresh. Samuel reassured me on this point, informing me that the Cock Inn sold the best beer in town, so we set off to this tavern. I purchased some beer, borrowing from the landlord a jug and two mugs – a borrowing that was much eased by the extra payment that I gave him for the liquid.

Samuel and I took the horse and trap to an area of grass in the town – more of the common land that was so plentiful in this era. There we found a horse trough full of the water that was so necessary in those days to maintain their transport system – a plentiful and renewable fuel, which contrasted sharply with the non-renewable fuel, oil, now declining in availability, which is used in my own age. Progress at far too high a price, I think! Is this squandering of such a precious resource, without regard to the interests and needs of future generations, not also a crime against humanity, as well as unethical? A question worth asking given the implications of what will inevitably happen when nations start fighting one another to gain control over the oil that is left.

While the horse grazed, Samuel and I ate game pie and drank beer, sitting on the grass, enjoying the warm sunshine. What a pleasure this was, to be free from the daily treadmill of life in the twenty-first century; I immersed myself fully in this idle pleasure, glad to be alive, to savour the simple joys that life has to offer.

Samuel devoured the half of the pie I had given him, so I gave him part of my share. "You are hungry," I observed, happy to see him enjoying his treat. He nodded in the affirmative by way of a reply. His mouth was too full of food for him to make a verbal response. "You like the pie?" I asked. He nodded again, indicating that he did.

I allowed him to eat in peace, while I consumed what was left of my share and sipped at the beer. I did not want to drink too much, as I was not used to consuming alcohol at lunchtime, knowing also that it, along with the pie, would begin to make me feel sleepy. And I did not want to sleep. So I sat on the grass, peaceful, taking in the sights, observing what was going on about me.

Eventually Samuel finished eating the pie and downed the remainder of the beer in his jug. He lay back on the grass and closed his eyes, savouring the experience of the warm sunlight on his face. He also was happy, for the moment, with his lot in life. He no doubt considered his chance encounter with me to be the greatest fortune, thus far, in his still short life.

"Hunger satisfied now, is it, Samuel?" I playfully asked him.

"Yes. I am full," he replied, adding, "At least for the time being."

"We cannot afford to stay here too long. I need to get these items back to the Cock Inn. Then we are off the tailor's to collect my new clothes."

Samuel sat up. "I am ready whenever you are, Benjamin."

He was keen, and also, I judged, loyal.

"Right then, let us be on our way."

We climbed back up onto the trap, taking the horse away from her pleasures, and set off for the Cock Inn, where I returned the items that I had borrowed. Soon we were back outside the tailor's shop.

I discovered that the clothes were ready for me. I tried them on and the tailor judged that they were a perfect fit. Thus I emerged from the tailor's shop looking and feeling a gentleman. Under my arm I carried a parcel containing my twenty-first century clothes and over my shoulder was slung a small canvas travel bag for the journeys that I might undertake while a resident in 1750.

"What do you think?" I said to Samuel after depositing the parcel and the bag into the trap and standing so that he had a good view of me.

"You look a real gentleman now," he responded. "Those clothes of yours looked really strange, but now you are just the same every other gentleman."

Perhaps in looks, yes, but that was the only way in which I could be likened to a gentlemen of the mid-eighteenth century. I climbed up onto the trap. "Take me to the solicitors' now, please, Samuel."

And, so, in a few minutes we were back outside the offices of Dome and Smith Solicitors, where I very quickly collected the money. On emerging from their offices I noticed a jeweller's shop on the other side of the road. "I am going into that place," I told Samuel. "I will not be long."

In the few moments in time that I spent in the jeweller's premises, examining the limited range of products on offer, I became the proud owner of an elegant eighteenth-century sterling-silver pocket watch. About me I also had secreted a number of the items of eighteenth-century jewellery, mostly gold rings, some broaches and a diamond ring. These I regarded as an investment, one that would yield me a profit on my return to the twenty-first century. Here you see my entrepreneurial spirit at work, timeless, one further way in which I was very similar to other people in this age. Only I could see the results of this; in 1750, Britain was on the cusp of the industrial era, when business men would flourish as in no other age before, and, as for the horrors that this new commercial thinking would lead to, no one could have predicted these, or at least this is what I believed, but they could, I now understand, have been avoided. This is the great tragedy of the industrial era and we should not forget this, for without doubt there are undesirable consequences, stemming from our actions in the early twenty-first century, which also can be avoided.

When I was once more seated next to Samuel, I informed him that I was now finished and that it was time to return, so I asked him to take me home.

"Aye, aye," he responded, sounding very nautical.

I glanced at the pocket watch that was attached to my new waistcoat by a silver chain – two o'clock.

"Two o'clock, Samuel. This is perfect timing. We will be home just before Miss Lucy is due."

The forty-five minute journey back to the Time House I spent as I had done on the outward trip, closely examining the surroundings through which we passed. Many times I had travelled along this road, but never under such circumstances. The route was familiar – after all, I did travel it five days a week to my office and then back to my home – but this was to me a unique experience and I was enjoying every minute of it. But thoughts of my environment were not the only ones that accompanied me on that short journey, for now, as the hour approached, I began once more to turn my reflections towards

Lucy, and that filled me with an expectation that I found very pleasing.

Soon we were arriving back at the house; time it seems in all eras flies by when one is having fun. Samuel parked the trap directly in front of the house, the lane being wide enough at this point for other wagons to pass while another waited or was parked. I collected my possessions and the two of us made our way around the side of the house.

"Do you not use the front door?" asked Samuel, surprised that we were using the rear door.

Up to that moment in time, I was not able to use the front door for the simple reason that I did not have a key, for the one that I had been given by the estate agent fitted a modern lock, not the eighteenth-century device that was originally fitted. My visit to the solicitors' was, partly, to collect original keys. The front door was going to be my only way of entering the rest of the house, since from the upstairs the way through the opening on the first-floor landing just led me back into my own time. Now that I did have a front-door key I was going to explore what lay downstairs, but I did not want to venture there with Samuel until I had investigated that part of the house on my own.

In response to his question I said to Samuel, "I did not have a key for that door, which is one reason I visited my solicitor." Then I added, "But I am not using most of the house, just two rooms upstairs, and they can be reached by the rear stairs just as well."

Thus it was that we entered the house by the rear door, and I led the way with Samuel following close behind. I took Samuel upstairs to my study and told him to sit for a while in one of the armchairs. I sat down in the other chair. "Quite an interesting day," I informed him. "Did you enjoy our visit to town?"

"Yes, indeed I did. It was very different from what I normally do."

"And what is that?" I enquired.

"Mostly helping Ma and Pa in the shop, but sometimes, when it is quiet, I go out and walk the country lanes and footpaths."

"So you know the area very well then?"

"Oh, yes, very well. I know how to get around using the local footpaths, all the quiet places, all the deserted buildings."

"And what, when you go to such places, do you do? Play?"

"Dream about the future, and think about all that I want from life. I make plans for when I am older, such as travelling, seeing the world, going to the American Colonies. Some will say these thoughts are nothing more than fantasies. But you do not!"

"You are right; I do not see these just as daydreams, wild flights of the imagination. No, if you want to travel to the American Colonies, then you can make that happen."

"What you told me the other day just makes me want to go even more. But I do not see how I am ever going to get there."

"Patience," I advised, "is what you need. Patience and a plan! If you really want to visit that place, and others, you will find a way, but a plan to take you forward is essential. And English lessons with Miss Lucy will help you – an important element in your preparations. For if you can read and write well, this will open doors for you, which will be closed to others. You could, for example, take up a seafaring life, become a navigator. That would take you to many parts of the world, and if you did not want to return home, then you could decide to stay and make a new life in a new world."

I looked at my watch – nearly three o'clock. I rose from the chair. "Come on," I said, Miss Lucy will be here soon, so let us go and greet her at the front gate."

Our timing was excellent for we reached that gate leading into the lane just as Lucy was arriving. "Hello and welcome," I said with a smile, being very happy to see Lucy again, such was my growing affection for her, and my interest!

"Good afternoon," she replied, also evidently glad to be with me once again. Then she noticed my new clothes. "You have some new clothes. Very elegant! Now you look a proper gentleman."

"Thank you," I politely responded, as I opened the gate for her.

"Hello, Samuel. It is time for your first lesson."

245

"Yes, miss. I am looking forward to it."

"Ah! A keen student! That is half the battle. The rest is hard work and some talent, of which I think, Samuel, you have both in more than ample measure."

Samuel was embarrassed by this praise, so I interjected by saying, "Let us go upstairs. This is the way you should come when I am not here. At the moment the front door is not in use."

"Very well. Lead on, then, and I will follow."

I led both Lucy and Samuel around to the back of the house and upstairs to my study, where I seated them in the armchairs by the fireplace. "I will leave you two to your lesson." Then, turning to Lucy, I enquired, "Will one hour be enough?"

"Oh, yes, one hour is quite enough for a first lesson. Perhaps later, once we have made a start and have a few lessons behind us, we can think about extending the length of the session, perhaps also increasing the scope as well."

"Excellent. In that case, then, I will be back in one hour."

Leaving them to their work I strolled to the front bedroom. Here I hid my money and the other precious items of jewellery that I had purchased. As soon as my visitors were gone I intended to return to my own time, taking these items with me, and to store them all safely at home.

I lay on the bed for a while, and it was at this moment in time that a possible difficulty occurred to me, a problem that I had not previously considered; yet another unforeseen, unconsidered issue that highlights the dangers of treading into areas where we have little understanding, even if we think we know quite a lot – the story of the modern age, especially technology, with all its unknowns that are conveniently downplayed or ignored, such is the determination to present technology as man's saviour, and I do here mean men!

What exactly was this new concern? It was a fairly simple one, but with profound implications. The worry that had arisen came as a question formed in my occasionally, and now less frequently, perplexed mind: What if Lucy and Samuel could see that the house looks different on the west side, through the opening that was for me a time portal? What if it were also a time portal for them, a gateway to a radically different world? What if they could step through it into the twenty-first century? Or was it just an opening that led to the stairs and other parts of the house, as it was in 1750? I was, as you may imagine, very concerned about this, but I was also curious to know what they could see. So I decided to find out once Samuel's lesson was over.

Rising from the bed and leaving the bedroom, I walked along the corridor, past my study where I could hear Lucy instructing Samuel about the pronunciation and the meaning of the words in a book that she was reading aloud to Samuel. Once downstairs I slipped out of the Time House and around to the front door, which I then opened with my new set of keys.

Exploring the ground floor I saw that all was, more or less, as I remembered it from my first visit to the house, back in my own time. One aspect was different, as I found an additional doorway located in the entrance hall, which I assumed must lead through to the south-east extension, but the door was locked. On my key ring were three keys, one of which was for the front-door lock. I tried the first of the remaining two keys, but it did not fit the lock on this door. This key, I therefore assumed, was the one for the rear door of the house, as that was the only other door that had a lock. Trying then the second of the keys, the lock moved and I soon had the door open. I stood for a moment and examined the profile of these three keys, memorising their shape so that in future I would know which key to use on each lock. Happy that I now had this matter resolved, I began to explore.

The room that lay beyond this door was, as I suspected, the one with the red clay floor tiles, and it was just as it had been when I left it, a few minutes earlier, on leaving the house by the rear doorway. I walked over to the rear stairs that led up to the first floor and I could hear Lucy talking to Samuel. But I did not ascend these stairs, for my main interest lay elsewhere in the house. Retracing my steps, I stood once more in the entrance hall. Now I climbed the main stairs up to the first-floor landing, where I discovered the opening that led to the rooms that I was occupying. Once again I stopped and listened and could faintly hear Lucy speaking to Samuel.

Thus I had discovered that when I was in the year 1750 and I approached the opening – my time portal – from the west side of the house, from the first-floor landing at the top of the main staircase, my time portal was not there. What lay beyond was just the Time House in 1750; this building was proving to be more complex than I had imagined. The Time House was truly an enigma. Although I did not realise it at that moment in time, this was yet one more indication that I was not in control, only I still did not see the warning signs.

The thought of this complexity did puzzle me greatly. "Where was the gateway back to my own time?" I asked myself. I did not like the look of what I saw before me, so I retreated, not daring to pass under the timber beam lest I might damage my means of returning to the twenty-first century. So I went back downstairs, out of the front door, and then re-entered the house through the rear door, immediately proceeding up the rear stairs once more, until I stood before the time portal. I walked under it and immediately experienced the sensation that told me that the gateway was still working. Looking around I could see that I was back in my own age, and a glance out of the north-facing landing window confirmed this, so I hastily retreated back into 1750 again, not wanting to be away, or for Lucy and Samuel to see me emerge, I assumed, as if from nowhere, for that surely would be the sight that they would behold if they were to be standing, gazing at the opening that led into the west side of the house, seeing only what they would expect to see, until that is, I materialised. This was to be avoided at all costs, for it would be impossible to explain.

My small experiment had established that there was nothing unusual that I could ascertain about the opening, at least as it would be experienced by Lucy and Samuel. I had also reassured myself that the time portal was still working and that I was not trapped. But then I began to wonder what would happen if I were to pass under the timber beam from the stair side in 1750. This I had retreated from, but I did want to know the answer. I began to speculate, sorry, I mean theorise, and a number of possibilities occurred to me. The first of these was that approaching from the stair side in 1750 would just lead me to the south-east wing in 1750. But this then created an uncertainty for me, as when I passed back, would I be in 1750 or in the twenty-first century? Another thought that passed through my mind was that which I had already considered – that I might damage the portal if I were to pass through from the stair side in 1750. What would happen to me then? Might I be forever trapped in the past, never to return to the twenty-first century? Perhaps I would end up in a completely different time, not 1750 and not the early twenty-first century; then I would be lost in time!

But how could I find out the answer? There was only one way to discover what would happen and that was to do that which I had wondered about, to actually walk through the opening from the stair side. I thought about the circumstances a little more. Although there had already been many points in my adventure when matters were telling me of my ignorance, I had chosen to ignore these warnings. But now for the first time I started to comprehend that I was dealing with that which I did not fully understand at all. My eyes were beginning to open, if only for a brief moment in time.

Given the circumstances and my lack of knowledge, I considered it far too dangerous to undertake what I had considered. It just did not make sense to me that one could pass though the opening from west to east in 1750, and then walk back through it again and end up back in the twenty-first century. It was all too confusing, and my mind had started to become befuddled. The order that I assumed was a defining feature of the universe was not now so obvious to me. This was my first glimpse into the reality of the universe, that *out of order comes disorder*, and this challenged deeply held beliefs, which I found very disconcerting; this is the price one pays when one begins to open one's mind to the truth, to let the mist of self-delusion disperse. At first it is painful, but, as I later discovered, it would eventually become liberating and exhilarating.

The more I thought about the circumstance, about the potential to create a paradox, the more I felt that my intuition about this matter was correct. I resolved to stay away from the stair side of the opening in 1750 time, and to do so would mean that I could never use the front door of the house, or the newly discovered ground-floor access door to the south-east wing. From that moment in time onwards, while in 1750, I would confine myself to the front bedroom where I was sleeping, to my study and the lower floor in the extension. That way I would never run the risk of damaging the time portal, or becoming lost in time.

What I did not realise at that moment in time was that this was futile thinking, for even if I did not damage the portal, there would be other consequences to my actions, as the universe continued towards its increasing state of disorder, despite my puny attempts to remain in control – this is the self-delusion that is shared in common with other scientists, engineers and technologists.

Returning to the rear door, exiting, and moving to the front of the property, I re-entered the house through the front door, immediately locked the ground-floor access door to the south-east wing, and then quickly retraced my steps, leaving through the front door, which I also then locked. All was now secure. These doors would never again be opened by me; they would remain locked and unused.

I glanced at my pocket watch; nearly four o'clock. Samuel's lesson would soon be over, so it was time to return to Lucy and Samuel. Walking back into my study, I discovered that they were still busy with the lesson. Lucy looked up at me and smiled. "Time to finish, is it? How time passes!"

"Yes," I responded, "your one hour is over."

"Samuel, you have done very well today. You are a good reader. But that is enough for one session."

"Thank you, miss," Samuel responded, again showing his embarrassment at being praised. "When will we have another lesson?"

"Tomorrow, I suppose, if that is all right with you, Samuel. And, Mr Woodward, will you allow us to use the study again?"

"It is fine with me," Samuel said keenly, and then they both looked at me.

"I have no problem with tomorrow. Come every day. Use the place as much as you like. It is a big house so you will not disturb me."

"That is very kind of you," Lucy responded.

"Thank you, Mr Woodward, sir," added Samuel.

"So what time tomorrow?" he asked Lucy.

"Same as today – three o'clock."

No objections were raised by anyone present and so the time and place for Samuel's next lesson was set, and this was how it would be for the many days to come.

Then I said, "Now it's time for you, Samuel, to get that horse and trap back to your mother and father. And here is your payment for today's work," and I duly passed him a shilling.

Samuel's face lit up at the sight of the money. "Thank you," he said. "Thank you very much." And then he rose, saying, "Do you want a lift back, Miss Lucy?"

"No, it is all right, Samuel. Thank you for asking, it was very thoughtful of you, but I will stay on here a little while longer and then walk back." She spoke these words most graciously, showing some affection for this young boy. And as she finished speaking she glanced my way, and for a moment I saw a hint of desire in her eyes.

"Goodbye then. I will see you tomorrow," said Samuel.

I escorted him downstairs and to the front of the house. Samuel duly untied the reins of the horse and climbed up onto the trap.

"You enjoyed that lesson, did you?" I asked.

"Yes, Benjamin, I did. This has been the best day of my life."

"Good. If you work hard there will be even better days to look forward to. You will soon find that your reading and writing will improve tremendously, and that will open the door to reading books, of which I have many that you can borrow. Then we will think about doing some arithmetic."

"Sums!" exclaimed Samuel. "I do not like arithmetic."

I laughed light-heartedly and smiled, thinking to myself that some aspects of schooling never change.

"I will see you tomorrow," I told him.

Samuel spoke to the horse, "Walk on!", and off they went up the lane. Samuel turned slightly and waved and I returned his gesture. I watched until the trap disappeared around the bend and was out of sight and I then rejoined Lucy, who was still sitting in the armchair when I entered the study. I sat down opposite her.

"So what is your opinion of Samuel?" I asked, curious to know her initial reactions now that she had experienced her first lesson with him.

"As you said yesterday, he is very bright. And he is a quick learner too. He should be able to read very well once he improves his vocabulary."

"And his writing?"

"He needs more practice at writing," she began, "and his style is a bit of a scrawl, but I do not see any reason why it will not improve. And with a better vocabulary and some lessons in grammar he should be a competent writer before very long. His mother has taught him many of the basics."

"Good," was all that I said in response to Lucy's pleasing report on Samuel's abilities and learning prospects. Then I changed the subject of our conversation. "Did you know that his mother and father worked for Walter Smythe's father, and that when they left to take over running the village shop, Smythe senior was very displeased with both of them?"

"Yes, I did."

"That might be why Walter Smythe treated young Samuel so badly the other day," I suggested.

"Yes, that is probably true. He is the sort who would do that. A big bully! He is a most unpleasant fellow – arrogant, conceited and self-opinionated."

"You know him well?"

"To a certain degree. We have been to parties at their house, which is, I must add, far bigger than our own. But not many such events; just enough not to cause offence, for it would not do to turn down all their invitations. Mama dislikes the Smythes. All of them are very much alike really."

"They sound as though they are unpleasant company," I stated.

"Oh, yes indeed, they are absolutely awful people." Then Lucy laughed.

"What is it?" I enquired, wanting to know what was so amusing.

"He, Walter that is, asked me to marry him just over twelve months ago. Mama was appalled at the thought of having Walter as a son-in-law."

"And you, what was your reaction?"

"I would not want to spend the rest of my life with someone such as Walter Smythe. I would be badly treated by him, for he is no gentleman, even though he dresses as such. Appearances can be deceptive. I tend to judge people by their actions not what they say or wear."

"Very wise," I returned, adding, "I cannot see you accepting someone of his ilk."

"He would be a brute to live with," she replied, nodding as she did so to show her agreement with my statement.

"So you declined his offer."

"Oh, yes indeed. Of course."

"And what was his reaction to that? He does not strike me as someone who can take rejection easily."

"You're right. He cannot. When I told him no, at first he just thought I was teasing him. He really believed that I would have him. So he persisted, until I eventually told him, rather coldly and bluntly, that I would rather live the rest of my life as a widow and die alone and unloved than spend even one moment in time of my life in his presence."

"I do not suppose he liked that, did he?" I said, imagining the look of outrage on Smythe's face.

"No, he did not. Since that day we have not been invited to any functions at the house, and the whole family snub us whenever they see us. Walter glares at me every time he encounters me. Tries to frighten me, I think, but I am not afraid of him. And I was glad that you taught him a lesson, but you should be wary of him. Stay out of his way, for he will not forget what you did to him, or forgive you. If he sees a chance to get back at you, he will take it, so please be careful."

"He is going to be even more annoyed with me when he finds out that his tailor has sold to me the new clothes that he ordered."

Lucy laughed and said, "He is having a bad time of it, is Walter Smythe," but then she became more serious. "Please, though, do be careful. He is not to be treated lightly."

I could see that Lucy was concerned about my safety, so I said, reassuringly, "Do not worry for I will take very great care to avoid him. I do not think he will come near me again, now that he knows I can physically overpower him."

About this I was wrong, as I was to discover, and very shortly. However, I had managed to reassure Lucy and she smiled as she rose to depart.

"Time to be going now," she said showing her reluctance to leave. "I enjoyed our little chat."

I got up and moved over to where she stood. She placed her hand on my shoulder, and stared straight into my eyes; no reticence, just plain openness to her soul. It was a warm but penetrating look, and for a moment I felt a tingle run through my nerves. Then she removed her hand and started to turn away, making ready to leave, and the sensation was over.

We walked down the rear stairs and then to the front of the house.

"I will walk with you to make sure that you get home safely." It was a very twenty-first-century statement.

"There is no need. It is completely safe. You are the one who should be careful, not me."

"Very well, then," I responded. "I will obey and stay here."

"You are a tease! Do not worry," she said, smiling, and she gave me another peck on the cheek. Then she turned to walk away, touching the elbow of my arm with the palm of her hand as she did so – a final parting gesture of affection.

"Take care," she said.

"And you," I replied.

She walked up the lane and after a few paces waved at me, smiling, saying to me quite loudly, "There is no need for you to stand there and watch. Get yourself back inside."

I waved back, saying, "I will just stand and watch," adding, "if that is all right with you?"

"Please yourself," she responded, continuing to smile. And she continued on her way. When she reached the bend in the road she stopped and waved once more and then was gone.

"She is a character," I thought to myself. "So full of life and joy, and far too good for the likes of Walter Smythe."

It was clear to me that he would just bring unpleasantness to her life and drain her of all her joy, turning her into an embittered and disappointed woman. The bad times and losses in life have a tendency to do that to people, some more than others, even without Walter Smythe contributing to the process. He would be a poison in her life, destroying that which made her so attractive. She was definitely far better off without him, even if that meant remaining a widow all her life.

I realised at that moment in time that my feelings for Lucy were developing, taking on a life beyond that which came from her similarities with Helen. I was losing control.

"So much for your intention of being the impartial observer!"

It was the voice again, breaking its silence, speaking of matters that I did not want to hear about. It continued, saying, "You are going to get involved in Lucy's life, regardless of the consequences. Is that not so? There is no turning back for you now, is there? Whatever I say, you will not turn away from the course you are following. But do not say I did not warn you!"

To this I made no reply.

CHAPTER 18

With Lucy gone it was time for me to return briefly to my own era. After changing into my twenty-first century clothes and collecting the precious jewellery that I had bought and most of my money, a large part of which was in the form of gold sovereigns, I slipped back through the time portal, into a society that valued wealth and its creation above all that is truly important in life. These precious artefacts would be, as a result of the greed that has been encouraged by politicians of both the right and the left, very useful and make me a very wealthy person. But it was a heavy load to carry in both the literal and figurative senses. My reason for moving my valuable hoard was that I did not want to leave such valuables lying around the Time House. The money was my passport to exploring the world of 1750, and I felt more comfortable knowing that it was securely stored in my own time where I could access it whenever I wanted to.

As I walked back home, once again I checked my surroundings to see if any aspect of my world had significantly changed as a result of the time I had just spent in 1750, but there was no altered feature that caught my attention. It seemed that my first visit to the mid-eighteenth century had been the one that had had the biggest impact, and now there was little that was different, if anything, as a result of my recent adventures; this was reassuring. Of course this was just part of my delusion that I was in control; I would have to wait longer to discover the true extent of my delusions. This is how it is with such matters – the universe lulls people into believing that they are masters of their worlds, and then ... I will not say teaches us a lesson, for humankind is remarkably immune to learning such lessons, and people often resort to speaking about 'how next time it will be different' or 'with new technology' and so forth. And is it ever different? Why, yes, but only in terms of the details. So I would, instead, be inclined to say that the universe demonstrates to us the illusion of control, only we chose not to see, we being the scientists, engineers and technologists and others who subscribe to the delusion of control.

After storing away my valuables, I took a shower, knowing that this would be my last chance for several days to experience this everyday feature of contemporary life, this taken-for-granted aspect of modern living. Where I was heading to was an age where many people still did not even take a bath, and those who did bathe did so infrequently and in what I regarded as a state of extreme discomfort.

Having completed my mission it was not long before I had returned to the eighteenth century and established myself for the evening in my new study. There was no television – that instant source of effortless entertainment available in most twenty-first-century homes in the industrialised world – so I had to find a way of occupying my time. Hence, I turned my attention to the books lining the shelves, choosing one with a historical theme. I consumed half of the pie that I had

261

purchased earlier in the day, reserving the other half for next day's lunch. At about midnight I retired to bed, where I slept peacefully until about seven o'clock in the morning.

After rising and taking breakfast, which consisted of some bread, a few hard-boiled eggs, and cold coffee that I had brought from home, I dressed and set forth once more into the unknown world that lay waiting to be explored. I spent the morning examining the large garden, and surveying the neighbourhood of the Time House, familiarising myself with the local footpaths, the surrounding farmland, common pasture, and the nature of several buildings in the vicinity of the house.

I ate the remainder of the pie for lunch and then had a short nap. In the early afternoon I sat in my study, reading. Three o'clock was approaching and, with a sense of rising anticipation, I went outside to meet Lucy and Samuel.

The lesson ran smoothly, with Samuel once more demonstrating both his aptitude for English and the value of youth when it comes to the speed with which he was able to learn. The hour was soon over, and once again I was alone with Lucy.

"It is another nice day," she said, smiling. "Let us not waste it sitting indoors. Come, we should take a walk."

I was pleased at this thought, for I had enjoyed my explorations of the countryside that morning, and now, to spend time once again taking in the sights, but this time with Lucy, seemed doubly pleasurable.

"Yes, let us walk. You can give me a guided tour. I did go out this morning, but now I have someone who can provide place names and add background and history to what are, at the moment, to me, just nameless places devoid of context."

"I would love to be your guide," she replied, showing her happiness to be with me, to have me all to herself.

She looped her arm through mine and we walked, close together and not at all bothered about the physical contact that this implied. As we strolled along she explained to me all that she knew, not just that day, but during the many that followed. For this was the pattern of our days, the routine of our lives, with Samuel coming with Lucy for his lesson, and then Lucy and I spending the rest of the day together. On those days when the weather was against us, we sat and conversed about her life, her family, and countless other topics. These discussions served, over time, to enlighten me about her background, to the conventions of her age, and to the small, countless, insignificant details that people acquire and carry with them as a consequence of living in a particular place and time.

It was not a one-way flow of knowledge, for Lucy continually asked about my life, to which I responded by referring to how I lived in my own time, and translating this in a way that related to the age I was visiting. I tended to focus our conversations on business, and topics such as the American Colonies or recent history, which made me, in her eyes, seem very knowledgeable about what in my time are called world events.

While always cautious when Lucy was probing me about the details of my life story, I still found these encounters very pleasurable, and I easily became lost in the magic of the moment, the intimacy of just the two of us, together, growing emotionally closer all the time.

The world that I was visiting appeared to me to be innocent, as I was used to a less naïve age where the horrors of the world are thrust into people's lives on a daily basis through the constant barrage of news reports, often delivered in real time as events unfold. The mid-eighteenth century seemed an idyllic era, made even more enchanting by the presence of Lucy.

All seemed rosy in this new world, at least for me, who had both wealth and the good fortune of such a friend as Lucy. However, there was one unsavoury aspect to this otherwise pleasant life that tarnished my peaceful existence – Walter Smythe.

As time passed and the days and weeks slipped away, I became more engrossed in exploring my new circumstances, and, growing bolder, ventured forth further into the unknown. So I suppose it was inevitable and inescapable that I should have a further encounter with this unpleasant fellow Walter Smythe. And so it was that one night while I was in town that the inevitable did happen.

I had spent the late afternoon visiting shops, enjoying spending my money, buying small items for myself as well as presents for Lucy. I had decided to take my dinner at the Cock Inn, before heading home in the horse and trap that I had borrowed from Samuel's parents, who were always generous in this respect, allowing me to borrow this means of transportation as often as I liked.

The Cock Inn is a coaching stop. I had discovered that a stagecoach for London departed from this hostelry every Tuesday evening at six o'clock, but other coaches, heading for several other destinations, called there en route at different times of the week. It was the London coach that was of most interest to me, as this was a journey that I had plans to make, wanting very much to see the capital city as it was in the mid-eighteenth century.

Being a stagecoach stop, the Cock Inn was therefore an ideal place to leave the horse and trap while I undertook the tasks that brought me to town. The establishment was one that I had frequented on several occasions during the time that I had already spent in 1750, but it was a place that I had only visited during the daytime. This was my first experience of the inn after the daylight customers had departed, they being mostly shopkeepers and visitors from out of town such as farmers and itinerant tradesmen.

As I was a regular customer, I had come to know the innkeeper, Mr Bartholomew, well. He was a large man, very muscular, resulting from the physical labour of shifting and lifting large wooden beer barrels, but with a friendly disposition. He was always attentive to my needs, recognising that I was both able, and well inclined, to spend my money in his establishment, to an extent that often exceeded that of many of his other clientele.

As was normal in this period, he brewed his own beer in a small brewing house at the back of the inn. It was a good brew, and his reputation for serving good beer meant that he was never short of customers. Unfortunately, this also attracted several undesirables from whom Mr Bartholomew would tolerate no trouble – his physical size and strength ensured that these miscreants complied with Bartholomew's house rules.

Thus, when I entered the Cock Inn that evening I was greeted by a more boisterous scene than I had hitherto been used to. Mr Bartholomew spotted me straight away, and guided me to a quieter area, close to the exit.

"Good evening, Mr Woodward," he said warmly. "Welcome. Take a seat over here – it is a lot quieter."

"Thank you," I replied, grateful to be away from the noise and activity that was as though it were a volcano, threatening to explode, just waiting for the right moment, when the pressure has built to a point when it can no longer be contained.

"I have not seen you in here before at this time," he said, sounding slightly concerned. "Now do not be alarmed by what you see, though," he said, continuing, "Mostly it is just high spirits, that is all. Very rarely comes to fighting." Reassuringly he added, "I make sure of that!"

"I will be fine. I do not mind people enjoying themselves, and I am sure that you can cope with this lot."

"Indeed, I can," he replied. "Now what can I get you?" he asked.

"Food," I returned. "What have you got?"

"You are in luck today, sir; we have a nice piece of roast beef. The cheese is also excellent. Cheddar! Very mature! And the wife has been baking this afternoon – fresh bread, scones and cakes."

"Sounds delightful! I will have some of the beef and the cheese with some of that fresh bread. And I think I will have some scones with jam."

"Right, coming up in a moment. And what will you be having to drink?"

"Half a pint of your best beer, please, Mr Bartholomew," I said in response to this final question.

"Now, you should not be getting up from your seat. Best you stay right where you are. If you need anything just wave and me or the wife will be there to serve you."

"Excellent," I responded, understanding his meaning, and grateful for his special attentions.

It was not long before Mrs Bartholomew was placing my order on the table before me. "There you go, Mr Woodward, sir. Hope you enjoy that," she said with genuine honesty.

"I am sure I will, especially your fresh bread and scones," I returned in the most complimentary way I could.

"Oh, now, do not go flattering me, Mr Woodward."

"No harm in that," I joked.

"Now, remember, if you need anything else, just catch Mr Bartholomew's or my attention. We will be keeping an eye out for you."

"Thank you. You are very kind."

Left alone I consumed my meal, which was as good as Mr Bartholomew had promised, and when all was eaten I sat quietly supping at my beer, enjoying the simplicity of the circumstances, watching life in the inn, thinking to myself that some facets of life never change. Although the details and the quality of the surroundings might improve with time, what I saw before me was a setting that I was familiar with from the twenty-first century.

It was while I was lost in thought, pondering the timelessness of the scene, that I heard a familiar voice – Walter Smythe. He had been sitting at the far end of the inn, lost in the crowd that had congregated there, all taking advantage of Smythe's hospitality, as he was providing free drinks for those he wanted to exploit in some way or whose services he might require. He was a man who bought friendship and companionship, for not many would otherwise wish to keep company with him.

He emerged from the melee, and began shouting at Mr Bartholomew in his usual arrogant and rude way, showing no respect at all for the man. "Bartholomew," he shouted, with a note of contempt in his voice. "Bartholomew, man, where are you?"

Mr Bartholomew looked up when he heard his name being shouted, but I could see in Bartholomew's facial expression that there was no hint of emotion or dislike for Smythe.

"Mr Smythe, sir, what can I do for you?" he asked warily.

"Bartholomew, this is just not good enough. I am completely out of brandy. The bottle is entirely empty. Look!"

And he turned the bottle he was holding upside down to demonstrate the point, showing on his face an expression that spoke of annoyance at such an inconvenience.

"I expect service from you, man," he continued. "I am not one of your common customers. You need to show me more respect."

"That is right, Mr Smythe, you tell him," shouted a voice from within the group of rift-raff and hangers-on that constituted Smythe's entourage.

Mr Bartholomew glanced at the man who had made this remark; the look on Bartholomew's face told the offender that he had said enough, and the man said no more.

"I am sorry, Mr Smythe," Mr Bartholomew began, apologetically, "but I did not know it was empty. I will get you another one straight away."

"I should think so. And bring it over to my table. I am not going to wait here for you."

He turned to walk back to the place where he had been seated when he suddenly noticed me. He stopped and gazed at me for a moment, his face full of malice. Then he was gone, lost within the crowd that had gathered around him, and a rough bunch they seemed.

I decided to drink up and leave, but before I could, Smythe re-emerged and headed straight over to my table, and without invitation, sat down and began to speak.

"Do my clothes suit you?" he asked snidely.

"Not your clothes," I replied coldly.

"They were intended for me, until you bribed my tailor to modify them to fit you."

"I needed clothes, and this was all he had, and I had the financial means to persuade him that my need was greater than yours."

"Yes, you may have money, Woodward, but you are no gentleman," he said sneeringly. "And you never will be. People are born gentlemen – they do not become so just because they have money, and you were not born to be a gentleman. You are no better than a peasant."

"I do not think so," I replied. "You are no gentleman. You are rude and arrogant. No gentleman would speak to Mr Bartholomew the way you just did."

"Him!" Smythe responded, showing his contempt. "He is just a peasant, as the rest of them are in here."

"Is that what you think of people?" I enquired. "Just peasants?"

"Yes, just peasants. Stinking wretches of humanity. And that includes you as well."

"You do not have a very good opinion of anyone, and you hold yourself in high regard. What matters is what you do and, so far, what I have seen of that does not warrant any merit," I told him.

"Fine words, Woodward. Fine words, indeed, but let me explain to you that what people think about me is of no importance. What matters is that people do my bidding and I have the means to make sure that they do. And if anyone crosses me, they will be sorry."

As he said this we were joined by a shaven-headed acquaintance of Smythe's. He was a brutal-looking fellow with a hard gaze coming from cold unsympathetic eyes. He had a manner that spoke of aggression and violence as a way of life.

"Is this the one you were telling me about?" he asked Smythe, while looking at me, making me feel nervous and uncomfortable.

"Yes, Spinks, this is the one."

"My good friend here," the rouge said threateningly, now addressing himself to me, "tells me that you pushed him to the ground."

Although I was apprehensive and felt a twinge of fear rising on hearing these words, I was not prepared to be intimidated by this ruffian.

"I intervened to prevent Smythe physically assaulting a young lad who had not done Smythe harm, nor spoken in a way that would warrant the beating that he was receiving," I stated defiantly. "In the course of protecting the boy, Smythe did fall to the ground. Those were the circumstances surrounding the event to which you are referring."

"Fancy talker, colonial," Spinks responded. "I do not take to your sort. In fact, I dislike you."

Smythe was looking on, observing, and taking pleasure in my obvious discomfort. But I was determined not to allow Spinks to bully and threaten me.

"I am not intimidated by you or your threats," I said.

This, without a doubt, annoyed Spinks, but before he could respond, a large hand descended on his shoulder.

"Now then, Spinks, what are you up to, sitting here with this gentlemen?"

It was the hand of Mr Bartholomew, who now stood towering over Spinks like a giant.

"You will be wanting to return to your own crowd now, will you not?"

This was, although phrased as a question, not a question at all, but an instruction.

Spinks rose, frustrated that he had made no headway with his attempt to provoke me into a fight, and angry that the innkeeper had intervened.

Spinks looked at Mr Bartholomew as if to challenge him, but thought better of the idea. Disgruntled, he returned to mob from which he had emerged, looking and behaving as though he were a wild dog that had just been brought to heel by a forceful hand.

"Now, Mr Smythe, you keep some bad company. You do not want to be mixing with that sort, and bringing them into contact with decent people such as Mr Woodward here."

Smythe stared at Mr Bartholomew, a look of disdain on his face, but he said no more. He rose, glanced at me coldly, and said bitterly, "This is not the end of the matter."

Then he too returned from whence he had come, absorbed by his acquaintances who flocked around him to hear his venomous words about me, until at last, his hatred satisfied for the moment, he moved on to other subjects of conversation.

Mr Bartholomew sat down next to me, a perplexed look on his face.

"A bad one is that Spinks," he said. "Mr Smythe's not very particular about whom he drinks with. Mixes with bad company. Always drinking, gambling and going with whores. And no good will come of it, that is for sure. He will meet a bad end one of these days."

"Yes," I agreed. "Smythe's an unpleasant man, but Spinks, he, I think, has criminal inclinations."

"Oh, no doubt about that," Mr Bartholomew responded. "He has already been in prison. End his days on the gallows, that one. But what I do not understand is why they both came over to your table. It was obvious what they were up to, trying to provoke you – that is why I came over."

"Ah! Yes, well, you see, I had a run-in with Smythe when I first arrived. I found him attacking a young boy. He was about to beat him with his walking cane so I intervened and stopped Smythe, and he came off the worse for it."

"Oh! Well then, it is good for the boy that you did stop Smythe for he has a foul temper and likely as not he would have beaten him to death, and would have gotten away with it as well, given his father's connections. But that puts you in a dangerous position. Smythe is unlikely to forgive or forget.

Watch your back, is my advice. Keep well out of his way. And that means not coming in here in the evenings, for this is where he is usually to be found at night time."

"I will remember that," I said gratefully. "But is it safe for me to leave? Any chance that they might follow me?"

"Not very safe at all, I would say, judging by what he was up to," Mr Bartholomew said, looking and sounding very concerned. "It is quite possible that they might follow you, then who knows what they might do to you out there in some dark corner. So this is what I suggest. I will get the stable boy to harness up your horse and trap, and when it is ready I will sneak you out of here, and then make sure that those two do not follow you."

I was uncomfortable with the idea running away in the manner suggested but, caution being the safer option to follow, I agreed to this plan. And thus it was that I escaped from circumstances that could have turned out to be harmful to my physical wellbeing.

I learned later that Mr Bartholomew's caution was well placed, for Spinks had made an effort to follow, but had been discouraged from doing so by Mr Bartholomew, who was big enough to persuade even the likes of Spinks.

So it was that I left the town that night without incident, and, after returning the horse and trap, I finally reached home, relieved that I was safe and that I had avoided being subjected to physical violence.

Once home I pondered the fact that some aspects of human existence never change. If Spinks were transported to the twenty-first century he would be at home in some dingy back-street pub, as he was in the Cock Inn in the middle of the eighteenth century. Plying himself with life-shortening alcohol and tobacco, he could, in either age, live an illusion of a life; in truth he was no better than a warring barbarian from the dark days of prehistory.

In all ages, violence has been a deliberate decision. This is the way it was; this is the way it is. And in the twenty-first century the same choice is exercised by those who fill the world with death and destruction, regardless of what badge they may wear, or what cause they claim to be pursuing. Terrorists, violent criminals, torturers, vigilantes, murderers, child abusers, and many more, all make the same choice and in doing so make the hell that will eventually consume and destroy them, and probably also the rest of us as well.

This encounter with Walter Smythe in the Cock Inn was just the first of several that were to follow, although it was perhaps the most dangerous, until, that is, the one that took place on a day that lay in the not-too-far-off future. More about this I will tell you soon, but for the time being I will say that while out walking in the neighbourhood, our paths crossed a number of times, but I did not feel threatened by these encounters; for it seemed that, without the likes of Spinks to do his dirty work, Smythe was only comfortable picking upon people he felt confident of being able to beat – such as young Samuel, for example. So while always cautious whenever he was nearby, I learned not to worry about him, and I just went about my business as though he were not there.

But there were times when I suspected that he was following me, observing what I did, where I went, which I found unsettling. Most times when we passed he would just smile at me, not a pleasant smile of greeting, but more a warning. But one time he did speak to me. This happened when I was with Lucy. We were sitting on a wooden bench on the village green when he approached and stood before us.

"Now, what a nice couple you two make," he said, mockingly.

"Walter Smythe," Lucy said, indignantly. "If you have no nice words to say, then better to remain quiet."

"I was being nice," he objected. "How could you say such harsh words to me?"

"Very easily," responded Lucy. "What do you want?" she asked.

"There is no matter in particular that I wanted to raise with you," he replied. "I was just being sociable."

"You need not bother," Lucy stated coldly. "I have no wish to socialise with you. In fact it would be perfectly nice, nay desirable, if you were never to speak to me again."

"I know where I am not wanted," Smythe responded with a smirk, and then he walked away from us.

"That was harsh," I said to Lucy.

"Harsh, yes, but necessary. I have always found it best to make clear to him that I do not want him near me. And he just stopped to mock us, so he deserved all that he got."

"You are very independent and know your own mind, so I will leave it at that," I responded, "but once you warned me to be careful with him, and here you are provoking him."

"Yes, indeed, but I do not think that he would try to hurt me. Too many people know about how I rejected him, and if harm were to come to me then the finger of suspicion would point to him. I am not so sure about you, though. You are a stranger around here, and he evidently has a strong dislike for you. That is why I warned you to stay away from him, and not to provoke him."

"I did not tell you," I began, "but I did have an encounter with him one night in town. He and one of his associates tried to provoke me into a fight while I was taking a meal at the Cock Inn. The innkeeper intervened to stop them, but the incident reinforced in my mind your warning."

"See, I told you. You must be careful," Lucy said, sounding very worried.

"I take your point. Do not be alarmed. Since that night, we have passed each other several times on my travels about the neighbourhood, and he has never attempted to harm me. He just smiles unpleasantly at me. Deep down I think he is frightened of me. He is a bully and he only picks on people weaker than himself."

"You are right, he is a bully, but knowing him, as I do," Lucy responded, "he is probably waiting his time, planning his revenge. Please, do not take this lightly. He is a real danger to you. And you live all alone in that big house. That makes you very vulnerable."

This of course was true, but what Lucy and Smythe did not know was that I had an escape route out of their time into the future. If necessary I could use this to remove myself from any danger that might arise while I was in the Time House.

"I will be extra careful, I promise you," I said as reassuringly as I could.

"I worry about you," Lucy responded, very tenderly, placing her warm soft hand on mine.

It was one of those moments in time that you do not want to end. Caught up in the essence of a simple touch, in the allure of physical contact between two people, it drove out all other sensations, leaving only a single-minded focus on one perfect instant, one perfect moment in time, when all was right with the world, when all was in harmony. But such enchanting seconds, for that is all they ever are, are over far too quickly, prematurely brought to a close by the fact of being in a public place. It was a foretaste of an intimacy that still lay in the future, of a coming-together of two souls and two hearts; we were, at that moment in time, two people whose lives were destined to become intertwined. Fate would soon play its hand and reveal what it had in store for us both.

The moment was over and we resumed our stroll around the village green, laughing and chatting about all sorts of subjects, none of which seemed as important as just being together. And so, having orbited the green grass and having taken in all there was to see and learn, with the light now fading away, and darkness enveloping us, our path brought us once more to the front door of Lucy's home.

"So, here we are back where we started," I said, stating the obvious.

"Yes, here we are," Lucy replied.

There was a pause for a moment, with neither of us speaking, just the looks on our faces saying all that needed to be said. But looks can be deceiving – were we reading the signs properly?

We stood there, silent, each of us wondering what to do next. I for my part was reticent to act for fear of causing offence. It was an unfounded worry for Lucy, to my surprise, took the lead and placed a kiss on my lips, where she lingered long enough to say what she meant. It was, unmistakably, an invitation to hold her, to kiss her, and to do it again and again every time we were able; this is how it is with lovers first stumbling towards the beginnings of intimacy – an eternal constant in a relationship between man and woman.

Thus it was that we held each other and kissed, until it was time to bring this moment in time to an end. And as is always the case, men, helpless to the passions of their gender, not wanting to be the first to break off such encounters, need to be guided in such matters by women. So it was Lucy who brought this to an end, breaking free from my embrace.

"That is enough for now. I must go in," she said.

I held onto her hands, saying that which I could no longer keep to myself. "There are feelings stirring within me. Feelings for you!"

"And within me, also," she replied passionately. "But there is a time and place for such emotions. Let us just proceed one step at a time."

"Yes, let us do that," I replied, smiling.

Lucy smiled back. She was happy. "You are so understanding," she said. "You remind me of my poor Henry. I think you and he are very much alike. Perhaps that is why I am attracted to you. I was made for you, and you were made for me – a perfect match."

I was not sure how to respond, so I just smiled again and then changed the subject.

"Time for you, dear Lucy, to go in, for now it is time for me to be getting back home."

"Yes. Until tomorrow, then. I will be thinking of you tonight, tomorrow, and the next. Every day."

I let loose her hands as she gently moved away from me.

"Goodnight," she said sweetly, turning to look at me.

"Goodnight, Lucy," I replied softly.

Then she was inside, slowly closing the door, watching me until no more could she see, and the door closed, and I was left standing on my own in the darkness that had descended upon the village green.

I stood there for a moment, savouring the experience, excited, longing once more to be with Lucy, to hold her, to kiss her. It was clear now exactly where we were both heading. It was just a matter of time. Nature would take its course. Here in a distant time, I was falling in love, not caring anymore about the consequences, just wanting to be with her, to spend all my hours and days in her presence, and to be part of her life forever. My intention of not getting involved had unmistakably failed, and as for my naïve belief that it was I who was in control, what can I say? Already matters were beginning to spin out of control, and the pace with which this was happening was about to increase. Hence it was that the disorder to which I was blind began to envelop me.

CHAPTER 19

Days ran into weeks, weeks into months. Seasons turned, from summer to autumn, to winter, then to spring and back again to summer. Before I realised how many moments in time I had experienced, mostly with Lucy, twelve months had passed. And love had blossomed.

As Lucy and I walked together, exploring the byways of the surrounding countryside, our conversations over the months changed from that of the past, of life lived, to that of the future, our future, and life yet to be lived, together. No longer did we just walk arm in arm, but we also held each other, each feeling the warmth of the other's body, kissing and cuddling, enjoying these moments, anticipating even closer intimacy yet to come, and the prospect of the excitement of uninhibited physical contact. We spent timeless moments just being together, content to be quiet, I sharing her company, she mine, bound together as though now one. And we made plans for a life in other places, in America.

From my new home in the Time House, I had experienced the seasons as time moved from 1750 to 1751. The summer months had drawn to a close, but it had been a summer of a different kind, the like of which I had never before experienced. The air was cleaner and much fresher than what I was used to, the weather warm and sunny, and there was a value attached to savouring moments in time and enjoying those aspects of living that really mattered and which no amount of economic wealth could provide. I had thought that such summers were the stuff of fiction, but there was quietude to life, with a pace more attuned to the natural world. In short, it was idyllic and I was glad of it.

When summer gave way to autumn, the colours I found were just as I had known them in my own time, but what came as a great shock was the coldness of the winter. For the first time in my life I knew the discomfort of living in a home without central heating. From December onwards the frosts were hard, and I awoke in the mornings to find the condensation on the windows frozen in intricate and enchanting patterns on the panes of glass. It was hard to imagine such a harshness, given the mildness of the winters that I was used to. And, of course, of snow there was an abundance, piled high in the lanes and across the fields, blown with the winds to form high drifts against trees and bushes. With no proper roads, no rock salt to keep the roads clear of ice and snow, and no means of removing the snow, I often had to wade, waist-deep, through high drifts, and I frequently arrived soaking wet at my beloved's home. By this stage, I kept a wardrobe in her place of abode, and often stayed there overnight in the guestroom. I found these winter days delightful, for now I understood where those Christmas-card scenes came from, how it was that people were able to skate on rivers and ponds, for I saw for myself the water freeze, as temperatures plummeted to levels that I had previously never known in my short life.

And I experienced my first eighteenth-century Christmas, which, as you might expect, was very different from the Christmases I was used to. There was none of the materialism that dominates the modern festivity. There was no Christmas tree, only simple presents, exchanged in the afternoon after a traditional dinner of roast goose, with the familiar vegetables, but no Brussels sprouts, for these had not yet been created by the hand of man, bred from other brassicas, which in turn had, across many generations of man and vegetables, been fashioned through artificial selection from what nature had itself evolved through natural selection over millions of years. And the absence of television meant that the day was similar to others, filled with people-centred entertainment and activities such as conversation, games such as charades, and reading aloud from favourite novels.

But spring returned as it must, and with it came warmer and longer days, and when the weather allowed, Lucy and I resumed our daily walks and the exploration of the land in which I now dwelt. Thus it was that spring passed by and once again we found ourselves in another delightful summer, with all the promise of warmth, light and seasonal pleasures. The sun warmed our lives, allowing us those moments in time when we were alone together, enabling the roots of our love to deepen.

Among this pattern of changing seasons and pleasant days spent with Lucy and her mother, I forgot, for the moment at least, where I had come from, of my life in the twenty-first century, of my life with Helen. This was now becoming more remote, and I did not miss it, nor did I venture back.

In my mind I no longer distinguished between Lucy and Helen, for now they just seemed to be the same person. In all ways Lucy was Helen, in her mannerisms, in her speech, and in her looks. This, I think, is why I found it so easy to become enchanted with her and engrossed in my new world. When I was with Lucy I was with Helen, and every day that I spent with Lucy brought us closer together. Thoughts of returning to my own time began to fade. I had found love, happiness, peace and contentment in the mid-eighteenth century, and saw no reason to return to an age that had for me lost its value.

Time passed by, but I was unaware that this was happening, and I was completely blind to the possible consequences. Back where I had come from, as far as I could tell and had experienced, life was suspended – a moment in time forever frozen, where I could, if I chose to, just return and resume my former existence as though my time in the mid-eighteenth century had never been. I could stay away for a long period and not miss a single second. Helen was with her parents in Abbotsbury, and would stay there for eternity if I so wished, for it seemed that I could step back into my other life and pick up exactly where I had left off. This is what I thought at the time, but, as I was soon to discover, I was creating for myself consequences and complexities that I could never have foreseen: *out of order comes disorder*.

The question of ageing did from time to time become a point of concern, and I did think about this. But I reasoned with myself that I was immune from the ravages of time, so long as I stayed in the past. I know that this may seem foolish, and it was, just like many aspects of my former life, especially that which I spent among those who practise engineering, who I now understand make many assumptions without solid foundation – ones that only time can reveal to be true or false – but I, like them, took comfort from my flawed analysis. I allowed myself to believe that if the natural laws of time could be broken to allow me to travel back to the eighteenth century, then surely time would have no effect on me.

I found the thought of eternal youth novel, and was pleased with myself for having been given such a gift. I was the master of time. It had brought me wealth, possessions, love, eternal youth and happiness. What more could any man want?

After such a long stay and with such a close relationship developing with Lucy, I had also become part of Lucy's family. Her mother accepted me and welcomed me into her home. On countless occasions we sat together, a family in the making, comfortable with each other and looking forward to a happy future.

And this is how the days passed. All was perfect, so it seemed, for there were no aspects to this arrangement that gave me cause for concern. No defect or flaw could I perceive, and no worry crossed my mind such was the state of my delusion, something I was well practised in, being an engineer and a product of the modern age, which is a place full of delusions, both individual and collective; take your pick!

I was in love and as happy as anyone could be. But there were storm clouds on the horizon, only I chose not see them, just as those in the twenty-first century chose to ignore that which must follow from the unconstrained consumption of the earth's resources, combined with all the other problems, that will ultimately lead to the destruction of contemporary civilisation. I was blind to the warning signs, took no notice, and went on with my new life, until eventually the storm broke, turning my new life into a nightmare.

How did such a perfect world turn into a living hell? It all began one day when, sitting with Lucy in her garden, I broached a subject that had, for quite a while, being floating in the back of my mind, which I had once raised in my early conversations with Lucy.

"Lucy dear," I said, "I have been thinking of going away for a few days."

"Away," she responded with a note of concern in her voice. "Why, my love, and where?"

"Why? Because, as I once told you, I have seen very little of this country, and I would like at least to visit London."

"London! Such a long way! It would take you days to get there and it is a journey of great discomfort, not to mention possible danger."

"Do not worry yourself, Lucy. I am well able to take care of myself, and as for the discomfort, I think I can bear that. The reward at the end of my travels will make the troubles of the journey worth the effort."

I did not elaborate on how interesting a visit to London would be for me, a person who knew the city as a twenty-first-century metropolis, complete with noise, pollution, and all the other aspects of modern life that combine to make cities unbearable to those used to quieter provincial environments.

"But I will miss you so much. I would be left here on my own, and your absence would leave a hole in my life."

"And I would miss you too, my love. Sweet Lucy, oh, how I would miss you."

"Then stay," she pleaded, "for, to be honest, I fear for you. I do not want to lose you. I have already experienced the loss of someone whom I loved dearly. I do not want that to happen again."

She looked at me once more, straight in the eye, and there for a fleeting moment I glimpsed the pain that she still held deep within her soul.

She continued her effort to dissuade me from undertaking the adventure that had taken shape in my mind. "Do not go. Please, I beg you," she said, pleading with me. "I have a sense of foreboding about this. I fear a terrible event is about to happen."

I am a man of the twenty-first century, rational and not at all inclined to take note of such emotional pleading. It was illogical to me, and I assumed that this sort of emotional response must be normal for the time I was in.

"Lucy, no dreadful accident or catastrophic event is going to befall me," I said confidently. "I will visit London and return to you none the worse for it. It will be good to have a little break. Once I have found somewhere suitable to stay, then perhaps you and your mother could make the journey on a future visit. You said yourself how much you wanted to travel, so think of this as a reconnaissance expedition. I will make a point of discovering suitable accommodation for you and your mother. Perhaps we could rent a house and stay in London for a prolonged period."

Lucy could see that I was not going to be swayed by her pleading, so she responded, "If you must go, then at least speak with my Uncle Ralf. He has been there himself on several occasions. He knows places to stay, as well as where to avoid. And it is what he has told me of the place that partially results in my concern. So please promise me that you will speak with him and take his advice."

"I will do as you ask, but who is this Uncle Ralf? No one has yet mentioned to me this person, and where does he live?"

"He lives in Dorset. He is my mother's younger brother. Mama received a letter from him a few days ago. In it he says he will be coming to see us in a few weeks. When he comes you can ask him. As for why we did not mention him, I cannot rightly say. The only excuse I can offer is that he is perhaps, let us say for kindness's sake, a little eccentric, and, from my perspective, quite boring. He is well set in his ways as you will soon discover."

"Very well, then, I will speak with your uncle. There is no harm in waiting. It is probably too hot at the moment for a trip to a big city. They can be awful places in the midst of a heat wave."

Thus the subject of my trip to London was dropped from our conversation, and the matter was not raised again until Lucy's Uncle Ralf arrived, but not immediately, for it would have been impolite to discuss the subject straightaway upon his arrival.

Uncle Ralf was a man of substance, living a genteel life on his country estate in Dorset. He came to his sister and niece every year in early summer, so it was no surprise to Lucy to find, one fine summer's afternoon, her Uncle Ralf standing in the drawing room, busy chatting away to her mother about the terrible journey he had experienced.

"The roads are in an appalling condition, my dear," he was saying as Lucy walked into the room.

On seeing his niece his face lit up for he had a soft spot for Lucy and was inclined to spoil her in whatever way he could.

"Ah, here comes my favourite niece," he said as if speaking to a child.

"Uncle," responded Lucy, "indeed I think I am your only niece, so I could hardly be described as your favourite one."

"Sadly it is indeed true that I have not been blessed with other young ladies whom I could call my nieces, but if that had been the case, then I think I could confidently state that you would be first among all of them."

"Well, that might be so, but it would still be a pleasure to see you even if that were not the case. Welcome, Uncle," and then Lucy kissed her Uncle Ralf on the cheeks.

Lucy's mother was sitting on the settee, and Lucy went and placed herself next to her. Uncle Ralf was standing by the fireplace, which was his habit on such visits, even though there was no fire lit, this being a season when such comforts were definitely not required.

"So," began Lucy, "how was your journey?"

"Ah, I was just telling your mother how bad the roads are. They seem to deteriorate with every trip that I make here. And, you know, no one seems bothered at all about it. I have complained and complained, but nobody takes the slightest notice. How the authorities expect anyone to travel about this land I do not understand. And when the winter comes … God forbid that I should have to travel the byways of this country at such a time of year. Disgraceful! That is what it is! Disgraceful!"

Now, this was a complaint that Lucy and her mother had heard on many occasions, and not wanting to hear any more on the matter, Lucy's mother tried to change the subject.

"Tell me, Ralf," she began hopefully, "how long do you intend to stay with us, for you did not mention it in your letter?"

"Did I not?" responded Uncle Ralf, sounding surprised.

"No, dear, you did not," replied Lucy's mother.

"Ah, an omission on my part then," said Uncle Ralf. "To be honest with you, I am not looking forward to going back home. Those roads are enough to make a man want to stay here till his days are over."

Lucy's mother's attempt to steer the topic of conversation away from the condition of the roads had failed, but she was not going to give up, and valiantly she persevered.

"Yes, but you must see Lucy's new friend before you go."

This did the trick, since Uncle Ralf's second most talked about topic was Lucy's future, and he was most interested to hear more about me.

"Ah, yes, indeed I must. I am intrigued to learn about this mysterious young man. Benjamin he is called, is that right?" he enquired, seeking confirmation of what he already knew and which was not in need of confirmation.

Uncle Ralf now left the fireplace to support itself, and sat down on the sofa opposite to where Lucy and her mother were seated.

"You must tell me all, every detail, the entire story, starting from the beginning."

And so the tale of how Lucy and I first met was recounted to Uncle Ralf, of how we had become close friends, and how that friendship had developed into so much more.

My own encounter with Uncle Ralf happened on the second day of his visit. By that time it had been established that he would be staying for several weeks, as yet unspecified, after which he would, as he put it, take his life in his hands and venture out once more on those dangerous highways, returning to his peaceful existence in his home county.

He was, as usual, standing supporting the fireplace when I was ushered into the room. Upon my entry he stood upright, placing his hands folded behind his back, assuming an air of authority, of one becoming the position of an elder about to be introduced to the lover of a cherished relative, with himself, in this case, taking on the position in lieu of there being no father figure in the Dent household.

I was, I confess, a little unnerved by this for I had become used to being the only male in a household, occupied in the majority by females, there being only one other male, the gardener, who also doubled as general hired hand, undertaking tasks that required a man's strength.

Lucy led me to her uncle and introduced me to him.

"Uncle," she said with an air of girlish excitement, "this is Benjamin."

"Ah," he began, as was his custom, for he seemed to begin all of his sentences with an *ah*. "Very glad to meet you, sir, very glad indeed. I have heard much about you, and all good, I hasten to add."

"Thank you," I replied. "It is a pleasure to meet you too. Lucy has spoken often of you." Not true of course, but it seemed polite to say this.

"All good I hope," he interjected.

"Uncle!" Lucy said, sounding alarmed.

"Just joking, my dear, just joking," he said, laughing.

This saved me from having to say words that would reassure him that Lucy had spoken of him in the warmest of terms, if not sometimes in a comical vain, for once the existence of Uncle Ralf and his planned visit had been revealed to me, he had been the centre of many conversations, along with the nature of his personality and his many idiosyncrasies.

Now that I had met Uncle Ralf the comical side of his character was becoming evident to me. He even looked comical, for he was a short, portly person with red cheeks and seemed forever to wear a smile. A cheerful man he certainly was, always ready to see the humorous side of life, and not averse to being the butt of a joke.

And, I have to say, he was well liked, for once the news of his pending visit had broken, there had been an air of anticipation about the household for many weeks before the date of his actual arrival. This of course was to be expected in a home that received few visitors apart from myself.

Once settled in his accommodation his amiable character added to the warmth of an already warm and cheerful household, and his light-hearted conversation, when he could be persuaded to talk about some subject other than the state of the nation's roads, was much appreciated.

"So, young man, I have heard that you have travelled the world."

"This is true," I replied. "I have been to many strange places."

"The American Colonies are indeed a strange place," Uncle Ralf responded. "Quite a wild place I have been told."

"It is a frontier country," I said explaining, "so wild, in every sense of the meaning of the word, is part of the culture. But it is not all like that. Boston is a very settled sort of town, but further out west it can be much untamed."

"Yes, exactly, and that is not to my liking. I suppose the roads are not up to much then?" he asked, wanting to know if they were any worse than those that he was familiar with.

"The roads," I said, sounding authoritative, "are much worse than the highways in this country. By comparison, your roads are in perfect condition."

"Hmm. Then I certainly do not want to go to the American Colonies. I cannot imagine any roads being worse than what I have experienced here. Sounds as though it is a hell on earth."

"But the American Colonies are not the only place that I have been to. I have travelled widely in Europe, and parts of Africa and Asia."

"My, what an adventurous young man you are. Very adventurous! Must have been dangerous though. I would not wish to risk my life going to exotic locations. I do not believe that it is worth putting one's life in danger just to see some foreign places. I have never being abroad and I do not intend to."

"It is a personal choice," I replied. "Everyone to their own."

"Hmmm. Yes, I suppose so."

Now I saw an opportunity to raise the subject of my proposed visit to London. "There is one place that I do desire to see," I mentioned.

"Ah. I sense a question coming," he responded, smiling.

"Yes, indeed, sir."

"So what place is it that you want to see?"

"London."

"London!" he stated, repeating what I had just said. "London!" repeating what he had just said.

"Yes, London," I said, adding by way of explanation that I had not seen much of England, and that I wanted to at least visit the country's capital city.

"London is a place that I know very well, Benjamin," he began to explain. "I used to have business dealings there. Not now of course, for I have grown too old for the noise and bustle of the place, but I can see its attraction to a younger man. Yes, I do recall having a number of pleasant stays in London when I was in my youth."

"Uncle," said Lucy, who had remained outside the conversation until this point, "I suggested that Benjamin ask you about London, since you do have such a good knowledge of the city. I was concerned that he may take accommodation in an unsuitable place and visit areas where no respectable person should venture."

"Ah, you are concerned about Benjamin. Quite right, too, for there are dangerous spots in London that need to be avoided. Takes experience to know these. And you have asked the right person, for I know exactly the place to stay, and what to see and what to avoid."

Lucy smiled at me while moving closer to me, looping her arm through mine. I smiled back, looking into her eyes, increasingly now a habit that neither of us sought to avoid.

"See," she said with a slight air of well-meant smugness, "Uncle Ralf knows. He can be your guide."

"Yes, indeed, Uncle Ralf knows," Uncle Ralf said, referring to himself in the third person, "and I am only too happy to impart my knowledge and experience to you, Benjamin. So fear not, Lucy. With me as his mentor, he will be as safe as houses."

"Thank you, Uncle Ralf," Lucy said softly.

"Yes, indeed, thank you. I much appreciate your giving time to this subject," I added.

"Oh, it is nothing. I am glad to be of help."

At that moment Lucy's mother entered the room.

"So what are you three up to?" she asked. "Huddled around an empty fireplace on such a warm day as this. Come, this will not do. Let us go into the garden. I have ordered tea and cakes and we can sit and talk outside."

"Ah, tea and cakes," Uncle Ralf responded, "how delightful, and in the garden on a warm summer's day. Delightful, indeed, and with such good company."

For the moment my interest to learn more about London from Uncle Ralf would have to wait. I did not think it polite to raise the matter again since Lucy's mother was plainly intent upon topics of lighter conversation, so I decided to wait upon a moment when I was alone with Uncle Ralf.

The conversation was indeed much lighter now that Lucy's mother had joined us. We sat by the Venetian window, on what today we would call a patio, and the tea and cakes were brought out to us. There was a repeat of the tea ceremony, with the precious leaves being added to the pot, the waiting and then the pouring of the tea into our cups, starting with, of course, the main guest, Uncle Ralf. Cake was also cut and passed to each and every one.

We sat quietly for a while, eating the cakes and sipping at the tea. It was all very English and just right for the period, so I imagined. It was Lucy's mother who was the first to speak.

"So, Ralf, what news do you bring? How is that country estate of yours? It is such a long time since I have seen it."

"All is well with the estate, Marjory dear. All is as it was on your last visit. You know that you are all very welcome to visit at any time, but I would not recommend the journey. No, indeed the journey would be very tiring."

"Yes, Ralf, I expect it would, but I want to see it one more time, so perhaps Lucy and I will take the risk and make the journey. Perhaps we will come this autumn. And Benjamin, you could come too."

"I would be delighted to come with you," I returned.

Ralf had not expected this response. Lucy's mother had never previously expressed a desire to visit Ralf's estate.

298

I sensed that Ralf enjoyed the bachelor existence, isolated in his own little world, and was not entirely overjoyed at the news that he was about to be visited by his sister, his niece and myself.

"But, Marjory," he countered, "think about the journey. It would be a nightmare for you, not to mention dangerous, with all those highwaymen on the loose."

"Oh, Ralf, stop fussing. We will be all right, and with Benjamin with us we shall be completely safe. Benjamin is a man of the world, are not you, dear?" she said turning to me with a smile. "And capable enough of looking after the two of us," she said, continuing and turning once more to Ralf.

Uncle Ralf turned towards me, as if looking to me to throw him a lifeline. I just shrugged my shoulders at him as I was not prepared to come to his aid and cross Lucy and her mother.

It quickly dawned on Ralf that he was trapped and that he had no option but to acquiesce to his sister's wishes.

"Very well, my dear," he said with good spirit. "An autumn visit it is, then. Shall we say the last week in September?"

"Yes, that will do fine," Lucy's mother responded.

And this was how the afternoon and the evening passed by, we four engaged in light conversation. We talked much about our forthcoming visit to Ralf's country estate, of the sights that Marjory was looking forward to seeing again, of the places we would visit, and the details of how we would get there.

At one point Uncle Ralf and I were left on our own, while Lucy and her mother were temporarily absent, arranging housekeeping matters, which, with the arrival of Uncle Ralf, had become less routine owing to his particular likes and dislikes. As we sat together, he began to speak of Lucy.

"I gather," he began in a fatherly way, "that Lucy is rather fond of you."

"Yes," I replied.

"And are those feelings replicated?"

"They are, very much so."

"Does that mean there are wedding bells not too far off?"

"I am not sure. We have not talked about such matters yet."

"Ah! Still getting to know each other. Very sensible! Very sensible indeed! One should not rush into marriage."

The truth was that I had never considered this as an issue. I should, of course, have realised that after being very close friends for one year, people would start to wonder and make assumptions, as this was the normal turn of events in such circumstances. All I could do was agree with Uncle Ralf.

"Yes, Uncle Ralf, there is no rush."

"Very wise. Marry in haste, repent in leisure is what I say," he said. "Take your time, but do not take forever. I am very happy that Lucy has, at long last, found someone." He said this sounding genuinely pleased.

"It has been a long time since her husband passed away, and I was beginning to think that she would remain a widow for the rest of her days. And that would be a terrible shame. Lucy needs to live her life, and not be shut up here with her mother. And you could give her that life, could not you? You have the means?"

"Yes," I replied, "I could, and as you say I do have the means."

Not wanting to continue discussing my relationship with Lucy further, nor our future plans, I thought now was a good time to ask him about London, and I was just on the verge of doing so when Lucy and her mother returned.

"Sorry to have left you two to your own devices, but one must provide directions sometimes to the servants, especially as they are not used to having visitors to take account of. They are too accustomed to the routine that they tend to forget that they need to pay attention to other matters. But it's all sorted now, is that not so, Lucy?"

"Yes, Mama, all is now running smoothly," Lucy responded.

"Now, it is time for some entertainment," Lucy's mother said. "How about a card game? Benjamin, do you play cards? Lucy and I play fairly often in the late evenings, and Ralf, I know, likes a good game of cards when he comes here, not having anyone at home he can play with."

"I have played card games before, but I am not a regular player," I replied. I tried to sound interested but, truthfully, card games had not been a big part of my life in the twenty-first century, there being many more interesting and stimulating activities that one can engage in for entertainment.

"Never mind, you will soon pick it up. Is that not so, Lucy?"

Lucy's mother stated this, being absolutely sure in her mind that I would enjoy playing cards.

We spent the rest of the evening playing whist, a game that I had never encountered previously, and I managed to prove Lucy's mother's predictions to be entirely incorrect, as I turned out to be a very poor card player indeed. The three of them tried hard to help me and to explain the rules, but as I was not in the first place very much inclined towards playing, all their efforts came to naught.

Thus, after a few hours frustratingly spent with a novice, this being exactly what I was, the three experienced card players who surrounded me gave up hope of enlightening me to the rules of play, and the game came to an end. The concentration that had been needed, not to mention the patience, had taken its toll on Lucy's mother and Uncle Ralf, who were now both ready to retire for the night. And with this went all hope that day of enquiring further about London. It was not in fact until the next day, in the afternoon, when I found myself alone with Uncle Ralf that I managed to steer the conversation onto the topic of my intended visit to London.

CHAPTER 20

I had already discovered that transportation to London was very poor, there not being a great demand in such a rural area to visit this city. A coach service to the capital city departed every Tuesday evening at six o'clock from the Cock Inn in the centre of the nearby town. Now I wanted to probe Uncle Ralf for his suggestions with regard to accommodation in London, as I, being a stranger in that time, might not know how best to avoid undesirable types and places.

"Uncle Ralf," I began, "you offered to advise me about London."

"Ah, yes, indeed I did," he responded, keen to display his knowledge of the subject and also to help. "But let me tell you first that it will be a most unpleasant journey. Dangerous as well! Too many highwaymen these days! Best not to take valuables with you! Chances are you will be held up and robbed. I do not suppose highwaymen are a problem where you come from. It is about time someone dealt with those blasted fellows. Hang them. That is what they deserve."

This was not a good start. I did not want to hear a speech, yet again, on the state of the roads or to hear Uncle Ralf's proposals for solving the nation's problem of highwaymen terrorising travellers. But as it turned out, he only briefly touched upon these matters, and went straight to the issues that were of interest to me.

"But enough," he said continuing. "I dare say that you do not want to hear my views on these subjects, having already listened to my discourses many times. It is somewhere to stay, and places to visit and to avoid that are of interest, is that right?"

I was relieved that he was being so brief. "Yes, that is correct," I returned, eagerly.

"Now, with regard to the former, I know the perfect place for you and it will not cost a fortune – the Strand Inn on The Strand. Comfortable beds and pleasant food is what they have, my friend. And it is very central for the places that you should visit."

"Sounds perfect," I enthusiastically interjected.

"Oh, it is. Excellent accommodation! Now, places to see. This depends very much on what is of interest to you."

I had not considered this as an issue, since I wanted to see London as it was in the mid-eighteenth century, not to visit specific attractions. I wanted to compare the London I knew with the way it was in the past.

"I am keen to see a sample of what the place has to offer, so that I can get a feel for it," I said, rapidly thinking of a logical answer to his question.

"Ah, right. In that case I suggest that you see the royal palaces: St James's, Kensington, Kew and Hampton Court. Alas the latter is someway outside the city, so be prepared for another journey, if only a short one. Then there are the churches of course: St Paul's and Westminster Abbey are the two most important ones. But there are some smaller ones worth a visit such as St Martin's. If you are interested in science then it would be worthwhile for you to visit the Royal Observatory at Greenwich. Yet another journey, I am afraid."

Uncle Ralf's knowledge of eighteenth-century London was extensive. He spent nearly one hour advising me, placing particular emphasis on the areas to avoid, highlighting Soho and the docks in East London as neighbourhoods that I should go nowhere near at all costs. He delved into some of the history of these places that he recommended, as well as mentioning points of interest that I should be careful to seek out and observe.

Over the course of this long session, during which he could not resist the urge to reminisce about his London exploits when in his youth, I patiently listened, occasionally nodding to indicate my continuing interest in the knowledge that was being imparted to me. And so it was that I came to know of the experience that awaited me – all that was now left to do was to make the necessary travel arrangements.

The days passed, and Sunday came, when we all gathered for lunch. I arrived at Lucy's early that Sunday morning to attend church with the family. Following worship, we had dinner, which had the proportions of a Christmas meal, Uncle Ralf's presence being an occasion worthy of such a celebration.

After dinner, Uncle Ralf started on the subject of the dangers to be found in London. A look of concern came upon Lucy's face, and, glancing at her, I saw the unspoken words telling me, still pleading with me, not to go.

Being Sunday there was no class for Samuel and it was on the following day that I saw my young friend once more. Following his lesson with Lucy, I told Samuel of my plans for the following day and I could see that he would have liked to come with me, but he said no more, knowing that I would say no.

"Tomorrow," Lucy began to tell Samuel, "we will have the lesson a little later, say five o'clock, as tomorrow afternoon I have to be with my mother and uncle, who will be returning home soon. Is that all right with you, Samuel?"

"Yes, I will be here waiting for you," responded Samuel. Then turning to me he said, "But what about you, Mr Woodward? I will not be able to give you a lift into town in the horse and trap."

"Not to worry, Samuel," I said. "I will walk. I think the exercise will be good for me."

"Are you sure?" he asked, seeking confirmation, and perhaps hoping that I might suggest cancelling the lesson so that he could take me to town and see me off on my journey.

"Yes, Samuel, I am certain. It will be a nice walk. I will be spending most of the time on Wednesday and Thursday sitting in an uncomfortable coach, so a stroll into town will be most welcome."

Samuel departed and once more Lucy and I spent the late afternoon and early evening together. We went out for one of our wanders along the paths and byways, which inevitably led us back towards the village and Lucy's home. But as the moment of parting grew closer, Lucy became more anxious and the conversation eventually returned to the now familiar topic of my safety.

"Please be very careful, Benjamin," she said, her concern written plain on her face. Lucy stopped and turned to look at me, placing her hand palm down over my heart. She edged closer and my left hand naturally went to meet hers, now resting on my chest, while my right moved around her waist. I pulled her closer and kissed her, and then I stopped and just looked at her. We gazed once more into each other's eyes and one word floated into my mind – surrender!

"Do not worry, my love," I said, trying to be as reassuring as I could. "I will be all right. And do not be concerned about those highwaymen. Uncle Ralf exaggerates the problem. My trip will be highly uncomfortable, but uneventful. And I look forward to telling you all about it when I return."

Speaking softly she said, "I will pray to God that you will have a safe journey to London, that all will be well with you while you are there, and ask him to deliver you safely back to me. But I shall not rest easy till you are back here with me. Only then will my mind be at peace." She paused for a moment as if reflecting on the matter, and then she became agitated. "Oh, Benjamin, please think again, for I have a bad feeling about this."

Once more I tried to calm her, and succeeded to a small degree. "Please," I said earnestly, "let us not part in such a way."

She forced herself to smile. "Very well. You are right. We should not say our farewells under the shadow of my apprehensions."

We resumed our walk, but each of us kept to our own thoughts and only when we had reached the steps leading up to the front door of her home did we speak again.

"So this is it," Lucy said, now sounding resigned to the fact that I was determined to make the journey to London, and no words she could advance could sway me from that intention.

"Yes," I replied gently. "This is it. Tomorrow I shall be on my way. When you come to my home with Samuel, I will be in town waiting for my coach. By the time the lesson is finished I will be embarking upon my adventure."

"I will be thinking of you always, until you are back here with me."

"And I will be thinking of you. Wherever I go, you shall be in my mind, my constant companion."

We kissed once more, and then she went in. I turned away and made my way back home. All was now arranged – all I had to do was to begin my trip.

CHAPTER 21

I set off on my journey very early on the Tuesday afternoon. The first part was a slow amble into town, where I planned to arrive in good time to buy, from the landlord of the Cock Inn, some provisions for the long coach ride ahead of me.

In the months that I had spent in my new life, I had travelled on many occasions along the lane that led to town. It was very peaceful – what a contrast with the world I had left behind. The mid-eighteenth century was an age without weapons of mass destruction, industrialised warfare, international terrorism, environmental pollution, traffic congestion, global warming, loss of biodiversity, resource depletion – challenges that if not properly addressed would lead eventually to dire consequences for the modern world. But the challenges are alas, in reality, only of secondary importance to those in power, compared with the dominating interest of ensuring continued economic growth, regardless of the consequences, and which is increasingly being driven by materialism and greed (private and corporate), which are, without a doubt, two key issues that need to be addressed as part of any effort to develop a sustainable world.

The mid-eighteenth century was a much simpler time and place. Technology was not very evident in people's lives. There were none of the complications of modern living, the stress of a fast-paced life, and the pressure to spend money. Yet, I also knew that in the early 1750s, the world was on the edge of a major transformation. Britain was on the cusp of the Industrial Revolution and the beginning of the age of industrial engineering. Society was about to be changed in ways that the people around me would not understand. The way of life that I was now part of, which had remained largely unchanged for centuries, was about to begin to disappear. It was the end of an era, or the beginning of a new age, depending on how one looked at it. Somewhere in England, men, pioneers of the Industrial Revolution, were taking the first small steps that would lead to my world, my time, with all its technology and drawbacks, but also all the items and facilities that made life for the majority, at least in the developed world, more than just an existence.

I am not fully sure why – perhaps it was the benefit of being able to see my own time from the perspective of an earlier period, along with insights that had come from knowing the past in a way that no historian had ever done – but I now realised that the world I had come from was also on the cusp of a momentous change. The direction that this would take was still unclear, for it was evident to me that the technological civilisation I had come from was beginning to disintegrate, as humankind continued to consume resources that were already in short supply, with each generation taking more than it was entitled to, and in so doing taking (perhaps robbing is a better word) that which belonged to future generations. And in this respect I realised that my own profession was right at the core of this behaviour, which I was in no doubt would be condemned by future engineers as unethical and unprofessional – that is, if the world survived long enough for such judgements to be made.

Survival, of course, I could now see was in doubt, as politicians, businesses, and people such as engineers were assuming that the civilisation that had emerged from the Industrial Revolution could actually in some way be adjusted to be sustainable. At that moment in time, it struck me as rather ridiculous to think that constructing wind farms, tidal barrages and the like, building more nuclear power stations, further increasing the industrialisation of agriculture, and implementing more and more resource-intensive projects would save the modern world. This thinking belonged to the mindset of people still trapped by the ideology of the industrial era, and in effect involved not responding to the real problems, but just dealing with symptoms and applying more of what had in fact created the circumstances that contemporary civilisation faced.

And it was not as though there was no alternative, for it was already apparent that people at grassroots level were taking control, in effect bypassing politicians and the professionals, creating for themselves, in their own lives, a more sustainable way of living. This other road, largely unexplored by engineers, and just as exciting as any resource-intensive project, already had a name in my own time – it is called *Transition*, a movement started by ordinary people who, it seems, know better than so-called experts that our modern world cannot be made sustainable without major changes. I made a mental note at this point to find out more about this when I did eventually return to my own age, and to ask my professional institution why they continually fed the profession with a diet of technology-based palliatives, while taking little notice of concepts that were better aligned with addressing the challenges faced by the people of my age.

Having the benefit of being able to see the world from two very different, yet in some ways remarkably similar ages also helped me to realise that people can be happy in many circumstances, including those that prevailed in the 1750s, but I knew that they could be unhappy as well. And so it was in the twenty-first century. We all have, regardless of the era in which we live in, the capacity to be both content and discontent, and I knew, given the place where I had come from, that to experience sadness in either age could be a bad experience. But in the end, where would I be better off? Was it in 1751 with Lucy, in a time and place where I would always be a visitor, or in the twenty-first century, with all that I valued, with Helen, where I actually belonged, even though there were increasingly many bad features of that age that I could no longer accept or tolerate?

This philosophical pondering would, I think, have gone on for most of the journey into town. I was definitely lost in my own thoughts when it happened. I heard the snap of a branch behind me and then all of a sudden there was pain. I had been struck on the back of the head. I started to fall to the ground, but before I hit it I blacked out. This was my last recollection before losing consciousness.

When I came around my head was hurting, throbbing at the back with the pain from whatever it was that had struck me. I was confused about my surroundings and not sure where I was. The place was dark, yet light was seeping through what appeared to be slits in the wall. At that point I was still not sufficiently conscious to assess the building. I had also forgotten that I was in 1751, and I wondered if I was in hospital. But this was just one of several thoughts running through my mind at that time.

My vision was blurred. I was vaguely conscious of the presence of someone else, sitting and watching me. I also realised after a while that I was not lying down, and I felt very uncomfortable, and it eventually dawned on me that it was not a chair on which I was seated. My arms were also hurting and I tried to move them, but found that I could not.

It took several minutes for my vision to return to normal and for the circumstances in which I found myself to sink in. I knew that I had somehow been hit on my head and that I had fallen. My twenty-first-century logic told me that in such circumstances I should expect to be in an accident and emergency department of a hospital. But such places are bright and clean, not dark and full of straw, for I had realised by now that I was sitting among straw. But, of course, I had had an accident in 1751, so my expectations were wrong. Then it further dawned on me that someone must have picked me up and moved me somewhere, for it was now clear to me that I was in a barn.

I tried to move, but strangely I was unable to do so. My hands were tied behind my back, but also bound in a way that prevented me from moving very much. I became conscious of the fact that I was tethered to one of the large vertical support beams holding up the roof of the building, and I was up near the roof in what I assumed was the hayloft. I began to wonder what was going on, and then I heard a voice.

"So you are back, you scumbag."

I recognised this voice, with its mocking and arrogant tone. It was Walter Smythe, and it was he who I had seen through my blurred vision.

He was sitting on a bale of straw, looking at me, contempt in his eyes and a grin on his face, sure in the knowledge that I was unable to escape and that all I could do was to lie there and take whatever punishment he wanted to bestow on me.

With a struggle I managed to position myself so I could better see my tormentor, who began to speak again.

"I understand that you are off to London," he said mockingly. "But you are not going anywhere except to hell. You see, I do not like people who humiliate me in front of a peasant such as that young Jones boy, and I certainly do not like people who take my clothes. But what really makes me hate you is that you have taken my woman from me. You are always together – walking, cuddling, kissing and embracing each other. Only yesterday you were with her, holding hands, you gazing into her eyes, she gazing back into yours, your love for one another so evident in your silly expressions.

314

Well, she is never going to see you again, never mind kiss you. One day she will be mine, and I do not want the likes of you touching my property again."

I looked at him in disbelief, but I did not want to risk annoying him further, for by this time my wits were returning and I had now realised that I was in a very dangerous situation. Lucy's concerns about my safety had not been unfounded after all.

"Very quiet, I see," he observed, when he realised that I was not going to be easily provoked into a reaction by his venomous words. "You might be wondering, though, what I have in mind for you," he said continuing his gloating.

This was very true, for I was beginning to have some concerns about his intentions, given his previous statement that I would never see Lucy again, but I did not want to ask. I did not, however, need to query him about this thought, for he was all too eager to tell me.

"When people cross me, I tend to make sure that they never do it again. A good beating from one of my more nefarious acquaintances if usually enough, but in your case you have crossed me too many times and to an extent that I do not think that I can allow you to live. What I have not yet decided is how to dispose of you."

My faculties had by this stage returned and I was fully alert. As his intention became clear my senses immediately became amplified. I felt fear and the adrenaline release increased the pace of my heartbeat, but there was no possibility of flight.

315

Evidently Smythe saw that I was afraid, for he continued to describe to me, tauntingly, what he might do to bring my life to an end. "No one is going to miss you, are they?" he asked rhetorically. "Your friends Lucy and Samuel think you are in London. But here you are with me in a deserted barn, miles from anywhere. You could yell and scream for days but no one would ever hear you. How does that make you feel?"

I did not answer this question, but remained silent.

But Smythe did not seem to want answers. His main concern was to talk, to tell me about my fate, to demonstrate his contempt for me, to subject me to his mental torture, to demonstrate his control over my life, and I listened, waiting for the news.

"I could leave you here to die of thirst and hunger, and come back once you are dead and remove the rope that binds you. Or I could have you hanged from one of those beams up there," he said, pointing upwards.

"Do you not think that someone might be suspicious?" I finally asked.

"The barn is disused and on my father's land. No one ever comes here. It could be decades before anyone ever discovered your body. I would remove traces of all that might cause suspicion. By the time you were found there would be no way of identifying you. People would assume that you had committed suicide or just died here from some illness."

I knew that he was probably right. No one would be coming to rescue me as they were not expecting to see me for well over a week. If I never came back Lucy might assume that I had deserted her, or that some misfortune had befallen me, far away in London.

It seemed that I was the architect of the circumstances that would enable Walter Smythe to exact revenge on me and to get away with it.

Smythe rose from the straw bale he had been sitting on. "I am going home now to think over your fate."

He climbed down the ladder to the ground floor and I heard him pass through the barn door, which had rotted from exposure to the elements. He walked away along the track that led to the barn. I was alone.

I waited for about half an hour; then I started to yell for help. Smythe had said that no one would hear me but I felt that I had to try. After a few cries, I would stop and listen in the hope of an answer or the sound of approaching footsteps – someone coming to see what was going on. But there was no response. No one came, not a soul, and I remained, as Smythe had predicted, unheard and helpless. So I yelled again, then again, and continued to do so for what seemed an age. I had no sense of time. Outside the world continued on its relentless journey through time and space, while I was constrained within the walls of some forgotten place. Here I would be entombed, and no one would ever know. I would be lost forever.

My throat was hoarse with shouting so I gave up that line of action and sat thinking about how I might extract myself from my predicament. I tried to loosen the rope that bound me to my position in the hayloft, but alas it was tied all too well. I then considered trying to break the wooden beam that I was tied to. If the wood were rotten as a result of age, which was quite possible, I might be able to snap it and free myself. However, there was a danger that I might bring down the roof in the process, thus saving Smythe the trouble of having to kill me. Nevertheless, I considered this a risk worth taking; it was better than just sitting and waiting for death.

So I endeavoured to push the beam, but I could not get enough leverage in any position that I could force myself into, and after struggling for a while I eventually gave up on this idea, for it was also evident to me that the beam, while old and rotten in places, was too thick to be completely damaged by age and insects.

I was now at a loss for what to do, not being able to see further possibilities for escape. It was at that moment that the nature of my plight began to dawn on me. My mind turned to contemplating the thought that I was probably not going to escape and that I would have to face death at the hands of Walter Smythe. He had told me that he was going to kill me and I did not doubt that he was capable of murder, and that he would do as he had indicated.

How cruel of him! He had deliberately told me that I was going to die, and then he had left me to ponder this.

Now, death is not a subject that many people think about in their life. We all die, that is for sure, but most folk die abed, or through an illness or as a consequence of an accident. Very few die at the hands of others, but to know that a person is intent on killing you raises an awful sensation in the mind. One can imagine the act, the pain, the desperation to live, the fear, the feeling of life ebbing away. One wants to block out such thoughts, but they loom like dark clouds on the horizon on a sunny day, threatening to black out the light and bring with it all manner of unpleasantness.

This is how it was with me on that summer's evening. I should have been onboard a stagecoach heading for London. All whom I knew in this time, my few dear friends, assumed that this is where I was. None were aware that I was tied up in a disused barn close by. While Lucy and Samuel thought of me on my way to London, imagining the sights that I would see, with Lucy worrying about the dangers that I might face in the capital city, they did not and would not know of my predicament closer to home. I would die but a few miles from these two good people and they would remain ignorant of this.

And far off, in a distant time and place, my other love, my Helen: what of her? What would happen when I died here in the past? How would that reshape the future? Would the consequences of my death ripple across the ages, changing the world beyond recognition?

Suddenly I felt a longing to be with Helen again, to see her, to touch her, to lie with her. Once more I wanted to feel her warm soft skin against my own, to wrap my arms around her, to be one with her, to share our love, but alas, no, this would never be again.

I knew this was hypocritical of me, for I had fallen in love with another, and had lost all rights to draw comfort from the thought of Helen at this time of need. How could I even dare to think of Helen, the one I had betrayed, who did not deserve such treatment?

I was doomed to die alone, not knowing how the complexities of my circumstances would change the future. Perhaps all memories, all knowledge of me, would be wiped away. Perhaps it would be as though I had never existed, as if I had never made a mark upon the world. It was likely that Helen would not grieve for me because she would never have known me.

I did not know the answers to these questions, because, like many in the modern world, I did not know what I did not know, and went about living my life as though there were no such thing as unintended and unforeseen consequences. The *risks can be managed*, we say. What nonsense!

I became miserable as a result of these reflections. The usual *Why me? If only* ... thoughts came into my mind. But of course one can think like this, but it is the nature of life to venture forth. Life is a risk, and to take no risks is not to live. To opt for safety over discovery, development, learning and growth is to choose to stagnate, to abdicate responsibility, to become uninvolved. I had chosen to take an opportunity that had presented itself to me, and now I was facing the consequences. I should have listened to that mysterious voice, now long silent, for it seemed to me, at that moment in time, that it had spoken words of wisdom: the *risks cannot be managed*!

I realised that self-pity would serve no purpose. I could just lie where I was, give up and await my fate, as if I were an animal being led to the slaughter. Or I could resist, fight back, and go down knowing that I had done all within my power to struggle against my captor, my tormentor, my assassin.

The moment of despair was over. Once more I was determined to overcome, to find a way to escape, or, failing that, to make Walter Smythe know that he was dealing with someone who would not submit quietly to whatever dastardly act he had in mind.

I returned to the matter of thinking through the possibilities for escape, but alas none presented themselves to me. So I considered what might happen when Smythe came back. Although my hands were tied behind my back, my feet were unfettered. That gave me two weapons to use against my foe. I also had my mind, which was now full of determination not to allow Smythe to murder me unopposed. And I also had the advantage of surprise, for he seemed to be the sort of person who underestimated people. He too did not recognise that life is full of the unexpected!

I thought through the likely scenarios, of Smythe returning alone, or with an accomplice or accomplices, and what might happen. I realised that I stood my best chance if he came alone; if he returned with others they would easily overpower me. I also reckoned that if I were to be untied before being killed, that too would provide me with an opportunity to attack or to escape.

321

I considered that the use of force, extreme and deadly force if necessary, was under the circumstances legitimate; my life was being threatened and I felt justified in defending myself with whatever weapons or implements I could lay my hands on. And there were many, for I was imprisoned in an old barn where there were several rusting, but still sharp, agricultural tools lying about that had obviously been abandoned ages ago, along with the barn. While these tools were self-evidently not as sharp as they once had been, and all the metal surfaces had accumulated a layer of rust, they would be adequate for the purpose I had in mind.

Then a thought occurred of using one of these implements to cut free the ropes that bound me to the support pillar. I quickly glanced around to see if there were any that might be within my reach. There were none, but there was a large pile of old straw close by, and being willing to consider every possibility, I began, with great difficulty, to manoeuvre myself into a position to explore with my feet whether there were any objects under this mound. It was then that I heard the sound.

I froze. My fear, which I had temporarily lost in the planning of my defence, quickly returned. I began to perspire and there was a churning feeling in my stomach. I knew that it could only be Smythe returning, and thoughts of what was about to happen to me began to take control. I did not want to die. I was not ready to die. I was too young to die. The rest of my life lay ahead of me. I was in my prime, and I was about to be prematurely terminated by a psychopath. Awareness of all that I could have done with the time that I had already had in this world, and with the time that was potentially still ahead of me, began to fill my thoughts.

But when one's life hangs by a thread, when one is faced with a life-or-death predicament, when one's continued existence depends upon making the right decision, and rapidly, it is surprising how focused the mind can become. I found all the thoughts that had, but a few moments previously, being filling my consciousness, now being driven out by alertness and a solidness of purpose that I had not experienced before. My mind became clear, and for a brief moment in time a feeling of peace came over me. Then I was ready – prepared to deal with Smythe and whomever else he might have in tow.

Outside the sun was now lower in the sky and the light cast longer shadows. Inside the barn was slightly gloomier than it had been, as the light that had earlier streamed through the cracks and slits in the walls began to fade. In this murkiness I heard the barn door open and perceived two people enter; Smythe had not come alone!

CHAPTER 22

The light was too dim to make him out properly, to see clearly Smythe and his accomplice. All I perceived were two dark figures, but they were whispering to each other and seemed to be looking about them. Then I heard a voice call my name.

"Benjamin. Where are you?"

I knew that voice, and it was full of concern. This was not the voice of Smythe, but a welcoming and friendly sound, one that I had not expected ever to hear again. It was fair Lucy who now stood below in the gloom, and I surmised that the person next to her was Samuel.

"Is that you, Lucy?" I asked, relieved, but already knowing the answer. "I am up here, tied up. Is that Samuel with you?"

"Yes, sir, it is me," came Samuel's reply.

"Come up and untie me, and hurry," I said. "But be careful. This place is old and no doubt the wood is rotten in places."

I heard someone climbing the ladder that led to the hayloft. Shortly Samuel's smiling face appeared, and he climbed off the ladder and ran over to me.

"I am glad to see you," I said happily. "Get me free of these ropes."

Samuel made an attempt to untie the knots but his small hands were not up to the task.

"I cannot do it," he said beginning to sound scared and worried.

"Do not fret about it. See that scythe over there," I said, gesturing with my head to indicate the direction, "go and get that and try to cut though the rope."

Samuel did as I suggested. While he was cutting at the rope Lucy, impatient to see for herself that I was all right, had climbed the ladder and stepped into the hayloft. She quickly moved over to where I was constrained.

"Here, Samuel, let me help you," she said. She took the scythe from his hands and began cutting.

"You should have stayed down on the barn floor. It is not safe up here," I said, concerned.

"Oh, shush, you," she responded. "You are a fine one to be talking. You men! I am quite capable of climbing a ladder, and poor Samuel here is struggling."

She smiled at me while saying this, and I smiled back. I was relieved to be rescued and in truth did not mind that Lucy had climbed what might have been a rotten and dangerous old ladder.

It took some effort to cut through the ropes, but eventually I was free. Lucy immediately hugged me and held on tightly.

"I thought I had lost you," she said, now sounding frightened. "I told you, but you would not listen. Never, ever, do anything again that puts you in danger. I have lost one love, and I am not going to lose another."

I did not respond at that moment in time, and just let her hold onto me. But my arms were hurting and eventually I had to struggle free from her embrace, and it was a relief to be able to bring my arms forward and place them in front of me. But there was cramp in my limbs from being tied up in one position for several hours. My head was also hurting.

I began to rotate my hands and stretch and contract, exercising the joints in my hand and arm. I rubbed my left arm with my right hand.

"Cramp," I said to Lucy.

She was kneeling down and she took my hands in hers and began to manipulate them, rubbing them softly, stretching and moving my arms.

"This will get the blood circulating again," she said, so softly and sweetly.

As she did this she occasionally glanced into my eyes, and I could see that there were no longer any barriers between us – nearly time for complete surrender! Over the months we had grown closer, and gradually she had slowly sought more physical contact. But one step she had not taken.

I smiled at her and then I enquired how they had come to be there, given that they would have thought me on my way to London.

"It was Samuel here who found you. He saw Walter Smythe and another man attack you while you were walking into town."

"I had been out wandering the lanes, and I was slowly making my way towards your house in time for my lesson with Miss Lucy," interjected Samuel.

"Yes," continued Lucy, "and he very wisely followed you here, and kept an eye on what was going on. He saw the other man leave and then later Smythe departed so he knew that they had left you here on your own. In the meantime I turned up at your house expecting to be greeted by Samuel, but he never came, so after waiting for a while I decided to return home. Then a little while later Samuel turned up at my door. I assumed that he had come to apologise for missing his lesson, but then he told me what had occurred."

"Most people would not have believed such a tale," I said.

"Yes, that is true," replied Lucy. "But I have known Samuel since he was a little boy and he is not the sort to make up stories, and I did warn you about Walter Smythe."

"Yes, you did. You are wiser than your years," I said in a complimentary way.

"My mother also says that as well."

"She is right. So once Samuel had told you about what happened you came to rescue me?"

"Yes, we did." She paused for a moment, as if not sure of herself, but whatever doubts she might have had, she continued. "What was Walter Smythe going to do with you?" she asked hesitantly.

I looked at here for a moment and then replied, "He was going to kill me."

327

She stopped massaging my hands and arms and she moved her hands so that they were holding mine and her grip tightened. She looked at me once more, straight in the eye, but did not speak. She did not have to. I could see all that she would have said written on her face and expressed in her eyes. And at that moment I knew also that from now on we would be inseparable.

I could have stayed with her, as we were, all evening, well into the dark hours of the night, but Samuel was there and I knew also that we had to get away from the barn before Smythe returned.

"We should leave this place before Smythe comes back," I said.

No sooner were the words out of my mouth than we heard the sound of someone approaching the barn. It could be no other person but Smythe.

A look of alarm appeared on Lucy's face. I placed my index finger on my lips, indicating to them both to be quiet. I waved them towards the back of the hayloft where they could hide behind some bales of straw. This they quickly did and then I returned to my sitting position, against the support pillar, and placed my hands behind me, pretending that they were tied.

Walter Smythe walked into the barn, alone, and carrying a bottle in one hand – he was obviously drunk.

CHAPTER 23

Smyth was a drinking man. He consumed alcohol regularly, both whisky and brandy, and in great quantities. He could afford to. But although he was hardened to the worst effects of strong spirit, it did cause him to slur his speech when he had drunk too much, and his balance was also affected. The worst impact, however, was upon his mood, amplifying his most unpleasant characteristics, and making him even more bad tempered than when sober. Thus, when he entered the barn he was, more or less, in control of himself, except that he was swaggering slightly and was even more out of humour than when he had left.

"I am back," Smythe shouted. "And I have come to tell you your fate, you piece of human filth."

The extent of his arrogance was evident in his voice. He wasted no time in shouting more profanities and headed straight for the ladder. Still holding the brandy bottle, he began to climb up to the hayloft.

"I am coming," he shouted. "I am coming to see my prisoner."

He stopped for a moment, took a swig from the brandy bottle and then continued to climb. It was not long before he was standing staring down at me, smirking, looking very pleased with himself.

"You know," he began, "your first trespass against me I might have turned a blind eye to. After all, you are a stranger in these parts and you were not to know who I am. To you it just looked as though I was attacking a young lad. How could you know that he was just scum, the offspring of a whore and a peasant? I might have even forgiven you for over-paying my tailor to have my new clothes modified to your own measurements. I have a sneaking admiration for that."

His tone was mocking, but that changed when he addressed the topic of Lucy. "But what I cannot forgive," he continued, sounding bitter, his voice full of hatred, "is stealing my woman. Lucy is mine, and by God I will have her one way or another, and no one is going to get in my way, not least some newly arrived colonial who does not know his place."

At that point Lucy, unable to tolerate being spoken about in such a way, stepped forward out of the gloom at the rear of the hayloft.

"How dare you talk about me in such a way," she said angrily.

Smythe was taken aback by Lucy's sudden appearance, and for a moment he seemed unsure of himself, but he quickly recovered from the initial surprise.

"Well, look what we have here," Smythe said. "It is Miss Lucy come to see her lover. Oh, and the Jones brat as well!"

Following Lucy's bold move to challenge Smythe, Samuel had also revealed himself.

"Do not dare to presume," said Lucy indignantly, "that I am, as you put it, your woman. I would never marry you. I would rather die than spend one moment of my life in your company."

Smythe carefully put down his bottle of brandy. "Marry me," he said in a sinister tone. "No, I do not suppose that you would, now that you have the colonial. But there are more ways than one of making you mine, of having you."

He stepped forward towards Lucy and grabbed her, forcing her to the floor. She tried to resist, but it was to no avail for he was too strong for her. Young Samuel was at a loss for what to do. He tried to pull at Smythe's coat tails, but Smythe just pushed him away with a force that sent Samuel flying across the hayloft.

"What you need, young lass, is someone to teach you a lesson, and I am the person to do just that. You need to learn some respect for you superiors. Learn some manners."

As he was saying this he was sitting astride Lucy, pinning her arms down by the wrists either side of her head. He moved to force a kiss upon her.

I jumped up and sprang to where he had pinned Lucy to the floor, where he was in the process of trying to force himself upon her, and in a moment I was pulling him off.

"Oh, no, Smythe. That is not how you treat a woman," I shouted.

Having forced Smythe to let go I could now see his face and he was obviously surprised to discover I was free. Then it dawned on him that Lucy had undone my bonds, for he glanced at her and then back at me. Being the worse for drink and in a foul mood he had not bothered to think through the possible consequences of Lucy's presence and he was too intent on forcing himself upon her to logically analyse what was going on. He was man blinded by his desires and now he was facing the consequences. Note the word, for it is key to understanding how to behave differently.

I stood up and went to help Lucy to her feet. I quickly moved her and Samuel towards the ladder.

"Quickly," I said with a tone of urgency, "down the ladder and get away from here. I will keep him at bay until you are outside."

"But what about you?" Lucy started, with both fear and concern evident in her voice.

"I will be all right," I said as reassuringly as possible. "Quick! Go!" I shouted.

No sooner had I said this than Smythe was back up on his feet, fully recovered, only this time he was holding his brandy bottle by the neck, preparing to use it as a weapon to hit me over the head. I edged sideways, intending to draw him away from Lucy, Samuel and the ladder. The ploy worked. His anger was exclusively directed at me for the moment and he badly wanted to hurt me. He was in a blind rage and solely intent upon doing as much damage as he could to me. I believed at that moment in time that he was going to fulfil his early threat and was about to attempt to kill me. He lifted the bottle and charged at me as if he were a wild animal, the precious golden-brown liquid flowing down his sleeve as he

332

raised the bottle further, preparing to strike with all the force he could muster.

I waited for him to reach me. It seemed an eternity, standing, watching him come closer, but it was in fact only a fraction of a second. Timing was of the essence for what I had in mind. He was nearly upon me. Out of the corner of my eye I could see that Lucy had frozen on the ladder and was about to scream, sensing that my time was up and that Smythe would be victorious. But I knew exactly what I was doing. It was time – the moment had arrived. I threw myself down to the floor, so that when Smythe reached the point where I had been standing, all that was left of me at that spot were my feet.

Smythe had gained some momentum and was not going to be able to stop. I thrust my right foot in front of Smyth's lower legs, tripping him up and sending him flying into the air. But there was nowhere for him to land in the hayloft, for we were very close to the edge of it. He went over and down headfirst. I heard a terrible cracking sound as his head, taking the full force of the impact, hit the stone-flagged floor below. Then the brandy bottle landed nearby where he lay, smashing into several pieces, the remaining contents spilling on the floor of the barn.

Lucy watched on as all this happened. She did not scream, but hurried back up the few steps of the ladder that she had descended and rushed over to me.

"Are you all right?" she asked, desperate for reassurance that I was not hurt. I sat up, and she held me, my

333

head resting against her breast. It was warm and comforting, and once again I knew we belonged together.

Lucy stroked my hair, but my head hurt too much to allow her to continue, despite how nice it was to have such a young and beautiful woman caressing me and allowing her breast to be a resting place for my throbbing skull. For, you see, the back of my head was cut and bruised as a result of being hit in the afternoon while walking along what I had thought was a quiet and safe country lane.

I raised my hand to hers and stopped her from stroking my head. I pulled it down to my chest and placed my other arm around her back.

"My head is hurting," I explained, in a soft, reassuring voice. "Otherwise I would stay here with you for eternity."

She set herself free from my embrace, gently placing my arm back where it had previously been, down by my side, and she moved my head away from her breast. She placed her hand on the side of my face and gazed at me once more – that look that spoke of giving herself to me.

"We think as one," she replied tenderly, "because to stay here with you for an eternity would be, for me, a state that I would gladly submit to. But we must leave now."

I had momentarily forgotten about Smythe, so lost was I in the gaze of this unusual woman. But as soon as she mentioned his name, my daydream was over, and the reality of our circumstance was pressing for my attention.

"Yes, let us go," I responded. "It will be a great relief to be out of this place."

We needed to see what state Smythe was in. He had hit the ground head first and the sound that the impact had made did not bode well for him. So with a little help from Lucy I was soon on my feet, but starting to feel the effects of being abused by Smythe, and being pushed around and falling on the floor. I judged that there would be a few bruises on my body by morning.

Together, holding hands, we stepped forward to the edge of the hayloft and looked down. There was Smythe, lying motionless on the floor. There was a pool of blood surrounding his head. Samuel had climbed down the ladder and was standing close by. He looked up and the expression on his face told us both that we could expect no more trouble from Smythe.

We descended the ladder and I checked to see if there were signs of life, but it was clear that there was no life left in Smythe. "He is dead," I announced, with a note of sadness in my voice, for although the man had tried to kill me, I would have avoided the present circumstance if that had been possible.

"What should we do?" asked Lucy, sounding unsure of herself.

I was silent for a moment. Lucy and Samuel both looked at me, waiting for leadership, for a decision. I thought about the circumstances in which we now found ourselves. I did not want complications, or anyone asking questions, or to place Lucy and Samuel in a position where they too would be probed. I knew from what Smythe had told me that the barn was deserted and not visited by anyone. He was lying there on the floor smelling of alcohol, his clothes wet with the stuff, and his broken bottle lying close by. Up in the hayloft there was only one sign that suggested anyone else had been there – my bag and the ropes that had bound me.

I knew also that there were no forensics, and no police force to carry out an investigation into Smythe's death, just magistrates and local constables, who probably would not believe any of us if we were to report what had happened. Smythe's social standing would work against us as well. The risk was not to be taken.

"Stay here," I said forcefully.

I climbed back up into the hayloft, recovered my bag and the ropes, placing the latter in the bag. I quickly tidied up, removing all signs that there had been a struggle. I placed the scythe on the spot where it had previously lain, forgotten for many years, and then rejoined Lucy and Samuel.

"Smythe is beyond our help," I began. "In his short life he persecuted you, Samuel, falsely imprisoned me, threatened to murder me, attempted to rape you, Lucy, and then, but a few moments ago, tried to kill me. I had no choice but to defend myself. What happened to Smythe is a result of his own obsessions, bitterness and hatred. We have not committed here any actions that we should be ashamed of. We should feel no remorse. I say that we leave him here where he lies and say no more of this. If they find him it will be concluded that he fell while drunk. That will be the end of it. There is no point in becoming involved."

I now looked at Lucy and Samuel, an unspoken question hovering in my mind, which both understood without any need for articulation.

"What about the other man who helped Smythe to abduct you?" asked Samuel. "Will he not speak of the matter?"

"What will he say? That he attacked me along with Smythe, knocked me out, and then imprisoned me here with the intention of killing me?" I said in reply. "I do not think so," I continued. "He will not want to let on that he was here. It might raise suspicions that he attacked Smythe. No, I think we can be sure that he will not speak of this. What has happened here is natural justice. Smythe has paid for his crimes. We are not to blame. There is no point in reporting this matter. It will be seen as an accident arising from Smythe's drunkenness."

Lucy and Samuel listened carefully to my arguments. When I had stopped talking they were both quiet for a while, reflecting upon what I had said. Then Lucy spoke. "Very well," she responded, "so be it. We will not speak of this again." Then she turned to Samuel and said, "Samuel, it is up to you now. What is your decision?"

Samuel looked up, first at Lucy, then at me, and said, "You are both my friends. You have stood up for me, protected me, and helped me. Now I will do the same for you both. Never will I reveal to anyone what has happened here. Smythe will never persecute me again. We will leave him where he lies and say no more of him or what happened here."

And then he held out his hand and offered it to me, and I took it, and with a handshake we sealed our agreement.

"Well said," I replied. "Spoken as a true man."

Then he did the same to Lucy. She accepted the offer, and so it was that our pact was sealed: there would never be further reference to the incident; it would not be revealed to anyone; we would hold true to our promise for the rest of our lives.

And it was as three friends – bound together by our common encounter with a man who in the twenty-first century would be regarded as suffering from some psychological disorder – that we stepped forth from that barn into the fading light of a glorious sunset.

And I have to say that our minds were not troubled at all by what we had agreed. No doubt, at some future moment in time, we would reflect on what had occurred, but for now we were all glad to be out of danger.

I stood for a moment looking out across the fields. Insects darted about, and on the horizon the sun has taken on the appearance of a large orange ball. This was freedom. I had only been imprisoned for a few hours, but in that brief interlude, my life had been threatened in both word and deed. Now, for the first time in my short existence, I knew the value of life and liberty. I also realised that it is not just ropes that can bind a person; people make their own prison bars through their conventions, dogmas, self-imposed limitations and unwillingness to explore the new and the unusual.

Lucy stood beside me and looped her arm through mine. We stood there looking as though we were a couple. To be honest I felt we were a couple. We had only known each other for twelve months, but already it felt that there was longevity to our friendship that spanned a lifetime rather than months.

"Come, Lucy," I said in a firm and commanding voice, "let us be away from here."

And we walked, arm in arm, away from the barn, with Samuel leading the way. If anyone had seen us they would have thought us a family, husband and wife with their child, out for a walk on a summer's evening. And in many respects we had become a family. We were bound together by a mutual experience, a shared secret, a common foe. Together we had faced this enemy and defeated him. We were all now free from his tyranny – Samuel from the persecution that he had suffered over several years and Lucy from the menace of unsought and unwanted attentions. As for myself, I could now walk in this world free from the danger of being physically attacked by a dangerous man.

So, onward we strolled, all three of us, quiet and reflective, until we reached my house, the Time House. When we arrived, Lucy spoke to Samuel. "Now Samuel," she began, in a tone indicating that she was not prepared to hear any objections, "you run along home. Your mother and father will be wondering where you are."

Samuel looked at me, the expression on his face pleading for my intervention. "Go on, Samuel," I said, "get yourself home. We have had enough adventure for one day. Time to get some rest."

Samuel looked disappointed, as if he was relying on me to save him from Lucy's strong will. But I sensed that Lucy had a purpose in sending Samuel home, for she had not indicated that she would be heading for home herself.

Samuel relented. "When will I see you again?" he asked me.

"I am not sure," I replied. "I should have been on my way to London by now, so I am going to have to reconsider my plans, and see what my options are. I will let you know, one way or another, what I decide."

"All right, then. I will wait for your message," he said rather disappointedly. "Good night then, Miss Lucy, Mr Woodward."

"Good night," responded Lucy.

I added my own farewell, and then Samuel walked off, and we watched him for a while. Then Lucy took me by the hand. "Let us get those scratches and cuts cleaned up," she said, and then she started to lead me up the front path around to the rear of the house.

In my bag I had a small twenty-first-century first-aid kit, one aspect of my own time that I was willing to risk bringing with me, thinking that the potential benefits outweighed the dangers. I took some paracetamol tablets for my headache and some ibuprofen tablets to reduce the inflammation around my head wound. Neither of these did Lucy see. Having poured some antiseptic into a small bowl I handed it to Lucy along with some cotton wool.

"Here, clean the wounds with this," I instructed. She looked at the cotton-wool balls with some surprise, for she had not seen anything of this kind before. I noted that she was curious.

"They are from the cotton plant," I said. "There are a lot of them in the American Colonies."

"Oh," she replied. "And the liquid, I have never smelt the likes of this before. What is it?"

"It is called antiseptic. It kills infections in wounds. It stings as well, so do not be surprised if I flinch when you wipe the wound."

I sat down in my chair and I demonstrated to Lucy what to do and she then gently washed the cut on the back of my head.

After she had carefully attended to my injuries, she put down the bowl and knelt down in front of me, placed my hands in hers, and gazed at me, her stare penetrating and meaningful. I could not resist her. I did not want to stop looking into those beautiful blue eyes. It felt as though I was in a warm sea, and I was lost in her gaze, enchanted and spellbound. All the while I felt emotions stirring and physical sensations travelling through my body, stimulating and heightening the senses.

I rose from the chair, still holding onto her hands. She rose from the floor with me and, when standing, I then placed my hands on her waist. She wrapped her arms around my

341

neck and slowly we moved closer together, until our lips met and we kissed, very gently and just for a few moments, and then we stopped. Continuing to hold each other, we spoke only with our eyes. Written in them I saw a multitude of emotions, thoughts and feelings – love, passion, submission, yearning and desire.

"Is this what you truly want?" I said softly. "We are not married and ..."

She placed a finger over my lips to silence my words. I stroked her hair, all the while gazing into her eyes, knowing that I loved her, that I wanted her, and that I could not resist.

"I do not know why," began Lucy, speaking with feeling, "but the first moment I saw you, emotions stirred in me. Here with you now, after all the months that have passed, after all the time we have spent together, I feel there is an aspect to our relationship that goes far beyond that which I had with my late husband. It is a strange sensation, but I know that I just want to be with you, to hold you, to give myself to you. Part of me is telling me that it is wrong, but it is only the conventions of my upbringing and I do not care anymore about them. I just want you. I am frightened that I am going to lose you, for there is a strangeness about you that speaks of worlds far away, a place where you belong but I cannot go."

I did not know what to say to this. I was hesitant, unsure of myself, not wanting to make assumptions, unsure about how people behaved in this age in circumstances such as this. Perhaps the gentlemanly act would have been to stop before we went too far, but I did not want to end that which I was enjoying.

I was about to reply when she kissed me again, but a much more passionate kiss than the previous one, not just lips gently placed against lips, but a kiss with real force; more inmate, more seductive, more inviting.

She stopped, looked at me and said, "It has been over nine years since my husband died. That is a long time never to have a man hold you close, to feel the warmth of human flesh, to be touched and caressed tenderly, to lie next to someone."

She stopped speaking and once more gazed into my eyes, all barriers down, no defences, nothing hidden, telling me to make love to her. Then she spoke softly, but with a forceful tone. "I give myself to you."

And then she took my right hand and moved it up, carefully placing it over her breast. The she looked at me once again, submissively. "I want you," I said.

"Take me," she replied lovingly. "I am yours."

I kissed her again, and deep down inside, I knew that I should not be been doing this. Here she was, beautiful Lucy, so close to me, offering herself to me. I could feel the warmth of her body. My passions were stirred and it was too late for reason. A stronger man might have been able to resist but, alas, strong I am not. A wiser man would not have put himself in a position where such might happen but, alas, wise I am not. Someone more in control would have taken control of the circumstance and directed Lucy away from where we were headed, but I now realised that I was not someone who was in control; so much for my self-delusions.

Such is the nature of life; everyone makes mistakes, and here I was doing just that. I knew that it was wrong, and that I would probably regret what I was about to do, but the biological need to reproduce was stronger at the moment than my intuition. Body and mind had taken precedence over soul.

I continued to kiss Lucy passionately, and she responded with equal fervour. Several times I ran my hands over her covered breast and down the sides of her body to her hips, and then back up again. Then the nature of the circumstances and the emotions of the moment took a hand. We were both caught up in a wave of passion that had now gone beyond the point of no return. She was offering herself to me; I wanted to make love to her and she wanted that as much as I did.

Within moments we had moved into my bedroom, had quickly removed our clothing, and lay together naked, bare flesh against bare flesh. Then it began, the consuming fire that made us both oblivious to the world, all inhibitions gone, a single focus on each other and the pleasure of the moment, leading to that brief instant of oneness with another human being, with the universe, and then the comfort of lying together, intertwined, in the knowledge that between us no more were there any barriers and that we had entered into a bond that no one could ever undo – my surrender was now complete!

So it was that we came to know one another. This is how we came to be intimate in a way that moves relationships into sacred ground, how we came to be close in both a physical and a spiritual way. As we lay there on my bed, holding onto each other, we were both silent, she gazing into my eyes, and I staring right back, speaking that language that only those who have experienced such a bonding can understand. This was not just casual sex, a one-off encounter, but love, the giving of one's body to another, freely and with joy. There was no dark shadow cast over us, just a knowledge that we had both found our soul mates.

We belonged together, but I knew that I had to choose, between her and Helen, but that my choice was not straightforward, for I did not belong in 1751. It was not my time, my era. I was of the twenty-first century, and how could I leave all that behind?

Although at that moment I was dwelling in a place and time that was not my world, I needed to be with Lucy, and not belonging in her age was an aspect of my circumstances that might come between us. By the normal laws of nature, as far as I understood them, I had no right to be where I was. As for Lucy, she did not belong in my time, nor was it likely that she could make that journey to the future, although I was not entirely sure of this. There was only one way to discover if this was possible, and this I would have to consider.

And there was Helen. I could not, and would not, divide my loyalties between Lucy and Helen. I knew too that this would not be easy, and as I lay there, I realised that I had created circumstances where I was going to have to hurt someone whom I loved, and in doing so I would hurt myself. Either way, be it Lucy or Helen that I said farewell to, I would have to bear the pain of losing someone whom I loved, but that was a minor issue considering that my predicament was one of my own making and that I alone was to blame. I could not transfer to anyone responsibility for what had transpired, and I would have to suffer the consequences of my actions and learn to live with them. I was beginning to see why the voice had warned me about what I was getting involved in.

But for now I was lost in the magic of the moment. Lying next to me was a beautiful woman, with character and intelligence. And at that moment in time, she was mine, and I was hers, and there was nothing separating us, dividing us, or driving us apart. We could be together for the rest of our lives, together for as long as we both lived. Only death would divide us, and even in death we would be as one, because we would always be remembered, by those who remained, as being one.

But precious moments in time such as these must all come to an end. Time is forever pressing. Lucy stirred and spoke, breaking the magic spell that was cast over us, tying us to that place, that moment, making us unwilling to part.

"I had better be getting back home," she said, with reluctance evident in her voice. She rose and sat up.

I looked up at her, saying, "Must you?"

"Indeed I must, for Mama will be beginning to wonder where I am."

I also rose and sat up, placing my arm around her shoulder. We fell back, and she rolled over on top of me and kissed me.

"Will there be more times similar to this?" she asked.

This question came as a surprise. "What makes you ask that? I want to be with you. I love you." I hoped that I was sounding convincing, for I did really mean what I was saying.

"You are not in any way similar to other men I have met. As I said before, there are features of your character that are different, as if you were from an entirely different place. I do not know what I mean, really. I cannot put my finger on it. My intuition is my guide in life, and that tells me to trust you, it tells me that I can give myself to you, but deep inside of me I have a feeling that this happiness that I feel at this moment in time will not last. There is a dark shadow lurking in the back of my mind."

"I know that, given the circumstances, with my links elsewhere, life may seem complicated," I said, trying to sound reassuring, "but ..."

She would not let me finish. Once again she placed a finger over my lips. "Do not say a word," she said. "We can talk about this some other time. Just hold me."

And I did. I held onto her tightly, not wanting to let go, and she too held onto me. For the time being we were safe together and we were both glad of that.

We lay there for a while, and then she rose once more, got off the bed and started to dress. I followed suit. We walked out of my bedroom and I looked sideways, at the

347

archway that led back to my own time. She noted that I was looking to my right, and she also glanced in that direction.

"Some time you must show me around your house," she said. "I would love to see what lies beyond that opening."

I smiled, but also at the same time wondered what exactly she could see. Perhaps she could pass through that opening, into my age, my world, and my life. We could be together in a different time and place, but would that work? How would I explain it to her? The idea seemed to raise innumerable questions.

I escorted her home. Hand in hand we walked, and all the time I was thinking of what we had just done together and of how I might take her with me, into a new life. Perhaps this, then, was the meaning behind the tragedy of which I have already spoken. Perhaps it was Lucy running away from her mother's home.

The thought that she might be able to accompany me back into my own time comforted me on my return journey as I strolled back to the Time House; I was very much looking forward to the next day and all the joys that it would bring.

CHAPTER 24

I was caught up in the excitement and ecstasy of a moment in time when just about every important aspect of my life seemed in place and aligned to ensure my happiness. I knew that I would be able to pass away my time with my beloved Lucy – tomorrow, the day after, and then the next, and onwards until an unknown moment in time, when nature, taking its natural course, would bring our relationship to an end. At least, that is how I imagined it. Until that moment in time came I wanted never to be apart from her.

As I made my way home, I focused my attention on Lucy and the physical intimacy that we had just experienced, and I became elated with the anticipation of further pleasures to come, of time to be spent together as lovers. Yet, even though I was full of joy, a dark shadow was present in the background, trying to spoil the perfect moment in time, moving my thoughts to Helen and my act of betrayal towards her. I tried to resist this, arguing to myself that this was an issue to be addressed in the future. This is how matters are when one is placed (when one places oneself) into a position where joy with one person comes at the expense of another. Although I tried to resist, I soon found myself falling from an elated frame of mind into a darker mood, as the prospect of the unpleasant steps that I would need to take began to become apparent, and then the inevitable feelings of guilt and regret began to flow through my thoughts. But then, I would recover, through a forced effort of focusing on Lucy, and all would then seem well once more.

Inherent in such mood swings was my assumption that I would choose Lucy over Helen, but it suddenly dawned on me while walking along that dark country lane that possibly I was being foolish. Perhaps I belonged with Helen, and maybe that was what Lucy was hinting at earlier. Lucy was no inexperienced young girl falling head-over-heels in love for the first time. Lucy was no novice. Her actions were those of a determined woman with experience of life and relationships. I was not the first to make love to her, and maybe she knew deep down that she had no chance of holding onto me. Time would, literally, carry me away from her, and while she genuinely had feelings for me, she may have been just grasping hold of a few moments of happiness, of physical intimacy, while she was able. When one has lost someone close, the awareness of how short life can be, of how little time we have, becomes more acute. People in such circumstances tend to value time, to reach out and grasp opportunities, no matter how fleeting they may be. And perhaps this is what Lucy was doing.

As I walked onwards, what Lucy had said caused new feelings to appear; doubt, uncertainty and apprehension dogged my footsteps home. I began to ponder the meaning of Lucy's words.

"There are features of your character that are different, as if you were from an entirely different place." That is what she had said. What did she mean by this? Had she guessed that I did not come from America, that I did not belong in her world, that I was a visitor from a far-off place, somewhere beyond the horizons of her imagination? She was an intelligent person. Surely she was not blind to the fact that my dress when we had first met on that fateful day was more than unusual. Perhaps I was only fooling myself with my explanation that I was a colonial from North America. How different could the dress style be between two continents, two countries, when one was just an off-shoot of the other, a possession, a dominion within a growing empire that would one day cover nearly one quarter of the world's landmass? Perhaps this explained her phrase "… as if you were from an entirely different place".

Was her feeling that the happiness that she felt would not last just an expression of her awareness of how fleeting true happiness can be, or was she declaring that she believed that I would depart, never to return, leaving her once more on her own? And what did she mean by a dark shadow lurking in the back of her mind? Those final few words were chilling and led to thoughts that I did not want to entertain, but which insisted on being heard. Did she foresee a blighted relationship with me, doomed to failure and disaster as a consequence of the wide differences in our backgrounds and experiences that would, perhaps, one day, drive a wedge between us? The gulf in time that had once separated us might prove, ultimately, to be unbridgeable.

Gradually, as I walked, the feeling of elation began to disappear. No more was I subject to the vicissitudes of moods as my emotions swung between peaks of sweet joy to troughs of depression. So far, I had been numb to the negative events of the day, but these now began to catch up with me, dragging me further down. In the space of a few hours I had been abducted, imprisoned, threatened with death, rescued, attacked, and then found peace and love in the arms of a beautiful woman who had wanted me, had given herself to me, and expressed the love she felt for me. But now, the one good experience that had happened at the end of what had been, by anyone's standard, a bad day began to move into the background. Assuming dominance in my mind were the dangers that I had encountered. Moving centre stage was awareness of how lucky I had been, and the realisation that I'd had a part in Smythe's unfortunate and messy end. And, as these thoughts began to fill my mind, and dark scenes began to replay themselves over and over again, I started to feel truly terrible. A sensation of sickness came over me, as my stomach became tense and panic momentarily raised its ugly head.

I found it impossible to drive out the disturbing thoughts that now ran through my mind. The only comforting idea that I could muster was to leave, to go back to my own time. For there I knew I would be safe. There was no danger there from anyone associated with the events of the day. I could stay there in the certainty that no one from 1751 could ever reach me. This seemed to me to be a way out of my present circumstances, of putting behind me, literally, all the events that had happened. I would, I knew, at least for a while, feel a longing to be with Lucy, a sadness that I had deserted her, but such emotions would surely fade with time, and I would be able to get on with my life largely as though these events had not occurred.

But having considered this option, another thought passed into my consciousness, one that lessened the attractiveness of running away. For a while all would be fine, but curiosity would start to gnaw away at me. I would with time, that great shaper of thoughts, come to be curious about Lucy's fate. Ceaseless questions would rise up and torment me until, unable to resist, I would be drawn back. Only what would I discover? That time had moved on? And what effect would my absence have had? Would Lucy welcome me back with the same warmth and love that she displayed when we came together earlier that night, or would she be cold and rejecting? Would I come to regret returning, of possibly learning that I had poisoned what was so joyful and full of life?

Actions have consequences; it is a lesson that life teaches everybody, yet few people learn that lesson, for to do so needs wisdom – a feature notably absent from the modern world, and I, as an engineer, am an icon of this deficiency. *Out of disorder I create order* – what a delusion!

Thus it seemed to me that there was no escape from the consequences I had created for myself. I could not run away. For although I could use time to separate me from my present circumstances, I could not positively shape events unless I remained where I was, in 1751. I was beginning now to see that *out of order comes disorder*. Denied the company of other engineers, the reinforcement of collective delusion was not possible, and adherence to ideology infeasible. Consequently, I was beginning to open my eyes, beholding for the first time the true nature of our actions as engineers and the associated damage that we wreak upon the world.

And having reached such a conclusion, a state of acceptance descended upon me, and I was all the more peaceful and calm for having decided not to leave, and for recognising that I had been the subject of self-delusion. I would face the consequences of my actions and stay to see events through to their logical conclusion.

CHAPTER 25

Thus it was that, in a calm and clear state of mind, I arrived at the Time House. Having entered and retreated to my study and lit an oil lamp, I intended to sit for a while with a small glass of whisky before retiring for the night. In the morning I would consider my next steps, whether to continue with my plans to visit London, or to abandon them and follow some new avenue, perhaps involving Lucy. I say that was my intention, but it was not to be, for it seemed the adventures and dangers of the day were far from over, and no sooner had I lit the lamp than I discovered I was not alone.

Standing in the room was a stranger, but it was someone whom I had seen previously, for I recognised him as the person I had briefly glimpsed at the front first-floor window, just before I had entered the Time House for the very first time.

My first reaction was shock at seeing someone in my house, because naturally I assumed that I was alone, and I had given no further thought to what I had observed on that first day when I arrived to check the electrics, having also dismissed that sighting as an optical illusion or a figment of my imagination. But here he now was, not at all an invention of my mind or a fantasy, but a very real person, or so it seemed. And of the man who now stood in my presence? He was not at all a pleasant sight to behold. He emanated a terrible aura of darkness, coldness and decay. He was dressed in black, but his clothes did not have the appearance of originating in the mid-eighteenth century. In fact I would say that his apparel spoke of no age or period in history that I was familiar with. His face was gaunt, pale, lacking any expression that might convey intentions or emotions. His eyes were as though cold pools of deep dark water and they lacked the sparkle and life that one sees in the living. Instead they were flat and lifeless. I did not have a good feeling about this person and as soon as I saw him I was frightened.

Logical, rational thinking, an old habit, now sought to assert itself, and the most rational thought that I could find was that this person had a connection with Smythe. Perhaps he was his accomplice or his father. But, aware as I was that this person was the same stranger I had seen while I was still in the twenty-first century, I began to consider other thoughts that involved considering options that were less sensible. The most obvious one was that he was a ghost. But he did not look as though he were one, for he seemed solid and real – of flesh and blood, just as I am. That left me wondering if he was someone who, similar to me, had accidentally stumbled upon the gateway through time. This seemed plausible, and being an engineer and not accustomed to thinking too deeply, I adopted this explanation. And with this now established as a fact, I began to react to his presence.

"What are you doing in my house?" I asked rather indignantly. "Whatever you have been up to, go now, get out," I ordered.

The man just stared straight at me and did not move, either to flee or to respond to my command.

He replied in his own time.

"Your house," he said, coldly. "This is not your house. This is my house."

I was at first taken aback by this statement, for I had, without further questioning of the circumstances in which I acquired ownership, assumed that the house was mine and I had the title deeds to prove it. But the fact that he had just stated that it was his made me wonder even more if he was from the future, or even someone of this time who'd had a similar experience as myself, and could travel back and forward between different ages. After all, if it had happened to me, why not to someone else? I continue to insist on my claim to ownership.

"This is my house," I repeated.

"Yes, I know what you mean. You may be the legal owner in the eyes of the law, but it is still my house, and you do not belong here, do you?"

This statement confused me. Here he was admitting that I was the legal owner, but nevertheless claiming that the house was his. But I was not confused about the second part of what he had just said. Here was a strong indication that he knew the truth about me and where I was from.

"What do you mean?" I asked. "I am the legal owner. I have the title deeds with my name on them. The house is mine."

"Yes," he said slowly, pausing for a moment, "but how did you come by these title deeds? You do not belong in this time. You are from the twenty-first century."

So he did know. I was not sure of what to say, but in the end I opted for a question, to give myself more time to think.

"Who are you?" I enquired.

"Ah. I see that you do not want to talk about your discovery of the time portal. Do not think I do not know about it. I saw you just before you came into this house, just before you discovered the gateway. But how could you see it? I am not clear about that at all."

I was surprised by what he said, and this showed on my face. Not only did he know that I was from another time, but he also knew about the time portal, and what it could do. And he spoke about it with a familiarity that both disturbed me and stirred my curiosity.

"I see that you are surprised that I know about it," he continued.

"Yes, I am," I admitted. "I asked you who you are. You did not answer me. And how do you know about the portal?"

"My name is Sgark," he said. "That is an unusual name, do not you think?"

It was a rhetorical question.

"You humans, you live in your little world, unaware of what is going on around you in the universe. Your eyes are blind to matters that others see with clarity. Take this house

358

for example. There it is, this great doorway between your world and the mid-eighteenth century, and very few people can see this portal or even sense its presence. Over time a small handful of your kind come along and, lo and behold, there it is, clear as day, and not only is it visible to them, they can also step right through it. And then here they are, in the mid-eighteenth century, travelling back and forward across time, free as a bird. And why does this happen? I must admit, I do not know."

There was now some clarity in my mind, where before there had been confusion and mystery. Sgark not only knew where I was from, but he evidently knew a lot about the portal. And he had used a strange expression, referring to humans as if he were not one himself.

"You refer to humans as if they were another species," I told him.

"They are!" he replied coldly.

That was all he said. It was short and to the point, and was stated this way to make that very point.

Now it might seem implausible to many that someone would suggest that they were not human, but in my circumstances, having discovered a gateway through time, and given his looks, which were, as I have already indicated, unusual, I was inclined to accept what he was saying.

"You are telling me that you are not human," I stated, to be sure that this was his claim.

"That is right. I am, I suppose, what you would call an alien, only I do not travel about using a spaceship."

"So if you are an alien, and do not use a spaceship, how do you travel?"

"In some respects you are in my means of travel," he replied. "That which you build I turn into the means of moving around the universe. This house is my means of transport."

I was for a moment lost. I did not really understand what he was implying and I said as much.

"I do not understand," I responded. "How could you possibly ..." But I did not finish my sentence, for suddenly it dawned on me what he was implying.

"I see you are starting to understand," he said.

"Yes, I am. This gateway that I have been using, it is a means of travelling through time."

"Not just time, but also space. You have only experienced the time-travel dimension, but there is more to it than that. This house is our gateway into your world. It is a point in space where we can enter from our world. But the house is full of time portals that can take us to any point in time where we want to be. And you have, for some inexplicable reason, found one of these time portals. And the house itself is just one of several places where we can enter your world."

Some of the apprehension that I had felt about this person was starting to wane, but there was an aspect to him, even taking account of the fact that he was not human, that I did not like, which made me feel uncomfortable and suspicious. For all his explanation about the Time House, the atmosphere he created in my room was unpleasant. I was curious, though, to know more about him and his world, so I asked where his world was located.

"All very interesting, but where exactly is your world?" I enquired.

He obviously did not want to answer this question for he replied with question of his own. "Where exactly is your world?" he asked in return.

I was silent for a moment, considering the answer to be obvious. But then I realised what he was implying. The earth is located in the solar system, which is in turn part of a galaxy, which is itself just one of hundreds of billions of galaxies scattered across the universe, which is expanding, but expanding into what? Sgark was not asking a question at all, but instead querying where exactly this universe was located. The answer, of course, I did not know and this is precisely what I told him.

"A very intelligent response," he returned. "You surprise me. I was fairly confident that you would deliver the obvious answer, but you did not."

"That may well be, but why do you come here? What purpose do you have?"

To this question there was no answer forthcoming. Instead he showed me that my caution about him was well placed. "Do not ask me questions," he said coldly. "I do not have to explain myself to you. You are interfering in my business. You have no right to be here. Not only that, but you seem to be a very lucky person, for you have survived all my attempts to drive you back into your own time. You have made friends here and I was not aware of this. These friends have foiled all my plans to force you to return, to drive you away, to discourage you, and, most recently, to eliminate you."

I was now aware that Sgark was a threat, a real danger, and I wanted to know more, but I also wished to ensure that he could do me no harm. For the moment I decided to stall him from taking action by getting him to continue to talk.

"You are claiming that you are responsible for the incidents that have befallen me?" I enquired.

"Oh, yes, indeed," he replied. "It was no accident that Smythe was outside the house at the very moment that you came out. I manipulated the events in his life to make that happen, such is the power I have as a time traveller. I thought that Smythe would have given you a beating when you first encountered him. That, I hoped, would be enough of a discouragement to drive you back to your own time, but no, you proved to be more than match for him, and I did not count on those two ladies turning up."

Interrupting him I asked, "So those events were not of your doing? They were not part of your plan?"

"No, they were not."

Then, without thinking and knowing why, I retorted by saying that which I had never said before: "Out of order comes disorder!"

"Very apt," he responded. "Yes, indeed, out of order comes disorder. I see that you are learning the natural ways of the universe, the ways that humans do not yet really understand – such is your state of development, your collective delusion of control, the nature of the soulless world that you have created."

I realised that he was indeed right in stating this. We, as a species, especially those involved in science, technology and engineering, do share a collective delusion that we are in control, that we can control, that in some way we are not part of nature; *out of disorder comes order* – what nonsense!

"But I digress," Sgark continued. "I was telling you about my plans, how I made sure that Smythe would be sufficiently annoyed with you to want to kill you. And if it had not been, yet again, for the interference of those friends of yours, you would now be out of my way."

Continuing to delay, I returned to what he had said about a few people being able to see the gateway.

"When you said that only a few people have seen the gateway, you seemed to be implying that I was not the first to discover and use the portal."

"That is correct," he replied.

"And what happened to them?" I asked.

"Most I managed to force back to their own time, and to keep them there, but a few, such as you, I had to deal with, or they discovered the other portals, and are now lost in time!"

"But how was it that I was able to find those title deeds, to take ownership, to acquire money? That does not make much sense. That could not have been your doing, if you had wanted me out of here."

He was obviously annoyed by these questions, and had no answer, which made me wonder if Sgark wasn't the only person or creature influencing the outcome of my circumstances. I also wondered whether he was as powerful as he claimed, for if he were, why did he not just deal with me himself? I decided to challenge him about this.

"You imply that you are powerful, but why did you rely on Smythe to do your dirty work? Why did you not change events in my life to prevent me from coming into contact with this house?"

"I have not come here to answer your questions," he screamed.

"No, perhaps not, but I do not think that you are as powerful as you make out. If you were you would have dealt with me by now, but you have not."

"Do not talk to me in that way," he said angrily.

This was the first sign of emotion that he had shown. "Why not? You're not going to do anything about it, are you?"

I was not entirely sure, but I was beginning to suspect that his ability to act in my world was very limited. In fact, I was almost sure by now that his only power was to influence people's minds, and only those people such as Smythe. I had invited him to act, but all that happened was that he had become angry. His inaction created an impression of impotence, and he was well aware of this, hence his anger. I continued to taunt him. "Come on," I said confidently, "show me how powerful you are."

Then I started to ask rhetorical questions. "Why is it that you act through other people? Is it because you cannot act yourself? You claim to be able to influence people, but all I have seen so far is that you can manipulate bad people. Those who are good such as Lucy do not seem to be so amenable to your manipulation. I wonder why that is? Could it be that you yourself are bad? Could it be that the good are too strong for you, that they can resist your pathetic attempts to interfere in their lives?"

My tone had now become mocking, and all the time I had been saying these words I had been edging closer to Sgark. Now I was in position to test out a theory that I had formed about him. The moment seemed to be right, so I lunged at him. He was surprised by this and caught off guard. I aimed for the chest, with the idea of bringing him down to the floor.

If my theory was incorrect, if I was mistaken, then we would probably end up engaged in physical conflict. What that might lead to I had not worked through, for to tell the truth I was not bothered. I had come to a conclusion that I did not like this creature from another world. He appeared to be arrogant, to think himself superior and to hold humans in contempt. If I ended up in a fight with him, it might teach him a lesson, for I knew how to defend myself, and Smythe had learned that the hard way.

But deep down inside I was not expecting that it would end up as such, for I was very confident of what would happen as soon as I came into contact with Sgark. And this is exactly what did occur. I had sprung straight at him and he just collapsed under me – we ended up on the floor, me in control of him.

"Just as I thought," I said with an air of satisfaction, "bodily form, but no strength, just physical weakness. Now I understand why you act through other people. You just do not have the ability to act directly, to do anything other than be present in my world. I do not know why that is so – maybe it is a consequence of travelling through time and space; perhaps the gravity of earth is not what you are used to – and I do not really care. All I see is a weak and feeble creature that I have no need to fear."

I stood up, letting Sgark free as I was no longer concerned that he could harm me.

Sgark also rose from the floor, but now he was even angrier. "Too clever by half, you are. Of course you are correct. I lack physical strength, so all I can do is manipulate people's minds to get them to undertake actions for me. People such as Smythe are easily influenced, but your two friends, they resisted my attempts."

"Too strong for you, eh!" I replied, making sure that the tone of my voice conveyed the contempt that I felt for this creature.

"You mock me at your peril," Sgark said with malice. "Oh, yes, you think you are clever, but no one can stop me. You will see. Just wait! I have a nasty surprise in store for you." Then he was gone. He turned towards one of the walls, stepped towards it and then passed right through it. I moved to follow him, but there was no way through. Before me there was just a solid wall, which I assumed contained a portal leading to some other place or time. But I could not follow. Only one gateway in this house allowed my passage and, in any case, I did not really want to pursue him, as I had no idea what sort of world he came from, and of this I was entirely happy to remain ignorant.

I could now understood why people speak of seeing ghosts, for Sgark with his aura, his coldness and grim features might easily be taken for such an apparition. But I knew the truth. Yet, still, what I had discovered left me feeling uneasy. I might not need to fear Sgark in terms of a physical threat, but there were far too many unanswered questions, not least of which was why Sgark and his fellow creatures, for I assumed that he was not alone, were coming into our world. What plan of mischief and evil did they have in store for humankind? What could they still do to me by acting through others?

All of a sudden the time portal that linked my time with this moment in time in the eighteenth century took on a sinister tone. Sgark's departing words were chilling. Even though he lacked the capability to act in my world, he was still dangerous to humans, for he had an ability to affect them and to make them do his bidding, to undertake evil actions towards others; this rendered him a dangerous creature. And what other powers did he have? So I was left wondering what was in store for me next. What new dangers would I now have to face?

But fatigue began to take over; I was very tired. The day had been long and eventful, and now my mind and body demanded rest. Even with the knowledge that my rooms were accessible to Sgark, and at any time – a thought that would have been discomforting in normal circumstances – did not bother me, for what I wanted and desired most was to lie down and allow myself to surrender to slumber. It was almost unnatural, this desire to sleep, and I could not resist.

And sleep I did, not even bothering to undress. I lay on my bed fully clothed, closed my eyes and sank into slumber instantaneously. And I slept deeply and peacefully. No terrible dreams disturbed me. Time passed by, until eventually I woke. But when I did wake, it was dark, and I assumed it was still the middle of the night. So, recalling that I was still dressed I discarded my clothes in the dark, throwing them onto the floor, and slipped inside the sheets. After this awakening, I did not sleep so well, and kept drifting in and out of wakefulness. Eventually the darkness began to give way to the greyness of the early dawn. It was still too soon in the day to visit anyone, so I lay abed, thinking about my options. After lying there for a while I decided to wash and shave; the stubble on my face indicated that I was much in need of the latter.

What happened next I was not prepared for.

CHAPTER 26

Once refreshed, smelling more pleasant and wearing clean clothes, I found myself feeling very hungry. The extent of my hunger surprised me, even when I took into account the fact that I had not eaten since the previous day's lunchtime. I felt as though I had not taken food for days, rather than just twenty-four hours. I ate a large breakfast and in the process discovered that my pocket watch had stopped. About this I was concerned, and began to think that it might be faulty, since I had wound it up only yesterday and it normally ran for forty-eight hours before requiring attention. So not being aware of the exact time, I decided to wait for a while before visiting Lucy.

I sat in my chair, thinking about all that had happened, when I suddenly heard a noise. Someone had entered the house and was climbing the rear stairs. I jumped to my feet and headed out of my study into the corridor just as Samuel reached the top of the stairs.

"Oh, it is you. You had me worried for a moment there," I said with relief. But the relief was only temporary for written on Samuel's face was an expression that alerted me to serious troubles. He had been running, for his face was flushed and he was out of breath.

"Benjamin," Samuel said, "where have you been? You did not come to see Miss Lucy as you said you would. Now she is—"

I interrupted Samuel, saying, "I was just preparing to come and see her. And what do you mean? What were you going to say?"

"But you said you would come on the Wednesday morning. It is now Friday morning, and Miss Lucy is seriously ill."

"Friday morning! That is impossible. I cannot have slept for so long. And what do you mean that Miss Lucy is ill? What is wrong with her?"

"I do not know. But it is serious. And she has been asking for you."

"You should have come for me sooner. I cannot believe that I have been asleep for so long."

"I was not sure what plans you had made with Miss Lucy. Remember I went home on my own. I came and stood outside the house several times, but there was no sign of you and I did not want to come in. It is your home and I cannot just walk in, and you did not respond when I knocked on the door. But this morning Miss Lucy is much worse so I thought I would come in and see if I could find you."

"Much worse! Then I must go and see her now. There is not a moment to lose."

So we set off at a fast pace along the lane heading for Lucy's house. As we walked I wondered what was wrong with her that could be so serious. And why had I slept for so long? I could not have been that exhausted. But then I recalled Sgark. I had momentarily forgotten about him and his departing warning. Perhaps he was responsible for my long sleep and this sudden illness that had gripped Lucy. The more I thought about this the more certain I was that Sgark was behind what had happened. This was his nasty surprise. It fitted with what I knew of him, insidious creature that he was, reaching out from his own world, poisoning this one with his evil manipulation of events.

Soon we were standing outside Lucy's house. I turned to Samuel. "It's best if you stay downstairs," I said. "Miss Lucy will not want lots of visitors. I will talk with her mother first to see what is wrong."

So I knocked on the door and the maid opened it. She had tears in her eyes. I did not wait for her to speak but strode forward into the house, saying with a determined tone, "I wish to speak with Mrs Dent."

The maid raised no objections and gestured towards the door that led to the drawing room. I entered, and there sat Lucy's mother, dabbing her eyes. Standing next to her was Uncle Ralf and someone whom I had never seen before.

As soon as Lucy's mother saw me, she rose from her chair and came over to me. "Oh, Benjamin, at last. Lucy has been asking for you since she took ill on Wednesday morning. She is so insistent upon seeing you, although she is not in a fit state to see anyone. We assumed you were in London, but she was adamant that you were not. At first we thought it was the

371

fever, but eventually we sent a maid to Samuel's home, and he only said that you might be on your way to London by some route he did not know, or you might be at home, venturing the opinion that since you had not appeared, the former was most probable. But it seems we were all wrong."

"Yes, no matter. It is a long story that is of no interest. I am sorry that I did not come sooner. I was delayed by unforeseen events. I have only just heard the news and I have come straight here. How is she? What is wrong with her? You mentioned a fever."

"Yes. The doctor here has just been to see her. I am afraid she has typhoid fever, and she is deteriorating."

And then Lucy's mother began to cry. Uncle Ralf helped her back into her chair.

"I am very sorry," the doctor began, "but there is very little I can do for her. The next twenty-four hours will be crucial. If she can make it through this period then there is a possibility that she will get better, but I feel that I must warn you that her chances of survival are very slim. I will come back tomorrow morning. Send for me if there is a change in her condition."

He touched Lucy's mother on the shoulder as he walked past her as a way of indicating his sympathy for her plight, and then he departed.

I waited until she had regained some composure. She looked up at me, sadness written on her face. "Come," she said, "let me take you to her. Samuel, please take a seat. I will be back soon. Ralf, please stop pacing about the room and take a seat and wait here."

Samuel and Uncle Ralf both did as they were told and sat down. Lucy's mother led the way up to Lucy's bedroom. We stopped outside the door. "Wait here a moment," she said. "I will go and tell her."

So I waited while she entered her daughter's chamber. A few moments later she came out followed by a maid. "You can go in now," she said, and so I did.

CHAPTER 27

It was as though death hung over the room, waiting its opportunity, which was not now too far off. Patience would bring its reward. The disease had done the work and death would take the prize.

Lying on her bed, weakened by fever and vomiting, hardly able to stir, Lucy looked at me with pleading eyes. I quickly moved to her side and took hold of her limp, cold hand. Her skin was pale, almost as pale as death itself, and her eyes, those once penetrating and engaging eyes, had lost their sparkle. There were beads of perspiration on her brow and her hair was damp around the forehead. Her body shivered involuntarily from time to time, but she had little energy or willpower left to move unnecessarily.

She tried to exert some pressure on my hand, but it was barely perceptible. Then she spoke.

"So you have come to me at last, my dear lover," she said feebly. "How I have changed since our previous meeting, since we were together. Oh, that night of love, how far away that now seems, that moment in time when we shared our passion."

I sat down on the chair that had been placed by her bed, on which the maid had sat wiping Lucy's brow and keeping vigil through the long night.

"Best not to speak," I responded, trying to sound optimistic. "You must rest and conserve your energy. Focus your strength on fighting the fever."

I said this knowing that her circumstances were grave, and that in her age there was no cure for this terrible disease – no antibiotics that would seek out and destroy the bacteria that were rampaging through her bloodstream. It would be a matter of luck, fickle chance, if she survived this mindless onslaught. It would be a matter of good fortune if she did not develop complications such as pneumonia and internal bleeding, which would send her on her way out of this precarious life into that which lies beyond. It would be down to her physical strength and her willpower. But I realised at that moment in time that fate was not on her side. Luck would not be her friend, nor time her ally. I knew, deeply and instinctively, that no matter how much she resisted, struggled, and fought back against the disease, she was going to die. For now I saw it all so clearly; this was the tragedy of which I have already spoken. Lucy would die young, as many people in her era did, struck down by a deadly disease that we, in the twenty-first century, have largely tamed, or so we think. And Lucy knew that her life was coming to an end.

"My time is short," she said quietly, "and I have so much to say to you."

"There will be time to say what you want to say when you are better," I said, trying to sound genuine.

"You are not a good liar," she replied, and the beginnings of a smile appeared on her face, but she did not have the energy to bring it to conclusion, and it hung there for a moment as if it were a lost child unsure of itself, and then it vanished.

"I know I am dying," she continued, sounding at once both saddened and reconciled to her fate.

I made to respond, to object, but she slowly moved her head from side to side, sighing as she did so, gently and silently reproaching me for trying to be so optimistic in the face of undeniable truth.

"There is no need to hide, Benjamin. When one is dying one knows it. The world becomes more distant; fears and hopes all become unimportant, all far-off matters in the realm of the living. I hover here on the edge of life, and see death not as an end but as a beginning. I will go where you, and everyone else, must all eventually follow, but not now. You will be left here while I journey onwards. Soon I will be with my dear Henry. I die by the same hand of death as he did. But you! You have your own journey to make."

I had never encountered the death of a loved one before, never sat by the dying, nor experienced the grief that follows from loss. But at that moment in time, with those words ringing in my mind, I could see the importance of living a good and decent life. For surely that is what Lucy had done. In her short life she had done no harm to anyone. She had made her best efforts to lead a blameless existence, and here was her reward – to face death unafraid, to be at peace with herself, sure in the knowledge that no ghosts of past bad deeds were about to come to haunt and torment her. Surely this is the goal that we should all aspire to, to know at the point of dying that we did our best, and that if we did transgress at all, to be able to forgive ourselves for such, through the merit of an otherwise worthy life.

I pondered for a moment on what Lucy had meant by my journey. I did not see immediately what she was implying.

"My journey," I said mystified. "What journey is that?"

"To go on without me," she replied. "Death is harder for the living than it is for the dying. I am at peace now with myself, but for you the pain is just beginning. But do not falter. Go on living. Never forget me, but do not bind yourself to me, for all that I can be to you is a memory. You and I were not meant to be. We have had our time together, and now you must move on. Go back to your Helen. Live your life to the full."

On hearing Helen's name, I responded involuntarily with a look of surprise. Lucy noticed this and spoke.

"Remember when we first met," she said with a hint of tenderness in her voice, "you called me Helen, confusing me for someone else. Somewhere in your life, Helen is there. Perhaps she is in your past or maybe in your future – I do not know, for you have never spoken of her, and I have never asked. But women have instincts about these matters. So go and find her, and live the life with her that you would have spent with me."

I bowed my head slightly, not wanting at that moment in time to look at her, such was the guilt that I felt. But she had not finished.

"Benjamin, look at me," she said gently. "I am not angry with you. Please, know this, for this is how I truly feel. We have only known each other for such a short time. But lying here, coming to the end of my life, I know that, truthfully, I would rather it be this way; better only to have known you for the brief time we have been together than to have lived a lifetime and never have met you."

I listened to her words and I was full of sadness. She managed to squeeze my hand, summoning up the last remaining energy in her body. She raised her right hand, which had lain limp by her side, and reached for my face. I moved closer to her and she stroked my cheek, but she could not maintain the action for long, so weak was she, and Lucy soon dropped her hand back on to the bed.

"I have waited for you, Benjamin. I wanted to see you one more time, to touch you, to tell you how much I love you. But now that you are here I no longer feel the need to hold on. You are here with me, and already I feel my grip on life is slipping away. Kiss me one more time."

There were tears forming in my eyes as I stood up and bent over her, placing a kiss on her lips. Her skin was cold, and I sensed that I was witnessing the closing moments in her life.

"Thank you," she said slowly and softly.

"Please try to fight this," I begged.

"It is no use, Benjamin," she returned. "All my fighting is over. There are no reserves of strength left within me that I can use to win this battle. You are the one person who was keeping me alive, for I did not want to die without seeing you one last time. Now it is time to go. It is my time."

I did not know how I should respond to this statement. What I was witnessing was beyond my experience. Of death and dying, and what it was like, of this I knew little, nor how to respond. So I turned my attention to other matters that I thought appropriate.

"Should I go and get your mother?" I asked quietly.

Lucy did not answer with speech, but just indicated a negative answer to my question with a slow sideways movement of her head.

"Stay with me," she said. "Stay until I have gone. I will go home with you by my side and no one else. This is not a time for sharing with others."

Then she was quiet and just wanted to gaze into my eyes. And for a moment there she was, the bright vivacious woman whom I recalled from a few nights previously when, full of life, we had made love, shared our bodies, imagining that we had all the time in the world to be together. She managed a smile. For a moment she looked as though she was better again, that all would be well. Then she spoke. "I love you," she said tenderly. "I love you so much, my darling."

"I love you too," I returned, with a lump in my throat, holding back the tears.

There we were, more moments in time, but unlike the many gone before, there would be no more to come; no more time to be together, to be happy, to look forward to the future.

She closed her eyes and seemed to rest, but she was falling into a sleep from which she would not wake. Lucy had spoken her last words. Quietly she slipped deeper into slumber, breathing steadily, but then her breath changed, becoming less regular and shallower, and very quickly she ceased to breathe. Lucy was no more.

I sat holding her hand, not wanting to let go. Tears began to trickle slowly down my face, but I did not burst into a flood of emotion. That would come later. For the moment I was feeling sad and lost, and I did not want to leave her. So I stayed there, sitting by her side, holding her now lifeless hand. But eventually I realised that I had to let go. Her mother had to be told, so reluctantly, and with a heavy heart, I rose and kissed her lips for one last time, knowing that death had been there before me and stolen my love away.

"Goodbye, my love," I said sadly. "Go in peace in the knowledge that I will always love you."

Then I placed her hand by her side and I slowly walked away.

I went downstairs to announce to all gathered there that Lucy's final battle was over, and that she had succumbed to the terrible disease that had sprung from nowhere to attack her. As I entered the room my demeanour said it all. Lucy's mother, who had been pacing to and fro in front of the fireplace, doing what she had asked Ralf not to do, halted her movement and looked at me as I entered the room. Uncle Ralf, who had been standing gazing out of the window, watching life carry on, watching the people who were going about their daily business, completely unaware of what was transpiring within these four walls, also turned towards me as I entered the room.

I sighed and said, "I am sorry," and more tears rolled down my face. Her mother began to cry. I walked over to her and held her. "She died very peacefully," I said reassuringly. "There was no pain."

"Lucy was holding on just for you," she began to say, sobbing also. "As soon as you arrived I knew it was all but over for her. She loved you. I could see it in her eyes, in the way she spoke about you, in the way she behaved every time your name was mentioned."

"And I loved her too, since the day we first met. So strange!"

"Love at first sight," Lucy's mother said.

Then she tried to recover some of her composure. Uncle Ralf walked over and placed his hand on my shoulder. "I am so sorry," he said with emotion. "Marjory, dear," he said, addressing his sister. "What can I say? I will of course stay for as long as I am needed, to be with you at this terrible time."

"Thank you," she replied. "But I must go to her now."

"Yes," I responded. "Yes, of course. And I will leave you, for I need to be alone for a while."

"Yes, dear, I understand, but please come back, though," she said kindly. "Lucy would not have wanted you to be on your own."

"Yes, I will come back."

While all this was going on, Samuel was sitting quietly, but he understood what had happened and his eyes were full of tears.

"Come on, Samuel," I said.

Samuel got up and followed. When we were outside, Samuel spoke.

"She was good to me," he said, crying, "always looking out for me."

"Yes, I know," I replied. "That is the way she was, always thinking about others. But she has gone now, and this we cannot change."

I crouched down, looking into Samuel eyes, and spoke to him. "Go home now and cry, but never forget her. Remember her through your deeds and actions and what you do with your life."

"I will," he said sadly. "This I solemnly promise."

I gave him a hug to comfort him and he hung onto me, seeking reassurance and support.

"I am going back to my house now," I told him. "I will come and see you when I am ready."

"I do not want to be on my own," he replied, still crying.

"You will not be on your own. You have your parents. Go and talk to your mother about Lucy. Cry with her."

"I will," he said.

Then he turned and headed over the village green to his parents' shop.

I walked back to the Time House, full of sadness, experiencing emotions that were entirely new to me.

CHAPTER 28

To have found love and then to have lost it again in such a short a time! For so much to have happened in such a short period! All seemed incomprehensible. But as the days passed by I began to see it all as a consequence of my foolish actions. Nature did not allow humans to travel back through time. What I had done was unnatural and now I was paying the price. But what I was experiencing seemed small and insignificant compared with the consequences for Lucy and her family. And one question kept haunting me – would it all have been different if I had not become involved, if I had not used the time portal?

There was no answer to this question and there would never be one. I could not undo what I had done. There was no going back. I realised that I was not the master of events, that I was not in control. I was able to travel back in time, but I could not go anywhere that I wanted to go. The *risks could not be managed*. My link with the past was to a particular age only. I had no power to go elsewhere, or to change the past so that what had happened to Lucy could be undone. I was as helpless as the next person, unable to stem the flow of events that resulted from my own thoughtless actions. What had started as an exciting adventure had turned into a tragedy, and it was a disaster of my own making. I had found my soul mate, the one person whom I knew I belonged with, but I had lost her. And what would I do with the rest of my life, living in the knowledge that my true love had lived long ago, was dead, and probably was so because of me?

And yet again I found myself saying that which hitherto I had not believed. "Out of order comes disorder." I stated this slowly and clearly even though there was no one there to listen.

I lay on my bed feeling the pain of loss, which was now growing and spreading through my mind as if a dark storm cloud were gathering, obliterating the light and joy in my life. And I was angry. I knew that what had happened to Lucy was Sgark's doing. This was the nasty surprise that he had threatened me with at the end of our encounter. Sgark's final words echoed in my thoughts. They had been spoken with a malice that I had not previously encountered. And this knowledge tormented me. I started to believe that if I had not spoken to Sgark in the way I had, then perhaps Lucy might still be alive.

Thus it was that my emotions swung from grief, to guilt and to then to anger, and back to grief, an endless circle of self-pity, remorse and helplessness. In the face of events that I could not control or change, I felt that I was both victim and perpetrator. And so this continued throughout the day and all through the long night. I was unable to sleep.

Dawn came, the beginnings of another day, the first of many without my beloved Lucy. And similar to the night, the day passed in much the same way. I ate no food. I drank no liquids. I cared neither about myself, nor what might happen to me. I wanted to go where Lucy had gone, to follow her.

Mentally I stretched out to her world, the place that lies beyond life, the place of eternity, the place of death, but found the ties of the living too strong to break. My will to live was so much stronger than my wish to die, and this tormented me even more.

The day wore on. Morning changed to afternoon, which once more slipped into night, and blackness once more engulfed me, for I could not be bothered to make a light. As the darkness blotted out the day, I, being now in a state of utter exhaustion, lost consciousness and slept deeply.

In my dreams my dear Lucy came to me. She spoke gently and soothingly, reassuring me, lifting my spirits.

"Remember what I told you," she said softly. "Do not give up on life, my love. You must be strong. You must go on."

I wanted to answer her, but was content just to listen, to feel, for what I experienced was the beautiful warmth of a kind that I had never encountered before. All was peaceful. Her presence calmed me and all my grief, along with its mind-churning pain, became less of a burden. We were together once again and I slept soundly in the knowledge that she was with me.

But it was not to happen again, for although my suffering was intense, the depths of despair into which I plunged that night were never repeated. Lucy's healing touch had reached out to me and seeded in me a strength that would see me through the days to follow.

I must admit that I longed to experience the peace of her presence one more time, but it was not to be. And when day broke and light once more streamed into my room, it seemed that it also illuminated my senses, for I was no longer so preoccupied with my own feeling. There were others to think of. Poor Samuel was feeling Lucy's loss. And Lucy's mother, what must she be experiencing? I had promised them both that I would come back and I had already been away from them for far too long.

And my body was also telling me that I needed to pay attention to my physical needs. I realised that I was extremely thirsty and my lips were cracked. I recalled that I had not taken liquids for nearly forty-eight hours and the thought of this frightened me. I rose from the bed where I had lain for most of the time. I felt dizzy and weak. I began to drink very slowly from a glass of water by my bed. Only taking sips at first, I began to increase the volume of my intake, pausing for a few minutes after each drink, unsure about the effects of consuming large quantities of water after such a long fast. I kept this up for most of one full hour.

The life-giving liquid began to do its work. I started to feel much better and stripped off all my clothes, which had become rather smelly, and began washing my body. Finally I put on fresh clothes. I was still not inclined to eat, but was sufficiently recovered to be able to set off back to Lucy's house.

I first called in on young Samuel. He was sitting by the front of his parents' shop, gazing out across the village green, his eyes firmly fixed on Lucy's abode. Thus he did not see me at first, but he eventually noticed me approaching the shop, and as soon as he caught sight of me, he jumped to his feet and ran over to meet me. Instinctively I dropped down to his level and embraced him. I could see that he had been crying for his eyes were red and sore.

"I thought you would not come," were his first words.

"I am sorry," I said with real regret.

"I have never felt so bad before," he continued, despairingly. "I hate these emotions."

"I know! I know! They are not nice; so much pain, so much grief. We all share it, Samuel. It is the other side of life. With joy, comes pain. They seem to go hand in hand," I said philosophically.

"Well, I do not want these feelings. Best not to become attached to anyone. That way I will not have to put up with pain when someone dies."

I looked at him, understanding what he meant, but I shook my head. "No, Samuel, that is not right. If you did that, you would never experience anything worthwhile in life. Think of all the good times, the pleasure, and the laughter that came from knowing Lucy, of being close to her. You would have missed all that if you had never come to know her, if you had never become part of her life. It is a risk we all take when we become attached to someone, a risk that one day we will be hurt. But if we never took that risk, just think of all the joy that we would miss, of how empty our lives would be. No, Samuel, the pain we feel now is part of life, just as much as the pleasure we feel in the good times. Life is about living both sides of the story, riding the high points and accepting the lows, taking the joy along with the sadness. We will survive this. You will always remember this time, Samuel, but the pain that you feel now will fade. This I promise you."

I was speaking as though from long experience, but in reality the emotions that Samuel was experiencing were just as new to me as they were to him. Of the experiences that hurt us most, such as betrayal, injustice and bereavement, of these I had very little knowledge. But I was learning fast. And there would be more to face, for at home, in my own time, there were bound to be repercussions of what had happened here. The emotional scars, the change in demeanour, the sadness, all these would be difficult to hide. I was a man who stood on the verge of losing all that he had and it seemed to me that I deserved to.

Samuel looked at me thoughtfully and did not initially respond. After a brief moment of silence, within which he seemed more than the boy that he still was, he said, "I suppose you are right, but it does not seem that way right now."

I nodded in agreement. "Yes, Samuel, that is correct. At this moment in time life seems unfair. I have lost someone I loved dearly, and ..."

I did not finish the sentence. My emotions were welling up again and tears formed in my eyes, preventing me from continuing. What I wanted to say to Samuel was that Lucy was more than just someone I had fallen in love with; she was also my friend. We belonged together, but between us there was an insurmountable obstacle – death. I wiped my eyes and stood up.

"Now I must go and see Lucy's mother and find out when Lucy's funeral will be held."

"The funeral is the day after tomorrow," Samuel said. "I will be there with my mother and father. The whole village will be there too."

Samuel lived in a small community. It was clear to me that I was probably the only person who did not know about the funeral arrangement. "Oh," I began. "I fear that I have stayed away too long. I must go and make amends. I will see you at the church the day after tomorrow."

And so I left Samuel, who went inside as soon as we parted company. I walked over towards Lucy's house, now home to her no more, now just a place where she had once lived, where we had become friends and lovers and shared so many happy moments in time. The house would always remain in my memory, though I should probably never grace it again after the funeral, since already I knew that I could not stay. For here, in the village, in this age, there were too many memories. Yet in my own time there would also be reminders. But surely it would be better than staying here, seeing every day all those people connected with my lost love.

This was a matter to deal with later. For the moment my main concern was to do what I had promised Lucy's mother and to return to her and share with her the mourning of a dearly loved daughter.

CHAPTER 29

I was admitted into Lucy's mother's home. I now no longer referred to it as Lucy's.

On entering the sitting room I found Lucy's mother sitting alone, gazing into the fireplace. She rose on seeing me and came over and wrapped her arms around me. "You poor boy," she began, sympathetically. "I see it all in your expression. I was deeply worried about you, all on your own in that big house. I did not know what to do for the best, whether to leave you to your grief or to come to you. But the dilemma is no more. Here you are."

"I am sorry. I know I should not have stayed away so long, but all was just a blur to me. Time no longer has any meaning. I was lost in myself. But, as you say, I am here now."

"Yes. Come and sit with me," she said with warmth.

We sat down, side by side, and fearing silence, I began to speak.

"I have just been to see Samuel."

"Oh, yes, poor Samuel. He was very fond of Lucy, I know. How is he?"

"Confused and hurting, as we all are."

"I will speak with him at the funeral. Make sure that he knows he will always be welcome here. Lucy took him under her wing. She was teaching him, as you know, to read and write. This I must continue. It would be a shame if all Lucy's good work with him went to waste. I understand he is a fast learner and keen student."

"Yes, he is, and it would be good if you could continue with his lessons. He has potential, does Samuel." I paused for a moment and then continued. "Samuel told me that the funeral is to be held the day after tomorrow."

"Yes, that is right," she confirmed. "At ten o'clock in the morning, in the church on the village green. After the service she will be interred in the family plot. It is a nice spot. Catches the sun all year round," she said, with great sadness evident in her tone of voice.

Lucy's mother was trying hard to control her emotions and was succeeding. She did not want to be seen crying, but her eyes told me that she had done much weeping. On her own, in her room, she had mourned long for her dear Lucy.

She continued describing the funeral arrangements. "At a quarter to ten, six pallbearers will carry the coffin from this house – all people whose lives were in some way touched by Lucy. You will walk with us behind her coffin, and sit with us in the church."

"Thank you," I said gratefully.

"After the funeral is over, family and close friends will come back here. I hope that you will join us. You are part of the family. Do you think that you will be able to cope?" she asked, looking at me with a concerned expression.

"I will try," I said sadly, and I hung my head.

The she looked at me. No words passed between us for a while and then she sighed and shook her head.

"What is to become of you?" she asked rhetorically. "So much sadness at such a young age; such a tragedy for you! But you have your whole life ahead of you – time to heal, time to love again. But will you? Will you lock yourself away? It happens, you know. But it is not what Lucy would have wanted. Or perhaps you will go away. Disappear forever back to the place that you came from."

Of what she spoke I was familiar with, for she touched upon the very ideas that had passed through my mind over the previous forty-eight hours. But my circumstances were far more complicated than Lucy's mother knew, and I could not explain these to her. She was concerned about me and for that I was grateful.

I had decided upon departing and it seemed to me the sooner the better. So I resolved at that moment in time to leave the day after the funeral. This would be my exit. I realised I would be abandoning Lucy's mother at a time of great sadness in her life and that perhaps my continued presence might help ease her pain. But I felt that I had no choice. I wanted to be far away from 1751 and for me that meant only one action, returning to my own time, to face whatever was waiting for me there.

I wanted to communicate to Lucy's mother the warmth and affection that I felt for her, of my sorrow at her grief, but I did not know what to say. No words seemed adequate given the circumstances. And so I spoke no more of these matters, preferring, through my attention to her in this time of hurt, to convey my feelings through my presence.

And this is how I passed the rest of the day and the next, until the day of the funeral.

CHAPTER 30

The day of the funeral dawned, grim in our hearts. But nature, not knowing of our sadness and grief, behaved as though naught were amiss, and offered not gloom and dark clouds, but brightness as though sunny and cheerful were the requirements of the day. Summer delights beckoned to all those light of spirit, those with minds and hearts welcoming the offering of warm sunshine and the promise of delicate fragrances that would drift on the slight breeze that gently stirred the already warm air.

The heavy cloud that darkened my day amidst this paradise hovered over me as if it were a hawk waiting for the moment to strike, to kill. On this day I would not only say my final farewell to my love, but would also prepare to leave that age, never to return. I had reached the final parting, the drawing of the curtain on an episode in my life, but it would not be the end. Step by step I would proceed through life sure in the knowledge that I was the maker of my own heartache, of my despair, of my feelings of helplessness, and that these would accompany me all the days of my life, stalking me, until I became just as Lucy now was – no more.

Slowly I walked the lane that led to the place where my beloved lay. Cold now, lying in her coffin, lifeless and stiff, looking as if she were Lucy to all whom would have claimed to have known her, but in truth only a passing resemblance now. Gone was the warmth and joy that had been Lucy, her defining characteristics, the personality that shone out to capture my heart; all that remained was but a mere shell.

I walked and walked, placing one foot in front of the other, as if I were an automaton, not noticing the life that went on all about me. Time passed. The clock of life ticked away, but few can hear the ticking. Only those sensitised to it, either through gift or life's traumas, heard the quiet sounds of life ebbing away. But for me there was no gentle soothing rhythmic noise. With every footstep that I took, the hands of time did hammer in my brain, heralding the end of my time. But that demise seemed far away.

I wore black, a representation of what was left of my life. Colour no more would venture here and no welcome sign would be found to welcome such. No warm reception would the rainbow ever find, nor light ever discover the dark chambers left within me. Grey and monotone my life would be forever more, though those who cared might colour decree.

I stood before Lucy's mother's house, knowing that I must enter, but holding back, preparing myself for what would come. Raw emotion was what I was expecting, tears flooding down my cheeks, but not yet. What would be the trigger? It was just a question of when, not if. And so I entered this once cheerful abode that was now a place of gloom. Dear Marjory, plainly on the verge of tears, just as I was, but doing her utmost to control herself, at least for now, greeted me as if I were her son. I was a lost child and she a lost mother. Together, our two lost souls found some solace.

"Come Benjamin," she said gently, taking me by the arm into the midst of family and close friends who had gathered in the sitting room. All knew who I was, but most to me were strangers. Introduced to each and every one, I took no notice of the names that streamed through my ears, and the soft kind words of condolence spoken with concern. I acknowledged all, but was in no mood for company or conversation, and indicated this to Lucy's mother, after taking her to one side. "There are many people here," I quietly stated, "but to tell the truth I am not sure that I have any inclination to speak with so many strangers."

She looked concerned.

"It must be very hard for you," she said sympathetically, "to be thrown among so many new faces at such a difficult time. But they will understand if you do not feel up to speaking."

She led me to the Venetian window that stood ajar and then out into the garden, along the path and then seated me on the bench, where, on my first visit, I had sat with Lucy, our first moment alone with one another; a poignant place indeed on such a day. "Just sit here quietly on your own till we are ready," she said soothingly.

And this is what I did. The sun shone down upon me, and I felt its warmth on my skin.

Just as the sun, bursting through a cloud-laden sky on a windy day, can bring bright sunlight into the dullness of a grey day, I felt for a brief passing moment the joy of living. But it was short lived. The clouds of my hurt and suffering soon blocked out the light and brought me back to the reality of my grief.

I remained, positioned on this bench, sitting in the warm sunshine, but not appreciating it at all. Then Lucy's mother reappeared. "Time to go," she said softly. "Be brave, be strong."

Looking up at her, I accepted that what was about to follow was necessary, and at that moment in time I became resigned to that which I had to do, and then I rose. She looped her arm through mine. "We shall support each other," she said, on the verge of tears.

I made no reply to this, but just allowed myself to be navigated back into the house, across the room and into the entrance hall. And there it was, the coffin, held aloft by six pallbearers, including among them Uncle Ralf and Samuel's father.

Now was the moment. When we entered the hall, the undertaker looked at Lucy's mother, waiting for a sign. She nodded, indicating that he should proceed, and so he stepped forward through the open doorway that led to the village green. Walking slowly, he was followed by the pallbearers carefully carrying upon their shoulders Lucy's coffin, using their free hands to steady it. Once through the doorway, Lucy's mother and I then moved and walked slowly out of the house, with the others following behind in procession.

We proceeded on our way towards the church, which lay to the left of the house. Some women in the cortège sobbed, but most kept their composure in a very English way.

And so it was throughout the funeral service – words of God, death and resurrection spoken by the priest, interspersed with muffled sobs from members of the congregation. And then it was over and time for the internment. Through it all I had remained in control of my emotions, but this closing act was the hardest part of all for me, the final farewell.

I watched as the coffin was slowly lowered into the deep grave that had been dug for my dear Lucy. Soon Lucy would lie beneath a heavy weight of clay and soil, never to be seen again. Her body would rot away, until all that was left were bones, a weathered tombstone and our memories. With the passing of time those who remembered her would, in turn, pass away, and then only the stone would bear witness to her existence. This is the way of life. But it would not be the case with Lucy. Somewhere in a distant time, my future, a man would stand by her grave and mourn for her as if she had only just passed away. Lucy's spot in the churchyard would, eventually, be surrounded by those who in the time following her death had also departed this life. Her grave, as was the case with others, would become overgrown with weeds and grass. Ivy would take its hold, clinging to the stone, seeking life in a place full of death. And amidst all this, a man would stand, tears rolling down his face, grieving for someone over 250 years dead. And that man would be me.

The tears began to flow. My head was bowed and the salty droplets fell to the ground at my feet, a small element of me joining with the earth that Lucy would eventually become a part of, bringing us together once more. Oh, how I longed for it not to be so.

Quietly I sobbed. I cried for what would be no more, for the days that would pass, here in this world, alone without the one I had come to love. I cried for the missed opportunities, for the experiences that we would not now share, for the joyous moments in time that we would not now spend together, and for not appreciating fully the time we had been given. I wept knowing that we had been united on that one night of love, yet it could have happened so much earlier, and there could have been so many more nights of sharing. Regrets filled my mind. Always there is the assumption that there will be more moments in time to do that which matters. It is an age-old assumption, but one that life has a habit of proving incorrect.

The ritual was over. People were filing past the open grave, halting only briefly to throw handfuls of earth onto the coffin. But I remained standing there, fixed to the spot. I did not want to leave. Lucy's mother stood next to me. Together we gazed into the opening in the ground and at the coffin that lay within. She was weeping, as was I, and those around us left us alone. But we could not stay there, crying all day. There was a wake to attend, and our presence was required. So slowly we departed the place where the dead dwell, and proceeded back to the world of the living.

For a while our grief was satisfied. We had cried and felt better for it. Now we had to face the final part of the ceremony. And somehow we managed it. The day passed, people began to drift away, until just the three of us were left.

The sun was beginning to set as we walked out into the garden, and once more I found myself sitting on that bench, but this time with Lucy's mother, Uncle Ralf having retired to his room, exhausted.

CHAPTER 31

"It is over now," she began, speaking softly. "It has been the hardest day of my life. I recall what we experienced when poor Lucy lost her husband. How I felt for her then, seeing her grief, remembering also how I felt when my dear husband died such a long time ago. And here I am again, experiencing the emptiness, the loneliness, the pain. But the worst of it is the knowing that I will never see her again. No more will she sit by me reading her books. Never again will I feel the comfort of her presence. And that, Benjamin, is so cruel. It is a cruelty that life inflicts upon all those who love someone else, because all love leads, eventually, to pain."

Tears began to trickle down her cheeks and she dabbed them with her handkerchief. I knew what she meant, for her words reflected exactly my own thoughts and feelings.

"Yes, it is true, but there is also the feeling of regret," I replied sympathetically. "Assumptions! Always there is the assumption of time; time to be together, time to talk, time to touch, time to grow old together. It is always the same. There is always the assumption of time. Yet illness, accident and death lurk around every corner. They are but one step ahead of us all; the uncertainty of when, where, and in what form they will strike blinds us to the certainty that one day they will descend upon us. Yet we ignore this certainty. We live our lives as if we had all the time in the world, putting off that which really matters till tomorrow, and filling the present with the trivia of life."

Time was a feature of the universe that I now understood more about, and of its value I was keenly aware, more so than perhaps any other person, past, present or future. I was a man with what I thought was all the time in the world, but it was all a delusion. In the end I was just the same as everyone else, wasting precious time on that which did not matter, while all around me that which was important went unattended. This is the pathway that leads to regrets. I had learned this the hard way.

Lucy's mother had listened attentively to what I had said and reflected for a moment on my words. "I fear that you are correct," she replied. "We do assume too much and take what we have for granted. I am as guilty of that as anyone. And now it is too late."

She sobbed and I placed my arm around her, trying to comfort her. But my eyes were full of tears as well and I, too, succumbed and began to cry. Together, holding on to each other, we cried, letting out the anguish that we both felt at our loss.

After a little while she made an attempt to stop weeping and I tried to do the same, but it was not easy for either of us. "Come," she said, "let us change the subject. We should not dwell too much on that which is in the past and cannot be changed. Time is irreversible. We can go only forwards and we must learn to carry the burden of our loss."

"Yes, let us not dwell on what now cannot be reversed. What is done is done and cannot be changed," I replied philosophically.

Then, changing the topic of our conversation, she asked the inevitable question. "So tell me, what plans if any do you have? Do you intend to stay, or will you go back to where you came from?"

I looked at her for a moment, not sure if I should declare my intentions. I had given the matter a lot of thought. To go, to stay; these were questions I had pondered, and I had made my decision, but I did not want to upset her, though neither did I want to deceive her. I decided to be open and truthful with her.

"I am torn apart by the question of whether to go or to remain," I began. "To be truthful I am not really sure of the consequences of either. If I stay, there will be reminders of Lucy all around. If I go, then ..."

I was not sure what to say next. If I left, there would also be reminders, not to mention the difficulties of returning to Helen, who did not know what had happened. Helen was, as far as I could be sure about such matters, still visiting her parents in some holiday weekend in the far distant future. But of this I could not speak. So what to say?

As it turned out I had no need to speak. Lucy's mother saved me from having to continue. "I know, dear," she said softly, "if you go then you will be cut off from the familiarity of the places where you spent so much time together. What a dilemma for you."

"Yes, it is a dilemma. But what of yourself?" I asked, not wanting to dwell on the matter of my intended departure. "How will you cope?"

"Cope, yes I will cope, somehow," she returned. "But I do not know how. I feel weary. A mother should not outlive her child. It should be the other way around. Children can survive the loss of their parents, but it is not so easy for parents to have to bury their children. I am not sure how I am going to manage. There are moments when I feel that all I want to do is to join my sweet child."

On hearing this I was even more inclined not to speak of my plans. I had not until this point fully understood Lucy's mother's feelings, but now for the first time she was opening up to me, telling me her thoughts, and this provided an inkling of the trauma that she was in the midst of experiencing. How could I tell her that I was leaving?

"I did not fully realise," I said, trying to comfort her, "what you are feeling. I have been too much caught up with my own sorrow that I have ignored that which you too must be experiencing, and for this I am sorry—"

"Do not worry about me," she said, interrupting. "I am not the first mother to lose a child and I will not be the last. It is only natural that you are engrossed with your own grief. It is hard under such circumstances to appreciate what others are feeling."

"This is true, but perhaps I should have tried harder to understand your sorrow," I continued, apologetically.

"No matter," she said kindly. "I do not expect anything. You must do what you think best and you should not delay on deciding upon your own future because of me. Nevertheless," she continued, with a hint of sadness in her voice, "I sense that you have decided and that your decision is to leave. Is that not the case?"

"Yes, I will leave," I said in as gentle a way as I could.

"When?"

"I was intending to leave tomorrow."

"So soon!"

"Yes, I just feel that it would be best for me. I know that will leave you with only Ralf for support."

"It is all right," she said reassuringly. "You must not think of me. You must do what you feel is best for yourself. I am sure that I will be fine. I should not have burdened you with my darker thoughts. Time is a great healer. The grief, I am sure, will ease with the passing of time."

Time! Yet again it creeps into our thoughts and considerations. I remained silent, wondering if I was right in what I was about to do. Then I spoke, trying to soften my departure. "Perhaps I should stay for just one more day, and leave at first light the day after tomorrow, for to tell the truth I am somewhat exhausted by this day, and one more spent resting might be best before my journey. But, I will manage. Tonight I think exhaustion will take me to a place of deep sleep, and tomorrow I will spend my time quietly, so that the following day I expect to be rested enough to be able to travel."

"I am tired as well," she responded, sounding very weary, "and I am ready for my bed."

"Yes, and I think it is time for me to leave. It is growing dark and an early night would suit me."

"Do you want to stay here tonight? I can ask the maid to make up a room for you. It would be no trouble, I can assure you. As I have already said, I worry about you all on your own in that big house."

"There is no need to be concerned about me. The solitude of the place suits me at this time. And I have become accustomed to its quietness."

She said no more about this matter, not wanting to force company upon me.

For a while we were both quiet until she spoke once more. "Let us not linger over this," she said, her voice conveying the kindness that she had always shown to me. "Come, let us say our goodbyes," she said with determination. "I fear that I may never see you again. If that is to be, then let me say that I will always think of you with kind thoughts and if you ever do want to return, there will always be a warm welcome here for you."

Then she rose and I too stood up. "I am very glad that I got to know you," I returned. "I am sorry that I am not staying, but I feel that I must go. Maybe one day I will come back, but this I cannot promise."

She took hold of my hands, moved them together, and held them between her own in a posture that looked as if she were praying, and perhaps she was. "Farewell then, Benjamin.

Look after yourself. Keep yourself well for the sake of Lucy's memory." She paused. Her eyes filled with tears, but she forced herself to continue. "I want you to know that I am glad that you and Lucy fell in love and I was very proud of you both. Go in peace with my love, Benjamin."

"Thank you," I replied, grateful for her warm words of farewell. "I will always remember you and the times I spent here. I will think of you and pray that time does heal your suffering."

"And I will pray for you as well, my dear."

I did not know what else to say and she for her part had also run out of words. She placed her arms around me and embraced me. And there we stood for a while, locked together, two people grieving for the one person in their lives who had brought each of them love and joy. This was our common bond, what united us.

Then she let go and turned away from me and walked towards the house. I followed.

Once in the hall, she headed for the front door, which she then opened, and there she stood waiting for me. I drew up beside her and she looked at me and placed her soft warm hand on the side of my face to comfort me, holding it there. I raised my own hand to hers and gently lifted it from my face. Both of us were on the verge of tears one more time. I gently and slowly kissed her hand, then let go and stepped through the open doorway.

She did not stand at the doorway to watch me as I made my way away across the village green. I turned once, to wave, but she had closed the door, not wanting I presumed to linger over a painful parting. The door was shut, a symbol of the way I was shutting myself out of her life. It was over. I had said my goodbyes. Tears once again streamed down my face. But I knew that my farewells were not over yet, though these would wait until the next day.

The closing of the day was in keeping with what had gone before. Nature presented itself in all its beauty, putting on a show, colouring the sky bright orange as the sun set. Nature was unaware that I took no notice of this marvel, being once more engrossed in my own thoughts; and then came the darkness of the night.

I passed the hours of darkness as I had done the previous ones, alone, sometimes sleeping, other times awake, tossing and turning, unable at first to reach the expected peace of a deep sleep demanded by my state of exhaustion. Though the day had taken its toll on me, I was unable to find the rest that my mind and body craved. Thoughts of Lucy kept invading my consciousness. I tried not to think of her, but alas it was no use. Many times I succeeded in driving visions of Lucy from my mind, but on each occasion it was not long before she was back with me. But often she was not alone.

Many characters came to haunt me that long night, for it seemed that the hours dragged on more than they had done on the other nights since Lucy's death. Walter Smythe appeared on several occasions, taunting me, laughing at my misfortune, smiling in his peculiar way, as if to say, *I could not have her, so neither could you.* It was a hard taunt to bear, but there was nothing I could do, for he was just a figment of my imagination, a part of my own mind. I had created his image and what he said was only what I imagined he would say if he had been alive to say it.

But most sinister of all was the spectre of Sgark. Creature of another world as he was, in my mind I recreated him, experiencing again his malice. I heard once more the words that he had uttered, and with these came the feeling of regret. Once more I was acutely aware that my persistence in remaining instead of returning to my own time, after I had been so clearly warned away, had, without doubt, sealed Lucy's fate. How I wished I could exact revenge upon Sgark, but there was no way that I could reach him, and even if he were to reappear, I knew that he was beyond destruction.

Through the long hours of the night the ghosts of my sojourn in this long-past age came back and forward, as if to remind me of my folly. But towards the end of the night, a new figure appeared on the stage of my imagination. It was someone who had not figured in my life of late, but nevertheless was a person who was very much a part of my life in the era to which I belonged. That figure was Helen, who had become almost a distant memory. All that was about to change, and I began to fret over our meeting.

She had been gone for a few days, but I on the other hand had been, in that same short period, away for over twelve months. In that time I had found my way through a time warp into the past, acquired a house and a fortune, been kidnapped, held prisoner, nearly murdered, fallen in love with Lucy, encountered a creature from another world, and lost my love to a terrible disease. Now in the midst of my grief, I was about to return to my other love, Helen, whom I had betrayed and who would not understand how I could have changed from a happy and optimistic person into one sunk in the midst of despair and gloom.

I knew for sure there was no way in which I would be able to hide my present state of mind from her. And how was I going to deal with the fact that I had betrayed my Helen? I had fallen in love with Lucy, when it was within my power to have avoided this by leaving. I had chosen to stay. And I had made love to Lucy, shared my body with her, a body that, up till my meeting Lucy, had been for Helen and Helen alone.

It was at that moment in time that I realised that we all are, through our own actions, often the originators of our own problems. We exercise free will and, through the choices that we make, create the difficulties that follow us to our graves. And I also understood that my quest, the challenge, for the rest of my life would be to find within myself forgiveness for what I had done to the two people in my life whom I loved in ways that are beyond words to describe. Somehow I had to find a way of atoning for my sins, and I could not see how this would be possible.

I was tempted, as many are in such circumstances, to run away. I felt that I could not go back and face Helen, to look into her eyes and to whisper sweet words of love in her ears, in the knowledge that I had betrayed her, had been unfaithful, had not lived up to the trust that she placed in me. So I contemplated remaining in the mid-eighteenth century, but not in the Time House. That would not do at all. The plan that formed in my mind centred on making true what had been the lie that I had lived. I would catch the stagecoach to London, the one that I should have taken on that fateful day when Walter Smythe had kidnapped me and held me prisoner in his father's disused barn. There in London I would enquire about travel to the American Colonies. Using my wealth, I would establish myself in business, using the knowledge that I had of historical events to make more money. The thought was very tempting. I would be able to evade the consequences of my actions.

But would I? For a short while I was convinced that this was the right course of action, but then doubts began to creep into my mind. Very soon I realised that running away to America would not work, for there was nowhere I could run to that was far enough away. Wherever I went my problems would go too. There was no escaping them, for they were inside me and would remain with me all the years of my life, or until I had somehow found a way to find forgiveness within myself.

Thus it was that I resolved upon the course of action that would lead me back to Helen. I knew that I could not tell her what had happened to me. Who would believe such a story? And for a while some peace did settle on my mind and at last I drifted, with great relief, into a deep sleep. It was an untroubled sleep and when I awoke the feeling of exhaustion that had dogged me for days was no longer present. It seemed that fortune had taken pity on me and that I would at least be able to return home without looking a complete wreck.

I lay in bed, just wanting to lie there and be inactive. I was oblivious to the time of day and my mind wandered for a moment, as I was still hovering between sleep and waking.

In my study, the sun streamed through the window, and eventually I went and sat there, trying to enjoy the warmth. The room was flooded with sunlight, stimulating my brain with sensations that I had thought I would never feel again. I got up and reached for my pocket watch. Ten o'clock in the morning. Should I stay another day or should I go immediately? Did it matter? Either way, the time for going home was rapidly approaching, but first I had two more tasks to undertake, two more farewells to make before I stepped for last time through the opening that would lead me to the twenty-first century and the remaining years of my life.

CHAPTER 32

For the final time in 1751, I set off for the village. I made my way along the lane that had now become so familiar to me, on which I had strolled with Lucy on countless occasions.

As soon as I trod upon the grass that spread as though it were a green blanket across the open space at the heart of the village, I was spotted. The person to whom I had come to say farewell, young Samuel, had been sitting outside his parents' shop, as he had done so often, lingering I think in anticipation of my appearance. And at long last, there I was. I had shown myself and he wasted no time by waiting for me to come to him, but ran as fast as he could to meet me. It was a scene that had been played out so many times in the past, but this was the final time that he would dash to greet me in such a way.

We met and slightly out of breath he said, "You are leaving?"

"Yes, Samuel, I am leaving," I replied, but in a way that indicated that I was doing so with a heavy heart.

"Why?" he demanded to know, obviously angry with me. "Why are you leaving?"

There was sadness writ large across his face, and I felt for him.

"I cannot remain here," I said gently. "After what has happened, I could not face staying. There are too many memories here. Every time I walk down a familiar lane where

414

Lucy and I once strolled I will be reminded of her. Every time I see a preferred tree where we once sat seeking shade from the summer sun, I will recall her and how happy we were together. Every time I visit a favoured spot where we held each other and were just glad to be alone together, I will feel my loss. Everywhere in this place I will be haunted by the memories of Lucy; there is no escape here, Samuel, just memories."

But I could not tell Samuel the truth – that I would still be here in the village, only in another era. Yet I had concluded that it would be more bearable being in my own age than to stay in Samuel's time. In my own era I would not see anyone who would remind me of Lucy. The environment would be similar, but different enough to for me to know that what had happened had occurred in the past, in some distant and now forgotten time. By leaving I would be able to break the link with the events that had taken Lucy from me. The chains that bound me to the past, so to speak, would be broken, or at least that was what I thought. Time, however, would soon prove me wrong about this.

For the moment I was living yet another delusion, that this was an episode in my life that was now over. I would not forget, but I hoped that with time, that supposedly great healer, I would be able to accept what had happened and learn to live with it, for it seemed to me that this was all I could expect. People do not get over the loss of a loved one, or some traumatic event in their lives. To suppose such is foolish and naïve. But it is possible to adapt, to learn how to accommodate the memories, and to live life anew, a changed person, and wiser perhaps as a result. This is the hope that all who have the misfortune to live through difficult times must harbour, that one day the thread of life will be picked up once again as we wander through the maze of life, as time moves us forward to whatever fate awaits us.

"Please do not go," he pleaded. "Stay. Please stay."

"I know it is hard for you, but I have to go. Please do not make it more difficult for me. It is not easy leaving, but it would be even harder to remain."

"Your mind is made up, that I can see," responded Samuel.

"Yes, Samuel, my mind is made up about this."

"Are you going back to the American Colonies?" he asked, curious to know about my plans.

"I am not sure where I am going," I told him.

I did not want to discuss my intentions in detail with Samuel, for I did not want to deceive him, so I felt that it would be better to say as little as possible.

"It is all over so quickly," he said. "One moment you are here, appearing out of nowhere, then you are gone again."

Samuel was starting to sound very philosophical. Evidently the education that he had been receiving had not been wasted on him. Then came the question I had been expecting.

"Will you take me with you? I would not be any trouble. I would do whatever you asked of me."

I smiled. "I am sure that you would be a perfect travelling companion, but you have responsibilities here. Your mother and father need you. They would be sad if you left them. There will be a time for such travelling, for experiencing the wider world, but that time is not now. You should be with them. Make the most of the time that you have together, the time you have left with them. Make the most of it, for as surely as the sun rises in the morning and sets in the evening, there will come a day when they will not be here. Live as though today was your last with them. Do not do what so many people do, and put off till tomorrow that which you can do today with them, for when tomorrow does come they may not be around anymore."

It was my turn to be philosophical. But it was a point that I wanted Samuel to understand. This, it seemed to me, was one of the most important lessons that life can teach anyone. Time, you see, has taught me this, although I should have known it instinctively.

"Samuel," I began sincerely, "know this. The past and the future do not exist, except in our minds. Now is all you have. The present is all there is. It is here, at this moment in time, that you create regrets or happy memories. Do not live your life in the past, sad for all that could have been but was not so. Take hold of life and make for yourself a future that will deliver contentment and fulfilment. Follow your dreams and know that time is your enemy. It is in the now, the present, where lies the potential to make your dreams come true. You cannot travel back in time and do that which you regret not doing. You only have one chance, so seize the opportunity while you can."

I spoke these words knowing that they were as true for me as they were for Samuel, and for all other living souls. Yes, it is true that I had broken some aspects of this universal truth; by some unknown and perhaps ungodly means, I had been able to break free of the constraints of time, but in reality I was as much a prisoner of time as anyone else. Through my own deeds in the present, no matter where I might be in the great continuum of time, I, as is the case with others, determined my past and my future by my actions and also by that which I had left undone. There was no escaping from this fact. No matter how far I travelled in time or space, this single unchangeable truth would follow me every step of the way.

Samuel listened to what I said and he understood. I could see this from the expression on his face, which had changed from one of yearning to one of acceptance. But his eyes told me that while he accepted this, he did not agree with it. In this, he was not alone, for he stood with all men and women across the centuries, raging at the circumstances in which he now found himself, but unable to change the situation. Some aspects of life are outside our control and that is the way it is. But other aspects are within our control, as I had learned at a high cost.

"It is difficult to let go," he said sadly. "I have lost Miss Lucy. Now I am losing you."

"I cannot say that what you utter is untrue. We may never meet again, Samuel, but I will always remember you.

But you must persist with what you have started. Lucy's mother has promised to continue as your teacher. Be a good pupil, for Lucy's sake. And when you are ready, go out into the world and do whatever it is that you are destined to do."

Tears began to form in my eyes and I knelt down and held Samuel. For his part, Samuel also burst into tears and he wrapped his small arms around me, held onto me tightly, and wept.

He did not want to let go; this I sensed. But it was time to go. "It is time, Samuel," I said kindly. "I must be away now. Farewell."

I gently undid the embrace in which he held me. He looked at me. He was sad, but he was now beyond the point of hope that I might change my mind. He did not speak again.

"I am leaving now," I continued. "But first I want to stand one last time by Lucy's grave and say my farewell to her. Then I will be gone."

He motioned to indicate that he would come with me. "No, Samuel," I said softly, "this I want to do alone."

Then I stepped away from him, turned and strode towards the churchyard.

I looked back once, but Samuel was gone. He had returned to the life that would lead him to wherever he was bound. My involvement in his journey was over and I could never know what influence I'd had upon the final outcome of his quest to find whatever it was he was seeking.

Once more I stood by my beloved, now buried deep beneath my feet, never again to see the light of day. And I wept, not for her but for myself, because Lucy was right. In her dying words she had said that death was hardest for those who are left behind and not for those who do the dying. Oh, what truth!

I wiped my eyes and looked around me, taking in, for one last time, the sights and sounds of this place which held my dearest love in its earthly embrace. I wanted to remember every small feature. The plants that grew, the shadows cast by the trees, the details of the surrounding headstones. I took it all in and then, turning to the new gravestone that had been placed at the head of the grave, I spoke aloud to dear Lucy, though my words fell on no ears but my own.

"My darling Lucy," I began. "I miss you so much, my love. And now I must leave you forever, for in this age I will never cast my eyes upon your grave again. Though I may stand once more upon this spot, it will be in a time far distant from the one in which you lived and died. Now I travel onwards, my love, but I will never ever be without you, for I shall, for the rest of my days, keep you within my heart. It is there that you will live on, in a time when no one knows of you, when all your family and friends are long gone and have been laid to rest, and I ... I will stand by your grave and mourn for you. Farewell for now, my sweet angel."

I had previously changed my mind about leaving immediately and had intended to stay for one more day, as I had indicated to Lucy's mother, but whether today or tomorrow mattered not, for where I was headed was a different time altogether. So I departed from her grave, not once looking back, heading straight out of the churchyard, out of the village, and out of that time where I had experienced so much joy but, in the end, only found pain.

CHAPTER 33

I did not witness the ravages of time that had brought a once new headstone into a state of decay. Time had passed by, and sun, rain, frost and ice had taken their toll. Yet it was plainly her gravestone. Carved on it, still legible after 250 years, I could read her name, Lucy Bamford, died 1751, age thirty. But she was no longer alone. In the space below the name of the person whom I had fallen in love with was that of Marjory Dent, died 1753, age fifty.

So it was, standing on the very spot where I had been only a matter of an hour ago, but which was in fact over two and a half centuries past by natural time, that I learned that Lucy's mother had outlived her daughter by only two years. I wondered if she had died of a broken heart and I wondered too about young Samuel. Had he lost another close friend? How had his education fared once Lucy's mother was gone?

There were no answers to these questions and no way for me to discover them, for I did not intend to go back to the past to find out what had happened to my dear friend Samuel. On that I was determined, but the house, the Time House, was still part of me, still in my possession.

I stood and reflected upon the scene that I beheld. It was different, that was certain. Headstones that had once stood upright were now inclined at angles, or had been placed upon the ground lest they should fall and hurt someone. But not the gravestone of my dear Lucy; hers stood true, although the stone had turned green with the growth of mosses.

How strange to stand by on old grave and feel such grief for someone dead these past 250 years. I had defied the nature of time and this was my punishment, grieving for someone who was now no more than a collection of decaying bones. But what I would have given to hold her once more in my arms, alive or dead, for even her dead body, though lifeless, motionless, and lying in her grave, was still my Lucy. I even began to imagine in my mind what she would now be like, after lying down there for centuries. This, you see, is the result of tampering with time, for surely I must have been the first human ever to have experienced such circumstances, to stand by the grave of a lover, over 250 years dead, and to know that I still had my whole life ahead of me.

And then my mind turned from thoughts of the dead to those of the living. Helen! Fast approaching was the time of reckoning.

I had been away for over twelve months, but I had no idea of what day, week, month, or year I was now in, for I had not bothered to take note of my surroundings when, after returning to the twenty-first century, I had left the Time House.

My return had been uneventful. Upon leaving Lucy's grave in 1751, I had gone back to the Time House, quickly changed into my modern clothes and, for the final time, passed through the opening that led back to my own age. Once more I had looked up and read the words carved into the wooden beam that spanned the opening into the world where my dear Lucy had been taken from me. *Alpha and omega, beginning and end, and in between an eternity of time for those who wander into here*, was what it said, and now for the first time I began fully to understand what this meant. Or at least I considered that I did.

I had once thought that it might be a warning. I now realised that it was just that. But it was more than a caution concerning the potential dangers that lurked in the Time House; it was also an accurate statement about what the Time House was. Reading those words now, I could see that it was someone's interpretation of the very words that Sgark had spoken me; the Time House was a gateway to other periods in history, not just the mid-eighteenth century. Throughout the building there were portals to the different ages of humankind, from their beginnings, to their end somewhere in the far future, and every age in between. And it was also a gateway to other worlds, perhaps better left unexplored.

For me, my adventures in time were over. It was the moment in time to go home, to see what awaited me there, but I was apprehensive about returning. I recalled how, after my first trip into the mid-eighteenth century, on coming back, details of my surroundings had changed. The consequences of staying in the eighteenth century for such a long period of time I had never seriously considered, so wrapped up had I been in my own life. But this concern now crept into an already over-burdened mind, further adding to my worries and emotional turmoil.

But I was set on facing the consequences of my actions and delayed not, heading back home as quickly as I could, wishing to get it over with as soon as possible.

I need not have been concerned. All was just as I had left it when I had departed. Once in the house I discovered that small everyday items, such as food in the fridge, were still exactly as they had been on my departure. There was no decay. I switched on my computer and established the date. Just to be sure I visited a website giving the time and date in various places around the world. This agreed with the time and date information on my computer. All was in order. The date had not changed; it was still the Sunday of my departure and I had arrived back shortly after the point in time that I had left for my adventure, so I had in fact only been away for a few hours. I was relieved by these discoveries, although I was in fact a year older, which was not a thought I found comforting.

I noticed that I had an email from Helen. I was eager to read it, since it was sent earlier in the day:

Dear Benjamin,

I won't be able to phone you today as we are going out to an area with poor mobile reception. My sister is here, but no boyfriend – seems she dumped him before coming down.

Did you find the problem with the electrics in the Old House? More importantly did you get any of the work done that you were supposed to do?

Missing you. Love you.

Helen xxxx

425

Helen remained part of my life, but her email did not indicate that she knew about my ownership of the Time House. The problem of trying to explain to her how I had come to own a large house in the village still remained, but perhaps this was the least of my worries.

I was alone in my home, exhausted by what had happened to me, but nevertheless glad to be back, for I felt here some relief from the troubles that I had created for myself. Perhaps there was some hope for me after all that had happened.

After showering and putting on clean fresh clothes, I sat down to ponder my circumstances, when I heard the front door open; someone had entered the house. This alarmed me, for it could not be Helen, who was far away in Dorset. A feeling of coldness descended upon me, for knowing it was not Helen, it could only be an intruder. Had I left the front door unlocked? Had some opportunist thief, counting on the occupiers being away for the holiday weekend, discovered an easy entry into the house?

I did not want to confront this burglar without first sizing him up; he might be large and muscular or even armed with a knife, such is the danger of twenty-first-century life. So I hid myself where I could observe him, but remain unseen. And not a moment too soon for he was into the room quicker than I had expected, seeming to know his way about, showing a familiarity with my home that I had not expected.

At first I thought I had made a mistake. I looked again at the person and examined him closely, making sure that I was certain about whom I was seeing. A familiar sight was before me, for I knew this man very well. That face I had looked upon countless times, those mannerisms I had seen over and over again, and those clothes were so familiar to me. The person I now observed, the person in my home, was none other than me!

I was confused and alarmed. What had gone wrong? Had I come back too early, in effect before I had left? I looked carefully at what he, that is to say I, was about, but had no recollection of doing that which he was now doing. I did not recall wearing, before my departure, the clothes that this doppelganger now wore. But I had been absent for twelve months; in that time I might have forgotten the details. But what I did recollect was the time that I had left the house, and having checked the present time, I was certain that I had not returned earlier than I had left.

This was a mystery. Undoubtedly something was wrong. I was reminded once again that I had been messing with matters of which I was ignorant. Perhaps this too was a consequence of defying nature, of travelling back in time. I had already come to terms with the fact that I would probably never understand what forces were at play, forces that had enabled me to do what should have been impossible. Now I began to realise that the consequences of my actions might be far more serious than I had anticipated.

I watched myself looking at the computer and wondering why it was switched on. I saw myself reading the email from Helen, and smiling to myself. It was all surreal and unbelievable, and it was as though I were watching a home video. But it was also a nightmare, only one that I could not wake from.

I began to feel sick. The consequence of what was taking place before me began to dawn upon me. I realised that I now had two existences, completely independent of each other, and that I had become cut off from my own life and that it would go on without me.

This thought upset me and I wanted to talk, to scream and tackle the spectre of myself who sat there leading the life that was mine. But I could not. I needed time to think, to get over the initial shock of what had happened, to analyse what I might be able to do to reverse these circumstances. So I waited for an opportunity to quietly slip away from my home. It was not long in coming.

My doppelganger did not stay long. He prepared himself a sandwich in the kitchen, ate it and then left. When I was sure that he was gone, I slipped upstairs and collected a few possessions that I might need. I was unsure how the present circumstances might develop, so I took several items from the house that I might find useful in the days to come, including the title deeds for the Time House and all the money and valuables I had acquired.

On leaving my home I immediately returned to the Time House. I had nowhere else to go, so no choice in the matter; this was now my only place of refuge in the sea of uncertainty that I had created. Suddenly the Time House was providing me with a home, until, that is, I could figure out what to do. But I did not venture back through the time portal, choosing to remain in my own time, and relying on luck that no one would be venturing into the property to view it.

I slept that night on the landing, using a pillow and sleeping bag that I had brought with me from home. I was well supplied with food, taken from the fridge and freezer, so I wanted for nothing in the way of immediate needs.

On Monday, the day of Helen's return, I stayed in the Time House, and spent the day writing down an account of what had happened to me – this diary. Later, I departed and hid myself in the garden of my home, watching and waiting to see what would transpire. Then the moment in time that I was waiting for happened.

Helen arrived, parking her car on the drive. There was my beautiful Helen, just as she was when she had departed, leaving me follow the course of action that would lead to my present predicament. But also there was my double, rushing out to greet her, embracing her, kissing her, holding her warm sweet body in his arms. I crouched behind the rhododendron bushes, hidden from view, watching my life proceeding onwards right front of me. I was an observer of that which I was participating in, at once part of events and at the same time excluded from them.

I felt lost and abandoned, for what was unfolding before me confirmed what I feared was the case, that I had indeed become detached from my own existence, and that my life would go on, without me, but at the same time with me. It was a paradox, and one that I had created. Now you know what can come of messing with matters that one does not fully understand.

I knew then that there was no way back. Helen was embracing her lover and her life would continue as if all that had happened had never been. Only I would know about the circumstances that had led to this terrible state of affairs. I was a lost soul and no one would ever realise it.

Helen disappeared into the house, what used to be my home, but alas was no longer, escorted by her Benjamin, he too unaware of the events that had taken place in his own life, but which he had no part in.

I was devastated by what I had seen and dejectedly I slipped away, unnoticed, unseen, never to grace my home again or to share, anymore, moments in time with my Helen. There they were, more moments in time, similar to the many gone before, and the many to come, together, happy, looking forward to the future. But I was not a part of it. From now on my home would lie elsewhere, but where exactly I did not know, nor in what time, for now the issue arose of whether to stay in the present, or to step back, once more, into 1751, a time that for me held no comforts anymore. Perhaps I might do what I had previously considered and travel to a far distant place. It was too early to decide. So once more I returned to the Time House, the place that was the cause of so much heartache.

Then, in a final act, the Time House seemed about to inflict one more blow upon me. And it started with the voice.

"So, Benjamin, look what state of affairs your actions have brought you to."

The voice, once silent for so long, returned, so I thought, to mock me, to taunt me. But I was wrong about the latter.

"I see you despair of your circumstances," the voice said softly and gently. There was no tone of reproach or gloating; it seemed genuinely concerned.

"Who are you?" I asked, playing the game until the bitter end, but in truth no longer caring what it was or what happened to me.

"I am," it returned, "the quiet voice that you have ignored. All through your life I have talked to you, but most times you have not heard. Call me your intuition if you wish, or your soul. It does not matter what name you give me. What is important is that you take notice of me. You need to realise that you cannot always analyse, theorise and design your way through life. There are moments in time when insights that stem from deep within you, from your soul, are needed, as was the case when you should have left the time portal well alone."

The voice had my attention now, for I was beginning to see that it had no connection with the Time House, but was a part of me.

"If that is so," I said, "then surely this is one of those moments in time, for try as I might I cannot reason my way out of my present circumstances."

"Indeed, this is true," the voice confirmed, "but you have already seen the way forward."

"You mean I should go back! Return to a time and place where I do not belong?"

"You do not belong here, in this time or place, so it can be no worse to return."

"But back in 1751 there is only pain, grief, suffering."

"These emotions you carry with you wherever you go. They are not part of the time in which you dwell, but exist within you as your own creations. You cannot run away from these feelings. This you know already."

What the voice said was true.

"I don't know," I stated, unsure about the sense of the idea.

"There you go again," the voice responded. "Always the logical and reasoning person, hardly ever taking note of your intuition. You should learn to trust me, for I would never hurt you in any way."

I thought about this for a moment. Perhaps the voice was right.

"This is your destiny now," the voice said, sensing my hesitation. "Go and meet your future. You may be pleasantly surprised at what you find."

Then there was silence. No more did the voice speak out. It is decision time, and as I sit here, in the Time House, writing this, more than time has passed by. My life with my dear Helen has also slipped away. She will go on living with the man she loves, me, in their time, and he will not know what has happened. But I, the person trapped between two worlds, between two times ... I have lost everything – my Helen, my Lucy, my work, and my chance of living a normal life. It seems that I have become a slave to time. For, you see, time has its price. I have time, but it seems I am doomed to wander through it for the remainder of my life. Only the rest of my days may be countless, endless, eternal. There is no way back for me. I am caught in a trap of my own making. And thus I have decided to return to 1751 and, there, face my fate, whatever that may be.

EPILOGUE

Benjamin closed the notebook in which he had recorded the details of his experiences and secreted it away in a place where only the most curious and determined would find it, for he did not want just any person to stumble upon the contents.

Benjamin stepped back through the time portal and went to his study and there he noticed for the first time small notes scribbled on the wall. The strangeness of the Time House never seemed to end. In all the moments in time that he had spent in this room, not once had he seen these scribbled notes, but is it not the case that people rarely see that which is directly in front of them? There were many of these small annotations, probably written by those who had wandered through the portal and found themselves caught up in the power of this mysterious house. And although there were many of these short messages, they all spoke of one truth – there are many paths through life, but be careful which ones you choose!

It was not difficult for Benjamin to see how apt these scribbles were and how other people, if they had encountered experiences similar to those he had lived through by the means of the Time House, would resort to such philosophical graffiti. Benjamin immediately knew that he too had to leave a note on the wall and exactly what that should be. So taking a pencil that was in his pocket he wrote: *The risks cannot be managed because out of order comes disorder: this is one of the most fundamental laws of the universe.*

As soon as he had finished writing this, through the open window of the front bedroom came the discordant sounds of someone shouting. The voice was strangely familiar to him so he ran to the front bedroom, the place where he had spent most of his nights during his adventure, and where he and Lucy had become as one in their love. Looking through the panes of glass he saw a familiar sight – Walter Smythe was standing in the lane in front of the Time House, shouting at young Samuel Jones. Benjamin was quick to realise the implications. Glancing to his left, peering into the distance, far along the lane, still some way off, he saw two now familiar ladies walking towards the spot where Samuel was about to receive a beating at the hands of Walter Smythe.

At first it truly seemed to Benjamin that he was living a nightmare. Everything was about to happen all over again – the joy as well as the pain and suffering. This was too much, and it was at that moment in time that Benjamin realised that he was caught in a loop, truly chained to the past by unbreakable chains, and that he had indeed become like Prometheus, only there was no Hercules to save him!

Then Benjamin smiled to himself. Mysteriously, some complex and unfathomable change had occurred within him. There was a chance now to modify the future, to create different outcomes, ones that would lead to happiness rather than tragedy. This was an opportunity to take a different road,

435

to depart from a course and, with luck, reach a changed end. He had within himself found the way to save himself.

He wasted no time in running downstairs to deal with Walter Smythe, but this time he would do it in a way that would not alienate Smythe and make him Benjamin's enemy. And very quickly, there they were, Benjamin and Lucy, more moments in time, in some ways different from the many gone before, but with many more to come, together, happy, looking forward to the future.

The End

www.ingramcontent.com/pod-product-compliance
Lightning Source LLC
Chambersburg PA
CBHW030928020726
47498CB00001B/163